Frost at Midnight

Also by James Henry

First Frost (with Henry Sutton)
Fatal Frost
Morning Frost
Blackwater

Frost at Midnight

James Henry

BANTAM PRESS

LONDON • TORONTO • SYDNEY • AUCKLAND • JOHANNESBURG

TRANSWORLD PUBLISHERS
61–63 Uxbridge Road, London W5 5SA
www.penguin.co.uk

Transworld is part of the Penguin Random House group of companies
whose addresses can be found at global.penguinrandomhouse.com

Penguin
Random House
UK

First published in Great Britain in 2017 by Bantam Press
an imprint of Transworld Publishers

Written for the Estate of R. D. Wingfield by James Gurbutt
Copyright © The Estate of R. D. Wingfield 2017

A CIP catalogue record for this book
is available from the British Library.

ISBNs 9780593073636 (hb)
9780593073643 (tpb)

Typeset in 11.5/14.25pt Caslon 540 by Falcon Oast Graphic Art Ltd.
Printed and bound by Clays Ltd, Bungay, Suffolk.

Penguin Random House is committed to a sustainable
future for our business, our readers and our planet. This book
is made from Forest Stewardship Council® certified paper.

1 3 5 7 9 10 8 6 4 2

Frost at Midnight

Prologue

'That'll be an extra fiver,' she said in a business-like fashion, already out of bed and perched – still naked – in front of the dressing-table mirror brushing her long auburn hair.

'I beg your pardon?' He reached inside the bed, fumbling to find his underwear.

'An extra five quid for all that . . . all that funny business.'

'Oh . . . you never said before, I haven't got that much on me.'

She turned to face him. 'That's because it never used to take that long, and look' – she pointed with the hairbrush – 'look at these marks. I can't have this, can I. What if my other punters start to notice?'

He felt himself colour.

'I'm sorry,' he mumbled. In truth, though, he did it on purpose – the blemishes; he didn't want her having any other punters. He wanted her all to himself but he could barely afford a fort-nightly visit these days, let alone with this surcharge. It incensed him that she'd go with others – she occupied his thoughts every minute of the day. He'd once asked her on a date, to the cinema (not in Denton, of course he couldn't risk that; Reading or one of the bigger towns). She'd laughed in his face. Date clients? 'You'll be wanting to pimp for me next,' she'd snorted in a common way that made his skin crawl. As if he'd do that. The very idea.

He watched as she stood to pull up her suspender belt; in less than an hour she'd be taking it off again for someone else, probably some scum with more money than him . . . she never stopped going on about what she called her 'richer gents'. He couldn't stand it.

What if she couldn't work? Just for a while maybe; out of action for a spell, needing somebody to help out . . . He'd be well placed to assist, what with—

'Come on, out of there.' She scowled. 'You better not have made a mess!'

He got out of bed and dressed hurriedly, his mind working away feverishly while he made a show of smoothing the sheets, plumping a pillow. Some minor accident, a fall maybe. Nothing too serious.

He handed over the cash, and thanked her obsequiously. She took it without comment and seated herself again at the dressing table. 'Same time in two weeks?' he ventured.

'I can't. Sorry, have to be in September.' Her attention now, having received her payment, was on her make-up. He was forgotten.

'Why?' he croaked. Not to see her for three weeks, what would he do? Maybe she was going away . . . with another man? 'Why? I need to . . .'

'Just because,' she said to herself in the mirror. 'In the meantime, you can always . . .' and then that annoying titter of hers slipped into her voice. He froze. 'You can always do some knitting.' She held a tissue to her lips. 'A nice long scarf for the winter?' She was laughing now. Laughing at him.

He scrabbled for his clothes to cover himself. He should never have mentioned his hobby. It was not the first time she'd poked fun at him: that time he'd given her a gift, she couldn't control her laughter either. How he'd hated her then. And now a red mist descended, anger welled like he'd experienced before, extinguishing any lingering pleasure and affection in an instant. *No one can mock me, least of all her, unholy harlot that she is.* He glanced down at her exposed white neck; if she insulted him like that again he'd do more than shove her down some stairs—

'Call me later in the week' – her voice abruptly assumed the rigid formality of earlier – 'I'll see if I can squeeze you in, otherwise it'll have to be next month.'

He stood, lingering over her a second or two longer. He was steady again, but he was not himself; desire and anger had fused into a black poison that still pulsed within. If she paid him the slightest attention, turned from her own reflection, she'd see just how much danger she was in . . .

'Go on then, off you toddle,' she commanded. A retort rose in his throat, but the words wouldn't come. 'And shut the door on your way out, there's a love.'

Sunday (1)

'Right you – off.'

From underneath the eiderdown he sensed she was holding the child; that horrible milky smell – the odour reached his nostrils. Boy, it smelt bad. He hugged the cover tighter.

'I mean it,' she said, closer this time. The baby was gurgling – any second now it would start wailing, he could tell. He cringed down into the settee, steeling himself – babies and hangovers definitely did not mix.

'. . . you were supposed to go yesterday. My mother will be here at midday. It's not fair, Jack. The place is a tip – I just can't keep on top of it, what with you and Philip.'

The gurgling was growing louder. Any second now . . . He stretched a foot out tentatively; but withdrew it hastily on contact with something soggy. Last night's Kung Po? And then off it went – a deafening wail. Christ alive! The next thing he knew the eiderdown was wrenched away from him.

'Oi!' he protested.

'God, you pong.'

Frost, lying prone in his string vest, was greeted by the silhouette of Sue Clarke and her hungry baby. His skull throbbed like the devil was playing the bongos right behind his eyeballs. He blinked rapidly then sat up. A cluster of empty beer cans that had been nestling overnight in his crotch clattered to the floor.

'And get rid of that beard. You don't only smell like a tramp, you look like one too.'

'Never mind me – oughten you to feed the nipper? He's making a helluva racket.'

'He's fine,' she said, impervious to the god-awful din. Clarke bent down to pick up the empties, bringing the baby to eye level with Frost – prompting a renewed bout of screaming. 'Stop looking at him, though – you know you scare him.'

'I—? Oww!' Frost winced in pain, as he propped himself up. 'Me back!'

'I've booked you in to see Dr Mirchandani on Thursday, I'm sick to death of you whining like an old dog every morning.'

'That's very—'

'At nine sharp. And get in the bath. Haven't you to be at the vicar's by ten? You can't enter the church looking like that – or wait, maybe you'll get struck down? That'd teach you a lesson.'

'Ha ha.' Frost got up from the settee – the proximity of the baby and its lactic tang had made him nauseous.

'You know, it wouldn't be half so bad if you weren't so damn messy,' she sighed, surveying her tiny front room. The small glass table doubling as a bedside *and* dining table; ashtray, cutlery, crumpled trousers, Scotch bottle . . .

'Well, you could always let me sleep with you?' He beamed.

'Yeah, right,' she said flatly, 'and you could get yourself some-where proper to live. There's nothing to stop you. Your house was sold ages ago. You've been here months.'

'I keep telling you it wasn't *my* house. Never has been.'

'Well then. If it *never* was your house, waiting for it to get sold *never* had any bearing on you getting sorted out, did it?' She was angry and upset. He knew he'd outstayed his welcome – it was unfair to put her through this, what with the kid and everything. And tomorrow was a big day for her, he knew. She was anxious on top of everything else.

'Don't worry, you know it'll be fine – I'm telling you.'

'You don't know for sure. I don't know why you're so confident.' She regarded him with consternation. 'Anyway, it's not just that – it's you. I don't want to kick you out, really I don't, but it's the only way you'll ever get yourself together.'

Frost frowned and picked up his flattened pack of cigarettes off the makeshift bed. 'Don't you worry, love. I'm sorted . . . nearly.'

'Jesus, Jack, are you or aren't you?'

'Am I what?'

'Sorted?'

'Almost.' Frost scratched his unruly beard.

'Define "almost".'

From across the kitchen table, Waters appraised his friend and colleague. Granted, Frost appeared marginally fresher, with an unfamiliar smell of soap about him and hair that had glanced at a comb; but the huge bags under his eyes were an indication the man hadn't had a decent night's kip in a long time. Unsurprisingly.

The big sergeant tutted. 'Seriously, Jack, you can't just go from couch to couch any more. You're not a bloody teenager.'

'Well, I'd be all right, if flamin' Hornrim Harry hadn't kicked me out the police digs on Fenwick Street.' Frost flicked ash angrily at the large blue crystal ashtray. He missed, sending the cinders skittering across Waters' fiancée's highly polished table instead.

'You know why he did that, man,' Waters said gently, not

wishing to rake over old ground. 'I'm not saying I agree, but you know Mullett's a stickler for what he sees as proper conduct.' Waters shook his head. When he'd moved into this place – his fiancée's – they'd offered his old lodgings at Fenwick Street to Frost. It had all been fine at first. Then there was the carry-on with Suzy Fong and her pals, impromptu parties and playing unorthodox games of Twister into the small hours (something he'd preferred to watch rather than participate in). Then the complaints from the two female occupants . . . He sighed and looked sadly at his pal, sitting hunched across from him, staring into his mug of heavily spiked coffee. Of course it had all reached Superintendent Mullett's ear and, quite rightly, he'd had to do something. Frost's antics set a bad example to the junior policemen and Mullett knew it. In truth Frost knew that too; his anger was shielding a sense of shame. And here he was now, slumped and half-stale from Sue Clarke's couch.

'So what have you got lined up, in an "almost" type way?'

Frost smiled slyly. 'As of today I'm house-sitting and pet-minding for a friend.'

'Really?' Waters was surprised. 'What friends you got that would (a) let you loose in their home, and (b) trust you to look after their cute and furry ones?'

'I'm keeping an eye on the Jade Rabbit for a fortnight,' he said proudly.

'You are kidding me, man! Old Fong must be losing his marbles; you corrupt his daughter then he leaves you in charge of his restaurant?'

'Suzy and I are just good friends.'

'Yeah right.' Waters scratched his head in mock confusion. 'Now remind me, what were we just talking about at Fenwick Street?' He reached over for the Rothmans lying on the table. 'What the hell do you know about running a Chinese restaurant?'

'Bugger all,' Frost admitted, spinning his newly issued bleeper on the table. 'Mr Fong's cousin from Rimmington is looking after the kitchen. I don't think he trusts him to be honest, and he thought I'd be some sort of security; you know, watch over the place.'

Waters tapped the cigarette tip on the box. 'I'd be amazed if he didn't think *you* needed watching.'

'I'm a highly valued customer – what I shell out on Kung Po a month feeds and clothes all the little Fongs.'

'And the rest.'

'Now, now. If you must know, he's taken Suzy back to Peking.' He stretched across with a lighter.

'Safest place for her, undoubtedly.'

'He won't be back until some time in September, so I'm sorted for a month. Moving in this afternoon. Suitcase is in the back of the motor.' Frost looked smug. 'And the family pets,' he continued, 'are not furry; no, it's feathers and scales.'

'Wha—'

The phone on the kitchen wall shrilled, interrupting them. Waters reached behind him.

'Mr Waters, sorry to disturb you.' Waters recognized the polite, elderly voice. Holding his hand over the mouthpiece he said, 'It's the vicar. What's the time?' Then he added, 'Father Hill, I'm so sorry, we must have lost track of—'

'No, no, dear me, it's not your rehearsal I'm calling about. No, I'm afraid it's something quite terrible. Maybe I should call the station – it's just I was already expecting you . . .'

'What is it, Father?'

Frost craned in to hear.

'There's a dead body in the cemetery.'

'I'm sure there's more than one,' Waters said, confused and pulling a face at Frost.

'Mr Waters – what I mean to say is . . . this one's above ground.'

*

Sue Clarke plonked the baby down on the bathroom floor and approached the bath. 'Eugh,' she said.

The child started to whimper.

'You may complain now, but if you could see the state of this bath you'd refuse to get in. Just a minute . . .'

She sighed and plugged the shower hose on to the bath taps. Frost had left a tidemark to end all tidemarks. And there were what could only be described as an array of 'bits' – some sizeable – left in the dregs. She couldn't bear to think where or what . . . When was the last time this man had bathed? Goodness, to think that she had shared a bed with him once upon a time. To think that he—

'Hey! What's that you've got in your mouth – we don't have any purple face flannels . . . Oh my Lord, no!' She yanked the material away from her son and held up a pair of heavily stained Y-fronts. *That man has got to go.* Baby Philip let out an almighty squeal – as though Frost's pants were a life-giving source. 'Believe me, honey, you'll wind up in Denton General sucking on those. Yuck, yuck, *yuck*!'

After scrubbing and hosing the bath down she ran a shallow one for her boy, where she teased him with the bright yellow duck Frost had brought him. She allowed herself to breathe easy for a minute. She'd get the baby looking respectable first, then whisk the hoover round, nip to the corner shop – she'd just about be straight before her mother arrived. It was imperative to get off on the right foot with her mother, show her that her household was in order, prove herself capable. If she appeared in disarray it would add fuel to the flames of disapproval ignited over her possible return to work. She could hear her mother now: if she couldn't even keep the place in shape while she was off work, what hope would she have of juggling both?

Sue did not want to fall short of her expectations; Mrs Clarke had been the model mother. Given up the library job until Sue was at school. *Kept house.* Then again, she never had Jack Frost lodging with her. Sue smiled down at her baby and imagined her mother meeting Jack. God, they would not get on, on any level. All the more reason to remove any traces of him.

The truth was, she had slightly fudged the details with her mother, work-wise. Things were still up in the air. She had a meeting with Superintendent Mullett on Monday morning to 'discuss the possibility' of her re-joining the force. Clarke had walked out on the job towards the end of last year following her assault on a suspect. She'd known she was for the high jump and didn't care.

Superintendent Mullett had been all for firing her outright. Not only had she attacked DC Simms' murderer, she had also scarred the woman's face, leading to subsequent problems with the court hearing. But when he'd learned of her pregnancy, Mullett had shown clemency and they had agreed a temporary leave of absence on half-pay.

She'd had time to think it over. Nothing would bring Derek back from the dead. Clarke had been dating a young energetic detective, DC Derek Simms, who had been murdered nearly ten months ago. His death occurred the week she'd discovered she was pregnant, and the poor man died thinking himself the father. This belief, however, might not be justified; for Clarke had had a fling with Jack Frost prior to getting together with Simms – there was this flicker of doubt . . . Now, though, Clarke could not bear to consider the question, it hurt too much and she missed Derek terribly, not realizing how much she cared about him until he was no longer there. And perhaps this had influenced her decision to return to work so soon; keep her mind active with police work, she was sure that's what Derek would have wanted. Besides, what the hell else was she to do? Be a single mum? Work part-time in Bejam to support the pair of them? No, it was the force or nothing.

But would Mullett have her back? Frost was of the opinion that a return to CID was a mere formality. She thought Frost blasé; the super was not the compassionate type – he wouldn't give a fig if she and little Philip were on the breadline. Mullett cared only for order and discipline; her behaviour last November would not be easily forgotten, regardless of what Jack Frost thought.

Sunday (2)

An early morning start was the only way to play golf in the summer, so Superintendent Mullett was disappointed with today's arrangement for a 9 a.m. tee-off at the Denton & Rimmington Golf Club. If – no, *when* – he assumed the role of club chairman, there'd be no more of this 9 a.m. nonsense; the club would be open by seven prompt, even on a Sunday. He spied his companions ambling idly towards the green; *'come on, come on,'* he willed them under his breath. It was already ten past, and who was it they'd been waiting for? The outgoing chairman himself, of course: Hudson, that corpulent old toad of a bank manager. Rumour had it he was set to retire by the end of the year, too. Bennington's Bank could certainly do with fresh blood . . .

The sun already had strength in it, and Mullett felt beads of perspiration forming underneath the peak of his golfing cap as he watched the trio grow nearer. Sir Keith, MP for Denton and Rimmington, graciously slowed his step to allow the gasping financier to catch up. Harry Baskin, the local nightclub owner, bowled along full steam, gesticulating with a cigar and talking animatedly to no one but himself.

'Ah, good morning, gentlemen,' Mullett greeted them tightly when they eventually reached the first hole. Each nodded. Hudson was deeply flushed and for a second the superintendent wondered whether he was quite well enough to make it round the course. He better bloody not cark it yet, not until he had cast his all-important vote. Like it or not, he needed that man's blessing.

Mullett stepped back to allow Baskin on to the green.

'We were just talking about that London sort who's doing up the Old Grange out at Two Bridges,' Harry said.

'Oh, I hadn't heard. Who would that be?' Mullett's knowledge of the comings and goings in Denton was poor despite his standing in the local community.

'Has a pretty penny, I can tell you,' Hudson wheezed. 'In fashion, or some such.'

Fashion was a subject on which the four golfers were unified in their ignorance.

Mullett despised the way the banker would drop snippets about clients like that into conversation. Granted, golf was the vehicle the town's dignitaries used to swap and share information – indeed Mullett learned practically all he knew of the town out on the greens. Still, he thought divulging personal financial details like this the height of professional discourtesy. Not least because moving house had left him mortgaged up to the eyeballs, and the thought of them all chuckling away at that titbit around the tee-off made him cringe.

'Yeah,' Baskin was saying, 'and flashing it about he is, too. But not, I might add, my way.'

'Oh, how so?' Mullett feigned interest as the four moved on to the first green.

'Ripping the place apart, improvements left, right and centre. Massive swimming pool now,' Baskin said, disgruntled.

'Ha, yes, the local residents are not best pleased with their new neighbour,' Sir Keith added. 'But we want to encourage new wealth to settle out here and stimulate the community somewhat. I say the City pound is more than welcome in Denton.'

The politician himself lived on an expansive estate near Two Bridges; no disruption short of an earthquake would trouble him all the way out there.

Hold up, thought Mullett. 'This the fellow who threw a huge party that went on a bit?' he said, pleased to have something to offer. And indeed, it transpired, it was. Mullett recalled an area car call-out that way the previous evening, a disturbance of some sort. Mullett thought maybe the locals had overreacted, and was inclined to agree with Sir Keith; some degree of tolerance was necessary to encourage the prosperous into town.

The game proceeded thus, but the banter and jokes were not as fluid as usual, the chatter somewhat subdued. Mullett (not usually the most sensitive of souls) discerned a slight edge to the morning's round. By the time they'd reached the last hole, they were playing in virtual silence. Indeed, Hudson and Baskin had barely exchanged a word all game.

As they loaded up their various cars, the banker called over to the policeman. Mullett was delighted; he was hoping for a quiet word about the succession. Disillusioned with the Freemasons, dismissing them as nothing but a bunch of bawdy drunken junior officers, Mullett was now channelling his energies into improving his status through the golf club. The AGM was on Wednesday evening and he was pretty sure he was a shoo-in; his aptitude for procedure made him a favourite, surely.

'Yes, Michael.' He hurried across the gravel to the Jaguar, where Hudson was struggling to load his clubs into the car's capacious boot. 'Might I help you there?'

'Very kind.'

'Not at all.' The trolley was sizeable. Mullett took the strain.

The clubs weighed a ton. He couldn't begin to imagine how much this armoury must have set Hudson back.

'Thank you.' Hudson touched Mullett's sleeve lightly, then whacked the boot shut with an expensive-sounding click.

'Is there anything else?' Mullett hovered, expectantly.

'As it happens, there is.'

Mullett leaned in.

'What do you know of the goings-on at the Coconut Grove?'

The superintendent stepped back, bemused; this was unusual. A blast of car horn caused him to turn round.

'Harry's place?' Mullett indicated with his chin the passing Mercedes.

Hudson nodded affirmatively. 'In particular, what the young ladies get up to.'

Mullett frowned into the sun; the conversation was not heading in the direction he had hoped for.

St Mary's Church in Denton was considered by many to be one of the most beautiful buildings in the town. Not that it had vast competition. Denton was a so-called 'new town' – knocked up in the sixties in a hurry to feed the growing London overspill. Much of the original village had been trampled on and replaced with cheap housing. Nevertheless the church – an elegant Norman construction set back from the road, largely concealed from view by sweeping yew trees and dense pine – was indeed beautiful. A pleasant reminder of a forgotten past.

Jack Frost slammed the Vauxhall door, startling a flock of doves from nearby conifers and sending them scattering into the warm August morning. Though the church's gentle splendour was lost on him, the place itself held significance for Frost. He had married his wife in St Mary's; and he had recently buried her there too. Not that he thought much on Mary Frost now; their marriage had been far from ideal. All the same, a brief flit of something he thought must be shame touched him for an instant as he considered the noble building.

Outside the main entrance to the grounds, near a wooden gabled porch set within the stone-wall boundary, there stood twenty or so individuals that he assumed made up that morning's congregation.

'Busiest day of the week,' Frost mumbled to Waters.

Father Hill, a tall octogenarian with a shock of white hair, appeared from the midst of his flock.

'Ah William, good morning, my son. I'm sorry to bring you here under such dreadful circumstances,' the vicar said gravely. 'And to you, Sergeant Waters.'

Frost bristled at the use of his Christian name. With Mary now gone the old churchman was the only one who addressed him so. 'What have you got for us, Father?'

'Come this way,' Hill said. The congregation parted to allow them through. 'The poor soul is around the side.'

He guided them along an ancient path through crooked headstones which had long ago ceased to reveal who lay beneath. The earliest of Denton's forefathers were buried at the front of the building, the more ornate seventeenth- and eighteenth-century memorials clustered around the middle of the graveyard, and right the way round the back, in the 'new' section, lay Frost's wife herself.

'Who's that?' Frost said, spotting a middle-aged man with a sparse ginger beard.

'That's Mr Weaver, the verger, who found the body. He opens the church first of a morning.'

Weaver, standing solemnly, retreated a step respectfully as they approached the body.

'Here she is,' the vicar pronounced unnecessarily.

'Aha,' Frost said. He'd seen a lot in his time, but the prostrate body of a beautiful young woman dressed in black and white on top of a Victorian tomb in such an unnatural position sent a shiver down his spine. She lay on her stomach, her head turned back at an impossible angle to face them. The right leg lay across the left, in a way that indicated a double-jointed knee.

'Wait a minute,' Frost said under his breath.

He took a step closer and crouched down. Her eyes were shut, and her mouth ever so slightly open – as though emitting a gentle sigh. A small trickle of blood had run from ruby lips across the alabaster skin.

'I know this woman,' he said.

'An old flame?' Waters whispered right behind him, giving him a start, like a scene out of a Hammer horror film.

'Cut that out!' Frost tutted and stood back, regarding the grave again. 'You know her too, if you stop to think for a second, instead of pratting about putting the willies up me.'

'Christ, you're right,' Waters gasped, 'how the hell . . .'

The woman's clothing appeared ruffled; short black miniskirt askew, revealing bare pasty legs. Her white blouse was off one shoulder, and a black bra strap visible. He thought back to the girl found by the train tracks a year ago: the position was not dissimilar. Could she have just landed there? Jumped? He turned to judge the distance from the church roof; a good leap would make it possible.

'The roof, Father; is it accessible?' The lead from up there had been stolen several times so it was not out of the question.

'Not from inside the church, Inspector – there are no steps. Though, as you know, the building has been scaled from outside over the years.'

'She's hardly dressed for burglary, is she – what, and barefoot,' Waters remarked.

Frost hadn't even noticed the lack of shoes. He forced himself to turn away from the dreadful twist of her body, spun towards the verger and said sharply, 'Seen any shoes lying about on your morning perambulations?'

The poor man shrunk away in alarm. 'Err . . . I . . . no. I've not seen a thing – I . . .'

Frost reached out and hushed him with a touch on the shoulder; Weaver was obviously shaken and who could blame him.

Frost knelt down on to the wet grass. On closer inspection she was lying on a jacket, a black denim number. She was well made-up, as though she was going out with friends – or perhaps on a date? Her lipstick was smudged. Snogging in the grave-yard? Or worse . . .

He pulled out a cigarette and addressed the corpse: 'Well Rachel, honey, what on earth has happened to you?'

Ben Weaver watched the shirt-sleeved detective shuffle off down the uneven, overgrown path, the large black man at his side dodging men in overalls hurrying Weaver's way. Inspector Frost was the least likely-looking policeman he could imagine; an ordinary sort of chap you'd find behind the counter at Halfords. His big companion was equally surprising; he'd never seen a darkie in Denton. But these were small beer compared to the shock discovery of the dead woman that he'd stumbled upon earlier that morning.

He'd been going about his usual business; opening up the church, laying out the vestments, when he'd heard a dog bark-ing ten to the dozen outside in the grounds. Inwardly cursing, Weaver had scurried out to see what all the commotion was about. Father Hill strongly disapproved of dogs anywhere on sacred soil, and Weaver was keen to shoo away the intruder before the priest arrived.

And there he found her, flat out on the tombstone, dead. He had nearly passed out on the spot. For an instant he thought it was *her*, placed there by the Lord himself – his crime laid bare, the victim prostrate for all to see, the stray dog sniffing around her feet. He'd leaned over to get a closer look. Of course it wasn't the same girl; Janey had long auburn locks and this girl had shortish black hair. There was no way it could be her, but he had peered even closer, just to be sure. Janey was twenty-seven, this woman might be a bit older.

Weaver remembered the relief. And then remembered . . . and though his heart had been pounding mightily, instinct had made him reach out and touch her leg, touch that creamy skin, just the way he had done with Janey after it happened.

'I shall send an area car, that usually does the trick,' Wells said.

'We don't want any trouble . . .' the caller said uncertainly.

'A police presence in these circumstances will, I'm sure, prevent the situation from escalating. I'm certain there'll be no further trouble.'

The caller was reassured and hung up. A biker gang at the Cricketers pub on the Wells Road had grown rowdy, and had apparently hurled abuse at a neighbouring house because the man's dog was barking at them. Six of one and half a dozen of the other, the desk sergeant thought. As far back as Wells could remember, Denton had always been a stopping-off place for armies of bikers on their way to the coast during the summer months. Despite a somewhat menacing appearance and their sheer number, the leather-clad hordes had never really caused a problem and Wells wasn't particularly disturbed by the call.

Sunday shifts manning reception at Eagle Lane were always a walk in the park for Desk Sergeant Bill Wells. Until now that is, and the dawn of the computer age at Denton following the edict from up on high. They claimed the new machines would save time, but the reverse was the case for station stalwart Wells. On the face of it, it should be clear-cut: to record all the incidents reported at the desk either over the phone or in person. The training course was all very well, and he could see the logic of the exercise in theory. But Wells was no typist and that's what this whole computer lark required. He'd never in a million years be able to log an emergency quick enough on the computer, so in practice he'd scribble it all down as he'd always done for the last twenty years, then have to type it all up on extra shifts.

Gone were the days he'd saunter in on a Sunday and have plenty of time to mull over the *Racing Post* and do the Pools. He sighed and continued doggedly bashing away at the keyboard with two fingers. Though the Police Federation were in consultation over changes to working conditions, he knew nothing would come of it. The irony was, the only person competent enough to operate this equipment was Mullett's secretary Miss Smith, whose typing proficiency (an impressive 70 words a minute) would make mincemeat of all this guff. But, inevitably, she was deemed too lowly to be allowed near a computer.

He still had the radio, though, through which a mournful Paul Young droned on relentlessly. *Wherever I lay my hat . . .* Wells chuckled to himself. Not that he liked the song – he didn't – but it made him think of Frost; there was a running joke at Eagle Lane to whistle the tune in corridors when passing the homeless inspector.

'Blast,' he cursed to himself as he realized he'd typed a surname in the address field and the computer rejected his entry. Either that or he couldn't read Johnny Johnson's handwriting. They'd alternated running the desk for over ten years, but had never had the need to read the other's scrawl. This dual recording of reports was a waste of time, in Wells' view. 'Bleeding machine, I'll never get this done. And then there's that flamin' expenses report for Mullett – if the bloody printer will ever work—'

'Excuse me, sir.'

Wells turned round to see a lad of about nine or ten at the desk.

'Hello there, young man,' he said with a smile, 'how can I help?'

'It's me mum.'

'Yes?'

'She's not come home.'

Sunday (3)

Though it was high summer and in the mid-seventies outside, the odour of a Sunday roast wafted through the Mullett household. Mullett himself had vetoed the idea of a salad – 'Too continental,' he had said disapprovingly to his wife, Grace. 'We're entertaining, we're British, so it will and must be roast beef.' But as the time drew near for them to take their places at the table, he felt a window or two might be pushed ajar, as it was stifling.

The superintendent's sister-in-law commented on how ravenous she was. Mullett smiled politely at the small pert woman perched on his settee guzzling Bristol Cream.

'Yes, rather,' he agreed, though in truth he had no appetite whatsoever. The conversation with Hudson in the golf-club car park still troubled him greatly. The banker wanted him to have a dancer, one Karen Thomas, removed from the employ of the Coconut Grove nightclub. Mullett chose not to press Hudson on his reasons – he was, after all, nearly three times the girl's age . . . so how to tackle Baskin on such a . . . such a delicate matter? Frost, on the other hand, knew Baskin and the Coconut Grove well; he'd have to trust the matter to him – he couldn't rely on any of the others. Still, the problem remained – how to present the situation to Frost? This Karen Thomas that Hudson was after hadn't done anything . . .

Mullett was so engrossed in the dilemma that he failed to hear the telephone ring. It was only his wife's haw-hawing in the hallway (a noise that set his teeth on edge) that snapped him out of it. Who the devil was calling on a Sunday lunchtime?

'Oh Inspector Frost, you are awful!'

The words cut through him like a knife. Frost! On no account was Grace to speak to Frost! He darted out of the living room, ignoring his guest, into the hallway and snatched the telephone from his wife's grasp.

'Frost,' he barked, his temper racing from 0 to 60 in a flash, 'what is the meaning of this!' Grace returned sheepishly to the kitchen to check on the spuds. Mullett knew that he was playing into Frost's hands by flaring up like this. There should be no reason for a superintendent to be angry at being called at home by a colleague. No, this was all because of that *incident* concerning Grace, that paperboy getting run over . . .

'Wait, say that again?' demanded Mullett, sensing he'd not taken in a word the man was saying. 'A girl dead? Where? In St Mary's?'

Frost was calling from the rectory. Mullett frowned as he listened to the recently promoted inspector explain the discovery of a dead body in the grounds there – a woman who, it turned out, Frost had arrested the previous year for armed robbery. She had recently been let out on licence. Mullett felt his temples begin to pulse and fumbled for his newly prescribed pills.

'I see. Do you suspect foul play?'

'Well, yes, Superintendent. I think it's fair to say that someone has taken a dislike to our Rachel.'

They should never have let the woman out in the first place, and to compound things she'd gone and got herself killed, creating yet more work for him. 'Get Drysdale's assessment and I'll see you at the station, six o'clock sharp.'

Frost sat quietly in the car as Waters waited at the main-road junction to pull out. An endless stream of motorcycles poured past. He retrieved his Polaroids from the sun visor.

'I can see you on one of those,' Waters said.

'You may joke, but I've often thought about getting a bike.'

'Really?'

'Sidecar too, for you.'

'Would be an improvement on what you're driving now.'

'Hmm.' Frost didn't comment further. He had his late wife's Mini Metro. (He was sure his mother-in-law had only permitted that because to sell it in its current state was too much trouble.)

'What news on a new motor?' Waters slipped on to the main road.

'I've grown used to the rust-bucket, and I can claim an allowance.'

'But it spends more time in the garage than on the road.'

'Not at the moment; it's at Sue's flat, loaded with all my earthly possessions. I'm between moves, aren't I.' Frost settled his elbow on the windowsill, as warm air filled the car. 'Wouldn't do to turn up to a crime scene like some travelling tinker, would it?'

They'd left the church having interviewed the vicar and verger. Both clergymen were in a state of shock, especially the poor verger, who'd discovered the body. Indeed Weaver's complexion had been as pale as the dead girl's. Drysdale had been alerted, as had the County lab, and that was where the detectives were now headed. And so another weekend was to be eaten away with unpleasantness. Being as they were a man down – or woman, to be precise – in the form of DC Sue Clarke, Hornrim

24

Harry had had no alternative but to approve overtime. Frost had nothing better to do anyway, adrift as he currently was – he was still waiting for a share of the proceeds from the sale of his old marital home, but wasn't expecting much – the house had been originally purchased with money from his wife's wealthy parents, neither of whom were fans of his. His belongings were currently collecting dust in storage, or crammed into the Mini Metro. With Suzy Fong gone, he had nothing but jazz records and history books for company. Unlike Waters here . . . Suddenly, Frost slapped himself on the forehead. The wedding!

'Sorry we missed our extra rehearsal, John,' Frost said, emphasizing the 'our'.

'No big deal, Jack. The good father said we could catch him later in the week.'

'No, it's out of order. I didn't even think . . .'

'It's cool, man. I had a chat with Father Hill while you were on the phone to Mullett. We'll do it one evening next week.'

'Good, good. Let me know, eh?' Frost lit a cigarette. After a suitable pause he said, 'Seeing that woman there, horrible. Tragic.'

'What was her name again – her real name, not her stage name?'

'Rachel Curtis. And "stage name" sounds a bit posh for a stripper at the Coconut Grove.'

'Rachel Curtis, that's right. And Rayner was what she called herself at work, right?'

''Fraid so, yes.' Frost exhaled and remembered the grisly events of last November. Rachel Curtis, Rayner as she was then, had robbed a payroll – ambushed two men from the Gregory Leather handbag factory at gunpoint on their way back from the bank with the weekly wages. Both men were shot; one had died later in hospital. His name was Albert Benson; he was just a bit of muscle from the factory warehouse who usually accompanied the wages clerk. She'd been convicted by the jury but the judge had been very lenient. His decision had shocked the whole of Denton. The relatives of the deceased made a television appearance. The press was up in arms. The judge was lambasted for being a do-gooder lefty.

Mitigating circumstances had accounted for the leniency in the judge's sentencing.

Rachel Curtis had been the girlfriend of a local gangster named Robert Nicholson, who was now serving a life sentence for murder. He was a vicious psychopath with ruthless ambition and the court had heard how he'd tormented Curtis into carrying out the payroll attack. She had wanted to escape his control, but was terrified. Curtis's lawyers had pleaded mental torture and coercion, told the court the robbery was an act of sheer desperation. In an unprecedented move she was given a suspended sentence and released on licence. Now she'd wound up dead on top of a tomb.

The obvious place to start was the relatives of the deceased warehouse employee. They certainly had a motive, but it would seem unlikely. On the face of it, the death looked to Frost to be some hanky-panky that had gone gravely wrong. He winced inwardly at the pun.

'When did she get out?' Waters said.

'Actually on the street? Two weeks ago. She—'

Waters hit the brakes suddenly and took a sharp right turn. Frost, who still abstained from wearing a seatbelt, was flung forward. The County laboratory could be easily missed from the road. It had a discreet entrance in a wall of conifers and from the outside, with its manicured lawn and well-tended evergreen borders, it had all the trappings of a retirement home. It radiated calm. A deathly calm.

'Bloody hell! Wedding nerves getting to you?' Frost barked, straightening himself out. 'As I was saying before you gave me whiplash, she's only been out two weeks, so in theory her movements shouldn't be difficult to trace.'

Waters pulled up sloppily next to a 1960s Rolls-Royce Corniche. Drysdale was in, then, and on a Sunday too. The fact that the county's chief pathologist cruised about in a Roller was a fact that neither Frost or Waters could fathom.

''Ere, you thought of asking Dr Death to drive you to the church instead of paying Charlie £25 for that rusty old Jag?' Frost asked, peeling himself away from the Vauxhall's plastic upholstery and climbing out of the car. The back of his shirt was wet through. 'What a belter, let's try and squeeze a pint in after this, eh?'

'I don't know about that, Jack, I got things to do and Kim says . . .'

'"And Kim says"? Gor blimey! Am I going to hear that for the rest of our days?' He clapped the taller man on the back as they entered the building.

'Leave it out, Jack, let's see later how we are for time.' He pushed open the stiff double doors muttering, 'And that ain't any old Jag – it's an SS 100.'

The lab was as cold as its walls were grey. Summer never entered the place. The chill made them pick up the pace as they headed directly for the heart of the building, where in a large room a tall gaunt fellow in white stood, head bowed, over a steel table. The sour green lighting added to the macabre feel and general unpleasantness of the place. Frost gave an involuntary shudder.

'Ah, gentlemen.' Drysdale looked up from Rachel Curtis's body and scowled at them.

'Afternoon, Doc, what you got for us?'

'Very little, visibly, that is. A bang to the back of the head,' he said. 'The neck is—'

'A bang on the back of the head?' Frost spluttered. 'Is her neck broken?'

Drysdale winced. 'If you would let me finish? The neck is *not* broken, but the right ankle is. Apart from the knock to the head there are no obvious external wounds. The ankle fracture is consistent with a fall; the head injury is not. There was no blood.'

'So what you saying?' Waters asked.

'Could it be she was killed there, on the gravestone, after you know, a bit of . . .' Frost urged.

'I'm not saying anything as yet. There are grass stains to the skirt and jacket. She has had intercourse recently, but until we have the test results and I've performed the autopsy, that's all I can tell you.'

'Oh,' Frost said, disappointed. Though he wasn't a fan of the posh pathologist personally, he held Drysdale in high regard and relied on him for a lead in cases like this. He couldn't reasonably expect him to have the test results already; he did need to give the man some time.

'There is this, though; might give you a start at least.' With a long finger he pointed down to the corpse.

'What?'

'There's a small crab—'

'Crab? Be surprised to find any form of crustacean in Denton, let alone in the graveyard,' said Frost.

'. . . on the left buttock,' Drysdale continued with a sigh. 'See here?' He poked the white flesh. 'It's a *tattoo*, Inspector, done in the last couple of days or so, judging from the blistering.'

'So it is.' Frost leaned in for a closer look. It was quite tasteful, if that was the right word. Or perhaps intricate was more apt. 'Can even see its little claws.' The surrounding skin had reacted, suggesting as the doctor had said that it was recent. ''Ere, John, take a butcher's at this.'

Drysdale handed Waters a magnifying glass.

'You're right, Doc,' Frost said, moving back to allow his colleague a look, 'it is what we in the trade call a "lead".'

Drysdale smiled thinly, and held up a large scalpel which glinted dully in the weak green light. 'Indeed. Now, perhaps, if you might allow it to lead you both out, I might make a start on the autopsy. See what we might find, eh?'

'Absolutely, Doc,' Frost said perkily. 'One final thing, though – check out her tootsies, will you; she was missing her shoes.'

'Nice day for it?' Frost beamed.

'So much for moving house then,' Waters said.

'That'll take me five minutes. Why waste a lovely afternoon and good company. It is the weekend, after all.'

The pair sat in the very pleasant beer garden of the Bull pub, a sharp contrast to the gloom of Drysdale's lab. It hadn't taken much for Jack Frost to twist DS John Waters' arm – something his fiancée, Kim, was constantly pointing out; but, hell, it was a scorching day, his pint tasted good, and combined with the colour and fragrance of the huge hanging baskets on display it really was the perfect antidote to the lab. (And anyway, it was another hour before DC Kim Myles finished her shift; so long as Waters remembered to drop that old guy the deposit for the motor – a vintage Jaguar – then she could not accuse him of being a total failure.)

'So what do you reckon then?' Waters asked.

'She went for a bit of rumpo in the churchyard, and something went a bit wrong?'

'A fatal head injury and a broken leg? More than a *bit wrong*, wouldn't you say?'

'Broken ankle,' Frost corrected. 'Maybe she was adventurous, hell, I don't know? The grass stain on the skirt would match the churchyard.' Frost took a large gulp. 'Let's find out who she's seen since she got out. Her social circle can't have been that wide and a lot of them would be giving her a wide berth knowing her to be on licence.' Frost toyed with the pack of Rothmans lying on the wooden table. 'Wouldn't want to be seen fraternizing. Her probation officer would be the place to start – she'd have had to check in with one.'

'Which one?' Waters knew there were two in Denton, a young woman and a curmudgeonly Scot.

'Fergusson.'

'We'll pay him a call after this. Then tomorrow we'll visit the tattoo parlours off Foundling Lane. Hanlon and Simms junior will be back by then.'

'I still think it's a bit harsh to send young Simms over to her next of kin, don't you?'

'Nonsense. Besides, we don't have time to trek over to Sheffield, or wherever it is her old dear lives.'

Waters looked around him, at the lazy, enjoyable pub garden. 'No, quite.'

'Oh come on. It's a mere formality, and will toughen him up a bit. Besides, he's not alone. Arthur is driving. He can't spend all day dicking about with computers, can he, if he wants to be a detective like his late lamented big brother?'

The men reflected on Derek Simms in silence for a moment. The deceased detective often gave pause for thought among those at Eagle Lane, though he was seldom discussed openly. The episode cast a long shadow over the station for many months, and most would rather not comment, preferring to keep their grief private. The manner of his death – stabbed outside Frost's home – left most feeling uneasy, and then there was the respect due to his kid brother, David. Who knew how this brave individual might really feel . . .

'I don't know that he does, though, do you?' Frost said eventually. 'I mean— 'ello, what's happening 'ere?'

Lying next to his cigarettes, the small black device, not much bigger than a matchbox, had started flashing red angrily.

'Flamin' bleeper.' Frost sighed. 'Another one?' He rose from the bench. 'I mean, we've not had a break all day. I'm bleedin' parched. Won't be long.'

'What about that?'

'I left it in the car, didn't I?' He winked playfully.

Your car's at Sue's flat, Waters thought as he watched Frost amble off towards the pub's rear entrance. Maybe he was right. One more wouldn't hurt, and he needed to drink something in this heat, after all.

Sunday (4) ─────────────────────────────

'Afternoon, sonny,' Frost said softly to the young lad dwarfed by the large interview room. 'Let's start from the beginning.'

After two further swift pints, Frost's conscience had got the better of him and he had returned to Eagle Lane at just after one thirty. He hated that bleeper, didn't like the idea that he could be got at, 'paged' or whatever, just like that. He wasn't a flamin' doctor. Nevertheless it was a Sunday, and Bill Wells would not have bleeped him unless it was urgent.

'Me name is Richard, Richard Hammond. I live at flat 14, Clay House.' The boy spoke clearly, with a touch of West Country. Clay House was a block of flats on the Southern Housing Estate, the grimmest part of Denton.

'Here you go, young man.' Desk Sergeant Bill Wells elbowed his way into the room clutching two dripping ice-cream cones. 'I got you a double flake.'

The boy's eyes lit up as Wells passed one over.

'Oi, where's mine?' Frost snapped at the desk sergeant who'd already begun to devour the remaining cone with gusto.

'I've only two 'ands,' Wells complained, winking at the lad.

'Tch, tch, honestly.' Frost played it up to amuse the kid, who smiled at Wells.

The inspector stood and circled the boy, who must have been about ten, and took in the lad's appearance. Richard Hammond was wearing a Denton Juniors school jersey. From behind, Frost could discern a dirty neckline on the white shirt collar. Neglect. It was tangible.

Frost knew the Clay House flats well; just off the Brick Road, many of them housed prostitutes.

'When was the last time you saw your mum?'

'Saturday teatime.'

'What time is that?' Keeping no regular mealtimes himself, Frost had no idea what the norm was.

'Four thirty,' the boy replied, ice cream dribbling down his chin.

'And you've been alone all that time?'

He nodded.

'Does she often do that, leave you on your own?' Wells asked, concerned.

'Sometimes.' The boy shrugged.

'Any idea where she'd gone?' Frost continued.

'To see a man in Rimmington.'

'Did she say what time she'd be back?'

'About seven.'

'So she'd gone for dinner,' Frost said disingenuously.

'Maybe, but usually she'd just 'ave it off with him, then come home and have cheese on toast,' he said confidently.

In the corner Wells spluttered into his 99 Flake.

Frost smiled at the young lad and said, 'A close friend of your mum's, is he, this fella in Rimmington?'

The boy bit the end off the cone, and sucked noisily before answering, 'Nah, don't think so, just a regular.'

Frost sat down and, crossing his arms on the table, leaned

forward. 'Is your mum what they call a "working girl"?'

'She's a prozzie, oldest profession in the world, she says, up there with soldiers and religion.'

Donal Fergusson lived in a flat in Baron's Court, behind Market Square. DS Waters had come into contact with the man only once before and, in spite of his reputation, had found him to be helpful.

Waters climbed the stairs to the second floor. After rapping at the door he looked down over the balcony. He knew the man was at home as he'd called ahead to arrange it – it was a Sunday after all. Fergusson had enquired as to the nature of his business. He'd told him it was concerning Rachel Curtis, said it was important they discuss it face to face, and the probation officer had appeared satisfied and told him to come round.

Two boys on bicycles were taunting an elderly woman struggling with a walking stick. The three-storey block was popular with the retired population due to its location: quiet and secluded yet close to Market Square. One of the boys wheeled in close to the old lady and she cowered. From up on the second floor, Waters whistled mightily through his fingers. The two kids jumped out of their skin, the OAP barely moved. Deaf, probably.

He recognized one of the pasty faces looking up at him, mouths agape. 'Deering!' he bellowed, leaning over the railing. 'I see you, sunshine – don't move an inch! I'll be down in five to give you a lift home myself!'

The pair scarpered, leaving their prey mystified but alone and safe.

'Detective Waters,' came a broad Glaswegian accent from behind him. 'That's some whistle you have there.'

'Mr Fergusson, thanks for sparing the time.'

'Not at all. Please.' Fergusson, tall and thin, stepped back to allow the detective in.

'It's serious, I'm afraid, hence the house call.' Waters walked into a spacious lounge-diner.

'Please take a seat.'

Pulling out a chair from an oval table, Waters sat. There was dreary classical music playing in the background.

'She's dead, isn't she?' Fergusson said plainly.

'What makes you say that?'

'Why else would you be here?'

'She might have skipped town,' Waters suggested.

'But then I'd be the one calling you?'

'Ha, yes.' Waters stretched his legs in front of him. Fergusson himself remained standing. 'You don't sound surprised?'

'I'm not. She was heading for a crash, that one.'

'Why?'

'Her mental health: she was clearly traumatized. What happened was the result of years of cruelty from that thug of a boyfriend, Nicholson.'

'You believe that?'

'What I believe is irrelevant – it's highly uncommon that someone guilty of such serious crimes would be released without a very good reason.'

'True,' the DS conceded. 'But then why not transfer her to a secure mental health unit, for her own safety if nothing else?'

'I'm not a judge, Sergeant. Though I believe the intention was that her mother would step in – from somewhere up north.'

'Sheffield. When was the last time you saw Rachel?'

'Thursday, 9 a.m. Billy's Café.'

Waters thought the probation officer remarkably detached. 'How long had you been meeting Rachel?'

'It was only our second meeting; once on the Tuesday when she got out, and then again last week on Thursday.'

'And how did you find her?'

'Lively.'

'Meaning?'

'Relieved to be out.'

'Any indication of what she was planning to do?'

'No, she had no immediate plans.'

'And so you thought her mental state was, what, disturbed?'

'My role, Sergeant, is to try to keep them out of trouble, and offer guidance. She was released on grounds of mental cruelty,' he said, finally pulling out a chair, realizing this might not take just a few minutes after all.

'I'm just trying to assess what frame of mind she was in. You might have been the last person to have seen her alive.' Waters didn't think so, but he wanted to impress upon Fergusson the importance of his last meeting with the deceased.

'Of course, of course.' Fergusson sighed. 'I'm not being a tremendous help, am I?'

Waters shrugged and smiled. 'It's not easy.'

The remark put the ageing probation officer at ease. 'She was certainly troubled.'

'How so?'

'Worried about reprisals from the victim's family. There was a big outcry when she was let off so lightly, you know. She decided it would be better to put the house on the market.'

'Yes, I read about the uproar in the *Echo* and *Gazette*. Did she come into contact with any of them?'

'She did mention the wife of the man she shot, I can't remember the context exactly – she brushed over it, didn't want to talk about it when I asked her. Maybe she felt remorse, I couldn't say . . . but I tell you who would know.'

'Who?'

'Sandy Lane.'

Sandy Lane, *Denton Echo*'s scurrilous chief hack. Interesting – but tricky. The press would find out about Rachel Curtis's death at the super's briefing tomorrow. If he visited Lane about it now, it could be front-page news come Monday's cornflakes.

Could he trust him to keep it under wraps? Somehow Waters sensed that, slippery though he was, if they wanted Lane on side they'd best bring him into the loop now.

'Good heavens, Susan, open the window!' Patricia Clarke waved a handkerchief dramatically under her nose. It was nearly two and Sue's mother had arrived late from Colchester due to dreadful traffic. 'It smells, of . . . I don't know what.'

I know exactly what it smells of, Sue fumed silently to herself. She'd had the windows open all morning but it clearly was not enough to combat the subtle but undeniable *Parfum de Frost*: takeaway food, cigarettes, stale body odour, *feet* – all subtly blended and ingrained for ever in the very fabric of her flat.

'Did you have a party last night? Poor Philip.' Patricia cooed at the boy on the carpet. Her mother had been in the flat a mere five minutes, and already Sue felt totally inadequate.

'No, just a friend over for a takeaway – I did have the window open but thought the breeze might be too chilly for Philip.' She looked down at the boy in dismay as he sucked on a Dinky Toy. Another inappropriate present from Frost – as if Philip would know who Captain Scarlet was. 'I do wish he'd not put everything he touched in his mouth,' she said, wincing as she remembered the underwear this morning.

The flat, unlike the kid who lived there with his mum, was spick and span. This came as no surprise to Frost. No self-respecting Denton prostitute would dream of keeping an untidy place of business and Jane Hammond was just like the others – she'd not risk putting off a punter for the sake of a few hours with a tub of Shake n' Vac and a duster. If the place was clean, so was the girl, local logic seemed to have it. The fact that her son went unwashed, and wore the same shirt all week, was no revelation either. No, Richard Hammond's lot was at best to keep out of the way, ignored, to the point of non-existence. The men who came to call at Jane's flat would not welcome such a reminder of domesticity.

Frost and the WPC crossed the threshold. He'd already briefed WPC Mitchell to search the mother's room while he occupied the boy's attention.

'Where's your room, sonny?' Frost said, as upbeat as he could muster.

'Through here.'

Frost pushed open the door to a boxroom. Something crunched underfoot as he entered. 'Didn't have Lego in my day,' Frost said enviously, surveying a sea of plastic bricks broken only by the small bed against the wall, 'it was balsawood aeroplanes and lead soldiers all the way, until packets of Woodbines and bottles of stout took over.' He moved gingerly across the floor to the bed, above which was the room's only tiny window. He looked out on to what appeared to be wasteland; tyres, prams and shopping trolleys, punctuated with tree-sized buddleia, crowned by clouds of butterflies in the hot afternoon.

'Ever play out there?' Frost asked, thinking it a veritable adventure-land for a kid Richard's age.

'Yeah, but my mum doesn't like me out there too late.'

'Why's that then?'

'She thinks I'll fall in the canal.'

'The canal?' By now the lad was standing on the mattress, shoulder to shoulder with Frost. 'Where's that?'

'Back of those bushes.'

'Of course it is.' The Denton Union Canal, the unofficial border between the Southern Housing Estate and Denton town itself, lay invisible two hundred yards away behind a scrub of bushes; beyond them the towpath, and then the old industrial estate on the other side. The abandoned mill sat shimmering on the horizon, majestic in its ruin. Frost sighed and moved back from the window, a bitter taste in his mouth at the prospect of having the canal dragged.

'When your mum pops out, who looks out for you?'

'Mrs Ridley next door. She's retired.'

Not ideal; Frost wanted the boy out of the area.

'Is there anyone else you can stay with while we find your mum?' he said, suddenly keen to be out of the child's room.

'Me aunt in Rimmington.'

'Oh, I see.' Frost had hoped for a father, but didn't bring it up. 'This aunt, does your mum keep in regular touch?'

'Now and then. Some Saturday nights she might stay over, after . . . work.'

'But not this Saturday?'

'Nah.' The boy picked up a Lego spaceship from the floor, and pushed a loose wing back in place determinedly. 'She'd have said before she left. She never doesn't tell me where she's going.' He held the toy firmly, staring at it and not meeting Frost's gaze. '*Never.*' He said the word again with a hint of anger.

'You're close to your mum, aren't you, Richard?'

The boy was struggling with his emotions; he wanted to be cross with her for going off without a word, but couldn't quite believe she'd do that, and the alternative, which hid just beneath the surface, scared him. 'We've only got each other, and if—' he started to say to the Lego.

'Sir,' WPC Mitchell interrupted softly from the doorway, 'found something.'

He could hear movement next door. It could only be the police. He stepped up close to the wall.

The boy would have grown concerned when Janey didn't materialize in the morning. She often stopped out, on a Saturday night – that's what he hated most, the idea of her spending a night out with another man; when she clock-watched with him like a hawk. And that's when he'd done it, when she was on her way out; like an accident, almost. Except it was no accident. It was pure rage.

The movements next door seemed to have stopped, so he backed away from the wall. The socks he was knitting for his mother lay innocently on the sofa, one needle tip proudly poking from the wool. Beside it sat a shrouded figure. She was still stiff. Weaver felt a pang of guilt in his chest. Poor Janey. He dared not try and move her yet. He shook his head and proceeded to pace the floor of the cramped flat anxiously.

Oh God, he never meant for this to happen. Any of it! He just wanted her to stop working. *Working* – that was what she called it but what she did wasn't work. She was defiling herself. Degrading herself. She'd tease him, saying there were plenty of prostitutes in the Scriptures. As if the Lord Himself had given her His seal of approval! Weaver would remind her of Proverbs 23:27: 'For a prostitute is a deep pit and a wayward wife is a narrow well. Like a bandit she lies in wait, and multiplies the unfaithful among men.' But, as the Lord was also fond of saying, and Ben was equally fond of pointing out, the harlot was not beyond salvation. Oh yes, Benjamin knew his Testaments, Old *and* New, and was fond of quoting from both – when it suited his purpose . . . He preferred not to think of Proverbs 5:3, for instance: 'For the lips of an immoral woman drip honey.' It only reminded him of the allure of beauty – reminded him, painfully, of that over which he had no control.

Whatever. He just wanted her to STOP. Rage pumped through him again, like it had before. He could feel his temples throbbing, a jealousy so powerful he thought he was going to throw up again. Calm, Benjamin, *calm*. All he ever wanted was her to stop for a little while . . .

He kept telling himself it was an accident. But the police would never see it like that; especially not now. He could hear someone with a hacking cough next door – it must be the coarse one he'd met in the churchyard this morning. It would only be a matter of time before they discovered that he, Ben Weaver, was Janey's neighbour. He must tell them – it would be expected, a man in his position. But not today. No, not today. He needed time to compose himself and come up with a plan about the – here he gave an involuntary shiver – the body. He'd need to be careful, what with the police crawling all over. He had to think of something subtle, something that didn't involve hauling her out of Clay House . . . In the meantime, if they came knocking, as they surely would, he'd keep silent and wait for them to go away. They weren't going to break down the door, she'd only been missing twenty-four hours. Tomorrow, he'd go tomorrow, to see the police. The scruffy one had given him his card in the churchyard . . .

Sunday (5) _____

'Had she . . . you know?' Mullett enquired.

Frost raised an eyebrow, feigning incomprehension. The evening sun sliced through the blinds, projecting bars across the far wall. Cigarette smoke drifted lazily towards the ceiling.

'Well?'

Frost cleared his throat, and said, 'Yeah, quite a bit actually.'

The superintendent winced, he couldn't conceive of what Frost's interpretation of 'quite a bit' might be versus his own. 'Rape?'

Frost shook his head in a pronounced way. 'Dr Death thinks not. There are no marks to indicate a struggle. In fact, there are no marks anywhere.'

'What, over the whole body?'

'Apart from the back of the head. Where she could have hit her head on the tombstone.'

'And that's it?'

'Yes, for now.' Frost stubbed out his cigarette.

Why must he make me squeeze every single thing out of him, Mullett thought. 'So what's your assessment?'

'At this stage?'

'Yes, at this stage.'

'I think young Rachel was in there for a bit of how's-your-father, got carried away and bang' – he clapped his hands – 'smashes her head on the tombstone. The fella panics, and scarpers.'

'I find that rather hard to swallow, Frost,' he said sternly. 'But I'd rather that than any hocus pocus.'

'How do you mean, sir? She's wasn't sawn in half.'

'You know – witchcraft, devilry, satanic ritual; found in the churchyard and what have you. Remember those young girls in Denton Woods? Prancing around in the middle of the night, chanting, and so on.'

'Ah, I don't think that's the case here, sir.'

'She should never have been released,' Mullett said to himself. 'Some do-gooder judge makes a mess and now we have to clear it up.'

'Well, if that's all, I . . .' Frost motioned to go.

'I've not finished.' Mullett himself rose. 'There's something else,' he continued as he twiddled with the blinds. 'The Coconut Grove, I feel it's time to pay Baskin a visit. I hear rumours.'

'Rumours? Why? About what?'

'The unsavoury treatment of the young ladies within his employ.'

'Sorry, sir, you'll have to be more specific.'

Mullett spun round. 'I have it on good authority the girls are . . . are . . .' He paused, searching for the right word. 'Are . . .'

'Are *what*?' Frost's crumpled brow indicated genuine confusion.

'Just . . . get down there and see if there's anything going off.'

Frost lit a fresh cigarette. 'The only things coming off, over there, are knickers. It's a strip club, sir, in case you didn't know . . .'

'I know what it is.' Mullett leaned across the immaculate desk, knuckles resting on its polished surface. 'Just find out if there's a Karen Thomas, twenty-two years of age, working there, and in what capacity.'

Frost shrugged. 'Twenty-two? She'll be working the pole like all the others, is my bet.'

'I beg your pardon?'

'Working the pole, it's all the rage – a new sort of strip dance.' Frost blew smoke rings in his direction. 'With a pole. Like what firemen use.'

Mullett dodged the smoke. 'I'm not with you, Frost. How might one dance with such a thing?'

Frost stood, and clutched an imaginary pole. 'They entwine themselves' – he stuck a leg out inelegantly – 'naked, poking legs at you in an erotic fashion. Like so . . .'

Mullett was at a loss. 'How ridiculous.' Was this what Hudson was getting in a fluster over? 'Well, get down there and find out if she's working there.'

'What's she done?'

'Nothing.'

'Then why am I going to see her?'

'Because I'm asking you to.'

Frost remained unmoved.

'Very well. The girl may be involved in blackmailing a local businessman.' Mullett felt he had to say something, and in a twisted way, it might even be true.

Frost exhaled and stubbed out his cigarette, but said nothing.

'I can't add any more than that for now. We'll catch up tomorrow – I know we're lean on staff, but I know if there's anything fishy, you'll sniff it out,' the super said, obsequiously.

'Yes, we are lean on staff, sir, you're right. Two men down.'

'One, Jack, we're one down.'

'You're one down, I'm two down – Derek Simms's brother David is in uniform.'

'The computers, Inspector, you're forgetting the computers.' Mullett smiled. 'They make all the difference.'

Frost snorted. 'Difference to what? The front desk may look like NASA Mission Control but Bill Wells looks as comfortable as John Hurt at teatime.'

Wells' progress was painstakingly slow, that much was true, but that was not Frost's concern and Mullett had had enough. 'Be that as it may, progress *will* be made – and if you really can't handle it, we can rely on Rimmington; Superintendent Kelsey informs me Inspector Allen has returned and may be called upon if necessary – Jim's a good man . . .'

'Forgive me, sir, but surely that's simply not necessary. Detective Clarke is fighting fit.'

'Clarke?' Mullett sat back at his desk. 'I'm not so sure of that. I've an appointment with Ms Clarke tomorrow. No, cast that from your mind. Jim Allen is our man.'

'Mrs Mullett was bouncy this morning,' Frost said, non-chalant as you like.

Mullett's jaw dropped.

Frost continued, 'Yes, she offered to take me for a spin in that MG of hers. Now the weather's improved, she can put the roof down.'

Mullett stared hard at Frost and for an instant, Jack thought he'd overstepped the mark. Mullett's wife was not a safe topic for conversation – but Frost felt confident he could push things a bit, given what he knew . . . He'd never had to bring up the paperboy hit-and-run incident – not yet – but it gave him some leeway.

'We sold it months ago,' Mullett said eventually. 'Now, if you'll be so good as to return to work, it would be greatly appreciated.'

Frost nodded and made for the door. There was a steeliness to Mullett's tone he'd not heard before. Got to hand it to the super, he gives nothing away. Oh, well, he'd see how tomorrow panned out. On his way out he winked at Miss Smith, who rolled her eyes.

John Waters elbowed the flat door open, holding his suit over his shoulder. He could hear Kim in the kitchen, back from her early shift at Rimmington. Tossing his keys on to the sideboard, he made to creep up on his fiancée. The diminutive blonde was at the hob, whistling softly to herself. He was a foot away when she spun round wielding a wooden spoon.

'You think I couldn't hear you? You great lunk!'

He lifted her up in a show of affection. He was the luckiest man in Denton.

'You'd never make a cat burglar.' She smiled up at him, show-ing off her pristine white teeth.

'I hope things never get to that state . . .'

'How'd it go?' she asked.

'How'd what go?'

She pushed him away. 'John – don't tell me you forgot to go? Wait – have you been drinking?'

He looked confused, then said, 'Ah, the church . . . yes. We did go – but there was no rehearsal. A body – a woman's body – was found in the churchyard.'

Kim Myles' annoyance evaporated as swiftly as it had arisen. 'Of course. I heard . . . That was St Mary's.' She looked so sad. 'I try to keep your work and our wedding separate—'

The phone rang, interrupting a thread that could have ended with another work/life argument.

'Hello?' she enquired politely into the receiver. 'Yes, he is . . . who may I say is calling?' Kim held the phone out and looked away in distaste.

'Waters.'

'Detective,' a familiar voice said. 'You're after me, I gather? Funnily enough, I was after you, too, but when I got home the wife said you'd been round.'

Sandy Lane. Bloody hack.

'Sandy. Yeah, I was after you, but it can wait until tomorrow.' Waters watched Kim saunter past, disrobing; she'd always have a bath after finishing a shift.

'What you want might wait,' said Sandy. 'But what *I* want won't.'

Waters immediately grew suspicious; Lane knew something.

'News and deadlines wait for no man,' Lane continued. 'Meet you in the Eagle at nine.'

The line clicked dead.

It was one thing questioning Lane, but another thing entirely being pumped for info for newsprint; he could imagine being stitched up. He'd bell Frost, or rather leave a message at the Jade Rabbit – best there were two of them.

Frost had arranged with the Hammonds' neighbour, a sweet old dear by the name of Ridley, to mind Richard for tonight. The WPC had cleared it with social services – as they were already over-stretched, they could offer no alternative on a Sunday. The lad was shockingly self-sufficient; the epitome of modern times, a typical latchkey kid. Tomorrow they'd move him to the aunt in Rimmington if his mum had not surfaced. Frost had called Clare Hammond from the station before setting off for Baskin's nightclub and advised her of the situation.

There were several vehicles in the club's car park. It was almost dark and the neon lights caught on a number of bonnets nearer the entrance. He turned off the engine and the cassette player. ELO's *Time* had been in there since he could remember. Who'd be there on a Sunday evening, Frost wondered, as he pushed the door of his Metro shut. It was balmy and insects bothered the air around him.

The Coconut Grove, Harry Baskin's nightclub, was on the outskirts of town, hidden beyond woodlands at the end of a leafy country lane (or as Frost had described it to colleagues, 'an outside privy at the bottom of the garden where jazz mags come to life'). In any case it was secluded. No way to know who was within, unless and until you banged on the door to find out. Frost nodded to the doorman.

'Wotcha Gary, Harry in this evening?'

'Sunday's his night off, Mr Frost.'

'Oh, never mind.' Frost pushed the double doors open and entered the club. He reckoned the bouncer would call Harry the second he'd crossed the threshold. Frost knew Baskin of old and they had sparred many a time over the years. They had grown surprisingly close after Harry was shot the previous year; but the old gangster had recovered his health, restored his inherent mistrust of the law and re-established a dignified distance between them. It was all very cosy Frost playing cards with Baskin, while the latter lay wounded in a hospital bed, but Baskin had to maintain his self-respect – he couldn't be seen to be growing soft – and since then the two had barely spoken.

Frost's eyes fought to adjust to the dingy atmosphere inside. 'Flamin' heck,' he cursed. Inside, the joint was reminiscent of a Soho sex club. He walked cautiously towards the rectangle of light that was the entry kiosk.

'Hello, love.' He beamed at the redhead behind the till. 'What you got showing tonight? *Twelfth Night, Romeo and Juliet*?'

The girl, she must have been all of nineteen, chewed noisily on some gum. 'You what?'

He flashed his badge; the girl was unperturbed. 'Only two girls on tonight, Karen and Sarah. If you hurry you'll catch Karen – she's about to go on.'

'Tell me, has Rachel been in at all?' This was why he'd really come to the Grove tonight, not Mullett's stupid errand (Frost had felt instantly that the super was telling porkies; as if he'd know that some stripper was engaged in a spot of blackmail! That was not the sort of tittle-tattle Hornrim Harry picked up on the golf course.)

'Rachel?' She pulled a face.

'Young, pretty, short jet-black bob?'

'Don't think so . . .'

'She used to work here. Robbed a payroll, shot a man last year, right little firecracker.'

'Oh *her*. You said *young*. Rachel – she's at least *thirty* – yes, she came in looking for Kate.'

'And is "Kate" in this evening?'

'Kate left months ago.'

'Any idea where?'

'Nah, manager might know – she'll be in there.' She nodded towards the *Bar* sign.

The manageress wasn't visible so Frost took a glass of wine from the bar, on the house, and went to find a booth. Only the bar itself was lit up, and it was tricky to work out which seats were occupied until you'd practically sat on some sorry individual nursing unpalatable French plonk. He eventually found a chair near the stage. The room was more airless and sticky than usual, heightening the fetid aura of sleaze. Frost settled in.

Soon the soft lounge music was replaced by loud lush disco – something from *Saturday Night Fever*? – and the lighting was adjusted; the bar lights went off, and a brash spotlight came on in front of him, illuminating a shiny silver pole centre stage. It was as he'd described to Mullett, like a fireman's pole. Frost felt his fellow voyeurs shifting in their seats, clearing dry throats, the signature tic of anticipation. He himself felt a quickening of the pulse – he'd been here God knows how often, and witnessed ladies of all shapes and sizes disrobe, but not for a while in the audience itself. He searched for his cigarettes. Damn, he'd left them in his jacket in the car. As he rose to leave, a lithe sequinned figure glided into view.

The girl, who was only a matter of feet away, was staggeringly beautiful. Frost was rooted to the spot. The dancer reached for the pole and hung there, gently swaying her free hand. And though he knew she couldn't see him beyond the glare of the lights, he felt her gaze fall on him, right there, standing in the dark. The girl wore her blonde hair up and her face had the fine features of eastern Europeans. She reminded him of the woman that was in that thriller with Jack Nicholson – he forgot her name – but the one with the scene on the kitchen table all the lads at the station were on about, which he still couldn't find on video . . . There was something in the eyes, the allure—

'Sit down, Jack, you're making the place look untidy,' a gravelly voice said in his ear.

Sunday (6)

Superintendent Mullett had not stirred from behind his desk since Frost had left his office several hours ago. He sat, vexed, staring ahead at nothing, his mind a mass of confused possibilities. He'd known this moment would arrive, sooner or later; but he was quite unprepared for it when it had, the shock of it as fresh as if it had happened this very morning . . .

Nearly ten months ago, on an autumn morning, a paperboy had come off his bike and been killed, halfway through his round. The first police to arrive at the scene thought it might have been an accident as the location was at the bottom of a steep hill; but the detective handling the case later thought it a hit-and-run. The dead boy was well known to the Mulletts. He had delivered their daily *Gazette*.

Following a door-to-door enquiry by his own men – which of course included his own house – Mullett had realized that his wife's daily departure for work coincided with the incident timeframe. He then discreetly inspected her MG sports car, only to discover the bonnet was marked in a way that suggested an impact, and the windscreen was also cracked. Confronted with these findings Mullett crawled into a cave of denial and kept the information to himself (he knew her to be an awful driver – there had been narrow misses in the past). He had not breathed a word of warning to his wife, for to air the subject would have made it real. And once it was real, the matter would have to be dealt with.

Meanwhile, at Eagle Lane, the division was swamped and the 'accident' was very much on the back burner, all the more so after Derek Simms, the detective leading the investigation, was himself murdered. The paperboy's death and the circumstances surrounding it were all but forgotten about. To all intents and purposes it might never have happened and thus Grace Mullett was off the hook . . . until now. He reached across the highly polished veneer of his desk for his pills. He didn't feel too clever.

Frost must have discovered something. But what? This sort of shifty behaviour was out of character for him. Whatever else you could say about Frost, he always played it straight. Unless . . . he'd just been biding his time? Maybe Frost had it in for him. It was certainly possible. Mullett had made his feelings about Frost well known; the pair tolerated one another at best, but underneath it all, maybe Frost wanted one up. If he *did* have some solid evidence against Grace, how would he use it? Blackmail him to get Sue Clarke reinstated? And then what . . . Mullett knew how these things worked. Clarke today, but what about tomorrow? No, no, none of this would do, not at all . . .

'Excuse me, sir.'

Desk Sergeant Bill Wells. The superintendent was suddenly aware of the hour. It was dark outside. How long had he sat here, stewing?

'Ah Wells, what is it?' he said, gripping the small tablet bottle firmly.

'Expenses print-out, sir. You asked for analysis of CID running costs . . .'

'Leave them here, thank you, Wells.' The man looked how he now felt – exhausted.

'Sorry it took so long. I couldn't get the printer to work, paper keeps clagging up, and . . .'

'Yes, yes, quite.' Mullett did not have the patience for this now.

'. . . then I thought I'd run it wrong as the figures were so big—'

'*Big?*' Now Mullett's interest was piqued. 'Where?' He snatched the reams of music-ruled computer paper and smoothed them across the surface of his uncluttered desk. 'Where and who?'

Wells edged closer reluctantly. 'Err, might be a mistake. There.' He jabbed a coarse finger at the faint grey type. The print overlying the green rules of the paper was barely legible. The imbecile had fed the paper in the wrong way, surely; was every technological improvement hampered by buffoonery? He ran a manicured nail along from the staggering figure until it stopped abruptly at the name: *FROST, W.*

'Hmm. Well, well!' Mullett exclaimed. 'Numbers this large can only be explained by fraud of the most heinous kind.'

'Jack wouldn't do such a thing. I'm sure these figures can be supported by paperwork,' Wells said unconvincingly.

'On car expenses? How the devil do you figure that? He loathes driving, avoids getting behind the wheel at all costs, he's idle that way. He'd much rather be chauffeured round and about by all and sundry.'

Detective Constable Arthur Hanlon had barely touched 60 mph in the unmarked Austin Princess. The drive was going to be much longer than his passenger PC David Simms had bargained on. Thankfully, Hanlon's tales of Eagle Lane police station were thoroughly entertaining. Usually David Simms would tune in to Simon Bates's Top 40 countdown – he loved his music – but any story pertaining to Denton's eccentric Eagle Lane division was worth listening to. Simms had been at the station ten months now, but his older brother Derek had worked there before him, in CID. Hearing about the goings-on in his brother's day made him feel connected in some small way. Hanlon hadn't known Derek well, but he excelled at recounting anecdotes of sparring between the station commander, Mullett, and Inspector Frost. The only disappointment was that Hanlon had not once mentioned Sue Clarke. Simms was curious about the CID detective who had been his brother's girlfriend. David had met her only fleetingly before she disappeared under a cloud from Eagle Lane. Then he discovered she had had a baby a few months ago. He was desperate to know more, but had yet to find an opportunity; he was keenly aware of his youth and was too polite to ask openly.

'Aha, there's the area car,' Simms said. South Yorkshire Police had offered to send two men to pick them up at the city limits and escort them to their final destination. Hanlon pulled over into the lay-by and wound down the window. A thin policeman approached the car and after a brief exchange, it was agreed they'd tailgate the last few miles into Brightside.

'Bleak up north,' Hanlon commented, 'nothing bright about it.'

'Denton's no brighter,' Simms said. 'This has some faded industrial lustre at least. Architecture. Denton has nothing. A new town, soulless, concrete thrown up like that, bish bash bosh.'

'I don't know much about "lustre",' Hanlon said as he followed the panda car through the traffic, 'Denton was once a market town, the old mill and that.'

'Pah. You'd not notice it. The Southern Housing Estate is Denton now, sprawling mass that it is.'

Finally they reached their destination, a Victorian terrace set amongst strings of identical streets. There was a fine drizzle in the air, and the temperature was noticeably a few degrees colder here than down south.

The Yorkshire policemen rapped on the door of the house.

'It's about Rachel?' a woman with crooked glasses asked, as she peered round the door.

'May we come in?'

Reluctantly she allowed the four men into her front room. Simms stood by uncomfortably as Hanlon delivered the news, and told her that she would be required to identify the body. In his brief time at Denton, the young PC had only twice been in similar circumstances. The woman, in her early fifties, absorbed the news calmly, nodding slightly as Hanlon finished relaying the discovery of her daughter's body.

'In a churchyard, you say? Tch, of all the places . . .'

'I'm sorry, ma'am.'

'Do I have to come with you?'

The policemen glanced at one another.

'I know it's tough, ma'am,' one of the Yorkshiremen said, 'but yes, you ought to come.'

'I don't see why. Rachel's dead; me going south won't bring her back, will it? She had it coming. Mixing with such scum.'

Hanlon was unsure what to do; for all his bravado on the way up, the big man was used to being led. Simms could see the fellow was crying out for Frost to tell him what to do.

'Ah, well, I suppose given the distance, it may not be necessary after all,' Hanlon said uneasily. A silence fell.

'May I ask when you last saw your daughter, Mrs Curtis?' Simms asked eventually.

'I ain't seen 'er.'

'What, not at all?'

'Not since last summer.'

'So . . . not since she's been out?' Simms said, unable to help himself.

'I wouldn't've known she were out, if it weren't for all that fuss in t'papers.'

The Yorkshire coppers looked to the Denton men expectantly.

'Now, if you don't mind, I don't want the neighbours seeing you lot round here any longer than necessary.'

After five minutes of stilted questioning, they were in the Princess again for the long ride back. Hanlon was far less chatty this time, and wore a frown. Once they hit the M1 Simms reached over and turned up the radio. Paul Young was still number one; this cheered Hanlon up, reminding him of Frost's nomadic existence. Simms stared out of the window. Frost might be laid-back about his sleeping arrangements, he thought, but he won't be so blasé when we show up empty-handed.

Sue Clarke laid out the blouse and skirt on the bed. She could hear her mother talking at her son in an annoying baby voice in the next room. She hoped she didn't sound so daft herself – it really did grate. He should be asleep by now. She hoped her return to work wouldn't unsettle the baby too much; he was too little to be affected, that was what she told herself anyhow . . . She picked up the pleated skirt and, holding it at arm's length, gave it a shake; it looked on the small side. Clarke took pride in her appearance, and since moving from uniform to CID she always did her utmost to look professional and smart. Plain clothes seemed little more than an excuse for her male counterparts to slob about.

She ironed the outfit and hung both items on the back of the bedroom door. In the sitting room her mother sat quietly watching *Tales of the Unexpected*, with the lights off. Philip was safely tucked up in his cot. The flat was now neat and tidy, all traces of her previous lodger gone. Her mother, primly sat there with a cup of tea in front of the telly, cut a very different figure to the previous incumbent – who'd usually slumped there spread-eagled with a can of Hofmeister lager. She sat down next to her mother and as she did so her foot caught on an object poking out from underneath the sofa. She bent down and pulled out an LP. Sidney Bechet. One of Frost's jazz records. Sometimes they would sit together on Sunday nights, when the baby was asleep, listening to music. Frost would talk about how he'd discovered jazz through inheriting his mother's collection, slowly working his way through the century's greats, from Jelly Roll Morton and King Oliver to Miles Davis. Clarke didn't like the scratchy old ditties herself but enjoyed hearing his passionate descriptions of the music. His own record player was in storage. If only he would get himself sorted. She wondered where he was now.

Sunday (7) ————————————————

Baskin thwacked on the harsh overhead light in his pokey office, causing Frost to blink rapidly.

'That dumpy ex-copper had enough of you, 'as she, Jack?'

'Eh?'

'Bird you're shacked up with. I seen you at the weekend mincing about Market Square with 'er and the nipper.'

'No, no, no. You got the wrong end of the stick there, Harry,' Frost spluttered, belatedly adding ''Ere, what do you mean, "dumpy"?'

Sauntering rather than jumping to her defence. Typical.

Baskin arched a cynical eyebrow. 'Whatever.' He peeled the cellophane off a cigar the size of a small truncheon. 'You're here for one of two reasons; the first being you ain't getting any.' He flumped down behind the desk, the leather chair farting as it smoothly accommodated his bulk, and worked on the cigar in silence, seemingly forgetting to conclude his thesis explaining Frost's appearance at the Coconut Grove.

'And the second reason?' Frost prompted.

'You tell me, eh?'

Frost pulled up the chair. 'Rachel Rayner?'

'Out on licence.'

'Out on a tombstone.'

'Eh?'

'Dead. Found this morning in St Mary's churchyard.'

'Bloody hell.' Baskin was genuinely surprised. 'How?'

Frost shrugged. 'Not sure yet. When was the last time you saw her, Harry?'

'She was here last week, as it happens. Just after she were released.'

'Why?'

'To enquire after my 'ealth. Why d'you think?'

Frost sparked up a Rothmans. 'You were shot,' Frost said dryly.

'Money.'

'Did you owe her? She used to work here, after all.'

'Nah.'

'Well, why?'

'After Kate.'

Kate Greenlaw, one of Harry's 'exotic dancers'; mid-twenties, four or five years Rachel's junior, but the two were friends.

'And did she find her?'

'Nah. Kate quit after all that business last year. Got a new one in. The one you was ogling. Karen Thomas.'

'She seems a cut above the usual?' Frost complimented.

'Eastern European extraction; Polish, I think. Thomas ain't her real name – it's summat unpronounceable. Old man flew a Spitfire in the Battle of Britain.'

'Blimey, that's a bit exotic for you.'

'Nah, you've seen one tit, you've seen 'em all.'

Frost had heard this line many, many times. 'Talking of tits, Hornrim Harry's not been in here, has he?'

'Who?'

'Your golfing buddy, my super.'

'You got to be joking. That one's so uptight, I doubt his blood pressure could handle it. He'll have a coronary before long.'

High blood pressure? Though this was news to Frost, it came as no surprise.

'I didn't know you were a medical man, Harry?'

'I ain't, but Avery has warned ol' Mullett to keep his cool on the green a number of times.' Avery was a snooty Denton GP. Baskin chuckled to himself. 'Yes, your gaffer don't 'alf get hot under the collar if he flunks a shot.'

Frost was eager to get back to the matter at hand. 'Why would Rachel be after Kate?'

'I just said. They're mates.'

Frost waited for more, but that was evidently all there was. Harry started shuffling papers on the desk. He clearly didn't want to hang around, this being his night at home. Frost had questions about the new dancer but now was not the time. Besides, he'd agreed to meet Waters and Sandy Lane and it had already gone half nine.

The Eagle on Eagle Lane was a coppers' pub and despite a recent paint job it was still a hellishly grim place to be for last orders on a Sunday night.

Waters spied the hack, Sandy Lane, sitting in the far corner as he paid the barman for his pint.

'There he is,' Frost said, 'like one of the dirty-raincoat brigade.'

'That's rich, you've a fondness for a grubby mac yourself,' Waters said.

'Not in bleedin' August. If ever there were a bloke looking ripe for nicking it's him. "Shifty" is not even close.'

The reporter spotted them, and raised a half-drunk pint of Guinness.

'Sandy! What gives?' Frost said cheerily as they approached.

'All right, Jack, as it 'appens I was hoping you might enlighten me there . . . Dead girl found in St Mary's? Legs akimbo on top of one of Denton's forefathers – that's not what the meek and 'umble line up for on a Sunday morning, is it?' He paused mischievously. 'Anyone we know?'

'Might be,' Frost said, aloof. For all his sniffing around Lane had clearly not gleaned the woman's identity.

The reporter looked suspiciously from one to the other. 'He wouldn't be banging on the door of my gaff on a Sunday, if it wasn't . . .'

'You can see the cogs grinding through, can't you?' Frost joked to Waters. 'Go on, put the bugger out of his misery.'

'You recall the hit on the Gregory Leather payroll last year? Girl desperate to escape her psycho boyfriend grabs the cash, guns down the minder?'

'How could I forget. Pumpy Palmer's sidekick – hacked the old porker to pieces on a snooker table. In Palmer's very own club.' He sniffed distastefully.

'Quite, but once Palmer's murder died down, and that psycho Nicholson was safely banged up, the girl that committed the robbery became the centre of attention. The case dragged on and on and eventually . . .'

'Wait, you're not telling me it was her in the church-yard . . . ?'

Waters nodded.

'Well, blow me down.' Lane's eyes lit up. 'How?'

'Under investigation,' Frost said. 'But you're to keep shtum, got me? I don't want to wake up tomorrow with this girl's boat race plastered all over the paper.'

'Ahh . . . come off it – this is a great story . . .'

'No, I'm serious: you can hold off a day or so. Tell us first what you know.'

'Not much, but all right . . .' Lane had spent his Sunday harassing shocked pensioners after a god-fearing friend of

Lane's mother had disturbed him at home. Once alerted to the discovery in the churchyard he was on to it, like the true newshound he was. And one had to hand it to him, he'd been pretty thorough – he even knew the name of the person whose tomb the body was found on (something the police hadn't bothered to note).

'The verger found 'er, apparently,' Lane concluded, 'but he'd scooted off by the time I got there.'

'That's about the sum of it,' Frost agreed. 'But that's not what we want to know.'

Lane's jaundiced complexion sagged.

'You covered the case extensively; Rachel Curtis getting released like that,' Waters encouraged.

'Ah, I see. The widow of that warehouse bloke that got shot, she vowed to— 'Ere, wait. You gotta tell *me* something first!'

'We just told you her name,' Waters said.

'Yeah, but I'd've got that meself in a day or so . . .'

'Hey man, and if that's the game we're playing *we* could just ransack the *Echo*'s offices – you'd have printed everything you'd been told. We'd just need to trawl through the last three months.'

'There might be stuff I kept back,' Lane protested indignantly.

'Yeah. Right. That'll be the day,' Frost said cynically. 'Look, we haven't got all night so, OK then, what do you want to know?'

The hack fidgeted uncomfortably; he wanted something, anything – the information itself was irrelevant, it was the bartering that was important, being in a position of power. Suddenly a sly grin passed over his face.

'All right, park the bird in the churchyard for a second.' He drained the Guinness. 'Is it true that roly-poly Hudson is having it off with some stripper tart at the Coconut Grove?'

'What, the manager of Bennington's Bank?'

'The very same.'

'I haven't the faintest,' Frost said flatly, 'it's hardly a CID matter, is it?'

'Be a huge scandal, though, don't you reckon?'

'If you say so . . . not my field.'

'Well, keep your ear to the ground, Jack, eh?'

'All right, now come on! They'll be ringing the bell for last orders any minute,' Waters interjected; this was getting tedious – this wasn't his idea of a fun Sunday night. 'Your turn. The family of the Gregory robbery victim, Albert Benson, what's the lowdown?'

'Keep your hair on.' Lane adjusted his pose, and peered into the empty pint glass.

Frost spun round and hollered across to the barman, 'Oi Dennis, another round, please, mate?'

'So,' Lane began, hunching over the table, savouring the moment, 'the deceased's wife was absolutely livid that Rayner/ Curtis got off the hook; she threatened merry hell, vowed all manner of retribution.'

'To be expected . . .'

'Nah, I mean when I interviewed her about it, she was seething – this was not grief, this was pure *hatred*. There was something dark and deep to it.'

'Meaning?' Waters asked, moving to allow the barman to place another pint in front of him. Only Jack Frost could command waiter service in a fleapit like the Eagle.

'Meaning? Meaning it's personal,' Lane said in a low voice.

'Cobblers,' Frost blurted angrily, 'of course it's personal – the woman has as good as killed her old man. That's pretty bloody personal if you ask me. What are you, some sort of psychiatrist?'

'All right, Jack, keep your hair on,' Lane apologized.

'Wait,' Waters said, 'I want to know what you're implying – that Mrs Benson knew Curtis? That's what that means to me – she hated her even before the shooting?'

Lane sipped the fresh Guinness thoughtfully. 'Yeah, you might be right.'

'Anything else?' Frost said, clearly tired.

'Her son is the bouncer at the Grove, would have known Rachel anyway through work.'

'Big Gazzer? Is his surname Benson? Well, that's something, I suppose.' Frost downed his pint. 'I gotta be off – got a lizard that wants his grasshoppers and a bird needs his seed.'

'Eh? What's that, some sort of police code?' Lane asked.

'Chinese code,' Waters said. 'Classified, I'm afraid we can't tell you.'

'But you got to tell me something,' Lane said, hurt, 'after what I told you.'

'We told you the woman's name?'

'Pah.'

'OK, she was shoeless,' Frost said, rising. 'Now, if you'll excuse me. I've to move into new lodgings.'

Waters followed suit as Lane looked up quizzically at them both.

'Shoeless? That all?'

'That's all we got. A real drag being a copper, you know.' Waters winked at the hack.

Outside the pub, Waters lit a cigarette and watched Frost amble off towards his car, and then presumably on to the Jade Rabbit. Frost had not found the time to shift his gear over there that afternoon as planned.

John Waters had woken feeling bright and alert on a beautiful Sunday morning, looking forward to a last extra run-through of his wedding with his best man before the big day on Friday, but instead they'd been summoned to the church to investigate a dead girl found on a tombstone; then – instead of enjoying a lazy afternoon with his fiancée – he'd had to go on to the morgue. And if that wasn't enough, rather than feet up watching the box, he'd spent the evening in a shabby pub with an even shabbier hack, only then to watch his pal wander off into the night to unpack a suitcase above a Chinese restaurant. It was at moments like this, one could, if one was that way disposed, question the way one lived one's life. But Waters chose not to. He drew heavily on the cigarette. He loved his soon-to-be-missus, he loved the job and he loved Frost: there could be no other way.

Monday (1) ───────────────────────────────

Dominic Holland stood impatiently watching the builder faff around in the cab of his truck, searching for a calculator. 'Tradesmen,' he muttered to himself contemptuously, as he stroked his neatly trimmed beard. Not that he thought the man a crook – he wouldn't have chosen Todd otherwise – no, the man had an honest air, and he was here punctually at seven thirty in the morning. He doubted the fellow's arithmetical prowess more. Holland himself possessed a calculator, of course, but he couldn't lay his hands on the infernal thing, which must be lying hidden in one of the many boxes he'd yet to unpack.

A crooked smile beneath squinting eyes in the bright August morning, and a wonky thumbs-up, indicated success on the driveway, and Todd marched bow-legged back up to the house, regarding the wrecked lawn as he did so.

'Want me to quote you on re-turfing that for you? Right bloody mess.'

'Let's just concentrate on the matter in hand,' Holland replied sharply; as he had no recollection as to how his front lawn had arrived at such a state, he chose to ignore it and the likely associated expense of repairing it.

'Now then, where were we?'

'The swimming pool tiles?' Holland smiled. 'My preference for the Mint Melt finish would appear to be costing me dear.'

'Dolphin Dream is cheaper, and as I said, it's the more popular.'

'Well, that's precisely why I don't want it.'

'Well, that's why it's costing more, ain't it? S'obvious.'

'Obvious? What's obvious about it? I fail to see how simply the colour makes a tile more expensive by forty per cent.'

Todd's weather-beaten face cracked an arch expression he usually employed to emphasize building complexity. 'It's yer economies of scale, ain't it?'

'Oh, come now.'

Holland had heard the savages in the office use the phrase repeatedly whilst knocking up his latest creation, the 'Dagenham Drainpipe' – a male trouser so tight, one could be fooled into thinking the wearer had had their lower half spray-painted on. Very tastefully done, but unfortunately the British figure did not lend itself to such a cut in suitable numbers to make mass production economically viable. That he could, reluctantly, understand – and he supposed there was a similar logic to the tiles argument, only not to the degree Pythagoras here was proposing.

The man went through the elementary multiplication again – it was painful to watch – and yet again failed to arrive at a consistent number.

'Tell you what, why don't we knock off a monkey for cash?' He pocketed the calculator, and nodded beyond the gravel drive. The pair proceeded round to the rear of the house.

'I beg your pardon? A "monkey"? What on earth are you talking about?'

'Five hundred nicker off the final price.'

'What, for the green tiles?'

'The whole job price.'

'But what about the colour of the tiles?'

'And the tiles. You can have them pussy pink for all I care.'

Holland's eyes narrowed. Was he being taken for a chump? The job was halfway through and yet the final price had yet to be fixed. He surveyed the work in progress; where once lay half an acre of quintessential English garden greenery, now was left, to coin the neighbours' phrase, *a post-apocalyptic hell*. And, to be fair, they weren't far wrong. The transformation had been brutal and merciless. To start with, the border trees had had to go – felled were a huge ancient oak and two enormous horse chestnuts – though they were still very much there, like vestiges from the Somme, poking above the ever-growing mound of earth and rubble. Then there was the earthen hill created by the excavation of the pool, which consisted of all matter of debris, polythene, paper, cardboard, even a tyre from heaven knows where. Holland was reminded of the dustman's heap from *Our Mutual Friend* . . . and . . .

'So are we set then?'

'I beg your pardon?'

'Agreed. I want a slice in cash tomorrow morning.'

'How much?'

'Two grand.'

He had just over a thousand under the bed, but would need to go to the bank for the rest. 'I'm afraid I have to go up to town on urgent business this evening and won't be back until Wednesday. Can't it wait?'

Todd shook his head woefully. 'Nah, I need the readies to buy tiles, don't I?'

'Do you? I had no idea it was such a hand-to-mouth existence. Very well, I shall draw out the cash this afternoon and you shall have it before you "knock off".'

'Leave it in the mixer, I won't be here this afternoon.'

'You won't be here ... but ... where will you be? It's the start of the working week! Surely Monday is a full day, even for you?' Holland had grown accustomed to an industrious start to the week quickly slumping to a minimal effort towards the end. 'What, pray, can be more pressing; it's not for the want of work here?'

'Got to price a job,' Todd said brazenly, and then realizing this wasn't an adequate response added, 'I got to look to the future, ain't I? We'll be done here end of the week, need to secure the next earner, building trade ain't like making dresses.'

Holland very much doubted Todd would complete the job by Friday, but there was little point rubbing the man up the wrong way. 'Very well. Where do you want it?'

'Just drop the dosh inside the mixer and I'll pick it up.'

'Inside the mixer?'

Todd pointed to the rotting cylinder, now more of a rusty bronze than its original bright yellow, resting dormant next to unwanted metal rods, left over from the pool lining. How quaint, he thought, that's how it's done in the country. He must try and adjust, blend in a bit.

'I like your cap.'

'Eh?' Todd touched the peak of his flat cap. 'Stops me 'ead getting burnt.'

'Very natty pattern. *Such* tasteful colours. I saw a chap wearing one just like that at the weekend – but not for the sun, because he had it on at night – a taxi driver, came up to the house to collect someone during the party. Where did you get it?'

'Castleton's, in the town ... About the money, you'll be sure to leave it?'

'Yes, yes,' Holland said, growing bored, 'just be sure to get it done. And for your information I do not "make dresses".'

*

Kenny –

Sorry to miss you. Tied up. Borrowed a couple of beers.

See you tonight, for sure.

Cheers

Jack

His stomach rumbled angrily. As an afterthought he then quickly scribbled: *PS: don't chuck out the leftovers – always happy to oblige!*

Frost pulled out a pound note from his overstuffed wallet and left it on the counter under the biro on the note, then moved to fill Monty's water bottle from the kitchen tap. Monty was a large – and unpleasantly loud – African Grey parrot. Frost wasn't complaining. He was more than grateful to Mr Fong for allowing him to bunk in the flat above the restaurant. It was ironic that he had Suzy's old bedroom, but his was not to question why, though he suspected one reason was so that he'd remember to feed the girl's gecko, who lived in a terrarium at the foot of the single bed. And indeed, he had fed it when he'd woken up. The other pet he was unlikely to be able to forget about even if he wanted to, given the noise it made in its cage by the restaurant's serving hatch. He turned off the tap and grabbed his keys.

'Noisy bleeder,' Frost said, re-attaching the bird's bottle. Monty eyed him closely as he fumbled with the wire clips. The only time the bird shut up was when you got up close to the cage; Frost had tried making it talk when he staggered in last night, but not so much as a *pieces of eight*.

He called out goodbye to both creatures, stepped out on to the street and slammed the door shut just as Monty piped up with something indistinguishable but almost certainly blue.

The white sunlight prompted a wince from the inspector as he patted himself down blindly for his Polaroids. He cursed. Were they in the car? Having arrived late last night at the Jade Rabbit, he'd missed the Fong boys who'd cleaned the place before closing, and thus missed any chance of scrounging a meal. He opened the Metro and scrabbled around on the dashboard for his shades; not there, but his crumpled panama hat was. He felt rancid from all the beer the previous day. He was, he discovered, at an age where drinking on an empty stomach didn't pay – something he'd not grasped until now. While living with Sue Clarke he'd eaten well; she would always cook enough for two, in the hope she could wean him off takeaways and thus rid her flat of used cartons. A fry-up in the mornings, too. As a consequence his belly was used to being full – missing one nosh was just about bearable; missing two in a row was decidedly not. He needed something urgently. Could he wait until the canteen? The station was in the next street. It would be quicker to walk, the traffic in Denton was dire at the moment; congestion everywhere, but he'd no doubt need the motor later . . .

He climbed into the car and thought for a second about the plan for the day. Rachel Curtis's bottom – or to be more precise, her crab tattoo – was on his mind so he'd need to make enquiries there. He needed to inspect her house too – better get a uniform posted outside until he had a chance. The place was up for sale, he knew that much, which meant he also had to get hold of the estate agent . . . But a bacon sandwich beckoned with more immediacy. He had time; it wasn't eight thirty yet.

He started the car. The radio came on simultaneously, filling his ears with Lieutenant Pigeon's 'Mouldy Old Dough'.

'Good morning, world.' He smiled and belched uncomfortably, flipped down the sun visor – finally locating his Polaroids – and drove the two-minute journey to Eagle Lane.

Detective Sue Clarke stood outside the station commander's door, awaiting the summons to enter. She gathered from overhearing snippets of a telephone conversation that the superintendent was late in this morning. But she wouldn't sit – that would indicate complacency, and should Mullett choose to open the door to her himself, she wanted him to find her upright and determined, eager to return to the force. She caught a glance from Miss Smith, Mullett's prim secretary, sitting behind her typewriter. Clarke tried a smile, but the woman looked away disdainfully. Always hard to read that one, Clarke thought; bit snooty. A nice girl when she first started but . . . too much like Mullett now. She paced away from the secretary, feeling her skirt pinch as she did so.

'Superintendent Mullett will see you now,' came the tart voice behind her.

'Thank you,' Clarke said in a clipped tone, as she passed Smith, hand still on the telephone receiver. She stopped at the door, looked down, cleared her throat then opened the door without knocking.

'Ah, Ms Clarke,' the superintendent said as she entered the room, though his attention was still on the huge computer monitor. Clarke was instantly wrong-footed by his not addressing her as Detective. 'Take a seat,' he added, after a pause.

She swallowed hard and pulled back a chair. The room was unpleasantly hot for the time of day. She'd always hated his fancy office decked out in wood panelling. Frost called it the old log cabin, but it reminded her more of a room out of a Miss Marple story. An electric fan stood dormant in the far corner, looking as out of place as the grey computer screen.

Mullett continued tapping away at the keyboard. She sat, not knowing what to do, and picked nervously at a ragged cuticle.

'Blast!' Mullett erupted, reaching for the phone. He didn't appear to be in the best of moods. Maybe it was the heat. 'Miss Smith, fetch me Desk Sergeant Wells.' The super nudged the keyboard aside and placed his hands there before his pristine tunic. Fingers locked together, he said, 'Now, Ms Clarke, what can we do for you?'

He must surely know, she thought, so replied simply, 'I want to come back, sir.'

'Come back?' he asked, genuinely surprised.

'Yes. To CID. I've had time away to think, and although I have a child, I see my place here at Eagle Lane.'

'Do you. Do you indeed.' Mullett's brow furrowed. 'And why should I take you back?'

She paused for a moment before responding, 'Because I am a good detective.'

'Hmm.' He slid open a drawer and retrieved a manila file. Hers, no doubt. 'You have had,' he said, opening the file before him, 'a colourful time in CID. How is the leg, by the way?'

He was referring to a stab wound she'd sustained whilst trying to apprehend two teenage thieves the previous May. 'Forgotten all about it, sir.'

'Quite the little villain chaser, aren't you.'

He proceeded to recount her successful capture of a rapist the previous autumn, after a chase on foot through the streets of the Southern Housing Estate. After an abrupt start he appeared to be warming to her; she felt a surge of confidence.

'Yes, commendable . . .' He smiled across the desk. 'A solid record, Susan, until—'

At that moment Sergeant Bill Wells lumbered in. 'Sir.' He flashed Clarke a quick smile. She was fond of Wells, Eagle Lane's old faithful; the station's mainstay.

'Wells!' Mullett's composure changed in a flash to one of pure annoyance, as he reached to pick something up from the desk. 'The data on this disk is corrupt.'

'Are you sure, sir? It was all right last night when I saved it.'

'Would I waste my time with this pointless exchange if it were not so?' Mullett waved a black flexible square as he spoke.

'I'm not sure you should do that, sir.'

'Nonsense. It's a *floppy* disk. Here, take it away and uncorrupt the information immediately.'

'I'm not—'

'Enough! It's not a debate. Is Wallace in yet?'

'He's just arrived, sir.'

'Tell Miss Smith to reschedule the appointment he failed to keep for after the briefing meeting. That gives you both extra time; I shall be expecting a solution.'

Wells nodded, and made to go. 'Nice to see you, Sue.'

'A *solution*,' Mullett said as he watched Wells leave, 'make sure Sergeant Wallace understands that.'

The door closed and Clarke focused on the superintendent who was scribbling something down on her file, or so she thought.

'Technology is the way forward, Ms Clarke,' he said, noting the time as he wrote. 'Alas, I can but dream of automated desk sergeants for now, but one day – mark my words.' He placed the pen to one side, and closed the folder.

'Sergeant Wells is an asset to Eagle Lane, sir, I'm sure,' she said, defending her colleague. 'The lynchpin to the station.'

Mullett looked at her as if she had taken leave of her senses and said, 'Wells is, indeed, unique in many ways, and though his contribution to law enforcement can only be quantified – generously – as minimal, he has nevertheless not impeded its progress with anything more than lethargy and bouts of staggering stupidity. Unlike yourself, Ms Clarke.'

Mullett held the file upright and tapped the cover squarely; this was it, she thought. Clarke's stomach fluttered, as she gripped the hem of her skirt and steeled herself for Mullett's verdict on her future.

Frost shoved open the door to Mungo's Tattoo Parlour and entered the shop, removing his crumpled panama hat as he did so. 'Parlour' was little more than wishful thinking on the proprietor's part; Mungo's was a slice of a place squeezed in between a 'Private' shop on one side and a bookie's on the other, at the far end of Foundling Lane.

It was a little after nine but already the soft buzz of a needle, like a trapped fly, intermittently punctured the low-level rock music that filled the shoebox-sized concern. Frost took in the dizzying display of art crammed on to the walls: motorcycles, dragons, tigers, women of Amazonian proportions. At the far end of the dark room in a pool of light sat a man in a leather jerkin with his back to Frost, presumably Mungo himself, at work on a blonde woman.

'Wotcha,' Frost called gaily. The woman smiled at him. She was topless and the tattooist was hunched over her chest with his pen.

'Be with you in a tick,' the man said without stirring from his work.

Frost mooched forward to get a closer look, practically peering over the tattooist's shoulder. He still couldn't discern what was going on – it looked as if the man was nuzzling her breasts. Frost stepped back feeling awkwardly aware he was intruding. For her part, the customer, dressed only in denim shorts and bright red lipstick, winked and smiled demurely.

'Right.' The man rose, placing his equipment in a small metal tray and picking up a cloth to wipe his hands. 'What can I do for you?'

But Frost was momentarily distracted, as he stood agape at the woman's breasts, newly adorned with what appeared to be a pair of cricket balls nestling between them. He checked himself and forced his eyes back to Mungo's face.

'Err . . . yes. Frost, Denton CID.' He whisked out a picture of Rachel Curtis. 'Remember this young lady?'

The man, who sported a spider's web up one forearm and a sword and snake on the other, took the photo and considered it for a moment and passed it back. 'Yeah. Cancer.'

'*Cancer?*'

'The Crab. Birth sign,' Mungo said, picking up a pouch of Old Holborn. 'Yup. That'll be her.'

'Can you tell me when exactly she came by?'

'Will have a note of it here, somewhere.' He reached for a scruffy appointment book.

Frost glanced around him. His knowledge of tattoos stretched not much beyond military history and the likes of Napoleon's Imperial Guard who covered themselves in ink. That and secret societies, such as the girls Mullett had alluded to the previous day but . . . Get off after a very serious crime and get a tattoo? Frost struggled with the logic.

'Yeah, in the morning. Came in 'ere with another chick at eleven on Saturday. They both had one . . .'

'What, she had a crab too?'

'Nah . . . Leo.'

'The lion.'

'You're quite the detective, all right.'

'Do ladies do that a lot? You know, come in and get tattoos together?' He regarded the woman still there, solo, and half naked.

'Some muffdivers.'

'You what?'

'Lesbians,' the woman translated, revealing a set of perfect teeth.

Frost grinned back and said, nodding at her chest, 'You're getting chilly sitting there.'

Mungo dogged his rollie, cracked his knuckles and picked up his instrument. 'Might have been a birthday treat.'

'Why do you say that?' Frost said, eyes on the woman still.

'We're in Leo, ain't we. Mind you, soon going into Virgo.'

'You what! Oh, I see. Can you give me a description of the other woman?' Frost scribbled a few lines in his notebook, wondering whether Kate Greenlaw, the woman who'd worked at the Coconut Grove and who Rachel had been looking for, was born in August. He thanked the man for his help.

'Bet Chris Tavaré wouldn't let Miller get his hands on those,' Frost said cheekily to the woman.

She glanced down at Mungo's handiwork. 'Eh?'

'The Ashes,' he said. But clearly she had no idea of the England side's spectacular test-match win in Melbourne last Christmas. 'A famous catch Down Under . . . Cricket? You know – those balls?'

'Ha, no, love,' she purred, 'these are *cherries*. Come closer.'

Frost edged closer, unabashed. 'Ah yes, I can see the stalks.'

'Nice, aren't they?' she said proudly.

And then throwing caution to the wind, he said, 'Don't suppose you fancy a drink tonight, do you?'

The woman's face registered surprise. 'A drink with a policeman on a Monday night, you are joking?'

'Most certainly not – there's nothing funny about drinking with a copper; it's not for the faint-hearted.'

Her face softened. 'How about tomorrow?'

'Done.'

The tattooist took that as his cue to continue, and switched on his needle. Frost hastily named a time and place and left the pair of them to get on with the job.

Outside, standing in the sunshine, it dawned on him he'd not got her name, but that didn't matter, there was always tomorrow; for the first time in ages he had something to look forward to.

Monday (2) _____

'Hold on!' Frost bellowed out of the Metro window.

Sue Clarke lifted her head glumly as she made her way across the station car park. He could see it had not gone well. Had she blown it? How? He parked sloppily across two bays and hurried over to Clarke's Escort.

'How'd it go?' He coughed. Thirty yards and he was wheezing uncontrollably.

'It seems my services are not required.'

'You're kidding! I don't flamin' well believe it! What did he say?'

'Mullett said he saw no reason to review the decision made eight months ago. Nothing has changed . . .'

'Other than we need you—'

'. . . and that my temperament was probably best suited to child rearing,' she added despondently. 'He's probably right.'

'Nonsense!'

'To think I believed you, Jack!' She opened the car door.

' "Everything will be all right, don't worry." I should know better by now than to have any faith in you.'

'Sue, Sue. I'm sure it's a misunderstanding,' Frost implored; he couldn't believe it – what was Hornrim Harry playing at?

'Oh, he did say one other thing,' she said, climbing into the car.

'Yes . . . ?'

'That now I was more mobile they could proceed with a full disciplinary hearing.'

Frost watched her disappear from the car park on to Eagle Lane. Mullett. Blast him. But *how*? Mullett must know he had him by the goolies for his wife's apparent guilt in the paperboy hit-and-run – what on earth would make him risk Frost blabbing about that? Maybe Frost had not got his message across yesterday evening.

'How flamin' obvious did it need to be?' he muttered to himself as he locked his car.

Or did Mullett think Frost too principled to act? Through some misguided loyalty? Surely not. Or maybe the time that had since elapsed made Simms's evidence invalid? Was there a loophole he'd not thought of? Frost cursed inwardly, he should have nobbled Mullett there and then months ago – traded the info for Sue's guaranteed return – and not given him time to plot and scheme, which he'd clearly done, master of such things as he was. The sun beat down on the troubled inspector as he felt for his cigarettes. It was going to be a scorcher again, maybe the heat had fried Mullett's noggin. Or maybe . . . could he have discovered something on Frost himself? He felt a chill in spite of the heat. Yes, that would have to be it. He knew the way the man's mind worked . . . but what could it possibly be? He scrabbled through his memory trying to recall what misdemeanour he could be guilty of. Trouble was, over a period of so many months, there were so many possibilities . . .

'Inspector Frost, please.'

'He's just slipped out,' a jowly sweaty officer in his fifties behind the front desk replied. 'Though he may have slipped back in while I was fiddling with this confounded thing. Let me try his line.' He stopped twiddling with a printer and picked up the phone. 'What can I say it's regarding?'

'Ah . . .' Suddenly, when confronted with declaring his purpose, the words froze in his throat.

At that moment another uniformed policeman appeared; this one was slimmer and well-groomed, with a tie that looked inhumanely tight for the weather.

'The disk, Wells. *The disk!*' he hissed.

Clearly this one was a superior, but despite his seniority he exuded a level of tension that made Weaver's legs go weak. Grave doubts flooded his mind – he didn't know whether he had the resolve to be able to pull this off.

'I'm just dealing with this gentleman, sir,' the sweaty one behind the desk said, replacing the handset. 'It would appear Inspector Frost has not returned to his desk. May I take a note of the matter you wish to discuss?'

'Ah . . .'

The superior one had suddenly clocked him and – unlike the desk officer – he'd apparently taken in Weaver's attire because his first words to him were, 'St Mary's?' Weaver was technically not supposed to be wearing his surplice – but he felt it afforded him some protection in the circumstances.

'Yes . . . I—'

'We're doing all we can, you know. Wells, page Frost immediately: he has been issued with a bleeper.' The man had intense beady eyes, shiny with anger. 'I shall call the bishop personally, as soon as we have concrete news. In the meantime, avoid the piffle in the press.'

Bishop? What in heaven's name? 'I'm sorry?' Weaver said, confused.

'The young lady found in the churchyard?' His eyebrows shot up in consternation. 'I assume that is why you're here?'

'Err no, I'm here about a neighbour of mine, who appears to have gone missing – I'm here to offer my services . . . If there's anything I can—' but the stiff policeman had lost interest at 'no' and marched off down the squeaky-floored corridor.

'Phew, thank goodness for that.' The desk officer breathed heavily and licked the tip of his pencil. 'Right, sir, if you'd be so good as to give me your particulars.'

The Monday-morning staff briefing could set the tone for the entire week, Mullett found, especially after an eventful week-end such as this. He stepped up to the dais as the digital wall clock clicked on eleven. Despite being late in he'd managed to catch up, due to his superb time-management skills. He surveyed the assembled officers, waited for a few more uniform to take their seats. A full contingent there thankfully, all present and correct, including Sergeant Wallace. Conversely, CID were woefully under-represented. Hanlon and Waters; that was it. *Where was Frost?* For heaven's sake.

Mullett was in two minds about Clarke – they did need a body, that was true, but all that . . . that . . . what-d'you-call-it with Derek Simms that had landed her in hot water in the first place. *Drama.* Yes, that was it: drama. A police station processed and solved other people's dramas; it was not the place to nurture dramas of its own. Then there was that child; fatherless, accord-ing to Miss Smith. Mullett didn't care to know more, suffice to say the boy didn't arrive out of thin air. Gossip and scandal had no place at Eagle Lane.

Just as the last man sat down Frost appeared at the back doors in a pink top, similar to those Mullett had seen at the golf club.

'Good morning, ladies and gentlemen,' Mullett said loudly.

'Sergeant Waters, without further ado, an appraisal of the dead woman in the graveyard, if you please.'

The sergeant stood and flipped open his notebook. Waters, in a tight *Starsky & Hutch* T-shirt, was an impressive specimen – a formidable build and speaking clearly, he instantly commanded the room's attention.

The circumstances were suspicious and unusual: the appearance of the body, the positioning, etc., suggested that the fatal wound itself might well have been sustained through a fall. That being said, a fall from the church roof would have been much messier. This was as much as he knew from Frost the previous day. The whole situation was odd, not to mention macabre. Waters continued: CID were intent on tracking the woman's last movements; and there was the possibility of a lovers' tryst that had gone fatally wrong. All of this would need investigating. The detective then touched on the details of her release, the history of mental cruelty, and that her behaviour might have been irrational due to an unstable mind.

Mullett thought this poppycock, psychological evaluations and the like. She should *never* have been freed, look where it's landed her . . . he suddenly noticed Frost at the back of the room. The inspector, in a pink polo top and frankly ridiculous hat, was staring directly at him. Such was the intensity of his gaze, the superintendent immediately felt unsettled.

Waters had now concluded and Mullett became aware of an expectant silence. He couldn't bring himself to ask Frost for his findings, and although he knew full well there was further business to discuss, he brought the session to a close.

The assembly filed out, but Frost remained.

'A word, Super, if I may,' he said, as Mullett was leaving.

'I don't have time; I have a meeting with Wallace now and then the press conference at noon and so forth – one can't expect this to stay under wraps given the congregation,' he said, trying to brush him off.

Frost was still at his heels though. 'The press, yes. I'm sure they'll have a field day. I hadn't thought of that,' he said, abstractedly, as though thinking of something. He had an agenda.

The super pushed open his office door, ignoring Miss Smith trying to catch his eye. 'All right, you've got thirty seconds.'

Frost tapped the door shut. 'Detective Clarke, sir. I believe you had a meeting this morning.'

'Ah, I might have guessed. Indeed I did. Though it's no concern of yours.'

'She's a highly valued member of the team.'

'Really? Well, you'll just have to soldier on without her.'

Frost stepped closer to the desk. 'I'm prepared to do anything to have her back.'

Mullett reached for a Senior Service. 'Bold words, Inspector.' Mullett was, he thought, ready for this confrontation. 'To go to what lengths, exactly?' He smiled sarcastically. He really did loathe Frost, only now did he grasp quite how much.

'Oh, anything,' Frost said casually, 'but in the first instance I'm keen to reopen that hit-and-run case – you know, *your* paperboy, the one who was killed last autumn?'

'Have you time? Being as we're stretched as it is.'

'Oh, I think we'd wrap it up pronto.'

'Really now, how so?'

'New evidence.'

'I see.' Mullett sucked hard on the cigarette. Frost, oddly, was not smoking. 'Before you do, I might mention there's an audit under way investigating expense claims. Technology is a wonderful thing. Yes, a thorough investigation. And I'm afraid to say you have already been highlighted for particular review. Any officer under investigation for false expenses claims is unlikely—'

'Really? That's great.' Frost smiled.

'You're pleased?' Mullett said, surprised.

'After the old lady died, the bank froze the account. I've not been able to cash a single cheque; be handy to know what I'm owed?'

Mullett was crestfallen. He could not believe it. If Frost had not actually cashed the cheques – however enormous the sum involved – he'd slip off the hook.

'You'll remember, sir, I'm sure,' said Frost, 'that I'm without a car at present and that you personally sanctioned me to use the wife's Metro? It has cost a small fortune to keep on the road, as your new technology no doubt tells you. But back to Detective Clarke . . .'

With that, Frost puffed on a newly lit cigarette with relish.

Monday (3)

Detective Sergeant Waters closed the door to the incident room behind him. With the morning briefing out of the way, the real work could begin. Frost was buoyant – whatever had transpired between him and Mullett after the briefing had evidently gone Jack's way; the energy with which he was berating Hanlon at the far end of the room could only mean he'd won a battle with the super.

Three uniform, including David Simms, were seated patiently waiting for Frost to finish lambasting Hanlon and issue directions on the Curtis case. Behind Frost a WPC was pinning photos and newspaper articles relating to the Gregory Leather case and Rachel Curtis's release to the incident board.

As Waters approached, the heated conversation subsided.

'What gives?' he said amicably.

'Would you believe this . . . this arse-head has come back from the bleedin' Midlands empty-handed!' He waved absently at the indignant Hanlon.

'Is Yorkshire in the Midlands?' Waters asked doubtfully.

'I don't care if it's north of flamin' Greenland; I give him a simple task, to bring back Rachel Curtis's mother. And even that was beyond him!'

'She'd not seen the girl recently, so she didn't see any reason to come all the way down here,' Hanlon said defensively.

'And *I* said she has to identify the sodding body!'

'Wait a sec – the probation officer said it was a condition of her release that she visit her mother once a week' – the two men turned to stare at Waters – 'help keep her out of trouble.'

'That so?' Frost said, his attention piqued. 'Interesting . . . what could that mean, I wonder – to break the conditions of her release so early . . .'

'I'm not surprised,' Hanlon said, 'the old dear was a right spiky misery.'

Frost rolled his eyes. 'Do me a favour; it wouldn't matter if the woman's mother was Medusa herself. If it was a matter of risking getting banged up again I'm sure she'd take the trouble, don't you think?'

Hanlon shrugged.

Frost shook his head and turned to address the remainder of the room. 'Right, you lot: we will assume Rachel Curtis did *not* leave Denton since her release a fortnight ago. This is her,' he said, banging the board behind him. 'I want you in every pub, shop, bookie's, you name it, until I have a minute-by-minute account of her movements over the last few days. And Wallace, I want a list of all the roads resurfaced in the last three months.'

The beefy sergeant started to protest.

'Cobblers, traffic's your responsibility. And traffic runs on roads last time I looked, so find out from the council. Albeit flamin' slowly at the moment with all the blasted roadworks. Now go, the lot of you.'

Waters leaned in and whispered Jane Hammond's name in his ear, prompting Frost to add, 'And another thing – a little boy's got a missing mum. So while you're at it . . .'

Frost filled them in on this as well; it was going to be a busy week.

Dominic Holland stood in a lengthy queue at Bennington's Bank, tapping his foot impatiently. He would miss the midday train to London at this rate. Not for the first time he wondered who on earth all these people could possibly be – why weren't they at work? They couldn't all be unemployed, surely; the unemployed had no money. He scrutinized those in front of him. A man in dungarees. *Awful*. A woman in a red-striped sun-dress, which the sun caught, rendering the garment see-through. *Tacky*. A middle-aged fellow with a comb-over in a bomber jacket . . . hold on, wasn't that one of the dreadful neighbour bores that had a pop at him about the devastation he'd wreaked on the landscape? There can't be that many looking like that around here . . . The man, sensing Holland's gaze, turned and caught his eye . . . Yes, that was him, sporting the additional aesthetic challenge of buck teeth. The fellow didn't seem to recognize him and moved up to the counter. Meanwhile, another till had just opened in anticipation of a lunchtime surge, perhaps. Holland reached inside his blazer for his cheque book, and slapped it lazily against his palm. His turn came eventually and he pulled out his gold Cross fountain pen and commenced writing a cheque for £1,000.

'Damn,' he muttered to himself. In his haste he'd brought the company cheque book.

'Is there a problem, sir?' the pimply clerk asked.

'No, no,' he said, signing above the Holland and Beswetherick Ltd account name – though there would be if Emma, his glamorous business partner, found out. The company cashflow wasn't too healthy at present. He'd have to transfer the money back soonest when in town tomorrow. That reminded him – he ought to call her this evening, to confirm their meeting in the morning. He'd not seen her since she'd come down for the party, where she'd laughed herself silly over the state of the garden. Wait until he told her about the pool tiles! Bet she didn't have this problem in Surrey.

Frost and Waters stood in the lobby at Eagle Lane. Frost had just recounted his visit to the tattoo parlour and the Kate Greenlaw connection to Rachel Curtis.

'Are you sure it's her?'

'More or less, just need to check her birthday. She's selling lipstick at Aster's according to Harry.'

'That's a damn good lead – why keep it to yourself back there?' Waters indicated the briefing room behind them with his thumb.

'Was preoccupied: Hornrim Harry had turned down Clarke's appeal to return.'

'Yeah, I heard – Bill saw her leave in tears.'

'Sue'll be back tomorrow, don't you worry.'

'How so?'

'Haven't got time for that now . . . 'Ere, what's that sorrowful-looking bugger want? Chap from St Mary's that found our Rachel, ain't it?'

Waters looked round and saw the St Mary's verger sitting on the visitors' bench underneath a peeling public information poster warning of the dangers of the Colorado Beetle. The man had a finger raised in a timid attempt to attract their attention.

'Psstt! Bill! What and why?'

Wells was frowning at the computer monitor. 'Ah yes. Sorry.' He beckoned them over and slid them the form with the man's details. 'Everything takes twice as long with this blasted thing.'

Frost picked up the card. 'I see,' he said, and handed it back.

'A man of the cloth living on the Southern Housing Estate? Unusual,' Waters remarked.

'Maybe he's doing missionary work – saving fallen women.'

'As good a place as any.' They ambled over to the verger; he appeared as nervous as he had the previous day. The man had clearly had a rough time of it.

'Sorry to keep you waiting, Mr Weaver, if you'll follow us.'

Waters loved the way Frost's manner could turn on a six-pence. One minute irreverent, bordering on crude, the next professional, polite and deeply concerned for a member of the community. The Frost who led them to the interview room now was an entirely different character to the one five minutes ago bragging about a date with a lady with cherries tattooed on her chest. No wonder a jobsworth like Mullett found him so exasperating.

'Thank you very much for coming forward, Mr Weaver,' Waters said, closing the door behind them.

'It's the least I could do.'

'If only everyone thought like that, it would make our job far easier,' Frost said, trying to put the man at ease.

Weaver tittered lightly. 'She has a hard time of it, I think.'

'Miss Hammond?' Frost said. 'Yes, I bet. I imagine you know how she makes a living.'

'Err . . . Yes, I'm sorry that is so.'

'Nothing to be sorry about.'

The man looked confused.

'We all have to make ends meet,' Frost added.

'Jane hates the way she's forced to live.'

This remark surprised Frost. 'Really? I'm sure that's the image she'd like to project to a respectable man such as your-self, but from what I gather she rather enjoys it – or at the very least is proficient,' he said, straight-faced.

'What Inspector Frost means is, she has quite a few clients,' Waters clarified.

Frost watched Weaver take this in. His bottom lip dropped a bit, as though he might just have been rendered speechless, but maybe that was just his general demeanour. He always found religious men hard to read – were they naive or innocent or both? Both qualities seemed at odds with the intelligence required to enter the Church . . . not that he had any idea how bright one had to be to get in, he'd just assumed this to be the case from the few conversations he'd had with Father Hill himself, a brainy bloke, who knew Latin and had read any amount of books.

'I see,' the man said eventually.

'Anyway' – Frost suddenly felt a wave of guilt at affronting the man in this way – 'that's neither here nor there, except in helping to trace her last known whereabouts – the fact that she's missing is what's important. When did you last see Jane Hammond, Mr Weaver?'

'On the stairs, to the flat, with some shopping, I think.'

'And that would have been when?' Waters asked.

'You know, I can't recall when exactly . . . Saturday morning?'

'And was Richard there?' Frost asked.

'Richard?'

'Her son.'

'Oh, yes – of course.'

'You know the kid?' Waters asked.

'Yes, Miss Hammond was keen I put him forward for the choir, but the boy wasn't interested. No, he wasn't with her on Saturday. How is he faring? Must be awful for him, his mother vanishing like that,' he said quickly.

'The lad is going to stay with his aunt.'

'Aunt?'

'Yes, one in Rimmington; Jane would often stay there herself on a Saturday.'

'I see.' Weaver seemed lost in a world of his own.

'The one fact we know is that Miss Hammond's sister was expecting her this Saturday evening but she didn't make it.'

'She was visiting a relative on Saturday?' Weaver said.

'Yes, we believe so. Tell me, Mr Weaver, how well do you know Miss Hammond? If she approached you to get the boy into the church choir, one imagines more than a passing nod good morning?'

The man frowned.

'You say she hates her work? Is that something she said over a cup of tea?' Frost prompted.

'She . . . I . . . can only assume she is unhappy, leading a sinful existence. We've never discussed it. I don't know her that well. A chat at the bus stop on the way into town; over the years one gets to know someone from a distance. I've been round for tea, yes, but I can't recall what was discussed . . .'

Frost didn't have time for this, nice as the fellow was. Aster's department store on Market Square and Kate Greenlaw beckoned. 'Did she ever appear frightened or mention receiving threats?' he said sharply.

'Good heavens, no.' Weaver's expression changed from one of confusion to one of horror. Frost thought the man simple.

'Well, thanks for dropping by, Mr Weaver.' Frost rose, and ushered the man, who cowered slightly, towards the door.

'Maybe vicars are like policemen, John,' Frost said as he and Waters parted company in the corridor.

'What do you mean, like moral guardians?'

'Eh? Do me a favour! Nah, I mean you get bright ones and not-so-bright ones.' They watched as the man exited through the double doors into the sunlight.

'Maybe he's in shock. Don't forget, he discovered Rachel splayed out on a tombstone. That would spook anyone out; let alone a god-fearing soul like him,' Waters said from behind him. 'Then the guy's neighbour disappears? Enough to give anyone a bad feeling.'

'Maybe . . . anyway, I've a bad feeling about his neighbour myself.' Frost pulled out a new pack of Rothmans. 'Pick the boy up from Clay House and take him to his aunt's in Rimmington. Then we'd better start thinking about a search of the scrubland behind the flats. Would hate the little blighter to discover his mother in the brambles while he's out playing with his pals.'

'You're not hopeful then?'

'The longer it goes on, the more uneasy I am. If the search of the town centre yields bugger all, we might as well make a start tomorrow.'

Frost approached the make-up counter at Aster's department store. The women that stood behind the glass cabinets were all dressed in white tunics, like dental assistants, Frost thought, but less sexy.

'I wondered how long it would take you,' one immaculately turned-out girl said sharply.

'How long it'd take me to do what?' Frost thought it 50/50 whether the news would have reached them by now. The press had been briefed less than an hour ago.

'Come bovvering me.' She had an accent. Thames Estuary.

'If you knew I'd want to talk to you, why not come to the station?'

'Sandra only just heard on the radio.' She glanced sideways at an older and more buxom colleague, who reminded him very much of Diana Dors from some dodgy comedy. 'What am I supposed to do, come rushing down to the nick and say how devastated I am?' she said coldly. The Dors look-alike beamed over at him.

'You were friends,' Frost stated, 'is there anywhere we can talk?'

'Outside. Cover for me, Tracey?' Diana Dors nodded. 'Ta. OK you,' she told Frost, 'follow me.' She reached beneath the counter and pulled out a packet of Silk Cut, and moved briskly to the store exit.

Outside, the glare of the midday sun forced Kate Greenlaw to frown, cracking layers of perfectly applied make-up.

'I'm not sure what I can tell you.'

'The last time you saw Rachel would be a good place to start.'

'Saturday. Was she . . . was she killed on Saturday?'

'We're still not sure of her time of death, but yes, Saturday night is likely.'

'Bloody hell.' She blew smoke over the tip of her cigarette, the enormity of the situation finally taking root. 'I'm sure you think I don't care, but you're wrong. I loved that girl. I can't imagine why anyone would want her dead. That psycho of a boyfriend – I'd shoot someone to get away from him.'

'She could have shot him instead of that poor sod Albert Benson from Gregory Leather.' Frost pulled out his Polaroids.

'Easy enough to say now, ain't it? She was scared, didn't know what she was doing. Besides, she didn't mean to kill him, we all know that. She didn't know 'e had a dodgy ticker, did she . . . It was the 'eart attack in hospital later killed 'im.'

'Did you know she was going to pull that job?'

The blare of an ice-cream van pulling into Market Square distracted them.

'Course I bloody didn't, and if I did I would 'ave tried to talk her out of it, and got 'er away from that madman. Rach never told anyone anything – just cos she worked for 'arry at the Coconut Grove everyone thought she was a slapper. She wasn't. She was a bright girl, that one.'

'A shame,' Frost said, distracted by a child throwing a tantrum across the road as his mother refused to get him a Rocket lolly. 'Now talk me through Saturday.'

'We'd decided to get tattoos.' Kate sighed and lit another cigarette. 'Seems so trivial now, but we thought at the time – sorry—' She turned in a shrug, fighting back tears.

This caught Frost unawares. Why? Because she'd been sharp

with him and – he was embarrassed to have to acknowledge it – her accent played a part. He should know well enough by now that people often need a protective layer.

He put his hand gently on her shoulder. 'Nothing trivial about it . . . I've often thought of having one myself, but never had the nerve to do one with a pal . . . must be a sign of true friendship.'

Kate Greenlaw looked him in the eye, trying to work out whether he was taking the piss. He met her stare with his best inscrutable no-nonsense face.

'Yeah, that's what we thought,' she sniffed, 'and it was my birthday an' all . . .'

'Nice.' He smiled.

'That's what we thought. "Nice" didn't mean we were dykes or nothing.'

'A lion?'

'Of course. You'd know. You'll have seen Rachel's, it's a—' The horror struck her again. 'Mine's on my shoulder. Rachel was terrified of her mum so . . .'

'Ah, I'm glad you mentioned her mum. Lives up north somewhere, that right?'

She nodded. 'Never met her.'

'A condition of her release was she was to visit Sheffield on a weekly basis, where her mother was to keep an eye on her; she was to relocate there after three months. But she ain't been up there in the two weeks she was out. Do you know why?'

'She talked about going, even on Saturday afternoon, but she was putting it off, because she hated her mother . . .'

'So after tattoos done, what next?'

'We stopped in the Bricklayer's for lunch then went to see the matinee of *Risky Business* as a birthday treat.'

'Then?'

'We went our separate ways; I went out with my boyfriend that night, for dinner.'

'You've a boyfriend?' Frost said, forgetting to temper his surprise.

'You *do* think I'm a dyke, don't you?' Her nose creased in annoyance.

'Of course not, I'm teasing.' He gave a wry smile, and asked for particulars of the cinema and restaurant. Not once in his note-taking did she object to the questions he levied at her; it hadn't occurred to Kate that he was constructing a framework of move-ments of both Rachel and Kate herself; being the last known person to see her alive she could be considered a suspect.

'And your boyfriend's name?'

'Adam King, twenty-seven Bath Road.' She dropped the cigarette and ground it out with her toe. 'But now he'll be at work at the garage on Eagle Lane, the one near the cop shop. Take it that'll be all for now?'

'Yes, you've been more than helpful . . . Just one last thing – did Rachel have a new boyfriend herself?'

'Would 'ave been fighting 'em off. Bees round a honeypot. Don't want to speak ill of the dead and all that, but one thing she was good at, and that was playing the victim.'

'Wouldn't have a name, would you?'

She stepped aside to let an old dear with a trolley pass by.

'We didn't really talk about fellas, to be honest. There sort of was one but she didn't want to talk about him, can't remember a name, sorry . . . and then on Saturday afternoon, after the flicks, I saw a biker drive up and start an argument with 'er as I left with Adam . . .'

'What sort of bike?'

'Do I look like the sort of girl who could tell one motorbike from another?' She smiled at him for the first time.

'Pardon me, *mademoiselle*.' He gave a slight bow.

'Look, I'll be missed. If I think of anything, I'll give you a bell, OK? Have a word with Adam; 'e's known 'er for donkey's years.'

She flicked her cigarette to the ground, crushed it underfoot, turned and left him on the pavement alone.

PC David Simms had spied Frost outside Aster's department store talking to an attractive woman dressed in white. The inspector was wearing shades and smoking. The woman had been talking animatedly, then abruptly abandoned him and entered the store. Frost, hard though it was to imagine, was considered to be a ladies' man by most of Eagle Lane. Certainly it wasn't his appearance. It must be down to his success as a detective; unorthodox but effective, was the station line. Even so, surely being good at one's job did not guarantee a pull with the opposite sex . . . And though he enjoyed Hanlon's banter about the Eagle Lane staff, David Simms – who had yet to turn twenty-one – was smart enough to know there was much he could not understand about a man who had spent as many years in CID as Frost had.

'Right, there you go.' PC Miller passed him an ice-lolly.

'Cheers. Are you sure we can have these on duty?'

'Without a doubt, mate, and we can now confirm Mr Whippy has seen neither of the ladies we're on the hunt for.' Miller, an unhealthy individual in his late thirties, had a questionable work ethic at times.

'We've done Woolies, Boots next . . .' Miller said, tossing his wrapper on the pavement.

'Odd, don't you think, both women were last seen on Saturday night.'

'Odd? Nah. Coincidence.' Miller was dismissive. His demeanour was one of jaded resignation. Simms hoped he wouldn't turn out that way. 'Come on, let's go. Not that we'll get anywhere.'

'Why do you say that?'

'Shops. Shop people never remember anything, do they?' Simms didn't know why the man was so sure of himself. 'So, we just whack one of these up on a lamp-post,' Miller said, waving an A4 sheet of paper in his face, 'and we'll be on our way.'

The paper was a Xeroxed poster. It bore both women's faces, with the word 'MISSING' under one, and 'MURDERED' under the other.

The two officers had posters for each corner of Market Square and were making last calls on the surrounding shops. Then they would head down Foundling Lane, where Rachel Curtis had visited a tattoo parlour. Another unit were out on the Southern Housing Estate making enquiries about Jane Hammond.

'Err, excuse me, mister.'

A kid on a purple bike wearing an *ET* T-shirt pulled up to them.

'What?' Miller snapped.

'The lady on the poster, I seen 'er.'

'Which one?'

'The dead 'un.'

'Where?'

'Outside the Codpiece on Saturday.'

'The Codpiece, what's that?' Simms asked.

'Fish 'n' chip shop on the Southern Housing Estate. More Jane Hammond's sort of place,' Miller said and turned to address the boy. 'Are you sure you've the right person? Jet-black hair? The missing lady from Clay House has auburn hair—'

'Yeah, woz 'er, all right, I ain't colour-blind, mate. Where's my reward?'

'Why, you cheeky little f—' the constable said, and raised his hand to cuff the youngster, but was interrupted by a wolf whistle from across the road.

The boy sat quietly in the car as they motored leisurely towards Rimmington.

'Are you into music?' Waters asked, as the radio tinkled quietly in the background, albeit abruptly interfered with by the harsh crackle from Control and area cars. 'Have a rummage in there.' He indicated the glove box.

'I've never been in a police car before,' Richard Hammond suddenly piped up, leaning forward to riffle through the cassettes.

'Glad to hear it.'

'We don't have a car. Mum always uses the bus or a taxi if it's late.'

'Cars can be a whole lot of trouble. Anything there you like?' The boy had a lap full of cassettes.

'I don't know any of these. I like Adam and the Ants.'

'Hmm, I'm not sure you'll find those guys there.'

'Status Quo? What does that mean?'

'Ah, you might not like them – and it means, the existing state of affairs' – Waters took one hand off the wheel and gestured – 'as in, the way things are.'

Nevertheless, he slipped *12 Gold Bars* into the player.

'The existing state of affairs,' the lad repeated.

'Yeah, so people might say such and such affects the status quo.'

'Like my mum missing affects the status quo?'

'Sort of.' Waters liked the little lad. He drummed his fingers to the rhythm of 'Roll Over Lay Down'.

'I like it,' Richard said, ''eadbangers, aren't they?'

'Dudes with long hair and denim up top 'n' down bottom do have an affection for this sort of music.' He turned off into an elegant Edwardian residential road that ran parallel with Rimmington High Street. 'Your aunt's quite fancy?'

'It's Grandad's house. He was a writer or something. It's that one behind the big tree.'

Waters edged in behind a convertible VW Beetle. This was a totally different setting from Clay House and the Southern Housing Estate. He picked up Jane Hammond's black address book, which Frost had found in the flat, from the dashboard and got out of the car.

He held the gate open to allow Richard up the steps first. He noticed how thin the boy was as he reached up to the huge cast-iron lion door knocker.

'These places must be worth a few quid.'

'I like where I live,' Richard said. 'This is too posh.'

'I know what you mean.' But Waters was wondering how Jane Hammond felt about it, out on the Southern Housing Estate.

'Ah Richard! You poor little love – oh . . . and who might you be?'

A tired-looking woman in a kaftan greeted them, the initial warmth draining on taking in a big black bloke on her doorstep.

'Detective Sergeant Waters, Denton CID; and might you be Clare Hammond? I believe you spoke with my colleague Inspector Frost.'

'I might . . . you best come in,' she said, clearly unhappy at having him lingering on the doorstep.

'I won't if you don't mind,' Waters said. 'He's a good kid.' He made to go.

'Is that it?' She came out of the house. 'What about Jane?'

'We're doing everything we can. A female colleague will call you later, to have a chat. I'm afraid I have to go.'

The woman stared after him in disbelief.

Closing the gate, Waters thumbed through Jane Hammond's address book. There were very few full addresses, mainly phone numbers of punters and girlfriends, presumably other prostitutes. There was only one address in Rimmington, alongside the name 'Tufty' and in brackets 'Saturday – no later than five'. And that address just happened to be in the next street.

Monday (4) _____

After his rounds with Miller, PC David Simms was to relieve
the constable posted outside the large house on Sandpiper
Close. Simms had collected the keys from the estate agent in
Market Square, as instructed. He stood on the sweeping driveway, awaiting the arrival of Inspector Frost, and surveyed the
property. If Rachel Curtis really was just a club hostess, as he'd
been led to believe, she'd done all right. A six-bedroom detached
place on Sandpiper Close off Bath Hill, North Denton. Fancy
manicured flower beds lined the drive.

It was two o'clock, and the sun's power was at its peak. Simms
was roasting hot in his coarse uniform and beginning to get
uncomfortable. Having already tramped around Denton town
centre this morning, he could do with a breather. And if he was
honest all he wanted was a bit of time at the station, fiddling
with the computers or even some paperwork, all in the hope he
might catch sight of Sue Clarke, who had been seen at Eagle
Lane earlier in the day. He was dying to know if she was coming
back but was too shy to ask. As he surveyed the area for a spot

of shade he heard the crunch of gravel behind him. Frost's red Mini Metro pulled up alongside him.

'Flamin' heck, John said she wasn't short of a few bob, but I wasn't expecting anything this flash!' Frost was in shades and a pink Fred Perry polo shirt, which was way too tight across the middle and probably better suited to someone nearer Simms's age than the inspector's.

'What you doing out in this bleedin' sun?' the inspector shouted, his creased forehead damp with perspiration. 'You have the keys, I take it?'

'I— I thought I should wait for you?'

'Tch, don't get into the habit,' he tutted, 'I'm very unreliable,' and marched across the gravel to the front door.

Simms stood rooted a second, taken aback by the senior detective's casual manner. 'Yes, I've the keys, sorry.' He fumbled for them inside his trouser pocket. This was the first time he'd come into direct contact with Jack Frost; most of Simms's time in Denton had been spent on the beat or in area cars.

'What was that scallywag Miller up to with those kids on the Market Square?' asked Frost.

'One of them thought he saw Rachel Curtis at a fish and chip place on the Southern Housing Estate.'

'The Codpiece?'

'That's the one.'

'Well, if he did, it's a long way from here to go for something to eat. And, you'd think, living in a gaff like this she might be after something more classy than a saveloy, tasty though they are.'

'I've not been . . . PC Miller has gone over there on his own to check with the owner.'

'Well, he's wasting his time – Andreas doesn't open until six on a Monday.'

'Oh.'

'I hear you're into computers,' Frost said, as Simms unlocked the door.

'Err . . . I know a bit about them, yes.'

They crossed the threshold. 'Well, when you have a minute, maybe you could give me a hand with mine. Wow, look at this!' The hall was done out with what looked like a marble floor and staircase. Simms thought it vulgar and OTT for the size of house.

'Sure, what sort of problems are you having?' prompted Simms.

But Frost was already in the kitchen.

'This stuff must have cost a fair few quid,' he said, surveying the solid German-brand appliances. He looked over at Simms and removed his sunglasses. 'Just how to turn it on for a start?'

'Turn it on?'

'The computer. I can't find the knob.'

'It's at the back – but . . .' Simms couldn't fathom this level of incompetence – the entire force had spent a week on the training course.

'Really? Hadn't thought of that. Thanks for the tip. The estate agent said there were no viewings, he hadn't even typed up the details. So we don't need to bother with that side of things. Now, what we're after here is signs of a boyfriend.'

Simms couldn't keep up, what with the inspector's train of thought jumping from one thing to the next. 'She was on her own, wasn't her boyfriend convict—'

'Yes, a very bad lot, that one; banged up, but Miss Curtis isn't the type to hang around. Know what I mean?' He winked and clapped him on the back. 'Come on, let's have a butcher's at the bedroom.'

The house was spick and span, one could say almost like a showroom. Even the bedroom was spotless, each pillow perfectly in place. Frost was disappointed.

'What were you expecting?' Simms asked.

'You never know until you see it, in this game.' Frost spun on his heels on the plush carpet. Simms moved to the next room, clearly a guest room, which was equally pristine; the hoover tracks were still visible. He went back to the other room. The same marks were just discernible, the pile being thicker, but they were there all the same.

'Inspector?' Simms called.

Frost had moved out of the master bedroom. Simms ran a finger along the dressing table. Clean.

'Inspector?' He repeated from the landing, 'Inspector Frost?'

'In 'ere,' Frost called from a room at the front of the house. 'What does that tell you?' he added as Simms walked in.

Three sparkly dresses were laid out across a single bed. Below them were half a dozen pairs of shoes, of varying styles. There was a full-length mirror on one of the open doors of a floor-to-ceiling fitted wardrobe.

'She had a lot of clothes?'

'Well done, young Sherlock . . . and maybe she was thinking of dressing up fancy?'

'Yes . . . Sir, also, I wondered, do you think a cleaner might have been in?'

'So what did the cleaner have to say?'

'Give us half a chance,' Frost said, 'the lad only just got the old dear's name off one of the neighbours. Bright boy, that Simms. Observant.'

Waters nudged the kerb. 'Anything else?'

'Zip. The place was immaculate – not even a pair of knickers in the laundry basket.'

'Right, we're here.' He released the seatbelt. 'This isn't going to be pleasant.'

'Of course it isn't, that's why I've got you to hold my hand.' Frost beamed at DS Waters.

'I didn't mean that – even you can handle a fifty-year-old housewife . . .'

They crossed the road and approached an end-of-terrace house.

'I don't know about that,' said Frost, lightly rapping on the door. 'Judging from the photos in the *Gazette*, she's no Mrs Mop.'

The door opened.

'Clear off,' a sinewy woman with short brown hair in a denim jacket said sharply.

'Ah, good afternoon, Mrs Benson,' Waters said nervously.

'She got what she deserved, and I'm glad – you can quote me on that, now bugger off.' She made to shut the door; Frost wedged his foot in the opening, but it didn't deter Albert Benson's widow, who shoved her front door with considerable might without batting an eye.

'Aaargh!' Frost cried out. 'Me toes – she's got me flamin' foot!'

Waters stepped in and pushed the door back forcefully, sending the occupant stumbling. 'I'm sorry, Mrs Benson, but you . . .'

'Police brutality! You lot think you can do anything you bloody well like.'

'Now, now, Mrs Benson,' Frost said, rubbing his ankle, 'we only want a couple of minutes of your time.'

'Is that all? Aren't you going to arrest me?'

'Why would we want to do that?'

'For murdering Rachel Curtis. I know what I said in the press . . .'

'Just because you said it, doesn't mean you'd do it—'

'Don't it just! I would if I'd had half a chance, but as it happens, I didn't.'

'You all right, Ma?' A deep voice came from within the house.

'Bleedin' coppers, Gaz.'

A tanned man in his twenties, equal in height to Waters, arrived in the hallway.

'All right, Gary.' Frost nodded. Sandy Lane had told them of the connection the previous evening, but Frost was surprised all the same to see Harry Baskin's doorman looming before him. Everyone had a mother somewhere, he supposed.

'Mr Frost,' the man acknowledged him. 'Is there a problem?'

'Just asking your mother – I presume the lady is your mother? – a few quick questions.'

'Yes, I am his mother – and Bert was his dad!' the woman shouted bitterly.

'Now, now, Ma,' Gary Benson comforted. 'What is it you want to know?'

'The woman who shot your dad was found dead in St Mary's churchyard.'

Gary Benson was understanding of the situation, and remained remarkably composed as Frost outlined their position, which was quite simply to ascertain whether his mother had been in contact with or seen the deceased.

'You've not seen her, have you, Ma?'

She shook her head.

'Jolly good,' Frost said. 'Of course, as your mother has openly made threats to Miss Curtis's life we may have to call again. And so I'd appreciate it if you remained in the Denton area while this investigation is under way.'

Benson nodded on behalf of his mother, who was now wedged under her son's arm.

'Very good,' Frost said, 'and Gary, you knew Rachel? She was running the bar at the Grove?'

'I knew her but not well.'

'I see . . . what about last week?'

'I was in Marbella until the weekend.'

'And straight back on the job, eh?' Frost had seen him last night. More words had passed Gary Benson's lips in the last two minutes than in the many times Frost had been at the Grove to see Harry. He seemed a reasonable sort, the direct opposite of his emotional mother. In fact 'Big Gaz', as he was known, displayed no feelings whatsoever.

'What do you make of that then?'

Frost and Waters sat in the Vauxhall watching the Benson residence from a discreet distance. The council house was on the corner of a residential street and the Wells Road. Frost was waiting for any movement to or from the house subsequent to their visit; he wasn't sure what to expect, but he felt he was missing something; something about the mother and son's behaviour didn't stack up.

'You'd have to be pretty daft to go out and kill someone after blatantly announcing to the press you'd kill them given half a chance. Unless it's all for show.'

'Hmm.' Waters flicked ash out of the window. 'She even repeated it to us just now.'

'Yes. Could it be a double bluff? An act; all this public ranting – might it be hiding in plain sight?' Frost frowned. 'All that guff in the press too. What was Sandy banging on about last night – "deep hatred"? I wonder about him sometimes.'

'He thinks in headlines.'

'Suppose so – wish he could say something useful for a change.'

'The son was cool as a cucumber, given the circumstances, don't you think?'

'Hmm, he might be a bit slow up here.' Frost tapped the side of his head. 'But you're right . . . too cool, compared with his mother. Might be worth checking out his movements with Harry just to be sure.'

'He looked like he'd been away though, nice tan – 'ello, what's that – looks like Mum's on the move.'

Mrs Benson shut her front door and hurried along the garden path. The two detectives sank into the seat on reflex, even though they were three hundred yards away with the sun behind them.

'Right, is it her we're after?' Waters had his fingers on the ignition key.

Frost urged caution. 'Wait for her to go round the corner, first . . .'

'She's moving at a fair pace, we're going to lose her.'

'In a sec . . .' Frost drew on the cigarette anxiously. 'We don't want her to see us.'

'Shit – look who's getting out of the Marina!'

'Blast! Sandy – bleedin' nuisance. He'll see us.'

The reporter had, and gave them a cheeky wave as he approached the Benson house.

'She'll be way down the Wells Road, we'll never find her.'

'Flamin' knickers!' Frost got out of the car, desperate to catch a glimpse of her. The traffic was solid on the main road.

'Jack, what you doing?' Waters had started the car, but Frost was still leaning on the door. 'OK, let's go.' Waters tugged at his buddy's polo top.

Frost got in, agitated. 'What's that git doing?'

'Annoying members of the public; it's what he does best.' Waters punched the Vauxhall down the road, but was blocked by a car coming the other way, which had pulled out to avoid a double-parked Audi. By the time they reached the Wells Road Mrs Benson had vanished.

Monday (5) ⸻

Superintendent Mullett was content with the press briefing. The sheer shock of a body in a churchyard had sent a jolt through Denton and a bonus was that the police were now suddenly a valued and needed part of the community. Serve them right for letting her out in the first place.

'Respect,' Mullett muttered to himself, 'respect . . .' as he battled with the lever to his office window, to let some air in. One individual troubled him – Sandy Lane from the *Echo*. A little too complacent, that one. The TV and radio people were suitably deferential and concerned about this slur against the Church ('Sacrilege' – Mullett had used this word more than once; it had a ring to it); yes, all understood the gravitas of the situation, apart from their own local man. Lane's questions about reprisals indicated a familiarity with the crime that the superintendent did not appreciate. He would bend Frost's ear later, once he'd finished dealing with the two halfwits in front of him. He returned to his desk to face the uninspiring presence of Sergeant Bill Wells and Sergeant Charlie Wallace, Denton's senior traffic officer.

'Gentlemen, I do hope you have something to report?' He interlaced his fingers proprietarily across the polished desk. The two men hesitated, unsure who should go first. The traffic congestion in Denton had reached crisis point. The centre of town was gridlocked by 8 a.m., hence the superintendent's own tardiness.

'Nothing to report as yet,' Wallace mumbled, 'but the summer is almost at an end – I'm sure the roads will ease up come September . . .'

'Piffle! The roads are set to get worse, the children will be back at school in a week or two – what on earth makes you think it'll get any better?'

Wallace started to bluster on about holiday through-traffic. Mullett was losing patience – he'd been late in again this morning because of congestion around Market Square. The situation had been growing steadily worse throughout the summer.

Mullett cut Wallace off with a raised palm. 'Wells, what news from the council? The road markings – the traffic problem is partly to do with the fact they're so worn nobody can see them. People are parking wherever they damn well fancy, especially in the centre of town.'

'They can't sort it.'

'Why the dickens not?'

'Well, sir, some blighter has half-inched the paint.'

Mullett sat there, unable to speak.

'Two hundred gallons of yellow paint, gone from the council depot end of last month.'

'Who'd want bright yella paint in their front room?' Wallace chuckled to himself.

'Quiet!' Mullett snapped. 'Have we made any progress at all on catching the thieves?'

'Not yet,' Wells said, 'the security guard was napping. I'm sure it'll turn up.'

'What do the council intend to do in the meantime?'

Wells shrugged.

'I shall intervene myself. And you' – Mullett jabbed a finger at Wallace – '*you* were late this morning.'

The policeman's silly grin was gone in an instant. 'Roadworks on the Bath Road . . . roadworks everywhere, which don't help none.'

'If it's repairs, get on to the council. Traffic is your responsibility. As for the town centre, put emergency measures in place – I will not tolerate this situation a day longer; and if you are caught up in traffic and late for duty one more time, I suggest you do not bother coming in ever again!'

Line 1 flashed before him on the desk. He reached out for the receiver sharply and barked, 'Miss Smith.'

'Mr Hudson for you, sir.'

'Put him through.'

What did the bank manager want, he wondered. Surely not an answer on that nightclub dancer already? Mullett dismissed the officers with a wave of his hand. Utterly useless, the pair of them. With all the nonsense over Clarke, Mullett had clean forgotten to enquire how Frost's errand was progressing.

'Afternoon, Michael, how can I help?'

'What the bloody hell are you up to?'

'I beg your pardon?'

'Frost was at the Coconut Grove last night, checking out my Karen.'

'How do you mean?'

'Do I need to spell it out – Frost was in the front row with all those other pervs, watching her show when he should be arresting Baskin.'

'Arresting Bas— Come now, Michael, you're overreacting, I'm sure Frost was simply checking he had the right girl.'

'Don't give me that nonsense. Get Karen out of there, Mullett, or you can kiss your chances of club chairmanship goodbye.' The line went dead. Mullett wasn't sure what to make of it.

Frost's being at the Grove was not a surprise, but Hudson's outburst was – if he really *was* in love with this woman, more fool him.

Clarke picked up the phone. She'd been shopping for baby essentials after the meeting with Mullett and had got stuck in traffic. She'd not been home long.

'It's all sorted.'

Frost.

'Honestly, Jack, it doesn't matter,' she said, fatigued, watching her mother cajole her hot and sticky son. Why hadn't she taken him out to the park, for heaven's sake?

'You're to start back tomorrow.'

She started to object but he interrupted her. 'Uh-huh. Am I not your superior officer, and therefore in a position to advise you of the change in circumstances?'

'I suppose so,' she said warily.

'But in the meantime, I want you to check in on someone. A young boy. His mum's missing and he's staying with his aunt, in Rimmington.'

Clarke heard Frost out on the Jane Hammond affair. Jack feared the worst, but did not want to be alarmist. When she queried why, he said bluntly, 'Prostitutes do not just go missing. When did you ever hear of one popping up a week later with a tan and a big smile to surprise her ten-year-old son, and say, "Sorry, honey, just fancied a breather"? Not recently, eh. Shallow graves on the moors or dumped in lorry lay-bys is more usual.'

'That's cheery,' was all she could think to reply.

'I'm a cheery sort of bloke. Now, I want you to go chat to the boy and his aunt and see if we've missed anything.'

'Why doesn't Waters "chat" to him?'

'He took the boy over this morning, but now he's tied up. Bit of the feminine charm never went amiss, did it? And you've bags of it. Sound the aunt out while you're about it – Jane

Hammond used to stop by sometimes after pulling a trick on a Saturday. It's vital we get her last movements.'

The line went dead.

'What was that all about?' her mother asked.

'Nothing, I've got to go out again.' She smiled at her son distractedly; Detective Sue Clarke was back in action.

Frost replaced the receiver, feeling pleased with himself. The CID general office, hot though it might be, at least had the benefit of a breeze flowing through the open windows. It was so unlike the stifling sweatbox he usually inhabited, rammed with paperwork and dormant computer equipment. For the last ten months he'd been taking advantage of Sue Clarke's empty desk – just spreading out a bit, as it were – but if she returned to work tomorrow he'd have to vacate. And he'd have to tidy up too; a half-eaten Mars Bar had melted into the desk, coating an upended stapler. Ignoring the chocolate he picked up an open Coke can, shook it, and discovering the dregs of something still lingering at the bottom, took a swig. Uniform had picked up a sighting of Rachel Curtis outside the cinema on Saturday afternoon, corroborating Kate's story; two boys had also seen her at the bus stop.

Clarke's phone began to ring, and he picked it up absently.

'You're a devil to track down,' Drysdale's clipped tone greeted him.

'Got to keep people on their toes.' He took another sip of the warm, flat Coke.

'Very apt, for it is feet that give me cause to telephone.'

'I'm sorry?'

'A splinter. The barefooted tomb lady.'

'Go on.'

'Not very big,' the pathologist continued, 'not discernible to the naked eye, because it's so pale, yes, lucky to spot the damn thing, one really does need the time to perform these operations to the fullest.'

A figure in dark blue loomed into Frost's peripheral vision, distracting him from the pathologist's self-aggrandizing sermon, and advanced towards him with purpose. He'd recognize that stiff, purposeful stride anywhere. *Mullett*. Frost turned his back on him and parked his sweaty rump on the desk.

'That's . . . that's wonderful, Doc,' he said, though he failed to see what use a flamin' splinter could possibly be in the circumstances.

Frost could feel Mullett at his shoulder, but he ignored him still. Drysdale hadn't finished.

'Yes, it's wood, but it's the shape that's interesting. Like the tip of a toothpick.'

'Toothpick?'

'Yes, a tiny wooden sliver, but that's what I think.'

'Really? That *is* interesting.' Frost sighed. So what – she had good oral hygiene? 'Anything else?'

'Her feet tell us a lot. This woman was not used to going barefoot, for a start. The soles of her feet are soft, hence the thin fragile splinter – it would not have pierced a more hardy foot. Also, I think this woman had been running.'

'Oh yeah?'

'Yes, her feet are marked, you see. There are indications of pressure being applied – small pocks and indents such as might be sustained while running. There are traces of what I think is bitumen from a recently tarmacked road. Yes, I think this lady ran along a newly laid road surface some time shortly before her demise.'

Frost perked up. This was more like it. 'Perhaps to evade capture?'

'Possibly.'

'The broken ankle, could that have happened from a fall while running? I'm thinking if the surface was tough underfoot . . .'

'Very possibly. Though one knee is scuffed, which would mean . . .'

'Maybe she fell twice?'

'Yes, quite.'

'Thank you very much indeed, Doc.'

Frost hung up, moving off the desk. 'Ooh, hello sir, didn't see you there. You gave me a fright,' he said to Mullett behind him.

'I thought I told you to get down to—' Mullett said loudly then, suddenly aware there were others in the room, continued quietly through gritted teeth, 'I thought I told you to get Karen Thomas out of the Coconut Grove.'

The commander's face was puce with annoyance.

'Sir, you oughtn't get so het up, not with your condition.'

The remark stopped Mullett dead in his tracks.

Frost decided not to push his luck; it was one thing winding him up in the privacy of his own office, but another in the general CID office.

'If I recall, sir, you asked me to find out whether she works there. I can confirm she does.' He grinned.

'What's so funny?'

'She's a corker, if you get me.' He winked playfully, to alleviate the situation.

'Well that explains it.' The super frowned.

'Explains what?'

'Nothing, other than the situation has escalated; get Baskin to fire her immediately.'

'What— What for?' The two men stared at each other. Frost knew Mullett well enough by now to know that the situation was not straightforward.

'Come with me,' Mullett said at last.

Monday (6)

After dropping off Richard at his aunt's, DS Waters had discovered that Jane Hammond's Rimmington punter – the one who lived a street up from her sister Clare – enjoyed equally enviable circumstances. He found the property empty, but managed to extract some details from an elderly neighbour he caught peering anxiously from a bay window. The old dear had clearly been troubled by the sight of a big black guy in denims sniffing around the next-door house. Once he'd flashed his badge at her window, the sixty-year-old widow was so relieved not to be robbed, raped and murdered, she dashed into her kitchen to fetch a business card.

Mr Rupert T. Cox was a lawyer at Cox, Drake & Elgin, whose offices were in Rimmington High Street. Waters flexed the card in his fingers behind the wheel of the Vauxhall; he didn't *want* to embarrass the man at work, but he was damned if he was going to wait for the lawyer to knock off.

Cox's neighbour's reaction was not surprising; Rimmington was posh, middle-class and white – very white. Apparently Frost had an Indian GP here – on the rare occasion that Jack mentioned his doctor, he described him as the 'outstanding Dr Mirchandani', a reference not only to the man's ability but also to his status as the only Asian in town. A statement that appeared to be true; Waters had never once seen a brown face here. The high street was populated with independent retailers – not for Rimmingtonians the Bejam, International and other chain retailers. No, the family-run greengrocer and the jolly local British butcher with his prime cuts, these were more suited to the discerning clientele around here. Waters stopped to buy a peach from one such place before entering the law firm.

Cox, Drake & Elgin operated out of the top floor of an imposing stucco-fronted Georgian building at the heart of the high street. Waters took a bite out of the ripe fruit and eyed the building with a hint of mischief.

'Well, *Tufty*, let's see what you've got to say for yourself,' he said, mounted the steps to the building and pressed the bell.

The receptionist buzzed him in over the intercom but, clocking him in person, she became immediately suspicious. Mr Cox was, she decided, about to become very unavailable. Her legal environment encouraged mistrust. Waters' credentials might look authentic – but a forged or stolen identity seemed more probable.

'I tell you what,' he advised, as she froze at her typewriter when he bore down on her, resting his knuckles on her desk, 'just pick up the phone and tell Mr Cox I'm here to see him about "Tufty", and if he doesn't want to see me, fine, I'll go away and leave you my number.'

She picked up the phone and spoke in urgent hushed tones. In less than thirty seconds, Waters was ushered into a corner office to meet a man in his late forties with longish sandy hair, wearing an open-necked shirt. An abundance of chest hair poked out over the top button.

'Mr Cox, thank you for finding the time.' Waters held out his hand.

'Thank you, Cynthia, that will be all,' the lawyer said, and shook Waters' hand limply. Once the door was shut he continued, 'Something has happened to Jane, hasn't it?'

'Why do you think that?' Waters asked simply, settling into an easy chair.

'Come now, Sergeant,' Cox said, 'unless you are a fraud and out to blackmail me.'

Waters gave a slight laugh. 'Ha. Yeah, I guess there's not much that gets past you boys. You're right. Jane Hammond is missing.'

'Since when?'

Waters filled him in with what he knew.

'I see.' The man seemed shocked. 'And all your information would point to me as her last port of call. But I didn't see her last Saturday, she didn't show.'

'Can you prove it?'

'No, I'm afraid I cannot.'

'Oh.'

'Does that make me a suspect?'

'Suspect? Suspect for what? She's only missing . . .'

'Don't play games with me, Sergeant Waters. Janey always caught the same bus over; she even knew the driver's name. Kev. Why not check at the bus depot?'

'All in good time.' The man was rude, but to be fair, he was holding up well. 'On a usual Saturday, when would you part company?'

'She'd arrive at four, and be on her way by five thirty.'

After the initial shock, the lawyer gave the impression of concern. He had known Janey three years, and was not ashamed of the relationship, it seemed. He was single, after all. Waters didn't see the guy in the frame, and emphasized that he was most interested in tracking the woman's movements. After five minutes he rose to leave.

'And Sergeant, please keep me informed. I want to help in any way I can. How's the boy?'

'He's being taken care of.'

'Of course, her sister Clare.' The lawyer pondered this, then added, 'As I said, I'm willing to help where possible, and that extends to the boy.'

Waters nodded and left. The man was a better person than he was prepared to credit when he'd arrived in Rimmington. You never can tell, he thought, and headed back to Denton.

Clarke sat in the bay window of the elegant Edwardian town-house with Clare Hammond. The woman, though pleasant enough, had an unhealthy pallor and instinctively Clarke had her marked as ill.

They had been discussing Richard's schooling, in a circuitous way; whether he should return to school given the uncertainty of his mother's whereabouts, and if so how he would get to Denton. Clare Hammond didn't drive. Clarke thought this a social services issue, but it was not quite the end of the summer holidays, so would not be an immediate problem, unless one was to take the bleakest view, and she was reluctant to pursue that with the boy within earshot at the far end of the room.

'I haven't got any money,' Clare said abruptly, reaching for the teapot, which sat on a small oval table between them.

'I'm sorry?'

'The house was left to us both by my father. I've not been able to work for some time.' Her hand shook as she poured tea into what Clarke thought to be a bone-china cup. 'I'm sure you must think it odd, me living here, and her and the boy over there in that flat.'

'Families are all very different,' Clarke said, thinking of her own small one. 'In any case, it's not our job to judge.' She reached for her cuppa. The ornate porcelain handle was too tiny for her fingers, and it slipped as she raised it.

Clarke watched as brown liquid splashed across a knitted tea cosy. Clarke thought the cosy – white, with a contrasting pattern in green – rather twee, verging on the ugly.

'Sorry,' she said.

'Oh, don't worry about that, it's ghastly anyway,' said Clare. 'Jane gave it to me for Christmas.'

'Does she knit?'

'Not that I know of, God knows where she got the damn thing . . . a jumble sale, probably. Do you have children your-self?' Clare asked suddenly.

'Why, yes, I have a baby.'

'Ah, I thought so.'

'Why?' She must look shattered, massive rings under her eyes.

'Oh nothing, just the way you look at Richard.' She nodded slightly towards the boy, who was sitting at a large table at the far end of the room drawing, his silhouette framed by the light coming through French doors at the back of the house.

Clarke's gaze dropped to the puddle in her saucer. 'I suppose I hadn't really thought of children as, as . . . anything beyond babies.'

'Oh, I understand that. Jane certainly never gave it a moment's thought. How could she?'

Clarke was surprised by the sharpness of her tone. 'Are you and Jane close?'

'You think I'm unsympathetic?'

'I . . .' Clarke stuttered to a halt. A silence hung in the neat Edwardian house for a long second.

'We are close, actually.' Clare Hammond's tone softened, eyes down on the teacup in her lap. 'I see her most weeks. I don't like the way she makes her living, but I do respect her; she's tough . . . and how she cares for Richard – never a mother more devoted . . . But this eventuality has always lurked at the back of my mind, that something would happen . . .'

'Do you think something has happened to her?'

Clare Hammond raised her eyes, and met Clarke's anxious stare. 'Of course, don't you?' She cleared her throat. 'I pray nothing has, but . . . but I'm steeling myself. I'm sorry if you find me hard-hearted . . . One reads about things in the papers all the time that happen to girls like Jane.' Her voice quivered ever so slightly on her sister's name.

'Has Jane ever confided that she's felt threatened?' Clarke said. The honesty was hard to absorb.

'No, not that I can recall. Ironically, she's often said she feels perfectly safe there in those flats. Protected from above and below by people like herself, looking out for one another. She'd not tell me anyway. And she never discusses her clientele. I only know there is one around here; and that's usually when I see her.' Clare smiled bravely. 'After work.'

Clarke was finding the episode depressing and wondered whether the time away had made her go soft, or if not soft, then vulnerable emotionally. She'd thought that with Frost staying so often at her flat she'd somehow maintain a rapport with CID. But he was seldom really present: he just ate and drank, made a mess and snored in front of the television. She felt a need to be back at Eagle Lane, back amid the chaos and coarse unpleasantness; let it toughen her up again. There was little more to do here. She didn't deem it necessary to talk to the child – in fact, she found the very thought conflicted with her maternal instincts. She scribbled down the social services number on the back of her own card and did her best to reassure the woman that her sister would reappear. Clare Hammond's expression was doubtful; her principal concern was at being landed with her sister's kid – something she felt at best ill-equipped for, and at worst pretty angry about. This suppressed anger was, Clarke thought, the overriding mood as she left the aunt and nephew.

*

120

Within the confines of his office, Mullett took a deep breath and settled into the comfort of his executive chair. He forced himself to regain his composure and not be riled. He knew Frost was baiting him, but he would rise above it. Miss Smith brought in a tea tray, and the superintendent politely encouraged Frost to partake.

'Now, how can I put it?' Mullett asked with more honesty than he'd intended. 'It would be beneficial to us all if Karen Thomas were no longer in Harry's employ.'

'How?'

'How what?'

'How would it be beneficial *to us all*?'

He sat there, slurping tea noisily, wearing that simpleton expression that drove Mullett crazy. After all their years of enduring one another, how was it Frost *still* had the power to wind him up so? (And – more urgently – how on earth did Frost know of his *condition*?)

'Let's just say it would help me in one way, and you in another.'

Frost set the teacup down with a clatter and reached forward for the heavy desk lighter. Even that gesture was carefully judged to annoy him! He knew full well the barbarian carried a Zippo; but no, why use that when there's an opportunity to scuff up his highly polished desk? The man was an ape.

'How would it help *me*?'

'In loose, unquantifiable terms.' Mullett gesticulated airily.

'Really? As beneficial as that?'

'Does everything have to be clear cut?' He leaned forward. 'You've got Clarke back, haven't you – can't you be satisfied with that?'

Frost drew deeply on the cigarette. 'OK.'

'OK? OK what?'

'I'll get Harry to sack Karen Thomas.'

'*Really?*' Mullett was speechless; he expected at least to have to twist Frost's arm, or come down hard. This was a surprise. 'Jolly good, thanks, Jack.'

Frost smiled back. 'That'll be all, sir?'

'Yes, yes.' He sat back, satisfied. 'Let me know when it's done.' Frost nodded and left the room, leaving Mullett feeling relieved, but nervous. Why would he agree so readily? It was not in his nature to do anyone any favours, him least of all, especially after their confrontation this morning. Surely? Unless he was stupid. Though Frost was many things, but not stupid. He must be up to something . . . The super scratched around irritably for his pills.

Monday (7)

With Waters out, Frost had seconded PC Simms to run him across Denton. Frost loathed driving, and was always on the look-out for an unsuspecting chauffeur. They parked outside the down-at-heel row of shops, and Frost exited the panda car with alacrity.

'I'm peckish,' he quipped over the car roof.

Andreas was a handsome man in his early forties, bald on top but with a heavy beard; powerfully built and wearing a tight white T-shirt to emphasize his physique, he was the proprietor of the Codpiece chippy on the Southern Housing Estate. With a lugubrious air he took an order from two teenagers in biker jackets.

'Hello, Mr Happy,' Frost teased.

'Frost? Jesus, what do you want – how many times do I need to tell you, you're bad for business? You frighten the customers away. Damage my saveloy margins.'

Frost had briefed PC Simms in the car, said the man was of noble European birth; well-educated, well-travelled but had

had a professional mishap, which had landed him here in Denton. What Simms saw before him was a fast-food chef, stuck behind a deep-fat fryer in thirty-degree heat, with little patience for sarcastic policemen. Andreas served the boys their chips, then removed his steel-rimmed spectacles and wiped them on his T-shirt.

'You can have a battered sausage left over from Saturday, but that's it. You'll have to clear off.' He spoke well and was clearly not intimidated.

'Talking of Saturday night . . .' Frost gestured to Simms.

'Sorry to bother you, sir, but would you happen to remember this lady?' Simms flashed a picture of Rachel Curtis, which they'd lifted from her house.

'Cute.' Andreas replaced his glasses. He raised his shoulders in a pronounced shrug. 'Maybe, when?'

'Saturday evening, between seven and eight?'

'Saturday evening there was a stream of biker gangs. Not local. Is she local?'

'Sort of . . . she's been away,' Frost said diplomatically.

'Sorry, are you saying she is in a gang or not?'

'Let's just say she was not from this part of town; we think she was with a man.'

'Couples . . . there's tons of couples come through.' He banged the metal chip fryer with a frown.

'Or she might have been on her own?' Simms put in, raising his voice. Frost shot him a glance with a cocked eyebrow.

'How was she dressed?'

'Short black skirt, white blouse. Too smart for those scruffy layabouts,' Simms said pointedly, nodding towards the two lads.

'A woman did come in on her own, I recall; it might have been her.'

Frost was impressed with young Simms. He showed promise in all the ways his older brother had but without the chip on his shoulder. He stood outside the Codpiece and watched the lad climb inside the area car as he sank his teeth into a saveloy. If Rachel Curtis had been here, it gave them no real clue as to where she went next. Beyond the Southern Housing Estate was the countryside. There was nothing closer than the village of Two Bridges over to the south-east, approachable only by narrow lanes. The Codpiece itself sat on a crossroads. Frost watched two bare-chested men in hard hats pass the police car and glance vaguely in his direction. He polished off the saveloy and tossed the newspaper wrapper in the bin.

As he slipped into the car beside Simms, a vicious drilling started beyond the bus shelter up ahead. He'd not noticed the temporary traffic lights earlier, which now switched to red in front of them: and why would he? The whole of Denton had been snarled up with congestion the majority of the summer and traffic moved at a snail's pace all over town. Frost felt hot and uncomfortable on the sticky plastic car seats, and after five minutes of going nowhere he abandoned Simms and the car and decided to walk. Though he had a fair distance to cover, the day was cooling and it was infinitely more pleasant to be on foot.

As the sun was going down, his mind turned to the conversation he'd had earlier with Mullett; the truth was that Frost was attracted to Karen Thomas, and until the super asked him to have the girl fired he had not realized to what extent. Suffice it to say, he jumped at the chance with such alacrity it surprised them both. The thought of any opportunity to be in contact with her was, well, rather exciting. He was in little doubt Karen Thomas was the girl to whom Sandy Lane had alluded in the pub, in connection with Hudson, but he was buggered if he'd let Mullett know that. No, he was content to allow the super to marvel at Frost's magnanimous gesture to help out, no questions asked. He'd call Harry at the club once he was 'home'.

The Jade Rabbit.

Frost had been determined to get there before Kenny and Mark Fong closed the restaurant, but as he hurried down Queen Street he could see Kenny Fong was already on the doorstep locking up.

'Ah Jack, there you are – all yours,' Kenny said. 'Left you some Kung Po Extra, just need to heat it through.'

'Cheers, Kenny,' Frost said as Kenny unlocked the door and pushed it open. He was going to eat all right over the next few weeks; that much was for sure. Frost and Kenny shook hands, and Frost apologized for his late arrival the previous night; this was the first time he had seen his host since emptying the Metro. 'See you tomorrow,' he called as he watched Kenny disappear into the night.

He switched on the lights and took in the garish oriental interior. The Jade Rabbit was for many years only a takeaway, but the owner had extended out the back of the building to develop a snug restaurant. Fong had figured out there was more money to be made by running licensed premises: Fong's mark-up on alcohol was as impressive as the average English couple's intake. It was growing ever more easy to buy French and German wines cheaply – and the Denton population, along with the rest of the UK, was acquiring a taste for the stuff. Who'd have thought Liebfraumilch and special crispy duck were a match made in heaven? What with the improved margin he could make on selling the same food only presented differently, Fong reckoned eventually he could ditch the takeaway (and the unpleasant late-night custom it attracted) altogether.

Frost would miss the convenience of the takeaway, though. He himself had been known to join the stragglers at the back of the queue for the Jade's chow mein and pork balls when the pubs turned out.

'I'll just have to adapt, like you, eh, Monty?' Frost said to the parrot cage on the mahogany serving hatch. The bird screeched and fluttered into life. For a spell Monty had whiled away his evenings at the takeaway counter, but drunken yobs had taunted the bird with football chants. 'Who ate all the pies?' in particular was felt inappropriate for a Chinese eatery, and the bird was soon relegated to the flat above the shop. Unfortunately there he proved unpopular with Mrs Fong – not on grounds of language (she spoke no English) but on health: feathers and dust. Poor Monty was soon reinstated below but this time in the restaurant.

Looking after Monty was straightforward; water, Trill and a sweep-out with a dust pan and brush every morning was all that was required. Frost quite liked the bird – they had chatted away quite animatedly when he'd arrived late last night.

'All right there, Monty?

'*Evenin' all!*'

'You learn fast, my feathery mate. Bill Wells better watch out, you're halfway to qualifying.' Frost poked a nicotined finger through the cage. 'Now hold on a second, I got to call the Big Fat Man.' Frost reached round through the hatch and pulled out the phone.

The bird sidestepped inside the cage, his beady eye on Frost the whole time. It didn't take long to get through; the club boss was expecting something – the previous evening having been left open-ended.

'Jack.'

'Harry. I won't beat around the bush, I need you to do us a favour.'

'A favour?' The surprise was detectable even down what was a very poor line.

'Yes, and bear in mind it's not easy for me to ask this.'

'It's easy for me to hear, though.' His gravelly voice cracked into a chuckle. 'Come on, Jack, what can I do for you?'

'Karen Thomas. That stripper. I need you to fire her.'

'Need me to?'

'Yes.'

'Any reason?'

Frost thought for a moment. It was best to say nothing. 'Make something up?'

'Me? Why me? You're the one that wants her fired. That's if I agree to do it. She's very popular – slides up and down that pole like it's one big shiny—'

'All right, all right,' Frost interrupted. 'She's your newest girl, right? Can't you say business is tight at the moment and you need to cut costs?'

'I don't know about this, Jack. You're right, business is tight, but she's the one bringing the punters in night after night . . . she is a stunner; I mean, look at you the other night, dribbling like a baby. I'll do it, but I need to be compensated.'

'Compensated?'

'Yeah. Two hundred nicker. For lost earnings.'

'Flamin' heck, Harry! That's a bit steep.' He couldn't see Mullett wearing that. 'A ton. And that's it, with no questions asked.'

'Deal.' Harry laughed. 'And if she asks – and she will, sparky one that she is – I'll give her your name.'

The day had been a success. From his armchair, Weaver smiled at Moira Stewart flickering on the nine o'clock news as he greedily devoured spaghetti hoops and Smash. His confidence and presence of mind had been rewarded. The Denton Police were grateful that he'd put himself forward, and had thanked him for his help.

The only fly in the ointment was the revelation that Janey had often stayed Saturday night at her sister's. He felt a tiny bit bad – he thought those Saturday nights spent away from the flat were with another man; she'd never allowed him a whole night. Anyway, it was her fault! All of it. If she hadn't teased him about his knitting, she'd be alive. Maybe with a broken leg, but alive!

He stamped his feet in annoyance, spilling his water into the mashed potato on his tray. 'Drat!' he cursed and stood up abruptly. A *whump* from the settee next to him caused him to turn. The body had slumped to one side, with an arm sliding from beneath the sheet and hitting the floor. The rigor mortis must have gone.

'I'm telling you, it's your fault. Knitting *is not* gay.' It was that one remark that had caused him to snap. Jonathan had always liked him to knit. He placed the tray on the cabinet, and moved towards the shrouded corpse. 'You'll be better off behind the sofa.' He pulled off the sheet. Weaver stepped back and scrutinized the young woman. The legs he'd so admired, now set at an awkward and ungainly angle, revealed too much thigh below the yellow mini-skirt. He moved the knitting to the floor and sat down next to her, tentatively patting her leg. 'I've a plan for you, my love.'

The fact that he'd been unable to move her yet, and was unlikely to move her in the immediate future, had initially vexed him. Now, though, an idea had surfaced . . . He moved closer; the pat became a stroke. Instead of pulling the skirt down as he'd intended, he found his fingers creeping up her thigh under the hem. He edged closer to her and began to snuggle up, until something jabbed his cheek. In the half-light, he'd not seen the knitting needle protruding from her neck, where he'd stuck it after she teased him at the wrong moment about his hobby. He adjusted himself on the settee then reached round and held her head firmly before tugging the needle out with a grunt. Placing the needle on his lap he clasped the dead girl's face. The mouth open; poised, frozen mid-gasp. Then, leaning forward, inches from her cold lips, he whispered, 'Not laughing now, are you?'

Tuesday (1)

Mist still hung in the air, spider's webs glistened in the early sun. It was 7.45 a.m. It was quiet, apart from the occasional bark from the dog unit.

Clarke felt ready and raring to go.

'Good to have you back, Sue,' Waters said.

'Good to be back,' she replied, and surveyed the scene. There were half a dozen uniform and practically all of CID on this patch of wasteland behind the Southern Housing Estate, awaiting instructions. 'Does it really require this many people to cover an area this size – it can't be more than an acre or so?'

'Be quicker this way, besides, we think she's close by.'

'Why?'

'Nobody saw her leave town. She didn't get her usual bus to Rimmington on Saturday; the stop is across the road, opposite the flats. A couple of the neighbours finish work and arrive home around the time she would normally be leaving so they'd usually see her either waiting for the bus or coming down the steps. The driver also confirmed that she didn't board his bus that afternoon.'

A huddle of uniforms suddenly parted, revealing Frost, who proceeded to march across the dewy grass towards them.

'Maybe she took an earlier bus?' Clarke suggested finally.

Waters shook his head. 'Uh-uh. Her son said she left at the usual time.'

'Morning, troopers,' Frost said jovially. 'Nice day for it.'

'If you say so. What's the plan?' she said. He had to be the worst-dressed man on the planet – the pink polo top was way too small and rucked up unflatteringly above the equally tight cheap nylon trousers.

'We'll be the rearguard. Sweeping behind uniform and the dogs.'

By nine thirty they had covered the area to the canal towpath twice, finding nothing more than discarded condoms and cider bottles. The sun now had some power in it, and Frost did not look as fresh as he had when they started out.

'Right, that's enough exercise for one day,' he puffed. 'I'm parched, and it's hours before opening.'

'Drag the canal?' Waters suggested.

'Nah.' He shielded his eyes with his hand and looked past him towards the flats. 'I think she's closer to home.'

Clarke turned to face the ugliness that was Clay House. 'Still inside there?'

'Possibly. Her son said she'd never stray far in the school holidays,' Frost said. 'Anyway, you chaps head back. I'm going to mooch around here a bit longer.'

Frost's expression was one of concern. Over the months, Clarke had grown used to seeing the sweaty inspector out of hours, but had not experienced this serious side to his nature for some time. She thought back to the discussion they'd had that spring as to what sort of house guest he'd make. Frost had claimed, on the rare occasions he finished work at a respectable time, he liked nothing better than to sit and read, preferably military history. She knew this to be true, the Napoleonic era was a favourite, but as it transpired the history books ended up in storage, and instead Jack would sit with his feet up, watching the television, guffawing at Benny Hill. The man needed to unwind somehow, she supposed; but it was nevertheless difficult to equate that hopeless figure with the one before her now, standing in the harsh sunlight, face creased in worry.

'The address book.' Frost squinted up at Waters. 'Did she list any punters in the building?'

'I told you, the book is just a bunch of nicknames – like Tufty the Lawyer.'

'Tufty the Lawyer?' Clarke asked.

'Body hair,' Waters said aside, as if that explained everything. 'His was the only address – maybe because he lived outta town. The rest of 'em do *not* have an address listed.'

'So she's either doing the homeless a favour, or she knows only too well where each punter lives?'

'Reckon so, but I don't see that helps us. I doubt those nicknames are common knowledge. Like, I only got in to see ol' Tufty by threatening to reveal it to his colleagues? I know that—'

'Not everyone is going to be as uptight as your poncy Rimmington lawyer.' Frost made to go.

Waters turned to follow. 'Yeah, some might be a bit more intimate, you know, like if a bloke is called "pumpkin dick", he's hardly going to spread that around, is he?'

' "Pumpkin dick"? What sort of nickname is that . . . is that in the book?' Frost's voice trailed off as the two made their way through the long grass back to the car.

Clarke was left alone next to a large buddleia. It was hard to equate this kind of conversation with the little boy she'd left drawing quietly at his aunt's dining-room table in Rimmington. This was the real world, though, and she better get used to it again. And soon, if she was to be any use in CID.

*

Weaver had watched the police staring up at the building. It was strange; here he was, invisible, and them down there searching for Janey. He pressed the side of his head to the window to see where the two men went. They stopped at a green Vauxhall, whereupon the black one got in and promptly drove off. The other disappeared from view. A woman PC remained behind, standing by a flowering bush facing the canal. They'd not find her there, no . . . And when they drew a blank, what then? Where would they look next? His audacious move had paid off; the gossip at the laundrette was that the police had questioned the entire block – all apart from him. By thrusting himself forward, Weaver had risen above suspicion.

He stepped back from the window, and slipped on a pair of trainers. He had to go into work later, but he could get the stuff first and do it tonight . . . He had a couple of hours before he needed to leave for his shift, so he could make a start on the preparation. He went to the bathroom and picked the razor out of the sink.

Weaver had quickly discovered that although he'd initially resolved to keep Janey for ever, he didn't actually miss Janey herself, but more the service she provided. Within a short space of time the powerful need grew again, ever stronger, within him. Pornography could not allay the necessity for touch. He was surprised at how quickly this had taken hold; Janey was barely cold before he felt stirrings towards the younger members of the church choir . . . he needed to act – it called for a trip to Foundling Street (where he knew Janey had placed her number in the phone box on the corner, advertising her services).

But Foundling Street could wait until later; he'd decided he still wanted to preserve Janey, and it made good sense on a practical level to keep her. Weaver wasn't an expert on policing but he knew that without the body she would remain missing, and that the police would soon tire of looking. If he kept her then she'd never be found; any number of fools had been caught through careless disposal of the body. Embalming was not something he knew much about, but he was no idiot – he had O levels in both Chemistry and Biology, and if it was good enough for Chairman Mao and Lenin, it was good enough for a Denton prostitute . . .

He knelt down over the bath and set to work. The body should be clean and hairless but it was no use – the razor blade was blunt and he'd need another to do the job properly. He might as well make a day of it – a trip to the library, then probably the chemist's and the hardware store. He'd wanted to do as much as he could before he collected the money required for France. He stood up and sighed. So much to do. He regarded the pile of clothes at the foot of the bath. Those could go in a bin on the way to the shops; not the blouse, that had blood on it, but the underwear and skirt. He picked the garments up, shoved them in a carrier bag and left the flat.

A tingle of excitement raced through him as he hurried across the landing to the stairwell, knowing the plastic bag under his arm contained her underwear; underwear that only minutes ago he'd held to his mouth. As he rounded the corner on to the musty concrete staircase he collided with a shortish podgy man in a pink top.

'Ooooff!' the man wheezed.

'I'm so sorry!' Weaver exclaimed.

'Not at all, I should have been looking where I was going. Better still, I shoulda got the lift.'

'It's broken,' he replied coolly on recognizing the man.

'Wait a minute . . . Mr Webb, the verger?'

'*Weaver*. That's right.' He hovered on the top step.

'Weaver. Sorry. Well, see you later.' He smiled and continued on his way.

What did he mean, 'See you later'?

Tuesday (2)

There was a terrible pounding in Dominic Holland's head. He had just sat down in an uncomfortable glass chair, half an hour late for the meeting in the company offices at South Kensington, one of London's most fashionable districts. He felt unwell and had slept badly at a friend's flat. Though the fan whirred and vibrated with all its might, the office was still excruciatingly stuffy for ten in the morning. He looked at a greasy croissant on the desk in front of him and thought he might be sick.

The launch party last night was a glitzy affair at Hanover Square; everyone from *Vogue* was there, Boy George *and* Marilyn, all of Depeche Mode, Terry Whatsisname from *The Tube* and a wrinkly Beatle (George or Ringo – he wasn't sure which). But the champagne was cheap and nasty. *Had* to be to explain the ferocity of the hangover he was currently experiencing.

Emma was wittering on interminably about the numbers; always the numbers, all the more so when they weren't good. And the July figures certainly were not good – they were very, very bad, as she was going to great lengths to make clear. She was a whiz on the figures. He needed to have his wits about him. Niles Tanklehurst, their PA, wafted in with some coffee.

Dominic, perspiring, said, 'No, just water. And might we open the window?'

'Are you all right?' Emma paused her monologue on the results.

'I'm grand, thanks; just a tad peaky.'

'Hmm.' She pursed neon-pink lips. 'I hope you're taking this in – it's not pretty; the overspend on marketing is not yielding results.'

He'd insisted on that extra cash. Hooting on about brand awareness, capitalizing on the success of the Tightspots campaign, which he later realized to his chagrin had been stuff and nonsense.

'And the cashflow is simply *dire*.' She drew the word out as if searching for another. Diarrhoea, maybe. Either way, he didn't want to think about it.

'Running low, are we?'

'Desperately low. We're five hundred off asking Coutts for an extension.'

Crumbs. If she discovered he'd drawn out money – even if by mistake – from their company account, the shock would straighten her shaggy perm in an instant. The phone at Niles's desk beyond the glass wall trilled fractiously.

'Might be your builder again, Dominic,' said Niles, reaching for the window.

'Eh?'

'Your builder. He's rung twice already.' Emma was annoyed. 'Go and see what he wants, will you, so that we might get on?'

Holland cursed but was relieved to be upright, and moved to answer the phone. 'Holland and Beswetherick.'

'There you are, at bleedin' last. No readies, no tiles.'

'I beg your pardon?'

'I can't get ya yer tiles, without some cash; I thought we . . .'

136

'I left it in the mixer, as you requested.' He smiled at Emma, sitting nonplussed the other side of the glass wall.

'Ain't nothing there.'

'It's there,' he persisted, 'I left it for you yesterday afternoon before coming up to town.'

'I'm telling ya, it ain't.'

'In a white Bejam bag.'

'Ain't no bag and ain't no cash, so I'm offsky. Might—'

But Dominic Holland didn't catch what Terry Todd might or might not be off to do as he was inconvenienced by the urgent need to vomit over a very carefully manicured and expensive imported bonsai.

PC David Simms had caught up with Rachel Curtis's cleaning lady between jobs. It just so happened that Tuesday was her slot for Sandpiper Close and the 'big 'ouses'. It was easily as hot today as it had been the previous day when he had stood in the same spot and elicited the woman's timetable from a helpful neighbour. Standing before him now on the pavement was a shrunken woman, stiffness etched upon her joints from years spent on her hands and knees scrubbing floors.

'So you kept the place spick and span while she was inside?'

'Once a month I'd pop round with a duster.'

'And then when she got out?'

'I came round Tuesday before last and she was out . . . Then she asked me to come back weekly.'

'What sort of state was the place in?'

She shrugged. 'A doddle. Give the kitchen a quick mop. It's a family-size house, she barely touches the sides.'

'Was there any trace of activity?'

'Beg your pardon?' The woman scowled unbecomingly.

'I mean, evidence that Miss Curtis had cooked, entertained perhaps?'

'Not that I could tell; not one for cooking, that lass . . .'

'So, all in all, it was a waste of time her employing you,' he said, growing impatient.

'I'm not going to knock a retainer, am I, what with me back an' all . . .'

A white Lotus turned into the close, like the one in *For Your Eyes Only*. The driver slowed on spotting a policeman. A horsey-looking blonde stared at them before pulling into a driveway further down. The sight of the Bond car had distracted Simms, and abruptly he was of the opinion he was wasting his time. This woman would tell him nothing useful. He had to be back for the catch-up meeting at midday but after that had the afternoon off, and he was desperate to get out of this uniform.

'. . . apart from the bathroom, which must have been a man.'

'What did you say?'

'A shave. Someone had had a shave in the bathroom.'

'A man?'

She eyed him warily. 'There's not many lasses do their legs in a washbasin.'

'Recently?'

'Well, must 'ave been over a week ago. Typical bloke. Can't be arsed to clean it afterwards.'

Curtis had lived there with her boyfriend Nicholson before they were arrested, so it seemed reasonable to think there would still be shaving equipment in the house . . . Was this evidence that she'd had a man back to hers since being released? This was something. He thanked the woman for her time and hurried back to the station.

Frost had dismissed Waters and Clarke, and now sat in Jane Hammond's flat alone, clutching her diary, which the WPC had found. It was a child's notebook; a colourful Little Miss Naughty beamed up at him. He'd already thumbed through it, but now it deserved closer scrutiny. There was only the one name that cropped up on Saturdays, and Waters had already dealt with him after checking her address book. All the remaining punters were identified with nicknames or codes: Mr Whippy, Mr Tickle, Socks-on-ears, and so on. She had also noted how much she charged them and what effort they required on her part at each encounter. 'Socks-on-ears, £7 – quick', or 'Spanky – drawn out'. 'Noisy – £23'. Illuminating, yes, but not much help.

How could he trace her movements?

She had to have had some punters calling at the flat or maybe even visited people in the same block. The old dear he'd left the boy with temporarily confirmed there had been frequent comings and goings during the day when the lad was at school. Frost walked into the kitchen to put the kettle on. The kettle was a new-fangled jobbie that had a bright light on its side to indicate it was heating up. He stood watching the white plastic object gently vibrate. The light reminded him of the new bleeper which he'd been issued and had promptly, conveniently, misplaced . . . The kettle pinged, the light went off. He lifted it off its pad and was about to pour water in a cup when . . . *wait* – the kettle's red light, like that on an answering machine. Surely she'd have an answering machine? He hastened into the living room, still clutching the steaming kettle, in search of the phone. Right on cue, it rang a couple of times; an answering machine clicked on, and he heard the soft purr of the missing occupant.

He located the phone next to the television set just as the caller rang off. A red light flashed: six new messages. Hopefully, the previous callers hadn't been as bashful. Frost pressed Play.

'Message for Miss, from Dirty Dan. Danny's been a very naughty boy, and deserves the rod,' a well-to-do voice said softly, but enunciating the 'R' stiffly. 'Yes, the rule of the rod must be observed. Firm and hard. No leniency for this dirty pup,' the man rasped out, and then switched to a mannered and more controlled voice to add, 'Thursday, if poss? Wednesday's out, I'm afraid, the wife's bingo's canned. Six if it suits you? Pip pip!' The call clicked off.

Frost considered himself a well-rounded sort of fellow, experienced in the world and familiar with the deviances of its inhabitants, but that message might as well have been in Mandarin for all the sense it made to him. 'But one thing I do know, chum,' he said to the answerphone as he rose from the settee, 'is you are not the sort of fellow that lives in Clay House.'

Clarke entered the station through the front entrance. There sat Bill Wells, Eagle Lane's front line, grimacing at a huge grey computer monitor. Two PCs in uniform stood to the left by the noticeboard, speaking softly. She instantly thought they were talking about her; this was her first official day back at the station. This morning in the field was different, and it wasn't until she'd stepped into the building that the unfamiliar air of paranoia touched her.

'Hello, Bill,' she said loudly, marching up to the reception desk, 'what's new?'

She'd seen him yesterday but hadn't really taken much notice of him. He was older than she recalled, worn and jowly. The inertia of the reception desk had not been kind.

'Welcome back.' He smiled softly.

'Thank you.' She loitered uneasily, she did feel different being here (yesterday didn't count; she didn't know where she stood then).

'How's the nipper?'

'Philip? Oh . . . he'll be fine.' Unaware she'd answered in the future tense, she did however feel a twinge of anxiety – maybe a maternal pull? 'He'll be just fine. My mum's looking after him.'

The station itself was exactly the same as ever; a bit grubbier – the magnolia walls were now more a jaundice-yellow, the plants had shrivelled and died in the heat and the posters warning of rabies and beetles hailed from another age entirely.

'Who the bloody hell is Inspector Jack Frost? And where is he?'

Clarke turned to see a striking young woman in a light floral summer dress march in. The woman stopped expectantly before them, confident in her manner, and unequivocally beautiful. Clarke shrank away feeling dowdy and inexplicably insecure.

'Where is he?' the woman repeated.

'Inspector Frost is away from the station,' Wells said dolefully, unmoved by the woman's presence. 'Can I take your name, madam?'

'My name is Karen Thomas.'

'May I ask what the matter is regarding?'

'It is no concern of yours.' She read his name badge and added, 'Sergeant W. Wells. Tell your inspector I'll be back.' And with that she was gone.

Tuesday (3) ———————————————

It was gone midday by the time Dominic Holland arrived back at Denton railway station.

He waited patiently for a taxi back to Two Bridges. Usually the type to grow exasperated at such inconvenience, he now discovered his anxiety had gone full circle: the desperation he'd experienced on the train home had now been replaced with a forlorn dread. What if Todd had exacted some sort of revenge for non-payment? Filled in the pool with debris, for example? What would he do then?

A car pulled up. An Austin Princess. He climbed into the back seat and gave the driver his address. How could everything swing from going so well to so very badly, just like that? He'd had a damn fine run of things until now. Last year's Tightspots – in particular the coup of Dave Gahan wearing them on the front cover of *The Face* magazine – had revived the company's prospects. They had started the year as a brand to be reckoned with – and Dominic had, in turn, rewarded himself with a rather nice bonus. A bonus he had used to engage the services of Todd, who would transform the place he'd inherited from his grandmother in Denton into his dream home.

All that seemed far behind him now. The results for the Drainpipe were not looking at all smart. Emma held him responsible; and maybe she was right – had he got too carried away? Too cocky after the Tightspots success? She had questioned him every step of the way, but he'd been dismissive, thinking her jealous of his success. She'd been snippy with him for moving out of London – said he'd been distracted. He stared out of the window; maybe she was right. The party last Saturday had been weeks in the planning and was intended to announce his glittering arrival on to the Denton stage. In fact it had done nothing more than upset the neighbours. And yes, he had to admit, the pool project had certainly grown into more than a distraction.

Clarke was horrified by the state of her desk.

'What the—' she exclaimed.

'Jack needed room to expand,' Waters said, busily typing at an adjacent desk.

'Expand? Like his pot belly?' Dear Lord. Finally evicting Frost from her flat only to be presented with his detritus at her place of work was too much. 'God, I'm so glad he's gone.'

'Gone? He'll be back.'

'I mean, from the flat.'

'How was that?' Waters released the sheet of paper, and eased back in his chair. 'I mean, Jack on the couch for what – three, four mo—'

'Four months, two weeks, and five days. Not that I was counting.' She pulled back her swivel chair; only to reveal a stack of files beneath the desk – she would not be able to sit down even if she wanted to.

'I just can't imagine that . . .'

'You should try it, sure you'd get on fine. You're like two peas in a pod as it is.'

'That is out of order . . . We're friends – that's it.' He laughed.

'Hmm . . . Like Cannon and Ball this morning.' She sat dejectedly, and picked up a crisp packet with thumb and fore-finger. She'd not had a chance to catch up with John Waters other than a brief hello this morning. The man's wedding was this coming Friday, and she hadn't even enquired about the prepar-ations. 'Sorry, John. I've been absorbed in my own sad little world, haven't I: how's the big day looking?'

'Almost there – three days to go.' He shook his head in dis-belief. 'We've a final run-through this afternoon.'

'How's Kim?'

'She's fine. Not deterred by Sunday's discovery, that was weird . . .'

'I heard. Rachel Curtis.' She winced. 'I wasn't a fan, obviously, but she didn't deserve that. Where are we at with her?'

'Close, but a step behind still . . . Only been out a coupla weeks, but she got around a bit, that one, and was seen all over town. Just last Saturday, tattoo parlour, pub, cinema, then seen arguing with some fella on a motorbike. Last seen on the Southern Housing Estate around seven thirty Saturday evening outside the Codpiece.'

'Town is full of motorcycles right now.'

'You're right.'

'Needle in a haystack.'

A phone began to ring from somewhere on the desk. She was momentarily surprised; who would know she was back?

'It won't bite,' Waters said.

'I'm sure,' she replied, 'but more a question of finding it, under all this.'

In desperation, she shoved aside several piles of paper, disturb-ing a layer of fag ash; after a scrabble she grabbed the receiver, which was sticky, and knocked over a can of Lilt in the process of bringing it to her ear.

'Hello?' she gasped.

'Detective Clarke.'

'Yes?'

'It's Clare, Clare Hammond. I'm sorry I was less than helpful yesterday. It was the boy in the room, I couldn't think straight. I'm sure you think I'm cold-hearted, but Jane chose her own path. She liked the power over them . . .' A sigh. Clarke glanced across at Waters, who was now also on a call and embroiled in a heated discussion. 'Anyway, that's not why I phoned. No, after you left I tidied up and threw away the tea cosy.'

'Oh, I'm sorry . . .'

'No, don't be; it's just that . . . I lied. About not knowing where she got it. One of *them* made it for her. I just couldn't, with Richard there . . .'

'What, *knitted* it? Are you sure?'

Waters hurried past her desk.

'Yes, strange, isn't it? I don't know who of course, but she did say he was always trying to talk her out of it.'

'Out of knitting?'

'Prostitution,' Clare said coldly.

'Do you think there was anything between them, other than sex?'

'I don't know.'

'But why a tea cosy? And why give it to you?'

'She gave it to me as a joke. The tea service is a family heirloom, you see, so she'd not expected me to actually use it. I can't really explain why I did, to be honest, and it's more than I know why on earth the man knitted it for her.'

'Maybe she discussed her family with this man?'

'Possibly.' A silence hung down the line. Intimacy. 'Anyway, I thought it was something you should know.'

Waters sat in interview room number 1 and heard the man out.

It was difficult to assess how serious this was; the guy – in fashion or something – would bluster one minute, burst into tears the next, then laugh manically. 'Oh, how could I have been so stupid!' he would lament, then rail against the builder, calling him every name under the sun.

'What's the name of the firm again?'

'A bandit by the name of Terry Todd.' Holland scowled. 'Does the name mean anything to you?'

Waters shook his head. 'And it was his suggestion to leave the money – cash – there?' The DS had difficulty keeping the incredulity out of his voice.

'The embarrassment!'

'Did you tell anyone, your neighbours, for example, the money was there?'

'Heavens, no! I don't know a soul here.'

'Didn't you throw a party at the weekend? Didn't you have a whole load of guests?'

'They were my friends, civilized people, from London,' he said pompously.

'So there was no one at your place from Denton or Two Bridges?'

'Well, there might have been one or two that gatecrashed; I mean, it did get quite frenetic in the early hours.'

'So much so that the police were called out.'

'But what on earth has that got to do with it! The party was on Saturday night – Todd didn't ask me for the money until Monday morning, and I left it in the cement mixer that afternoon, for heaven's sake!' he cried out in exasperation.

'Please calm down, sir,' Waters soothed, 'I'm only trying to ascertain who you've come into contact with in Denton—'

'Wait!' Holland sat bolt upright in the chair. 'The fellow that complained – I saw him at the bank, yesterday morning! He was in front of me in the queue – he saw me withdraw the cash.'

'How did he manage that, if he was served first?'

'That's beside the point, Sergeant!' He tapped Waters lightly on the knee. 'Arrest him immediately!'

Waters left Holland with a glass of water and made his way to the front desk to request the call sheet from Saturday night. He really didn't have the patience for this type of baloney . . .

'Ah, Waters,' said the superintendent as the detective approached reception. 'What was all that frightful wailing?'

'Man in Two Bridges has been robbed, sir – I say "robbed" in the loosest possible sense, he practically gave it away.'

The super tilted forward to catch the sergeant's low voice as he ran through the details.

'I see.' Mullett processed the information, then said, 'It's not unusual, Sergeant, for people to leave items, money included, discreetly hidden; not everything must be under lock and key. This part of the county is not exactly a den of thieves, contrary to what people like to think, and certainly not what you're accustomed to. I'm surprised, and not a little disappointed, that you've not shaken off your Bethnal Green roots by now.' The superintendent considered the matter closed, and strode off from whence he came.

'What a cock,' Waters remarked quietly, 'the guy's just been robbed, for chrissake; can't be *that* bloody innocent, can they, your charming country bumpkins?'

Mullett stopped in his tracks and pivoted round on the polished floor – for a dreadful instant Waters thought he'd heard. 'And Sergeant, I want this top priority. This man has only recently moved to the area, and I want people from the city to feel safe here. I want the culprit found, and I want him found soon.'

Time was proving of the essence on both cases. Frost had decided they needed to act, and held court at the two o'clock catch-up. The incident room was full, uniform and plain clothes listened intently. Two fans whirred, lamely circulating unpleasant air.

'It's called division of labour.' He puffed earnestly on the end of a Rothmans.

'Eh?' Hanlon asked.

'"Who's doing what", to you.' Frost stepped back from the board. 'Firstly we'll deal with Rachel, whom we know to be dead. Now, although she didn't own a motorcycle she is known to have associated with someone who rode one. Kate Greenlaw saw her on Saturday talking heatedly to a person on a bike; though Kate couldn't name the make of bike, she later called back to say the rider had a red helmet. I know it's not much, but it's a start.

'That evening Rachel was seen at the Codpiece fish and chip shop on the Southern Housing Estate. The proprietor reckons there were several gangs around passing through on their way to somewhere else. She had company at the house on Sandpiper Close; a man had shaved there. We've sent Forensics in to dust for fingerprints and they should be finishing up there shortly . . . Well done, PC Simms. What else do we know?' He consulted a slip of paper. 'Oh yeah, Rachel was banned from driving. A condition of her parole. Actually, where is PC Simms?'

A hand went up.

'We didn't check for motorbikes up at Sandpiper Close, nip back up there?'

'I checked already; nobody has seen a motorbike at or near her house, though bikes are often heard around there, though it's usually just a couple of teenagers screaming around on 50cc mopeds.'

'What about the garage? Did you check the garage?' Frost cut in sharply.

'I—'

'Arthur, run the lad up there too, snout around a bit.' Hanlon nodded, and he and Simms left.

'Detective Clarke.' Frost turned his attention to his ex-landlady. 'Jane Hammond? Nothing to report?'

'Clare Hammond just called. She recalled one of her sister's tricks knitted her a—'

'Knitting? What flamin' use is that? 'Ere, where you going?' he snapped on seeing Waters about to slip out.

'The super wants me to check on a theft over at Two Bridges.'

'Is that really a priority?'

'According to the super it is, yes,' Waters said coolly. Frost didn't want to question his pal in front of the entire room, even though it seemed a bizarre decision; the man had a lot on and Waters, unlike Frost, often gave Mullett a degree of respect he didn't deserve.

'Well, you better get on with it then,' he acquiesced, then returned to Sue Clarke. 'Where was I – yes, Jane Hammond. I need you to watch her flat.'

'Sir?'

'Covertly, see who turns up. Pals or punters. We've not much to go on; we need to find anyone who can shed light on her movements.'

'That's a job for uniform, surely.'

'Normally yes, but the type of bloke she consorts with might be put off seeing a plod outside the front door, don't you think?'

'I suppose,' she conceded.

'Good, and if they've knitting needles on them ask what the knit-one, purl-one they get up to. After the message I heard on her answerphone, nothing would surprise me. Now,' he said, addressing the room in general, 'back to Rachel Curtis: although Denton is awash with biker gangs, I suspect she's not part of one. I fear I'm going to do the unimaginable . . .'

'Shave?' shouted one.

'Have a bath?' cried another, followed by a whistle of the chorus of 'Wherever I Lay My Hat'.

'No, worse than that,' he said grimly. 'I'm going to have to go on the telly.'

Tuesday (4)

Superintendent Mullett was in a surprisingly good mood. A combination of fine weather, a holiday looming and Frost toeing the line for once, had for the first time in many months made him feel he could actually relax. The medication was doing the trick no doubt. And if he was being honest, the question of Grace's culpability in the paperboy hit-and-run had cast a long shadow for many months. But now it was gone, just like that. Yes, now he could focus with energy and confidence on what mattered most: the golf club. The command of which grew ever more a reality as the days passed. Indeed the outgoing chairman, Hudson, had this minute called to report that his girlfriend had just been on the phone, seething with anger. She had been fired by Harry Baskin. Hudson was overjoyed: Karen was his now, and his alone, 24/7, and he was eager to channel all his energies in her direction. Distasteful though the thought was, it was an otherwise excellent result for Mullett – the golf club would be the first thing Hudson would want to strike off his list.

The super smiled smugly to himself, switched on the radio and settled back with his afternoon tea. He deserved ten minutes listening to the news, before addressing the paperwork in front of him. It always paid to be up on world events before a conversation with the Assistant Chief Constable, which was pending later. The focus very much appeared to be on the weather. There was a serious account of the bad weather wreaking death and destruction across the globe, which seemed on biblical proportions, from a hurricane in Texas to the severe flooding in Bilbao. Grim, but the UK was safe, 'just a trifle hot', he muttered, pulling out a memo from County entitled *Woodentop*. The peculiar title was in reference to a television programme, and offered guidance for dealing with 'The dramatization of the police force'. Heavens, was this all they had time for? On the radio, the news presenter had shifted into an upbeat tone as he launched into an excited monologue about America's latest space shuttle mission, which was to herald the first black man in space. Much was made of this fellow. *Enough*, he thought and flicked off the receiver, his mind now transported back to his own earthly sergeant.

He was mindful of the conversation with Sir Keith, the local MP, on the golf course on Sunday, concerning new money being brought to the town, and he was pleased he'd intercepted Waters. He was fond of the coloured sergeant, but Waters was prone to be dismissive of lesser crimes. His inner-city background dictated they should be ignored in favour of more serious offences. Denton was a different kettle of fish. One needed to think of the wider picture. Mullett hadn't met this Holland fellow, but the last thing Denton needed was a chap from London being robbed and left dissatisfied with local law enforcement, badmouthing the force and the town to all and sundry—

The office door was flung open violently, causing Mullett to spill his tea.

'What in the name . . . Frost!'

'I'm sorry, sir, but I had no alternative, Miss Smith was otherwise engaged. I have to advise you we need to go public, urgently.'

'Go public? What, with the missing girl?'

'No, Rachel Curtis. We need to make an appeal for witnesses now.'

'Slow down. She's dead, why the haste?' Television only highlighted a difficult situation and was often counterproductive; it was a move that needed careful thought. 'I see there may be a point in the case of Jane Hammond, the missing prostitute. But Curtis, a convicted felon on parole?'

'Curtis was seen with a fella on a motorbike, and while I don't think she's part of a biker gang herself, she might have been seen by one or more of them. These guys are nomadic, travelling through, it's crucial for us to act now.'

'I see,' Mullett said, perplexed. 'Given the transitory nature of the motorcyclists, won't they have moved on already . . . and would they even see a television set?'

'All the more need to do it now, hope they might catch it in a motorway café?'

'Very well . . .'

Frost turned to go.

'On one condition.'

'What?'

'You shave that beard off. I can't have you appearing on national television looking like some sort of yeti.'

The unkempt inspector agreed with alacrity and left. Mullett sipped what remained of his tea. He was not sure what to think; Frost loathed public appearances. What with this and the current general agreeability of the man, it was natural for Mullett to be suspicious, but the super began to wonder if Frost had genuinely turned over a new leaf. The leaf of cooperation.

'Ah, there you are, Miss Smith,' Frost said unctuously. Mullett's prim secretary instinctively shrank back. 'Would you be so kind as to notify the BBC that we will need to record an appeal for help in time for the evening news?'

Frost turned the ignition over again.

'Come on, start! You've had a new starter motor and battery, there's no reason not to . . . At this rate you'll be a completely new car by Christmas.' The Metro cracked into life and whined as Frost over-revved the engine. He slammed the small car into reverse; he wanted to join Hanlon and Simms before they left Rachel Curtis's place at Sandpiper Close. The Forensics team were already back, excited at the array of prints they'd gleaned.

Frost had promised Waters he'd not ruin the wedding photos with a Serpico-style look, so a shave was not so disastrous. Worth flattering Mullett into thinking he'd deign to spruce himself up for his benefit alone. The only drawback was that he wasn't in possession of an actual razor. (Once or twice he'd used Clarke's kitchen scissors to cut away foodstuffs that had become lodged and crusted in the growth, but apart from that . . .) His shaving equipment must be in one of the boxes in storage. He could nip into Boots on Market Square, but then he'd have to find some-where to shave, which would involve too much messing around, and he needed to be at the church this afternoon for that run-through. They did, however, have the key to Rachel Curtis's place. Not far from the church . . . Simms said the cleaner had told him someone had had a shave there, so why not pop round, give the bathroom a once-over again? They'd only glanced at it before.

He motored up the Bath Road, and was surprised to spot Hanlon's Escort coming the other way. He flashed his lights at the oncoming vehicle. The other slowed down.

'Bleedin' hell, lads,' Frost said through the open window, both cars stopped in the middle of the road, 'that was quick?'

'Nothing to report, Jack. No motorbike. Capri in the garage, covered in dust, and with a flat.' Horns tooted angrily behind him.

'All right, chuck us the keys.'

Clarke rested her elbows on the balustrade that lined the walkway to the flats in Clay House and looked out across the estate. She was on the third floor, which afforded her a view of council-house roofs shimmering in the mid-afternoon heat. The noise of children at play drifted up from the street below. She couldn't imagine much in the way of traffic to a Clay House prostitute on a day like today; too hot, surely, for any sort of hanky-panky? Nevertheless she had positioned herself between the stairwell and Jane Hammond's flat, a few doors away. It was now nearly four. In the forty minutes she'd been there she'd seen one old biddy, Hammond's neighbour Mrs Ridley, and a couple of scruffy kids who'd regarded her curiously. She wasn't sure she could hang around that much longer without arousing suspicion. Maybe she'd move to ground level – she could watch the comings and goings from there, but it was breezier up here . . . Just then she heard heavy footsteps approaching.

Out on to the walkway stepped a middle-aged man clutching a bulging carrier bag in each hand. The man had pale skin and a sparse ginger beard. He moved towards Clarke, not noticing her until he was practically upon her, when he gave a slight start.

'Afternoon.' He had small eyes, of indiscernible colour, set too close to the nose. 'I didn't see you there.' The man – a resident, judging from his bags – expected a response.

'Waiting for a friend,' Clarke said, nodding towards the nearest door.

The man's eyes followed her gesture. 'I see.' He blinked and looked off across the balustrade fleetingly, before muttering good afternoon and moving on.

Clarke wondered if he was unsettled, and possibly with good

cause. There was every chance he knew who lived beyond the door she had indicated. Or maybe not? She watched until he stopped at his own entrance, just the other side of Jane Hammond's flat, where he shot her another glance. Damn. She might as well tell him, being a neighbour, why she was here, just to put his mind at rest – but he disappeared behind the door in a flash, shutting it noisily.

She walked over and was about to knock, when she heard the clip of shoes on the balcony. Approaching her was a well-dressed balding man in an open-necked shirt. The man had registered her hesitation and slowed his stride. Clarke took a step back from the door, which prompted him to stop uneasily. She instinctively pulled out her badge. The man was breathing heavily, whether because of the stairs, or nerves, she couldn't tell. If he was thinking of making a bolt for it, he lacked the energy, so he sighed and held up his hands.

Weaver's heart was beating nineteen to the dozen. Who was the woman waiting for Cath? Should he have told her she was on holiday? But if he had, might that have suggested a knowledge of what Cath did on the side for pin money? Maybe the woman outside her door was a prostitute too. Weaver liked the look of her, that white bra pushed to the limit beneath her thin summer blouse. He'd paused for a moment outside his own front door – but self-control had won through and he'd fought off the desire to make conversation and hurried inside quickly.

Ben Weaver had not had a very productive morning. The process of embalming was not as straightforward and common-place an activity as he'd imagined. The equipment required appeared to be the preserve of world leaders and morticians, the fluids were not to be had off the shelf at Boots, and he didn't have the time for the complexities of draining the blood. The only useful thing he'd learned from the medical textbooks in the library was that for preservation purposes alcohol was a primary ingredient and he'd been able to get hold of ethanol, in the form of methylated spirits, from the hardware store.

He had bought ten litres. Any more he thought might arouse suspicion. He had to get to work now, his shift started soon and they'd complain to the agency if he was late.

Frost pulled into Sandpiper Close and noticed a motorcycle parked on the road, close to the pavement. Nothing unusual in that, he thought – he had motorcycles on the brain at the moment – though having said that, he didn't recall seeing one yesterday.

He coaxed the Metro on to the drive. He gave the close a quick up and down. Dead: the quietness of a well-heeled residential street. He wondered briefly where they all might work.

The front door opened easily. Once inside he pushed it shut gently. In doing so he noticed the post on the floor. He had the immediate sensation that he was not alone in the house. Bending to the floor, Frost lightly touched a gas bill, which bore the unmistakable trace of a footprint. Still in a hunched position, he shut his eyes and listened.

Silence.

Above him a floorboard gave ever so slightly. Frost remained motionless, despite an acute burning feeling developing in his upper thighs. Then from behind he heard a dull thud. He spun round and up. Outside? He reached for the door; it had a compli-cated Yale lock, which in his haste he managed to double-lock before succeeding in opening it. Once outside he saw a helmeted figure scampering across the gravel. On reflex, Frost looked above and saw an open window above the porch. He heard the kick-start of a motorbike, the one he had seen on arrival. Damn! Flinging the Metro's door open he dived in and fumbled with the ignition. Mercifully, the engine being warm, the thing started immediately. Frost cleared the drive quickly and the bike was just visible turning left out of the close towards the centre of town. He pushed the Metro as best he could. It had a surprising amount of go – the MG badge on the front was more than mere decoration. The junction was clear and he was in hot pursuit.

In the first instance, Frost wondered why the rider had headed for the town centre, instead of the open road, but as he hit traffic he understood: the bike could dodge and weave between vehicles, leaving the Metro behind and the bike beyond reach. After half a mile Frost screeched to a halt before the Bath Road roundabout, narrowly missing a Ford Transit travelling the other way – also comfortably above the speed limit. The driver gave him the finger as Frost spun to a stop in its path. Slipping into first he floored the accelerator, but something was wrong – his left foot couldn't find the clutch.

'Flamin' heck,' he shouted and tried to see where the pedals were. He then realized his foot was indeed down hard on the clutch pedal. With his toe, he flicked the lifeless pedal upwards as the Metro rolled limply on to the scorched grass of the roundabout.

'Knickers.'

The motorcyclist had long since gone. Frost kicked open the door and stood in the centre of the roundabout as the town's traffic ground to a halt, and an orchestra of horns began to sound. He lit a cigarette and grinned ruefully, recalling how he'd often told his dead wife not to ride the clutch as it would go when she least expected it.

Tuesday (5)

'I am not, I repeat, *not*, going to be your bloody driver, Jack,' Clarke said as Frost got in and slammed the Escort's door shut needlessly violently.

'Flamin' heck! I didn't ask for you to come get me, or anyone else for that matter; I called in the registration number of the blasted motorbike then asked Bill to send a flamin' tow-truck.'

But she wasn't listening. He'd been marooned on the busiest roundabout in Denton, and had to walk up the Bath Road to a public call box and, given the length of time it took for Clarke to fetch him, he might as well have carried on walking. If it weren't for this infernal heat (and the fact that he did indeed need someone to ferry him around) she'd have made him do just that.

'Waters might like the proximity of you in the passenger seat, but I don't – the last few months—'

'All right, all right, point taken. But blame Bill Wells. He sent you – for all I knew you were still at Clay House,' Frost said, agitated.

'Oh, I didn't know that. I thought *you* had called for me to fetch you.' Her tone was on the verge of apologetic. 'But, after all, I could be forgiven for thinking that—'

'Never mind that. 'Ere, have you got the time on you? My watch has stopped.' He tapped the glass face of his wristwatch.

'Ten to five.'

'Flamin' hell, is it that late – and still so flamin' hot! Can you take me to St Mary's? I have a run-through for John's big day.'

'Yes, OK.' She swung the car into a U-turn in the middle of the Bath Road.

'Why aren't you at Clay House, anyway?'

'A punter showed.'

'Oh yeah, what did he have to say for himself?'

Rick Celba's doughy potato head emerged distastefully in her mind's eye. 'Middle manager, late forties, popped round there because Jane hadn't turned up at their Monday-afternoon rendezvous. They were due to meet at three at the Poplars Motel out on the A36, where Jane would usually thrash him with a riding crop until he begged for mercy.'

'Hmm.' Frost rubbed his beard distractedly. 'Seems to be popular, that sort of thing. I wonder whether it's worth a go—'

'Worth a go?' she said, dismayed.

'Eh? Just thinking aloud. Would explain the lack of addresses, if she met them at a motel. Maybe I'm barking up the wrong tree.'

'How do you mean?'

'I was convinced she would be close to home, and now we've discovered another posh twit she met out of town, like the lawyer in Rimmington.'

'And the Poplars Motel is not even just down the road like Rimmington; it's a good forty-five minutes away. Why did you think she was close to home, though?'

'Oh, nothing much really.' He shrugged. 'Only, it being the

school holidays, I thought she'd not stray far with a young boy. But what do I know? Never met the woman.'

Clarke softened; any anger at having had to pick him up evaporated. He surprised her even now, one second the crudest devil you'd want to meet, the next a sentimental soul searching for the good in everyone. 'Don't give up on that idea just yet, Jack. The reason Celba risked calling at her flat was because he was desperate; he'd not seen her since the last week in June. She'd been refusing to make the trip to the motel until September, but then he offered her double for this week.'

'That timeframe would fit with the school break.'

'Exactly.'

'But she was still prepared to leave the kid alone on a Saturday night, and spend the night in Rimmington.'

The spire of St Mary's rose in the blue summer sky as Clarke turned off the main road.

'That's different.'

'How so?'

The car drew to a stop, behind Waters' green Vauxhall.

'Family – she was visiting her sister, and it wasn't evey Saturday. If you've a hunch, stick to it; you've been right before.'

Frost got out. 'Thanks, Sue.' He smiled.

'Don't worry, I'll wait for you.'

Three area cars had been alerted to look out for a motorcyclist in the town centre. Frost's description of the rider was that he was wearing a green bomber jacket and a red and white helmet. One car reported a striped helmet shooting by on the Rimmington Road but the constable didn't catch the colour of the bike itself, though he identified an N or M plate ending with CAT – which tallied with Frost's report.

'They ain't going to like this,' Miller said. They'd been assigned to the Cricketers pub at the end of London Street. 'Us snooping around checking out their bikes.'

'I dare say Inspector Frost was right to send us here. Easy for a biker to blend in, and like looking for a needle in a haystack,' Simms said.

Frost's motorcyclist would have hit the town's busy Market Square, and what better way to lose yourself than to pop out the other side and park up at the biker-friendly Cricketers.

'But why aren't these people at work?'

'It's August, ain't it. Not just the kids who have the summer off, is it?' Miller parked the car. There were countless bikes.

The sight of two policemen, in white shirt sleeves and black ties, immediately caused heads to turn. Silence descended on the dense throng of hairy denim-clad men outside the pub. Between the officers and the eighty or so strongmen was a row of bikes some three deep stretching the length of the wide-fronted pub.

'Right,' Miller announced, 'you check round the back, there's a car park behind the beer garden.'

'Sure?' Simms said uncertainly.

'Yep, quicker if we divide it up.'

Simms was impressed with Miller's nerve; the experienced PC was not intimidated in the slightest. Simms himself, in contrast, was nervous as hell. Miller made off towards the pub sign, where the bike line started. Simms headed down the road which separated the pub from the surrounding housing. Almost immediately a motorbike came powering towards him. The rider wore aviator sunglasses but no helmet. Like on all modern bikes there was no front number plate. The rider came perilously close, swerving at the last second. Simms spun round to try to catch the registration; it was a blur already but he was pretty sure he saw an S. Not their bike. He continued walking to the rear of the pub, keeping close to the wall. In the car park stood a handful of motorbikes; it was otherwise empty apart from an old mustard Allegro, the only actual car.

As he drew closer he scanned the motorbikes' number plates;

there, one read CAT. He felt the side of it – the engine was still warm. It had to be the right one! His heart thundered in his chest. Crikey! What should he do? First off, he pulled out his notebook to write down the full registration. Should he now fetch Miller? But then Miller wouldn't be able to intercept anyone who tried to make a run for it out the front. Simms needed to check if any bikers were inside the pub. If he went in the back way, then at least he'd have the rear entrance covered.

Simms entered the pub cautiously, his eyes slowly adjusting to the dark interior. The place appeared to be empty. He approached the barman and asked if he'd seen any new bikers come in in the last quarter of an hour. The man indicated over Simms's shoulder; behind him was a skinhead with a bent nose in a Clash T-shirt, at a small round table. The skinhead was with a girl, and the policeman's arrival had clearly interrupted their conversation.

'Ah' – Simms approached the table – 'excuse me, sir, would—'

Suddenly the man shoved the table towards his companion, spraying her with Cinzano, and sprinted towards the front door of the pub.

Simms hesitated; the guy was powerfully built. The PC was no coward – or didn't think he was – but knew he'd not be able to apprehend him single-handed. He dithered for a second or two, under the cynical eye of the barman, before giving chase.

Outside in the blazing sun, Miller had already cottoned on. Confronted with a barrier of motorcycles, the skinhead dodged this way then that, frantically seeking an exit route, not thinking to dart along the side of the pub itself. The other bikers on the forecourt, a mixture of leather-clad men and women, were enjoying the spectacle. Out of options, the skinhead turned to confront Simms in the pub doorway. The young PC held his ground, barred his entry and braced himself as the man swore and raised an arm. Before the man could attack, Miller rushed up behind and caught him in a half nelson. Simms slammed into the door jamb but recovered quickly to tackle the suspect's ankle, causing him to topple over, bringing Miller down on top of him. It wasn't textbook, it certainly wasn't elegant, and it no doubt gave the onlookers a good old laugh; but it didn't matter. They had their man.

'Thanks for squeezing us in, Father,' Waters said appreciatively.

'Not at all, gentlemen, I'm just sorry the delay was caused by something so utterly terrible.' Though polite, the elderly clergyman was pushed for time and exasperated by John's best man's lack of preparation.

'Now, William, do you have the ring this time?' Father Hill asked.

Waters turned and looked dubiously behind him. His best man was leaning back on the front pew while desperately rummaging in his trouser pockets.

'Just a sec, just a sec.' Frost's nylon trousers were from another decade; pastel-blue, tight at the hips and bell-bottomed at the feet – trousers in which the pockets were practically inaccessible. Waters winced as he watched Frost's protracted efforts to wedge his stubby hands into the far crevices of such unyielding material.

'Wait a sec,' Frost gasped again.

'I do hope William doesn't intend to wear those trousers on the day?' The vicar sighed and stepped down from the altar.

'Nope, he'll be in a morning suit, like me.'

'Ah, yes; well, maybe recommend he use the breast pocket of the jacket for the ring?'

'Damn!' Frost exclaimed, stricken. 'I'm afraid I've not got it . . . Don't worry, I'll have it on the day. Third time lucky.'

'Let's hope so, William,' Father Hill said sternly. 'There'll not be a fourth time. Now, if you step forward here, on cue.'

In spite of Frost's general shoddiness, Father Hill talked them through a ceremony he must have conducted countless times before with patience and warmth. Waters was touched as the priest gently indicated the positions to be taken by each of the participants on the day.

'Ah, yes, the verger.' Frost's attention suddenly twitched when Father Hill's assistant was mentioned. 'Where is he today, by the way?'

'Benjamin will be at work, I assume,' Father Hill answered.

'Isn't his job here, with you?'

'No . . .' Hill hesitated. 'Ben Weaver is a layman.'

'A what?' Waters asked.

'A civilian – he's not ordained. His time at the church is purely voluntary.'

'What does he do then?' Frost asked.

'I believe he has a job as a care assistant at High Fields care home.'

The clergyman looked away and Frost sensed his unease. This man had married him and buried his wife; they weren't strangers to each other, and Frost knew something was wrong.

'What's up?'

'Oh . . . nothing. Now, where were we? Ah yes, the bridesmaids . . .'

'Come on, Father, you can't pull the wool over my eyes. Something's up. Weaver. What's the story?'

'What's done is done, and the past should be forgiven.' Hill looked at his feet.

'We are the forgiving type,' Waters said, stepping back from the altar, now curious himself.

'Very well.'

The three of them sat down on the front pew.

'Benjamin was never ordained because he was dismissed

from theological college due to an unfortunate incident.' His face was heavily creased from years of absorbing the woes of others. 'He's a good man, though. He is. Generous – he knitted all those, you know.' Father Hill indicated the kneelers lined up underneath the wooden bench. Waters was sitting on one – white with a simple blue cross.

'Knitted?' Frost scratched the back of his head – strands of thought were coming together in his brain. Waters was clearly making the same connections. They looked at each other.

'The tea cosy,' Waters said. 'Sue said that Jane Hammond's sister had one. Knitted. Jane told the sister it was a gift from one of her regulars?'

Frost nodded, regretting he'd been so dismissive at first of Clarke when she'd tried to tell him about this. 'Father, if it's not breaking too many commandments, may I ask why exactly Benjamin Weaver didn't cut the mustard as a trainee priest?'

The vicar let out a loud sigh and stretched his polished shoes out on the stone floor. 'Benjamin cultivated a very close relationship with another young man—'

'Describe "close" for me, vicar.' Frost stood and started pacing. 'I mean, were they reciting a few poems together' – he waved a hand speculatively – 'or should we be thinking more along the lines of exploring each other's privates in the vestry?'

Waters turned to see the vicar's reaction.

'I fear the latter,' Hill said. 'His friend, a nice boy, Jonathan Gunn, took his own life. All very regrettable.'

'Indeed, thank you for your frankness, Father.' Frost turned to Waters. 'We need to have another word with Mr Weaver.'

'What, you think . . . ?'

'Sex is sex. Grab Clarke and bring him in. I've got to face the cameras in half an hour . . . if the good Father has finished with us for now?'

'Yes, of course. Very good.' Hill paused. 'See you Friday?' he said with an air of uncertainty.

'Yeah, yeah . . .' Waters smiled reassuringly, but kept his eye on Frost who was shooting off down the aisle. 'Thank you. Thanks.' He hurried after the inspector, who was already in the porch.

'You better get a sprint on,' Frost said, sparking up.

'No need to waste time picking Sue up, then?'

'Won't need to, she's just over there.' He gestured towards the boundary wall with his cigarette. 'Always better to travel in pairs on a case like this.'

Waters wondered if this was a pointed remark, but dismissed it. 'All right, that means you'll be . . .'

Frost held out his palm. '. . . borrowing your motor.'

'Jack, you know I need the car in one piece – going to the airport Saturday; my honeymoon . . .'

'Flamin' heck, mate, I didn't total the Metro, you know . . .'

'I'm just saying.' By now they were at the lychgate. Clarke was indeed behind the wheel of the Escort. Waters tossed Frost the Vauxhall's keys. 'Easy does it, eh?'

PC David Simms waited impatiently in the station lobby for DI Frost to return. The man they held in custody was a known bad boy. Miller reckoned there'd be some excitement. The station was already buzzing with Frost's impending television appeal. The small town of Denton was manic. He'd never anticipated seeing such activity first hand when he signed up for what he thought would be a largely administrative role.

'Inspector Frost, sir!' Simms blurted as the station doors opened and in strode Jack Frost. 'We've caught your motor-cyclist.'

'Really?' The inspector beamed, but he was perspiring dreadfully.

'Yes, in the Cricketers, like you said.'

Frost turned to Desk Sergeant Wells. 'Still got it in me, eh, Bill?'

'Mullett's getting antsy about the television people,' Wells said, not looking up from the computer monitor.

'Good, good . . . keep him that way, for a bit longer. Now then, young Simms, who have you got?'

'A chap by the name of Wakely, tried to make a bolt for it at—'

Frost's smile vanished. 'Martin bleedin' Wakely?'

'Yes, a man known to you?' Simms said hopefully.

'Nose like this?' Frost pushed his nose to one side. 'Very much so.'

'He's got a record as long as your arm.'

'Hmm.' Frost was lost in thought.

'You don't seem convinced.'

'I've an open mind.' Frost mustered another smile. 'Reluctant to help with our enquiries, I bet?'

Simms nodded.

'Must be up to no good, then. Again. In the cells? Lead on, young man.'

'The super, Jack. Itching—'

'Scratch it for him, Bill; the starch Mrs M puts in his underpants plays havoc in this heat.'

Tuesday (6)

Frost felt a headache on the way; *must be dehydrated*, he thought.

'Police Constable David Simms, allow me to introduce you to Martin Wakely, or Spud to his pals, on account of his attractive hooter.'

'We've been introduced,' Simms said.

Wakely sat there scowling.

'Do tell me how, exactly,' Frost asked. Simms explained the incident in the Cricketers. Wakely had form – only last year he'd been in trouble for selling stolen goods; breaking and entering was well within his skill set. Furthermore, he had been caught in possession of a firearm. What would he be looking for in Rachel's house?

'Rachel Curtis, Martin. Know her?'

'Everyone knows her.'

'Knew her.'

'Knew . . . ? What you talking about?' He frowned.

'Dead.'

'Hadn't heard.' Not so much as a flicker of emotion.

'Know where she lived?'

'One of the big posh places.'

'Yes, and it's been empty since her demise. Mind you, it's been empty a lot longer than that; her case lasted months. Her fella having already been sent down. House has been a sitting target for a good while.'

'Wait a minute, what's this all about?'

The door went.

'Jack, he sent me to get you. They're all here.'

'Be along in a mo, Bill. Take young Simms with you. Hornrim Harry always likes a uniform presence.'

When the two were alone, Wakely muttered, 'Simms, I know that name . . .'

'Yes, it was his brother who tackled you last year, remember?'

'Yeah, yeah . . . well, I didn't cause a fuss this time, did I?'

'Well, let's not make a fuss now, eh? Rachel Curtis's place has been empty a while. News travels fast in your community . . .'

'Wait, wait, wait,' Wakely said, confused, 'what's all this about Rachel Curtis?'

'Why do you think you're here, Martin?'

'The bleedin' motorbike.'

'The what?'

'I didn't nick it, just borrowed it.'

'Borrowed it – from who?'

'Err . . . can't remember . . . err.'

'Leave it out!' Frost fumed. 'You don't seriously expect me to believe you "borrowed" a motorcycle?'

'Err . . . you put the frighteners on me, me mind's gone blank,' Wakely pleaded feebly.

'Cobblers! I haven't got time to deal with this nonsense now – you're staying here until you remember who you got that bike from.'

Mullett's unease had got the better of him. The super stood proprietorially on the steps of Eagle Lane Police Station. It was five thirty-five. He pulled the peak on his cap forward to shield his eyes from the glare of the late-afternoon sun. It wasn't so much having to step back from the spotlight that made him apprehensive; no, it was more the thought of Jack Frost stepping into it that concerned him. The media were arriving in force. The radio crew were here already, first in line to ensure a good position. Now before him a BBC van spewed forth an array of cables, microphones and various young people in T-shirts.

'You Frost?' a youth with unruly hair shouted from the side of the van.

Mullett just smiled into the sunlight; there was no chance he'd answer such an address.

'Oi, sport!'

Was he being bellowed at by an antipodean? Mullett turned to face in the other direction. Surely the BBC could source its staff from its own shores without recourse to the colonies? The surly individual brushed past him, hauling a camera.

'Quite a turnout.' The familiar tones of Bill Wells reached him from behind.

'Is Frost on his way?' Mullett enquired evenly. 'I thought I told you to fetch him.'

'He's just putting the finishing touches to his statement, I believe.'

The phrase struck Mullett as discordant. 'Preparing,' he sniffed, 'that would make a change . . . and so long as he's shaved.'

'Oh – I think he—' Wells stopped abruptly as Mullett turned to face him.

'Think *what*?'

'Nothing, sir.'

''Ere 'e comes.' The brash Australian's attention turned to his camera, angled towards the station's double doors. All heads looked up.

Frost appeared, beard still wildly intact, resembling George Best gone to seed.

'I thought I told you to shave?' Mullett hissed through his teeth.

'I was interrupted,' Frost said out of the side of his mouth as they faced the cameras.

'Just don't balls this up.' The super smiled as a man with sideburns and kipper tie moved to the front steps, and was relieved to discover the Australian was a mere minion.

'Good afternoon, ladies and gentlemen.' Frost beamed. 'I'm Inspector Frost, and I'm here to make an appeal to—'

'You bastard!' A female voice rang out from behind the assembled press corps. Mullett turned to Frost who raised an eyebrow slightly. 'Yes, you, Frost!' In the next instant the young woman was right in front of them. The man with the microphone stepped aside uncertainly. 'What the bloody hell you playing at, eh? Who do you think you are?' she shouted.

The reporters, surprised by this outburst, watched Frost intently for a reaction. Mullett fidgeted uncomfortably. Who the blazes was this woman?

'I don't believe we've had the pleasure,' Frost responded with a cheeky smile, which only served to infuriate the woman further; she lunged forward, clawing at his face. Mullett stepped back in shock, as Frost staggered sideways to escape the woman's reach.

The press clamoured for her. 'Miss, miss! What's the inspector done?'

Mullett barked at the two PCs standing behind him to apprehend the crazed woman.

Simms and Miller strong-armed the woman through the door. For one so slight she had phenomenal strength. Once inside the building, though, she ceased struggling and came quietly.

'You can't do this!' she spat.

'Oh yes we can,' Miller replied, 'believe it or not, it is an offence to attack a CID officer. Even one as badly turned out as that.'

As they reached the front desk, Simms saw the super-intendent storm off towards his office.

'Hello again,' Wells said genially to the woman.

'You've met before?' Simms asked.

'Young lady was enquiring after Jack this morning.'

'She found him, all right.'

'Right you, in here.' Miller shoved the woman into a free interview room and shut the door. 'Bloody hell, that was hilarious!' he sniggered to Simms. 'Did you see Mullett's face?'

'He left pretty sharpish,' Simms replied uncertainly.

'Too right, he'd hang old Frosty out to dry as soon as look at him . . .'

'Wonder who she is?' Simms peered over the other's shoulder into the room.

'Christ knows, some old sort Jack's had it off with. Tasty, though; the old bugger must have something.' Miller adjusted his tie. 'Anyway, I better get back out there. You keep an eye on 'er meanwhile.'

And with that he strolled off down the corridor.

Clarke and Waters mounted the Clay House staircase.

'I can't quite figure this yet,' Waters remarked.

'How do you mean?'

'This dude . . .' he didn't finish.

They reached the third floor and walked briskly along to Weaver's flat.

'Number fifteen. Right next door, if you can believe it,' he said.

'You're kidding!' Clarke stopped in her tracks.

'What's up?'

'I saw him. Weaver. Earlier this afternoon.'

'No way. Did he mark you as a copper?' Waters banged on the door energetically.

'I . . . I don't know. Maybe,' Clarke said. 'Something tells me he's not in now, though.'

'If he *is* in, he's either innocent or stupid.' Waters rapped again. 'There's no way he'd be sitting there otherwise; he's got to have seen all the activity.'

'But didn't he come forward?'

'So? Of course he did. Wouldn't you? He didn't say he was in the habit of knitting tea cosies for her, though, did he.' The sergeant reached up to a small frosted-glass window next to the door that was ajar. 'Nor did he mention that sorry business with the Church . . . Come here. If I give you a leg-up.'

Clarke checked the coast was clear. 'We don't have a warrant.'

'We heard a cry for help? C'mon. Quick.'

She put her foot in the cradle of Waters' linked hands.

'I mean, being chucked out of the Church for messing with another man is one thing,' Waters continued, 'but Jane – aargh' – an awkward lack of suppleness hit Clarke as she jolted upwards and clung to the windowsill – 'is a female prostitute.'

'But it's all sex when it comes down to it,' Clarke said, steadying herself.

'Yeah, that's what Jack—'

'Jesus!'

'What?'

'The smell, it's . . . eugh.'

'It's a bathroom, shit happens.'

'No, not that kind . . . God, it's foul,' Clarke said, retching.

She reached down inside the window, straining until her fingers found the lever, and she pushed it with all her might. The window gave suddenly, causing her to lose her balance, but Waters grabbed her and quickly lowered her back down.

She coughed violently; whatever it was, she'd breathed a hell of a lot of it in. The stuff was rasping at her throat.

'You all right?'

Clarke held out a hand and nodded; after a moment she stood up straight and said, 'OK. I'm good. Who's going in?'

'A slender lithe lady like you – be in and round the corner in no time. If you're OK?'

'Flattery will get you everywhere.' It was the first compliment she'd had in a long time, and though blatantly untrue, it was enough to propel her up through the window in one smooth move.

She landed squarely on the toilet seat. Her senses were so consumed with the pungent stinging smell that she didn't take in the contents of the bath until she'd climbed down off the toilet seat, steadying herself on the wall.

Weaver locked the Volvo door.

The afternoon had been a disappointment; he thought he might have been able to find something in the storerooms at work to help him with his task. God knows, most of them were destined for the grave any day now . . . What to do? He couldn't leave Janey in his flat indefinitely. He made his way across the road. A football skidded across his path.

'Oi, mister, some woman is climbing through your window!'

Weaver looked up at the flat. The bathroom window was indeed fully open. Panic rushed through him. It was as though in a flash the whole street could see him and his crime. He turned back to the car, fingers trembling so violently he couldn't open the door. The football thudded against the wheel, giving him a start. He would need to get away. Where? Where? Then it struck him, something that he'd heard at work, the perfect place. The lock finally gave, and he climbed in as naturally as he could manage, with the knowledge that the police were moments away from discovering his crime.

Tuesday (7)

'You're looking for me, Miss Thomas?'

Frost closed the interview-room door behind him and nodded to Simms. Simms was taken aback that Frost knew the woman, who sat bolt upright at the table, perfectly composed.

'Ah, at least you have the courtesy to acknowledge you know who I am.'

'Never forget a pretty face.'

Miss Thomas rolled her eyes. The woman was elegant, in an Eastern European kind of way. She had exotic oval eyes. Simms thought her a couple of years older than him, about twenty-five.

'You were at the club Sunday night,' she said.

'I'm impressed you noticed, what with the lights shining in your face.' Frost appeared genuinely surprised.

'Only because Baskin sidled up to you. You were in the front row,' she added distastefully, 'and you can always see Baskin coming, no matter what the light.'

Simms watched for Frost's reaction – if he didn't know the

old man any better, he'd have described him as looking nervous.

'Was there something in my performance that displeased you?' she continued.

'No, no, not at all,' Frost said, adding hastily, 'It was very . . . entertaining.'

'Then why did you instruct Harry to fire me?'

Frost shook a cigarette out of a half-empty packet and offered her one. She declined. He shrugged, lit his own and inhaled deeply. He glanced at Simms fleetingly, as if he'd only just registered he was there.

'Is that what Harry said?' he asked eventually.

She nodded.

'It's not true,' Frost said, standing opposite her, 'it just is not the case.'

The woman frowned, unsettled. 'Then why am I without a job?'

'I don't know, Karen, but I intend to find out.' He said this with a determination no one in the room could question. They made eye contact, and now her gaze never left him, as he paced about the confined room.

Simms didn't know what to make of it. Why was he addressing her by her Christian name? And what was the inspector doing in a strip club on a Sunday night?

Frost stood in front of her, hands on hips, cigarette smoke curling around a pronounced stomach. Both Karen Thomas and Simms waited expectantly for him to expand on his intentions. Eventually, he cleared his throat.

'Leave your contact details with Constable Simms, and I'll be in touch before the week's out with a solution.'

Frost leaned forward and ground out the half-smoked cigarette in the tin ashtray and left the room. What did Frost mean by 'solution'?

'Do you have a pen, please, Constable?'

Simms patted his tunic pocket urgently. It was an odd interlude and one that Simms, if asked, would not be able to explain.

Mullett held the phone tightly to his ear as Assistant Chief Constable Winslow delivered a verbal dressing-down over the Denton police force's appearance on the early evening news. Frost poked his head round the corner of the office door. Mullett beckoned him in. The inspector strode casually over and helped himself to a Senior Service from a packet lying on the super's desk. He wouldn't be so brazen if he knew the trouble his little incident had caused.

'Yes, sir, I do understand,' the super said emphatically into the receiver, 'but one can never tell with the public, they do have the habit of being unpredictable.'

This did not do anything to put Winslow off his stride. In fact, he warmed to his theme. 'Then hold press briefings in the building where you can control who attends! Use some common sense, man! What on earth did she want, anyway? I've had all and sundry on the phone wanting answers. I've always been of the impression that Jack Frost was quite a one with the ladies.'

Frost, as though he sensed he was being talked about, grinned and scratched his expanding stomach. He really had put on the pounds since his wife passed away.

'We've held the woman for questioning,' Mullett said, sensing a possible opportunity to taint Frost's image – Winslow had been a fan of Frost's, indeed it was the ACC who had pushed Mullett to promote Frost to Inspector in the first place. 'I assure you I will get to the bottom of the matter, and if there's been any inappropriate behaviour, it will be dealt with severely.'

'Very well, goodbye.'

Frost settled down in the visitor's chair. 'Go easy on yourself, sir.'

'I'm sorry?'

'The "severe dealing with".'

Mullett frowned. 'Any conversation with the Assistant Chief Constable is of the most confidential nature, and is not for the ears of the likes of you.'

'Oh all right, well, you did invite me in, but I'll just toddle off then. For some reason I thought I might be req—'

'Wait.'

Frost paused, eyebrows raised in anticipation.

'This woman. The one that atta— approached you, on the steps, was Karen Thomas?'

He nodded. 'Yes, took me a while – looks different with her clothes on, but yep, says she is.'

'Just what . . .' Mullett searched for the words. 'What did . . . how . . . how did you request Harry let the young lady go?'

'I didn't give him precise instructions; said, give her the old heave-ho.' He ground out his cigarette. 'What more could I say? You wouldn't tell me any—'

Mullett held up a hand. 'What did Harry say? Did he object?'

'Yes, he did. We owe him a ton.'

'*I beg your pardon?*'

'We owe him a hundred pounds. For loss of earnings.' Frost helped himself to another cigarette and pushed a slip of paper on to the desk.

'What's that?'

'Petty-cash chit – I forgot to give it to you this morning, what with all this carry-on.'

'I will condone nothing of the sort.'

'He wanted two hundred to start with, but I beat him down. Be more of a problem if we – or whoever – doesn't stump up in the long run.' Frost's eyebrows bounced playfully over the word 'whoever'.

'I'll take care of this for now.' Mullett took the slip. 'Did Baskin say anything else?'

'He did say she was a fiery one.'

'You don't say.' He shook his head as the telephone started to ring. The super ignored it. 'And where is Miss Thomas now?'

'Let her go.'

'Let her go? Good heavens, after that embarrassing display? Fetch her back and charge her with affray. Lock her up!'

'What?' Frost said, aghast.

'You heard me,' the super said, 'put her in a cell while we decide what to do with her.'

'You must be joking, sir, after such a public incident! They'll have your – or to be more precise, my – guts for garters!'

'That I can live with . . .' Mullett pressed his elbows down on the desk, kissed a knuckle in thought. What to do – he had not foreseen this eventuality when agreeing to deal with the girl for Hudson. 'What have you said to her, so far?'

'Nothing. Let her calm down, first.'

'While she's doing that, get on the phone to Harry and tell him to put the fear of god into the girl.'

'I can't do that – maybe if we give him his money, then we might . . .'

'He's not getting a penny,' Mullett said sternly. 'Perhaps we might be investigating the Coconut Grove with a view to suspending his licence instead? I can't believe you're so stupid!'

'Why's it my fault?'

'Sloppy handling, as with everything. I gave you this simple task, because I foolishly felt that sleaze-merchant afforded you some respect. But no, he's made you and the whole division look ridiculous.'

'You didn't give me a reason – I . . .'

'A reason? Why do I need to give a reason? You're a subordinate – you do as you're told and don't ask questions. Now get out of my sight!'

The super watched Frost shuffle away. Although this fiasco was, indeed, of Mullett's making, it felt good putting Frost in his place. With the threat of blackmail to Hudson gone, the balance of power was back where it belonged. The superintendent had the upper hand. The relief was palpable; he'd be off the tablets in no time. The telephone began to trill again. Mullett adjusted his tie and tugged his cuffs forward before picking up the receiver. He knew before he answered it would be Hudson's voice on the end of the line. *Let him just try, let him just try.*

'Ah, Michael, I wondered whether you might call . . . yes. Oh did you, indeed?' He picked up the petty-cash slip and twirled it in his fingers. 'Well, things have taken a nasty and somewhat expensive turn, it would seem . . .'

'Jane Hammond, Jack.'

'You what?' Frost's mind was on Karen Thomas as he hurried through Eagle Lane reception – he needed some air and time to think . . . he wasn't his usual self, that much was certain. Hornrim Harry should never have got the better of him, yet that's what he felt had just happened: Mullett, bellowing at him for what? For doing him a favour?

'They've found Jane Hammond,' Bill Wells called softly after him, 'Clarke and Waters, in Clay House.'

That got his attention. He turned and stared at Wells. He didn't need to ask; she was dead. 'Right.' He stood, still digesting the news. 'Why are you whispering?'

'They broke into a neighbour's flat,' he said quietly.

'OK. We'll say the door was ajar. But say nothing until I get there,' he cautioned. 'I'll make my way over.'

'What about Wakely?'

'What about him?'

'He's still in the cells. Do you want to keep him in overnight?'

'I'd forgotten about that toerag . . .' He scratched the back of his neck. 'Feed and water him. I'll be back in an hour.'

Outside the station he pulled out his Polaroids and then lit a cigarette. His mind touched on the dead woman's young son, and the prospect of informing the sister in Rimmington, but try as he might his thoughts swiftly returned to Karen Thomas. What was he to do? He climbed into the Vauxhall, and drove at a moderate pace towards the Southern Housing Estate. It was fair to say, and he'd be the first one to admit it, that he was in a confused state of mind. And it was down to more than just the addling heat.

Tuesday (8)

Waters let Frost into the flat. 'You took your time. TV couldn't get enough of you?' Waters and Clarke had been in the flat for over an hour.

Frost didn't answer.

On a second glance Waters noticed his friend was not his usual chirpy self. 'Did it go OK?'

'Don't ask . . .'

'Why? The super put out because you'd not shaved?'

'Huh. If only.' Frost continued into the lounge. Clarke, who was still very pale, got up from the settee. 'What've we got?'

'Back here. The bathroom.' Waters showed the way, pushing the door open.

Frost, though evidently weary, on seeing Clarke's distress had clicked back into life. 'Flamin' hell.'

Waters stepped back to allow Frost to take in the scene. A naked woman, fully shaved, presumably Jane Hammond, lying partially submerged in a shallow bath of methylated spirits.

Frost automatically patted himself down for his cigarettes.

Waters reached out to prevent him sparking up. 'Talking of flaming hell . . . you'd best not.'

'What make of bubble bath do you think she's using?' Frost remarked. 'Wants to be a bit more careful; made her hair fall out. *All* her hair.'

'Don't think it's fallen out, Jack. There's no sign of—'

Frost held a finger to his lips. There was no sign of clothing, just two empty plastic containers and a sink full of hair. Whoever had done this had taken great care. Not so much as an eyelash remained on the body.

'Open the bleedin' window before we all pass out,' Frost ordered as he left the bathroom. Waters did as asked and followed him into the lounge. 'I imagine he's not finished the job, probably out buying more meths.'

'That must have been what he was carrying in those bags when I saw him earlier this afternoon,' Clarke said. 'To think that she . . .'

'Let's not dwell on that,' Frost said. 'Where is Weaver now, I wonder.'

'Do you not want to know how? There's a puncture mark on her neck, looks like it's from a knitting needle.'

'She's dead, I think, and not from overheating in the bath. Let's leave it to Forensics, eh. What time did you see Weaver?'

'About four.'

'Right. I bumped into him this morning around ten. It's six forty-five now.'

'You saw him too?' The relief on Clarke's face was visible. The poor woman felt she'd failed in some way, by not questioning the man when she'd had the opportunity. Waters had tried to console her; it was well after the event and the girl was long dead. And who would have suspected the verger neighbour?

'Yep, on his way out somewhere. So you saw him coming home at four. Did you see him going back out?'

'No, don't think so. I was talking to that punter out on the walkway, so I would have seen him.'

'You and Waters can't have missed him by long – at most by an hour. Have you had a rummage around the flat?'

'We were waiting for you,' Clarke said.

'There's a couple of library books – taken out today,' Waters said.

'On what?'

'One on Egyptian mummies and another on embalming.'

'Anything else?'

'Nothing other than a church calendar which has shifts marked out for the High Fields care home; it was twelve to three today.'

'And the morning off for shopping and embalming.' Frost mulled it over. 'Nothing else look out of place?'

'Nope.'

'No sign he's left in a hurry?'

'No . . .'

'Then he doesn't realize we're on to him. He might be back any minute. Nobody else knows other than us. Don't notify anybody. Not Forensics, Drysdale from the lab, nobody. Only Wells knows, and he'll keep shtum if I tell him to.'

They exchanged glances.

'Right. You two'll have to stay here and wait for him,' Frost said finally.

'Us? Why us?' Clarke complained.

'You can't stay here on your own. Look what he did to her,' Frost retorted.

'Why can't *you* stay?'

'It might be a long wait, and I can't hang around tonight. I'll slip out down the fire exit.'

'Charming.'

'Call me if anything happens. The phone works.' With that Frost made to go.

'You are joking?' Clarke said, dismayed.

'We need to, Sue,' Waters added, diplomatically. 'If Weaver doesn't know we're on to him – and it looks very much that way – then we gotta try and catch him. No point all three of us staying put,' he reasoned. What Frost was up to he had no idea; it was unusual for him to bail out, especially in a case like this, but no doubt he had his reasons. Waters nodded his agreement.

Clarke sank back down on to the sofa as Frost closed the door behind him. 'Shit!' she blurted out as she leapt up.

'What is it?'

'I sat on something . . . wait. Oh no!'

Waters came over and saw a knitting needle sticking out between the cushions. When he took a closer look he noticed there was a brown and red smear along the length of it.

'You don't think . . . ?' Clarke asked nervously.

'Uh-huh. I do. Well discovered.'

'That must mean he did it there.'

'Yeah. Maybe sit at the table, you've had a shock.'

'Do you think he'll show?'

'Your guess is as good as mine, no idea where he could be. It's getting late now. Everywhere's shut . . . apart from the pubs.'

Clarke was holding her head in her hands.

'What's up?' he asked.

'I've forgotten all about my son!' she wailed. 'Can you believe it – been back at work one day, and I've clean forgotten all about him . . .'

Frost was exhausted by the time he arrived back at Eagle Lane.

He had stopped off at the Unwins on Piper Road and picked up a four-pack of Hofmeister. He sat in Waters' Vauxhall and downed half a can. 'Better,' he said and shut his eyes. He couldn't let on to his colleagues that he had a date later. He took a smaller gulp next. He didn't feel guilty. He still had Wakely to contend with; he couldn't leave him overnight in the cells without causing a stink.

Frost picked up the beers and headed for the front entrance. At least it was starting to cool down a bit. Johnny Johnson, the night sergeant, had taken over from Bill Wells.

'Evening, Jack, another late one?'

Frost raised his can. 'I'm just following the bear, Johnny, but he keeps leading me here.'

Superintendent Mullett surprised him on his way down to the cells.

'Progress?'

'Err, nothing confirmed, sir.'

'But Wakely was resisting arrest?'

'He's done that before. Martin Wakely is allergic to Denton Police.'

'But he was in Rachel Curtis's house.' Mullett looked to the ceiling, pondering. 'Must've been after incriminating evidence. The girl's shoes were not recovered?'

'It's not yet confirmed he was in the house, sir.'

'But he was identified as the motorcycle rider?'

'Simms and Miller picked someone up who fits the description.'

'Who then evaded arrest?' The super was fishing for good news on his way out, but Frost was not in the mood to jump to hasty conclusions just so that Mullett could sleep more easily.

Mullett was correct, of course. Wakely had run when approached; but Frost was of the opinion that there'd be something more wrong if he *hadn't* tried to leg it. Wakely was more often than not on the wrong side of the law – of course he'd not come peacefully; with him, it wasn't a question of *if* he'd been up to something, rather *what* he'd been up to. Frost knew the Wakely family of old; figured Martin for housebreaking, sure – but not murder.

All the same, he was surprised to find Wakely soundly asleep downstairs in the cells.

'Oi! Sleeping beauty. Wakey-wakey.' He pushed the cot with his foot. Wakely groaned. How the flamin' heck could he be asleep given the potential trouble he was in?

'Where am I?'

'In the nick.'

'Bleedin' hell.' Martin scratched the back of his shaven head.

'You wear your troubles lightly, my bald friend. I don't think I'd be able to sleep if I was in the poo as deep as you.'

'Eh? I'd had a few in the boozer, sleeping it off.' He yawned.

The publican had now stated that Wakely had been in the Cricketers over an hour, despite his original indication to young Simms that he'd only been there a much shorter time. Frost was dismissive; landlords always covered for villains for fear of retribution. No, he didn't give that any credence – but the fact that the toerag had been sparko made Frost wonder . . . A guilty man would be pacing the cell, agitating for a brief. Frost rubbed his back which was sore and said, 'The bike – has forty winks helped you remember where you got it from? Has that kip done anything for your memory?'

'I found it.'

'Make your bleedin' mind up. Thought you said you borrowed it?' Frost glanced down at the arrest sheet. The number plate was: CAT 93N.

This wasn't the flamin' motorbike Frost was after.

Tuesday (9) _____

Frost was late for his date.

After his frustrating chat with Wakely, Frost had had a lengthy telephone conversation with the vicar. Father Hill listened without comment to their discoveries at his verger's flat. Frost had pleaded with the vicar to allow him to station a PC at the vicarage, for his own safety, but the elderly churchman wouldn't hear of it. Frost even put himself forward for the job, but the offer was likewise rejected. In truth, once Frost understood that Weaver did not perform any actual religious duties, he doubted very much the man would venture on to church grounds. Frost didn't push the old clergyman, but instead asked for a special favour – which was granted.

By the time Frost entered the pub looking for his date, he really didn't expect to hear any more from Clay House. The night sergeant, Johnny Johnson, had details of his whereabouts should the need arise, but he thought it unlikely this late in the day. He knew he'd have to get Forensics down there before the end of the night, otherwise Mullett would have his knickers in a knot over procedure.

On his first hasty scan of the pub he missed his date altogether. Assuming she'd blown him out, he ordered a pint of Tennent's Extra (rather a pint here, than heading back to Clay House). After the day he'd had, he was not too bothered to have been let down. He seldom thought of women these days; he still fancied them of course, but since his wife had died, he'd not made any new 'special friends'. His lack of permanent abode hadn't helped matters (not even he would have dared bring Suzy Fong back to Clarke's, for instance). No, women hadn't featured in Jack Frost's life for quite a while, not until this week, in fact. Must be the weather; he grinned into his pint glass; the cherry woman in the tattoo parlour and – yes, yes, the girl on the pole at Harry's on Sunday night, with whom he'd made a strange connection only hours ago, standing in the sweltering Eagle Lane interview room. Karen. A 'connection'? What did that even mean . . .

He took a pensive gulp of the ice-cold lager, thinking of the pole dancer. She was a cracker, no doubt about it. Even angry as hell, screaming at him as she had this afternoon. What was he to do about the whole mess now, though? He said he'd fix it, but how? There was only one thing for it: he had to tackle Hornrim Harry head on. Then maybe he could ask Karen to the Jade Rabbit . . . He felt a tap on the shoulder. He turned to see an attractive blonde in her late thirties, dressed in the sort of sarong that was all the rage this summer.

'Sorry I'm late,' she stammered.

'You're late?'

'We said eight?'

He checked his watch. Eight twenty. 'And there was me thinking I was late. You look . . . lovely.' Pathetic, but it was all he could think to say. What he really meant was, 'Not what I expected.'

'Why, thank you. And you look . . .' She paused. 'Different

somehow? Ah.' She reached and touched his jaw lightly. He recoiled from the unexpected move. 'The beard? It's gone.'

'Yes. I forgot – I only just shaved it off too.'

They both laughed. Frost offered to get her a drink before realizing she already had one. She guided him to a booth.

'Cosy,' he said as they sat down. 'So what do you do when not in . . .' He left it hanging.

'Getting tattooed? I work in a solicitor's office.'

'Oh, that's unusual.' Frost took in the woman's full appearance for the first time; she was the right side of forty, slight creases beginning around the eyes when she smiled, bit younger than him.

'Always fancied a tattoo, but my husband would never allow—'

'I see.' Frost avoided her eyes and examined his pint glass.

'But now that he's gone, I can do what I like.' She beamed at him. 'What about you?'

'My wife died.' It was an awkward and blunt statement to make, and one he'd not made in a while. Goes to show, he thought, how few new people he met outside of the job.

'I'm sorry.' Her face dropped.

'No, no, it was some time ago, we didn't really get on; job got in the way.' He half smiled.

'Can you tell me about that, what your work is like? Or is it a secret?'

'Huh, if you really want to know?'

'Tell me,' she insisted, touching his hand. 'But first tell me your name, Inspector. I'm Julie.'

'Oh, I'm so sorry, how rude of me not to ask,' he spluttered, 'I don't do this . . . sort of thing very much.' He cleared his throat. 'I'm Jack. Jack Frost.'

He met her gaze; instinct told him she was a warm person. 'Well' – he downed the rest of his lager and ordered another pair of drinks with a nod towards the bartender – 'you asked for it.'

He proceeded to divulge the whole of the Rachel Curtis case. They were getting on well, and Frost chatted animatedly, spurred on by Julie's enthusiasm. If he paused to reflect, he was actually enjoying himself. She was simply indulging him, letting him ramble on – he couldn't remember the last time anyone had shown any interest in what he did (not that he'd gone out of his way to try).

'And so what has happened since we met at Mungo's?'

'Not much. After I met you, I went to see one of Rachel's pals at Aster's who said she saw her having a row with a bloke on a motorbike. Then when I went to her house I disturbed someone – someone had broken in; he leapt out of the window on to a bike and—'

'Wait a sec, this row you mentioned – when did that happen?'

'Saturday afternoon, top of Foundling Street, on the corner of Market Square.'

'Have you got a picture of Rachel with you?'

Frost rooted around in a pocket. 'Somewhere, yes, I think . . . here,' he said, retrieving the same photo he'd shown Mungo yesterday morning.

'Yes, that could have been her, right age . . .'

'Where were you?'

'On my way down to the tattoo parlour, to look at designs.'

'Did you clock the fella on the bike?'

'Yes . . . but it wasn't a man. It was a woman.'

'Are you sure?'

'Positive. After the girl – Rachel – stormed off, the bike parked up and the driver pulled off her helmet and went into Boots.'

'What she look like?'

'Nondescript – late forties, short brown hair, denim jacket . . .'

'Boots, eh?'

'That's right.'

'Boots . . .' he ruminated, 'very useful. Thanks, worth turning up for.'

Her face fell.

'Oh, I didn't mean it like that,' he added hastily. 'You have to forgive me, I'm not much good in polite company.'

'You're not so bad.' She sank her teeth into the glacé cherry that had come skewered on a cocktail umbrella in her Bezique and lemonade.

'I think you've been short-changed with that' – he pointed to the cocktail stick – 'from what I've seen of cherries this week.' The conversation settled back down to a more relaxed tone, and police work was mentioned no more. He turned the focus on her. She was a solicitor, it transpired (not a secretary, as he had assumed). Time raced by and before they knew it the bell was rung.

'Fancy a Chinese?' Frost said.

'Bit late for that, isn't it?'

Frost pulled out Mr Fong's spare key and jangled it over the table. 'Not if you've got the run of the restaurant.'

It was nearly eleven as DS John Waters fumbled wearily with his front-door key to Kim's flat. God, he was beat. Soft lighting and the murmur of the television greeted him as he slipped off his shoes. *Home sweet home*, he muttered to himself – Christ was he glad to be away from the Southern Housing Estate.

Supine on the couch with feet stretched out on the pouffe and still in a trouser suit nursing a glass of wine was the love of John's life: Kim Myles, soon to be Kim Waters. The thought of it still sent a tingle through him.

'Hi babe.' Kim stirred, her white teeth glinting in the flicker from the TV. 'Salad and vino in the fridge.'

'Hey, you look comfy. I'm done in.' Waters walked between her and the TV, squeezing a stockinged toe as he passed. On the telly, he caught women dressed in ragged clothes exchanging words in hushed serious tones. *Tenko*. What better way for a policewoman to wind down after a late shift than immersing herself in the hardships of a bunch of women in a Japanese POW camp?

In the kitchen, he pulled open the fridge and, ignoring the Mateus Rosé upright in the door, opted for a can of Kestrel instead. He downed the ice-cold lager in a matter of seconds. My, he had a thirst on him. The temperature had eased but it would still be a stuffy night. The window was open, and a light breeze caught the net curtain. He took another lager. Next to a stack of beers was a bowl of potato salad that Kim had made that morning. As they both worked long shifts the couple took turns to prepare meals; though they seldom ate together, they did eat the same food, which was a togetherness of a kind. When the pair had started co-habiting it was fun to see what the other could rustle up. They'd stuck with it, which was sweet, and Waters enjoyed a dabble with a saucepan; he found it relaxing to prepare a meal, even in the summer when it was mainly chilled foods. He took another dish, a beetroot and tomato con-coction, and lifted a Scotch egg from an open packet. He sat at the kitchen table and ate quickly in contemplative silence, enjoying the beer and food before returning to the lounge.

Side by side they sat and watched the war drama. It was grim viewing, but Kim and her pals lapped it up, recording every episode. John didn't follow it and was almost asleep as he felt a nudge.

'You're late,' Kim said quietly, her attention on the screen.

'Uh-huh.'

'All good?'

'Uh-huh, just stuff going on.' Where possible they both left their work on the doorstep. What was there to gain by Kim hearing of their failed stake-out? No need to disturb what little downtime they had together before bed by discussing an unpleasant murder case. Leave it behind for eight hours; he yawned. He hoped he had some reserve energy for Friday. The upside of them both working right up to the big day was it left little time for apprehension or anxiety; not that there were any doubts . . . There were some pre-wedding nerves, of course, but these were generally confined to worries of the job interfering; more 'what if' scenarios.

She snuggled closer. 'Even so I'd thought he'd cut you some slack this week of all weeks.'

'There's stuff going on,' he repeated. Kim viewed Frost in a dim light; she held him responsible for most things. Keen to avoid a conversation opening up about him (followed by doubts about his competence as a best man: he wasn't allowed to look after her wedding ring for instance, that duty had passed to Kim's sister), he said, 'Jack's bending over backwards to give me an easy time of it. We're lucky to have him; he's working flat out too – probably still in the office.'

'I know, babe, I know, I just don't want anything to go wrong, I'm sooo happy.' She gave him a peck on the cheek.

'It won't, honey.' Waters wondered if her wedding nerves were rubbing off on him: why then did he say that about Frost? He was pretty sure he *wasn't* at work . . .

Voices rose on the television. The Japanese commandant was shouting at two women. Waters opened another beer, wincing as the women defiantly took their abuse, but for all the drama a small part of him was churning over what Jack Frost might be up to. Then he couldn't help but think he should still be on surveillance on the Southern Housing Estate; that he'd left too early . . . he swigged from the can. A controlled gasp of wind escaped. He realized at this point he was overtired. Planting a sloppy wet kiss on his betrothed's forehead, he said goodnight. He knew they'd be all right. He knew Jack would be all right. He just needed to reach the end of the week safely: he collapsed on the bed and was asleep in seconds.

Wednesday (1)

Clarke pulled her toast out from underneath the grill. Burnt to a cinder. Frazzled, like her. She had slept badly. Having returned late, her mind was too active to sleep, and when she eventually did she was plagued by dreams of bald women in baths. But her fears for her son had proved to be unfounded. She'd expected to arrive home and find him screaming for his mother; as it turned out, both grandmother and child were sound asleep by the time she walked in the front door.

She and Waters had finished the night having 'officially' discovered the body at ten. How Frost planned to explain that one away to Mullett she had no idea. She dumped her failed breakfast in the bin, flicked the kettle on, opened the fridge for milk. She was reaching for a mug when the telephone began to ring, too loud in the still peaceful flat. She dashed into the hall as her infant son woke and started wailing.

'Yes,' she snapped into the receiver.

'Mornin', love.'

'Jack? You've a nerve.'

'Missing me already?'

'What do you want?'

'Hold the fort, will you?'

'I beg your pardon?' It was seven thirty, why was he even calling this bloody early?

'I'm going to have a word with the last people to have seen Ben Weaver – other than your good self.' He started to chuckle, which really grated.

'Why the hell are you so chirpy this morning? What were you up to last night while John and I were sitting in a council flat with a dead woman in a bath?'

Silence.

'Jack, you there?'

'Er, yeah. Nothing. One thing, on the Curtis Case: the motor-cyclist we're looking for? It's a woman.'

'A *woman*?'

'A woman, yes.'

'How do you know that?'

'There was a witness.'

'Who? Who else have you talked to? John ran me through the whole case last night. The woman at Aster's said a man in a red helmet.'

'Yes, but the rider took the helmet off and, like I say, we have a new witness. A woman in her late forties was possibly the last person to see Rachel Curtis alive.'

A clean-shaven Frost appeared outside the Jade Rabbit. A second later a woman followed. Simms couldn't quite see her properly at this angle, sitting behind the wheel of the panda car. She pecked the inspector on the cheek then hurried off down the street.

'Morning, sir,' Simms addressed the inspector as he opened the car door, 'where to?'

'High Fields Care Home, know it?'

'Yes, sir.'

'Right, now then, back to yesterday and Martin Wakely.'

'Sir?'

'He was wearing a T-shirt, when you nicked him. Did he have a jacket, or more to the point, a helmet?'

'No, sir, I checked in the pub after; he must have been riding a motorcycle illegally – without a helmet.'

Frost said nothing after that, and sat in thoughtful silence, presumably contemplating Wakely's fate . . . Simms, however, along with the rest of Eagle Lane, was preoccupied with Karen Thomas. At the station yesterday the staff canteen was buzzing with gossip and speculation; was this a very public lovers' tiff? Even Simms had found himself drawn to the drama; even outweighing his desire to see DC Clarke who was, it was said, back on the force. Simms had been cajoled by his colleagues into prying into the inspector's private affairs, something he was reluctant to do . . . Now, however, he found himself unable to resist wondering about the blonde who had left the restaurant with Frost. He racked his brains trying to think of an opening line that wasn't too obvious.

'That's it, then,' Frost said. 'I let Martin go last night, anyway. Helmets aside, you were given the wrong plate number.'

'Sir?'

'Bill needs his ears syringing. When I called it in, I said K-A-T as in KitKat, not C-A-T as in Top bleedin' Cat.'

Simms was baffled; the phonetic alphabet was there for just such a purpose, the avoidance of such miscommunication. C for Charlie and K for Kilo.

'Keep that to yourself, eh.'

'Yes, sir. Why are we going to the care home? If you don't mind me asking.'

'Not at all, son. I'm all for an inquisitive mind. We are going there because it is where Ben Weaver works part-time as a care assistant.'

'Oh? Does he work at High Fields? His name's not familiar.'
And then realizing an explanation was needed he added, 'My
mother is in there.'

'Really?' Frost said, fidgeting in the seat and turning to face
him. 'Been in there long?'

'A couple of years,' he said glumly, 'she had a stroke.'

'I'm sorry to hear that. Can't be easy.'

'Not that old, forty-seven.'

'Blimey, that isn't old at all,' Frost said, the surprise in his
voice evident. Part of the reason David Simms had applied to
come to Denton was to be closer to his mother.

'Booze and fags.'

'Your brother never . . .' Simms stopped at some lights. Frost
toyed with a cigarette packet.

'Mentioned it?'

'Not that there'd be any reason why he should tell me.'

'I suppose it's not something people like to talk about.' They
both watched a doddery old couple shuffle over the zebra crossing. Simms wondered what the odds were of him ever making
that age. His father was still alive, somewhere, as far as he
knew.

'No, course not. She in there today, your mum? Pop by and
say hello if you fancy?'

'Oh, I don't know, work is work. I'm seeing her tomorrow on
my day off.' The young PC didn't know how to respond
appropriately; the older man was being kind but Simms now
regretted having raised the subject of his mother, and was
uncomfortable.

'Dad not around, I suppose?'

How could he know that? 'No, not for some time.'

'How is she? Talking?'

'Oh, yes, compos mentis.' He was unsure how to describe
her.

'There you go then, she'll be pleased as punch to see you. I can tell her what a good job you're doing, eh?' Frost elbowed him lightly, as he shifted down a gear. 'Mothers love to be proud of their sons.'

'If you're sure, sir.' This really hadn't gone the way Simms had planned; instead of getting the lowdown on the DI's love life, he'd managed to divulge his own family history.

Frost pushed the panda car door shut. High Fields was named for its location, out on the North Denton plains commanding beautiful views. Before them, watching from behind a huge plate-glass window, were the residents, many in wheelchairs, a few standing, but all with a uniformly ghostly pallor; Frost, who considered himself hardy, was dismayed by the contrast between the pale faces within and the glorious summer weather outside.

'Flamin' Nora,' he muttered, 'why don't they let them have some air?' PC Simms didn't answer, walking ahead in silence. It wasn't only the deathly lot inside that troubled Frost; the story of Simms's mother had worried him. There was no denying Frost was not as young as he once was. The stairs at Clay House were a painful reminder of the fact; his legs were stiff just from walking up and down three flights (he wished they'd sort the lift out). He remembered Sue Clarke had fixed him an appointment to see Dr Mirchandani about his back; he might check he'd not missed it – be useful to get the once-over while he was at it.

'After you.' Frost pushed the door open for the young policeman. At the front desk they asked to see Mr Baxter – Father Hill had passed on the name as a contact. Soporific music filled the atrium at an unobtrusive volume. Nurses soundlessly passed them by, paying no heed to their presence.

'Inspector Frost, Mr Baxter will see you now.'

In a panelled office not dissimilar to Mullett's, a bald man with Himmler-like spectacles sat behind a large desk. Frost did not give specifics as to the reason they wished to see his employee Weaver, other than for questioning in relation to a serious crime.

'I did not imagine you would trouble us for a speeding ticket.'

'If only it were so. Mr Weaver was in work yesterday—' The door opened behind him, and a nurse entered the room. The woman in her fifties crossed the floor, and stood to the side of Baxter's desk.

'Sister, can you confirm Mr Weaver's presence at High Fields yesterday?'

'Certainly, Benjamin was here until three, he was with Mr Cassidy. They were chatting away.'

'Mr Cassidy?'

'Mr Cassidy, a patient, discharged from Denton General on Monday.'

'May I have a word with the patient?'

Baxter and the sister exchanged glances.

'Mr Cassidy's speech has been affected by his illness,' Baxter said.

'But he's the last known person to have spoken to Ben Weaver – "chatting away", you said so yourself.'

'The last person here, yes,' the sister confirmed.

'So, worth a try?'

Frost with Simms at his heels was led out across the atrium into a large day room.

'There he is in the far corner,' the sister said. Frost craned to see who she meant, the patients were indistinguishable.

'Sir, do you mind,' Simms whispered in his ear, 'my mother is just over there.' Frost turned to see an emaciated woman, struggling with a walker.

'No, son, you go ahead.' Frost couldn't believe this woman was only seven years older than him.

'Inspector, shall we?' the sister prompted.

Frost followed, dodging a middle-aged couple trying to coerce an old lady away from a group watching a television. Three people in wheelchairs sat facing the plate-glass window. The sister tapped one of them on the shoulder, and pulled his wheelchair away from the view.

The man registered the DI's presence and gave him a pleading stare. Frost could see how confused he was. With visible effort the man slowly opened his mouth to attempt speech, but no words followed. His gaze drifted lazily from Frost to the middle distance in disappointment.

'No chatting today,' the sister at Frost's side remarked.

'Give the poor sod a chance,' Frost appealed, and knelt beside the man. The sister gave a slight shrug of impatience. Cassidy leaned forward in the wheelchair, gripping its arms with shaking hands, and moved to speak. A pained expression in his eyes accompanied the soundless fish-like jaw movements.

'No chatting today,' the sister repeated, this time firmly.

Wednesday (2) ———————————————

'So let me get this perfectly clear.' Clarke felt Waters shift in his seat next to her in the super's office. Mullett's beady eyes flitted from one to the other. The wall clock behind them clicked to nine thirty. 'You returned to Mr Weaver's flat because the lady next door heard a noise and called you at—'

'Called Jack,' Waters said calmly. Clarke shot him a discreet look. That wouldn't bear close scrutiny; Frost was nowhere to be found.

'Telephoned Inspector Frost, who then in turn handed it over to you?' Mullett prompted. Clarke could tell he smelt a rat. 'At that time of night? Your devotion to duty is commendable, Sergeant.'

'Yeah, the inspector has a lot on his plate at the moment, moving lodgings, I said no problemo, I'd scoot round there with Detective Clarke to check the situation out.'

'Both of you?'

'Ever been on the Southern Housing Estate late at night, sir?'

'No.' Mullett sat back. 'No, most certainly not. So you turn up, and then what?'

'There's a weird noise coming from the guy's flat, we tap on the door and it opens, just like that . . .'

'I see, and what was the noise?'

'We clean forgot about the noise, when the stench of meths hit us. Probably rats?'

'In a third-floor flat?'

'They get everywhere, sir,' Clarke added, now caught up in the tale.

Mullett switched his focus on to her. 'And you subscribe to this story, Detective Clarke?'

'Absolutely.'

'I needn't tell you both that if you entered a private property illegally it could jeopardize a successful prosecution.' They both nodded. 'Very well, have Frost come see me when he arrives. Where did you say he was – at a *business breakfast*? With whom?'

'He didn't say.'

'Right. Moving on. Where do we think Weaver might be?'

They both shrugged. This much at least was honest; they had absolutely no idea where he was.

'We better launch a manhunt pronto. Presumably this fellow is in the frame for Rachel Curtis too.'

The detectives looked at each other. Waters eventually said, 'I can see why you would say that, but I don't see the crimes as related, there's no evidence to suggest Weaver ever knew Curtis.'

'Except that he can be placed at the scene of the crime.'

'He's a lay verger, sir,' Waters said, 'but he'd not necessarily be there in the church in the middle of the night.' The sergeant tried to dissuade Mullett from leaping to any conclusions.

'That, I'm afraid, won't be good enough. It'll be the first question the press will ask.'

'He has a point,' Clarke said outside.

'Yeah, but let's not get drawn into it yet. Jack can deal with Mullett on that score. I'm not doing him any more favours. First thing this morning, I had a garbled message to collect the Vauxhall from outside the Jade Rabbit. He'd left the keys in the ignition. I nearly got a parking ticket, but you couldn't see any yellow lines at all. Told the traffic warden to hop it.' Waters sighed.

'What's your next move?'

'Tedious. Seeing the super has reminded me: I've got to crack on with this case about the toff who left a pile of cash in a cement mixer. Hanlon has found the builder. Local man. Fancy that?'

'Can't. I've to officially identify Jane Hammond's body with the sister at the morgue.'

Waters considered offering to come but thought better of it – he'd no doubt spook the bereaved once more. 'OK, how about I pick you up at the General in an hour?'

'That'd be good. Then I can send Clare Hammond home with the WPC.'

Waters saw the van first, emblazoned with *Todd Builders*. The children's play area by Denton Primary School was being resurfaced. A heavy-set man, troll-like, was humping blocks of concrete from beneath the swings. A young skinny lad was levering up the slabs, freeing them for the other to move.

'Mr Todd.'

'That's what it says on the van,' the man said, his back to them.

'Might we have a word?' Todd looked from Waters to Hanlon. Hanlon knew all the local builders and had found out swiftly where the man was working.

'If you're quick.'

'Dominic Holland.'

Todd rolled his eyes. 'What about him?' he said and carried on lugging the slab.

'His swimming pool. Said he left you some cash in a cement mixer?'

'There weren't no money there.'

'Is it usual to leave cash in machinery?'

The man shrugged uninterestedly. 'Yeah, if the fella ain't around.'

'So you've done that before?' Hanlon said.

Todd nodded. 'Many a time.'

'Ever had money disappear?'

'Wouldn't do it if I had, would I?' He took off his flat cap, wiped his brow and pulled out a pouch of Old Holborn.

'Where are you picking up the dosh on this job?' Waters said, surveying the play area. 'Someone left you a roll of fifties in the middle of the see-saw?'

'The council are prompt payers.' Todd licked the cigarette paper. 'By cheque.' He'd said the last with the weight of finality, but then added, 'Look, people nick things from places they expect to find them. Burglars rob houses for jewellery and tellies. They rob banks for cash. In places they expect to find stuff, see. People do not go looking inside cement mixers unless they know something's there besides mortar.'

Waters thought the man practical and straightforward, and knew that he'd not survive in business for long if he nabbed down-payments from his customers. 'And you didn't tell a soul, right?'

'Why would I?'

'Do you think Mr Holland told anyone?'

'You'd better ask him that.'

'Did you see anyone coming and going from the house, in the time you were working there?'

'Not really. Apart from a delivery van on the Friday afternoon.'

'Delivering what?'

'Loads of booze for a party on Saturday, I think. I wasn't invited.'

Waters remembered there being a disturbance out at Two Bridges on Saturday, and Holland had mentioned it himself . . . It was marked up on the incident board on Monday.

'Right mess they made. Bottles everywhere. Tyre tracks all across the front lawn. Shocking.'

'Car tyres?'

'Motorbikes.'

'On Saturday night?'

'Couldn't say for sure, but they weren't there when I clocked off Friday, and there plain as day Monday morning.'

Inside the car the two policemen sat for a while. Waters drank a Pepsi. 'That's odd.'

'How so?'

'Holland said only his London cronies came to the party.'

'And?'

'You have to meet him to appreciate this, but he doesn't strike me as the sort of bloke that's gonna have pals on motorbikes carving up his front lawn.'

'What are you thinking?'

'I know this party happened before Holland's money was stolen, but prior to that Saturday night nobody in Denton had met Holland – he said himself he didn't know anyone local – but suppose the party drew attention to this flash new boy in town with lots of money to chuck about on home improvements? Some of the village kids get wind of the party; they show up uninvited and start larking about on the property; cause a bit of a disturbance, but at the same time are scoping the place out?'

'I'm with you; they'd have picked up that he works away from Denton, so come Monday, they watch the house and wait for him to leave?'

206

'Exactly. Imagine it; they return on Monday thinking they'll find him already gone, but instead can't believe their luck when they see our dandy friend place a huge bag of cash in a cement mixer! They'd not even bother breaking into the house with a result like that – all suspicion would be on the builder. Let's take a butcher's up there.'

'I can't. Jack has told me I've got to go all the way back up to flamin' Sheffield to bring Curtis's mother down for questioning.'

'That's a drag, all the way back up there.' Waters remembered he'd offered to pick Clarke up at eleven. The country charm of Two Bridges would at least be a change of scene from the hospital morgue.

Frost had spoken little since leaving the care home. Simms was preoccupied too, and was not of a mind to spark up conversation. The experience at High Fields had not been great in any respect; the lad had said his mother was disturbed at seeing him in uniform, out of context; the unexpected break from routine had agitated her.

'A woman,' Frost muttered.

'I'm sorry?'

'It might have been a woman Rachel Curtis was arguing with on Saturday.' Frost had not yet mentioned to Simms what his date had told him last night.

'Oh, so not Martin Wakely?'

'Wakely is no doubt guilty of something, but it seems unlikely he has anything to do with the Curtis case if the biker seen rowing with her in Market Square is the same person that leapt out of her window yesterday afternoon.'

'How old is this woman supposed to be?'

'Late forties.'

'Isn't Rachel Curtis's mum that age? Or thereabouts.'

'Yeah, I forgot you went up there with Hanlon. How was she? Not griefstricken, I gather.'

'No. No love lost between mother and daughter.'

'Don't suppose she rides a motorbike?'

'We didn't ask. But would she have come down here? It was part of Rachel's parole conditions to go up there . . .'

'Which she failed to do. We ought to see old Fergusson again.'

'Who?'

'Her probation officer; a grumpy Scotsman. Wait, stop here.' They were at the Market Square, right outside Boots. 'Worth a try.' Frost reasoned that if a shopper nipping into the chemist was on a bike, they'd of necessity be after something small that could be slipped into a jacket pocket.

He flashed his ID at a stern-looking man in glasses behind the pharmacy counter and asked to be told about all the prescription customers on Saturday afternoon.

'Dropping off or picking up?'

'Either.'

'We're quite busy on a Saturday.' The pharmacist sighed and disappeared below the counter.

Frost's attention was suddenly caught by two teenage girls giggling at the next desk. He grinned at them, and they laughed all the more. One held something in her hand. Photographs. Frost moved over to the next counter, and asked, 'Lady, late forties, on a motorbike, drop off a roll of film Saturday?'

'Yes, I remember, a very angry lady. One second' – the shop assistant looked warily at Frost – 'here you go.'

The assistant passed him a Boots Photography wallet. Inside were an array of snaps of Gary Benson, Harry Baskin's flabby doorman, larking around in the sun.

'That'll be two pounds, sir.'

'You what?'

'Your wife didn't pay for the photos.'

Wednesday (3)

Waters pulled into an ambulance bay outside Denton General Hospital and switched off the engine. Frost had insisted the body be brought to the General for identification – the lab had no immediate need as the cause of death was straightforward – believing the experience under the care of the hospital staff would be a fraction easier on her kin than a visit to Drysdale's morgue. Leaving the radio on, Waters tapped a JPS out of the packet. Twenty yards away in the shade of the ugly building a pair of ambulance drivers nodded, in silent recognition, as they too sparked up. On the radio the DJ gabbled on heatedly as Waters jettisoned smoke through the sunroof, his right arm dangling out of the open car window. The patter subsided and a familiar beat tinkled out of the stereo. He turned the volume up, and let 'Master Blaster' drift across the tarmac, where it received the thumbs-up from the other drivers.

What a week, he thought. It was hard to imagine he was getting married in two days – less than two days, to be precise, the church service was at midday on Friday. This time Friday he'd be 'ringed-up', as Frost had put it, and toasting his bride with champagne in the grounds of Chadwick Hall. Then a week in Barcelona on honeymoon. Waters thought himself diligent and hardworking, but he had no qualms about stepping away for a week. There'd be plenty here waiting for him when he return-ed, of that he was sure. Besides, Clarke was back; she and Frost might be rubbing each other up the wrong way now, but that was down to a readjustment in their relationship. They'd work it out eventually. Trying to bring the child up on her own and return to work must be stressful. Waters knew Clarke's mother was on hand and would be more help than Frost ever would, but still; it couldn't be easy with a job like this one, not exactly a straight-forward nine-to-five, and no sign of a dad on the horizon.

The absent father was never mentioned. Paradoxically the rumour that the boy might be Jack Frost's son had ceased when he announced he was sleeping on her settee. Waters had aired the question of paternity only once, when both were roaring drunk, whereupon Frost had said slurringly it was indisputably Derek Simms's child. And that was that. It was good enough for Waters; and the belief was corroborated by Frost's air of general nonchalance towards the kid (an air that had, at times, even come across as mild distaste). Frost was not well disposed to dealing with the infant's howls at the best of times, let alone during the slim window of the night when Frost did finally sleep. Still, it was tough on Sue Clarke . . . As Waters drummed his fingers along the warm outside of the car door to the music he saw two women exit the hospital. One was Clarke, wearing a worried face, and the other was Jane Hammond's sister, who appeared very shaky.

'They sure ain't feeling pretty, Stevie.' Waters flicked the cigarette, started the engine and turned the stereo down.

Clarke handed Clare Hammond over to a WPC, who helped her to a waiting car. Then she hurried over towards the Vauxhall, one hand shielding her eyes from the sunlight.

'I don't have to ask how that was,' he said as she shut her door. There was nothing in this world sadder than witnessing kin die before their time. Clare Hammond had looked haggard, and he might not even have recognized her as the woman he'd visited in the leafy Rimmington street on Monday.

And then it struck him. 'What about the boy?'

'With a neighbour.'

'Christ.'

'We have got to catch that bastard.'

'We will, we will.' He indicated to turn on to the main road. 'Jack won't let him get away.'

'Where are we going?' she asked quietly.

'A distraction,' he said grimly, 'see how the other half live.'

Holland first knew of the police presence when he saw them inspecting his lawn. He hurried outside. 'Oh, am I glad to see you!'

The muscular ebony chap he'd met the previous day had a woman with him now. She held out her hand and introduced herself as Detective Clarke.

'I left a message this morning . . .' said Dominic.

'Yeah? We were out. Having a chat with your builder.'

'Humpf. Him. What did he have to say for himself?'

'He said your lawn was in a bit of a state.'

'As you can see.'

'Your London friends, Hell's Angels, are they?' asked Clarke.

'Most certainly not.'

'But when I asked who came to your party you said it was just your city pals?'

'I—' He was tongue-tied for a moment. 'What can I say? You throw a big party and you get gatecrashers, even out here.' He held up his hands helplessly.

'You might have mentioned your front lawn being ploughed

up,' Waters said, a hint of annoyance in his voice. 'Hired a combine harvester for landscaping?'

'I forgot.'

'How can you forget *that*?'

'Quite easily, when one has other, more significant, problems to deal with . . . come this way.'

He led them both round to the swimming pool site.

'Wow!' Detective Clarke exclaimed, perking up. 'Why throw a party then?'

'It wasn't supposed to be an open-air bash; having lived in town all one's life one doesn't think of parties as taking place *outside*. It wasn't a . . . what's it called?' He wafted a hand about. 'Popular with Antipodeans?'

'Barbecue.'

'Yes, not one of those; frightfully common. Just a few tasty canapés, pineapple and cheese on sticks, you know. Bit more refined. But what with the weather, the windows open and that, people spilled outside . . .'

'What, here?' Clarke asked sceptically.

'Heavens no, common sense prevailed – you're likely to get impaled wandering around here in the dark.' Holland indicated the metal rods poking up from the earth. 'No, the front garden.'

'The police were called,' the sergeant said to his colleague, 'too much noise. So, what happened out in your front garden? Todd thought there were motorbikes?'

'Well, if you simply must know' – Holland crossed his arms defensively – 'I peaked too soon on the mojitos.'

'Beg your pardon?' Clarke asked.

'Cocktails,' Waters said. 'How badly?'

'I believe I passed out about nine-ish.'

'A nuisance, at your own party and all,' Waters commiserated.

Holland thought he might start to like this fellow, friendly and with a sense of humour. If only he weren't so spiky. 'I'll say – the place was drunk dry by the time I surfaced the next day. So, I'm afraid I'm pretty useless on what went on after dark. But nothing was stolen that night, I'm pretty sure. Why the interest in motorcycles?'

'We're thinking that local lads who'd been refused entry to your party may have decided to pay your place a visit again at a later date.

'Possibly after you left on Monday, and they came across your money by chance or, more likely, saw you drop it in the mixer.'

'Very good!' Holland was impressed. If only he could remember more about the party.

'There's been a spate of' – the woman looked to her colleague fleetingly – 'incidents involving a motorcyclist. So it would be good to rule out first anyone you might know who owns a motorbike.'

'Oh, I don't know anybody like that, and I can't even drive myself.'

'Going back to possible intruders. Be useful to hear what your guests recollect. Maybe we could ask some of your friends, see if they remember anything?' Waters asked.

'Hmm.' Holland tapped his forearm thoughtfully; which names could he give? All the lot from the office were out of the question; he could not have them knowing of this, Emma would laugh herself silly. . . Nigel? Or Matthew and Bruce? But were they reliable? He was pretty sure they had been out of it on fairy dust or whatever it was they were tooting. 'Let me think, eh? I'm sorry to be so damn useless.'

'So you called again? What did you want?'

'To know whether you'd caught the thief and found my money, of course.'

'Would you mind if we took a quick look around the house, sir?' Waters asked.

The house was spacious and light, Clarke would love to have

a place like this. Plenty of boxes remained unpacked but furniture was in place to give the house a habitable feel, the carpets were a soft ambient grey and the walls a soft honey sheen. She was unclear why Waters wanted to inspect the house other than to impress upon Holland that they were doing something. Clarke allowed her mind to wander. She pushed all thoughts of the Hammond sisters aside and tried to imagine little Philip having all this room to run around in, not to mention the garden. Fat chance on her measly pay packet – her outgoings on the flat alone were only just manageable, and now with all the extra she had to allow for nappies and baby food . . . They had to get out of that cramped flat. But how? She needed a man, preferably one with money. She stopped by the first-floor window and gazed out at the rolling countryside spreading away as far as the eye could see. What hope did she have of finding a bloke, as a single mum? Nil. One reason she'd been so eager to get back to work was to be part of the world again; but so far all the job had done was remind her of how unpleasant most of it was. And to highlight how far out of reach the nicer things truly were for most people, herself included.

Back down in the kitchen, Holland appeared with a plate.

'Cocktail sausage, anyone? Cheese and pineapple?'

Clarke was famished but hesitant.

'Don't worry, they've been kept in the fridge. Go on. I can't eat them all.'

Clarke took a wooden toothpick. Wait a second, she thought; the pathologist's report Frost had given her to read mentioned a sliver of wood found in Rachel Curtis's foot.

'May I have another?'

'Be my guest.'

'Guess it got pretty raucous? Did it take long to clean the place up in the morning?'

Holland raised his eyes to the heavens. He had long lashes and soft doe eyes.

'A veritable bombsite.'

'The floor?'

'Eugh! Literally, littered with all manner of detritus.'

Clarke pricked the tip of the toothpick against the palm of her hand; one of these could easily pierce the skin, if caught at the right angle.

'Well, thank you very much, you've been very helpful.'

'He's a funny one, all right,' Clarke said as they left the property. Holland stood on the front doorstep waving, as though seeing off relatives. 'How does he think crimes get solved? Clueless is spot on.'

'Ah, he's OK, just out of his depth in Denton.'

'And that can happen to the best of them, eh?' She smiled across the roof of the Vauxhall.

'Damn right.'

'What next?'

'Back to base.' Her colleague gazed out of the open window at the property opposite – a mock-Tudor detached, set back behind an immaculate lawn on which a sprinkler waved leisurely. 'What do you have to do to own one of these places?'

'Design trousers like our friend back there? I don't know . . . not police work, anyway.'

'What's that?'

'It's a toothpick for the lab. Rachel Curtis had a wooden splinter in her foot. Strikes me that this fits the description.'

'Wow, smart thinking – back on form, Detective Clarke.' Waters gave a whistle

PC David Simms was fast becoming resigned to the fact that he was now Frost's driver. Either by random allocation or, as he hoped, because the detective actively wanted him. The inspector sat beside him now chortling at the photographs, occasionally flashing one into Simms's field of vision. But pictures of topless girls by a pool did nothing to lift his mood. It wasn't just his mum who had been unsettled at the home; the staff were off with him, too. He felt as though he'd been deceitful or something equally stupid. He wasn't intentionally hiding from them that he was a policeman, for goodness' sake – it's just that he only came in on his days off. Why should it matter, or why should they know how he earned his living? It was of no consequence. He'd take it up with them tomorrow; he was off on Thursday . . .

On top of that, it transpired his drama with Martin Wakely yesterday had been pointless – according to Frost, the assailant on the motorcycle was a woman. Wakely was just a waste of time. Simms was sullen. He was much better suited to tinkering with the station database. And the young PC was very dubious about their next port of call.

He broke the silence: 'So . . . if we think we know who the woman is, why don't we just arrest her?'

'Good question. The suspect is, let's say, fractious – or excitable – and could react badly. We need to be a hundred per cent sure . . . so a word with Harry first might be useful.'

'You seem to have that effect, beg pardon, sir, if you don't mind me saying, on ladies this week.' Simms blushed as he said it.

'Hazard of the job. And this one is no Karen Thomas.' Simms took his eyes off the road and shot the inspector a glance. 'Though her flabby son does work for Harry Baskin, as did Karen until recently, but that's as close as they get. Right, here we are. Nearly eleven, the old porker should have opened up shop by now.'

Simms had never been to the Coconut Grove nightclub but had heard many a tale from the lads about crazy times in the strippers' bar. Simms followed behind the inspector. The place didn't look like much from the outside. The club was shut during the day, but Baskin worked at his office inside in the mornings. The front door was open. A large thickset man was talking to a girl a fraction of his size in the club foyer. The girl was wearing a scanty sequinned dress and nodding obsequiously.

'Ah Jack, can't keep away, can ya!' he growled.

The girl took this as her cue. Darting Simms a glance, she hurried away underneath an illuminated neon pink *BAR* sign into the dark club interior.

'Which of my girls are you going to ask me to fire now, eh?'

'I'm not after the girls, Harry.' So this was the legendary Harry Baskin. A squat, hairy hulk of a man, who wouldn't look out of place minding Don Corleone. 'Good job, too. After the slapping you got yesterday!' he guffawed. 'Come down to the office.' The man waddled round the corner of the ticket booth and down a dimly lit corridor. 'Didn't I say she was a spunky one?'

'I can't remember, you might have said something along those lines.' Frost rolled his eyes, and nodded for Simms to follow.

'After you, lads.' Baskin pushed the door open. The office was small and cluttered; golf clubs, boxes of spirits, and as Simms noticed as he stepped further, the pungent body odour of a man who drank and smoked a lot. 'Sit down.'

'We won't, if it's all the same.'

'Suit yourself.' Harry lowered himself carefully into a leather chair; Simms recalled he had a bullet wound from an attack last November. 'All formal in front of young spotty here.'

Simms felt himself blush. His skin was bad for a man of nearly twenty-one but he did his best to leave the thought of it behind in the mirror of his Fenwick Street bathroom when he departed for his shift.

'Young spotty, as you call him, has the makings of a great policeman, so I'd be careful how you address him – he might hold it against you down the line, when you're even older and less mobile than you are now. Now, your Gary Benson, tell me his story.' Frost winked at Simms, who was touched by the remark and started to feel better about things.

'Gazzer? What's he done?'

'Who's saying he's done anything? How long has he been on your payroll?'

Baskin sniffed. 'Two, three years.'

'Any bother?'

'Bother? He's the bleedin' doorman – it's his job to *prevent* any bother.'

'When his old man had a heart attack after being shot by Rachel – another of your employees – how did he react?'

The club owner reached up for a crystal decanter from a shelf behind him. All lightheartedness evaporated as he began to pour. 'Gaz is a muscle man, he's not going to go to pieces when his old man goes, is he? C'mon, Jack, you seen him – hardly likely to be blubbing in the bogs, is 'e?' he said coldly.

'So, no visible signs of distress? The old boy didn't even come up in passing conversation?'

'Eh? Do me a favour with the colourful talk. Look, I sat the lad down and give him the best advice I could – we all got to go some time. Old man Benson was as strong as an ox; a shot from her peashooter weren't enough to kill him. I mean, take me – I'm the same age Bert was – I took a plug at the same range, eh? Right here in this bleedin' office.' He beat his chest, but lightly. 'The fella had a dodgy ticker.'

'How did Gary take your warm words of consolation?'

'He understood.' Baskin took a gulp of brandy. 'And he held nothing against Rachel.'

'That's very understanding of him. Why not?'

Baskin shrugged. 'Maybe he listened to what I said, young fella of twenty-three might credit me with a bit upstairs' – he tapped the side of his head, a heavy gold ring glinting as he did so – 'just cos you don't.' He grinned. 'Ask him, he's a nice enough bloke, just back from a week in Spain. Nah, it was his old dear who took it hardest. Sent her loopy.'

'Loopy?' Simms said, annoyed that his voice sounded croaky from not speaking.

'Yeah. Swore she was goin' to kill Rach. Poor Gazzer didn't know what to do. Told him to take her to my place in Marbella.'

'Did he?'

'No.'

'He should. Mind you, I'd not want my mother there, with all that totty about.' Frost smiled lasciviously.

Baskin frowned, not comprehending.

'Have you ever met Mrs Benson yourself?'

'Once, when she came screaming down here on that bike of hers.'

'Bike?'

'Yeah, great big thing it was. When Rach was first arrested last year. I met her at the front door. Raging away, blaming me. Not nice. Not nice at all.'

'And?'

'Told her to clear off. Scaring the punters.'

'Did Rachel come back after she was released?'

'I already told you on Sunday night, she came looking for Kate. Bleedin' shame. Someone shoulda looked out for her, got her away from that scumbag Robbo Nicholson.'

'All right, all right. Tell me, Harry, in your opinion, would Maria Benson have it in her to kill?'

He paused. 'I wouldn't put it past her.'

Wednesday (4) _____

'Clear off!' The door slammed in their faces.

'That went better than expected,' Frost said to his young companion, pulling down the brow of his panama hat and stepping back into the sun.

'How?' Simms muttered quietly.

But Frost had wandered off back down the path and started examining the motorbike on the concrete drive. This machine wasn't anything like the vehicle he'd seen shooting away from Sandpiper Close, but he had her son's photos now. So that *had* been her arguing with Rachel outside Boots. Maybe she had two bikes?

The front window opened. 'Oi, get away from that!' Mrs Benson screeched.

'New, is it?'

The door was flung open again, and the woman, a vein throbbing angrily in her neck, rushed at him. 'This is harassment!'

'I have a witness who saw you arguing with Rachel Curtis Saturday afternoon.'

'Go on then, arrest me!' she spat.

It was tempting. He could, for lying. 'If you're innocent, why not admit it? You stopped on your motorcycle on Market Square.'

'I don't care whether you catch the person who killed that bitch or not. I'm glad she's dead.'

Frost was unsure of his next move. He looked at the young policeman next to him.

The press would have a field day if he was wrong; it was a punt. But he did have a witness, and Harry had reckoned she had it in her. Sod it. He'd have to bring her in. 'Call for back-up, son.'

At one o'clock, in the blazing heat, Maria Benson was forcibly taken from her house. The arrest had been an unpleasant affair; the widow's protestations had brought the whole street out to watch. She went defiantly, foul-mouthing Frost before mums with babies on hips. Ironically, it was only the return of her son Gary that had calmed proceedings. Not that Gary, himself on a motorbike, thought his mother was guilty – far from it. But he knew it was futile to resist arrest. As they bundled the mother into the back of the panda car, cuffed, the bouncer son said solemnly, 'I just want this over with quickly, the sooner you try and charge Mum the sooner you'll realize she's innocent.'

And maybe that would be so, but for now the woman, presently at Eagle Lane, refused to speak until her solicitor arrived.

'I hope she is innocent, I don't want to inflict any more pain on your family, Gary,' Frost said as Benson left his next-of-kin details at the front desk, 'but she needs to cooperate.'

The larger man's temples throbbed as he hurriedly squiggled out the family address.

'You don't know what it's been like for her, Mr Frost. Her and Dad were together since they were kids. Dad was her world. It's not the same place to her any more.' He paused, then said, 'Have you ever lost someone special?'

Frost reached and patted Gary Benson on the shoulder supportively but did not answer. Benson ignored the gesture, slid the paperwork and pen wordlessly back to Desk Sergeant Bill Wells and walked towards the front doors.

'Be in touch, Gary,' Frost called after him.

'Don't feel bad, Jack. She's not helping herself,' Wells said from behind the desk.

'I know, Bill, I know.' Frost felt momentarily adrift. He scanned the empty reception area. 'Water that before it expires, will you?' He pointed to the sorrowful rubber plant in the corner, Eagle Lane's one remaining concession to the natural world, before moving in the direction of the canteen.

The station itself was quiet; he knew Clarke and Waters were out, but there was nobody else around either. It was lunchtime. Many would be outside enjoying the last days of summer, if indeed they'd not taken holiday. His stomach nagged. He'd not had anything to eat since last night's Chinese. Billy had left a double portion of Kung Po on the side. He and Julie had tucked in by candlelight. They'd had a good time; whether it was to be more than 'a bit of comfort', as she put it, remained to be seen. All the same it had given him an appetite. He sorely missed breakfast at Sue's; her fried bread was to die for. Since moving to the Jade Rabbit, he'd not managed so much as a bowl of Kellogg's in the mornings. It didn't feel right to start messing around in someone else's kitchen; he didn't mind borrowing the odd lager, but dipping into Mrs Fong's Alpen felt as wrong as it was unappealing, especially when he had a guest.

Fortunately the station canteen was, he discovered, deserted, and he picked up a sausage sandwich at a reduced price before heading to the general CID office.

He had just settled down at Clarke's desk, out of habit, with the Curtis autopsy report, when the phone sounded, alarmingly loud in the empty office. The surprise caused him to squirt brown sauce all over the desk.

'Knickers!' he cried into the receiver.

'I knew you were a pervert from the moment I saw you,' said a female voice down the line.

Frost saw the woman sitting on a bench in the shade of the poplar trees. The recreation area, or 'Rec' as it was known, was the largest area of public green space in the town. The grass was teeming with children screaming out the last week of the summer holidays. Dogs, frisbees and footballs added to the scene.

'Thanks for agreeing to meet me,' he puffed as he sat down.

'I don't have a lot else on at the moment,' Karen Thomas said without turning to face him.

He removed his panama hat and fanned his face. 'No, quite,' he conceded. 'I'm sorry you're out of work.'

'So you said.'

Now he was actually here, Frost could think of little to say. He'd agreed to meet without hesitation, eager to see her again, but hadn't thought through any conversation. Mullett had been so furious with him yesterday and not in the mood to offer any reasonable explanation as to why he wanted Karen Thomas fired from her job. This indicated to Frost that the super had acted in haste, without considering the implications of the order.

'Someone wanted you out of there, can't you see that?' He regarded her profile, elegant and noble.

'What were you doing yesterday?'

'I beg your pardon?'

'I meant in front of the TV cameras.' She turned to face him. 'Was it important?'

The question was unexpected. 'Yes. Yes, it was important. A woman had gone missing, but we found her now.'

'Oh, is she all right?' Her eyes were intense. He couldn't hold her stare.

'No.' He turned away. 'She's dead. We found her in a neighbour's bath.'

'Oh, I'm sorry.' Karen bowed her head. 'I'm sorry to have interrupted your broadcast. I was angry. Jobs aren't that easy to come by. But it's fine.'

A frisbee landed on the ground to their right. A boy roughly the age of Jane Hammond's son scampered over to pick it up. Frost became acutely aware he was here for the wrong reasons and didn't have time for this: he should be doing everything he could to find the killer.

'I mean, how would you feel if someone took your job away just like that?'

'It's a daily worry, I assure you.'

'You're laughing at me.'

'No.'

'Can't you tell me anything?' He could hear the desperation in her voice. 'Yesterday you said . . .' She trailed off.

Frost watched the little boy with the frisbee. He struggled inwardly: he didn't want this woman to leave, but couldn't think of any reason to detain her. He felt his bleeper go off in his pocket, and this time he was grateful for the excuse it offered him.

'Look, someone wanted you out of the Grove. Maybe for your own safety?'

She turned sharply. 'Wait, you think I'm a hooker, don't you? How dare—' She made to go.

'No – wait – of course I don't!' He reached up and caught her wrist. 'But maybe somebody else does.'

'How do you mean?'

'For your own good, worried about you.'

Karen Thomas stood, sizing him up.

'There is no cause for concern there. Working at Harry's is insurance against that sort of thing.'

'I know,' Frost conceded, 'maybe a jealous boyfriend?'

'Pah. Jealousy is for children,' she said flatly. 'I thought I saw something in you back there, in the police station. Here is a good man . . .'

'I'd like to help, honestly, if I could.'

'What would you do, seriously, if someone took your job?'

'I dunno.' He stretched his legs out in front of him. He'd never thought about getting fired as a real possibility. True, there'd been plenty of close shaves, but what if Mullett really *did* get shot of him? He couldn't do anything else half as well as policing, except for drinking and smoking.

'You're good at your job,' he said, 'and I'm good at mine. But if someone had it in for me and caused me to lose my job – well, I'd get my own back.'

'How?'

He was aware she was watching him intently. 'Hit them where it hurt.'

'Where it hurt,' she repeated quietly.

He had to go, this train of thought was doing nobody any good. He fished his card out on reflex.

'I already have it,' Karen Thomas said. 'I phoned you, remember?'

He turned and met her stare. 'Maybe I want you to phone me again.'

'There were bikers present at Holland's party in Two Bridges on Saturday night,' Clarke said.

'So?' Frost said, gulping down a Coke greedily. 'There's motorbikes flamin' everywhere. I'd be suspicious if there wasn't.'

'You've lost your chirpiness,' she said acerbically. 'I think I prefer the grumpy you, actually.'

'Really?' He belched mightily and picked up his cigarette packet.

'God, you *are* disgusting.' He was really annoying her, and she couldn't put her finger on why.

Waters pretended not to hear, which made her suddenly embarrassed.

'But so what?' Frost waved a cigarette in front of them carelessly. 'Correct me if I'm wrong, but didn't the money go missing on Tuesday? Who cares what Mister Tight Trousers got up to the previous Saturday night?'

'Sue's right,' said Waters, 'you have lost that cuddliness. We thought it might have been gatecrashers that came back a couple of days later when the place was a bit quieter?'

'Not one of those posh twerps he invited? Laying the blame on the locals, are we, like Hornrim Harry? Tch, tch.' Frost shook his head. 'What a disappointment.'

'It's just a theory, Jack,' Waters said quietly.

'We have two young women, both dead, and one little boy who's now an orphan, forgive me if I don't weep over Mr Holland's two grand.'

'There were bike tracks on the front lawn; I thought you might be interested, given the episode at Curtis's place – the bloke leaping out of her window might have been the thief at Holland's. You know Martin Wakely has sticky fingers and a tendency to turn up at various places uninvited?'

'I see what you mean, but I don't have Wakely for the Curtis place. We have Maria Benson downstairs for questioning over that . . .' He exhaled. 'But be my guest over posh boy's money and get Wakely back in if you can. But I'd rather there was a tad more focus on the more serious crimes.'

'But Jack, Mullett said—' Waters touched Frost's arm lightly as the super himself hove into view.

'I don't give a monkey's what Hornrim Harry says, as you well know, Johnny boy. You are growing more like him every day. Maybe it's your impending marriage? Stiffening you up, eh?' He raised his eyebrows in wonder.

'Ah, Jack, a word if I may.'

'Sir? I was wondering when we might next have the pleasure.'

Clarke watched Frost troop off behind the super. She cursed under her breath; she was angry with herself for being so short-fused. Maybe leaving little Philip at home was nagging at her more than she realized. There was no need to be so sharp with Frost, especially as she'd just dislodged him from her settee; maybe that had upset him.

She felt Waters' hand on her shoulder. 'It's not your fault – he's not himself.'

'I do feel I'm not helping.'

'It's just the job. Much as he loves it, it can be unrelenting at times.'

'Hmm, maybe,' she replied, unconvinced.

'Why didn't you mention the cocktail-stick theory?'

'He had me riled by dismissing the motorbike – you know Rachel Curtis was seen at the Codpiece at the same time a load of bikers were there? – besides, I want to wait until I hear back from the lab, they'll confirm if the material is the same. They'll let me know in two hours.'

'Well, in the meantime, let's check out Holland's neighbour, the one that called the police on the night of the party. Front desk will have logged it.'

'Sure.' Clarke spied Rachel Curtis's autopsy report on her desk – she picked it up, revealing a dark brown smear underneath. 'Jesus. That man.'

'I apologize for firing off like that at you yesterday.'

Frost slowly pushed the super's office door to, an apology from his boss instantly triggering suspicion. He dismissed the comment, and sat down. 'Think nothing of it, sir.'

'No, you were put on the spot, a woman like that coming at you, unsettling, to say the least. Any news on that front?'

'I've not been to see Harry if that's what you mean' – it was only a white lie after all, given he was there on the Curtis case – 'what with Jane Hammond found dead.'

'Yes, I hope there was nothing inappropriate going on there.'

'Apart from her being stabbed in the neck with a knitting needle, fully shaved and left to fizz in a bath of meths?'

'You know very well what I mean: procedure – if you've not followed the correct procedure we'll come unstuck when it comes to the prosecution.'

Frost knew it was unlawful entry but chose to ignore the fact and simply said, 'We'll have to find him first.'

'Quite, one imagines he must have figured out you're on to him. What are we doing?'

'All ports and airports alerted. We know from the neighbours that he drives a maroon '79 Volvo 240. The last person to have contact with Weaver was a stroke patient at High Fields, the care home. We questioned him, but the poor fellow's mind is a jumble and his speech is shot after a recent seizure; we can't get a useful word out of him.'

'And the Rachel Curtis case, did the television appeal yield anything, in spite of the incident? And what of Wakely?'

'Nothing as yet. But Wakely's innocent.'

'Wakely, innocent? You saw him jump out of the window at Rachel Curtis's house and make his escape on a motorbike.'

'I think I might have misread the number plate . . .' Frost admitted.

'Oh?'

'And Wakely didn't have a helmet or jacket when Simms pulled him outside the pub.'

'Maybe he tossed them away to mislead you?'

'Unlikely; that would involve quick thinking and thinking – fast or slow – is not one of Martin's strong suits. Not to mention that he was fast asleep when I went to see him last night. Not the behaviour of a guilty man. No, I'm afraid it's not him.'

'That is disappointing.'

Frost nodded in agreement.

'Well, get your eyes tested, man.'

Frost was about to leave but thought he should mention Mrs Benson before the super found out via other means. 'Maria Benson is in for a chat. She was seen arguing with Rachel Curtis on Market Square last Saturday.' He didn't think it necessary to say he had arrested her, and was equally loath to mention the new witness's name – he'd have to tell folk about his relationship with Julie eventually, but if he could squeeze something out of Maria Benson first, it might be avoided . . .

'Tread carefully, Frost. I needn't tell you the press would have a field day there . . . And let me know if Karen Thomas shows again.'

Although vexed by the Rachel Curtis case, Frost was more upset by Jane Hammond's fate, but had not let on. Outwardly he maintained his carefree flippant manner; this was his armour, and for the benefit of appearances and morale. He'd been witness to countless deaths over the years, many brutal; no, it was not the loss of life that disturbed him as much as those left behind. In particular young children, those whose lives from that day forth were changed for ever, cast out in the world without a guardian.

Frost had quietly slipped over to Rimmington to see Clare Hammond, who was back at home after identifying her sister's body. Frost sat in the window alcove with her nephew Richard opposite him; his aunt stood behind the high-backed settee close to a WPC.

'Now, Richard,' Frost said softly, leaning forward, so near his knees almost touched the boy's bare legs on the edge of the settee, 'I want you to be brave and listen very carefully.'

The boy, his head down, nodded. Another tear dripped from the end of his nose.

'See, I'm all on my own too. And though I'm much older it gets very lonely. And I can tell you a very big secret.' His voice dropped lower. 'I always wanted a son, but sadly my wife passed away before we got there. So if you wanted to be friends, that would make me very happy. We could help each other. What do you think?'

The boy nodded again.

'Hold out your hand.' The boy unclenched his hands clasped in his lap, and held out his right timidly. Frost placed a black oblong in his palm. Richard's head moved up slightly. 'Now, squeezing this box sends a signal to me. It's called a bleeper. I have the other one, see?' He showed him the matchbox-size responder. 'Any time you want me you just press this and I'll be right here for you.'

'How,' Richard sniffed, 'how will you know it's me?'

Frost pulled the chair forward and said in a whisper, 'Because it's the very latest technology, they've only got one of those. That was my boss's, but I don't think he'll miss it.'

The boy turned the bleeper over in his hand. Frost sat back and forced a smile towards the women, but Clare Hammond had turned her back, sobbing quietly into the WPC's shoulder.

Wednesday (5)

Reg Stirling was asleep on a sun lounger in the afternoon heat, strands of a sparse comb-over plastered across his forehead. The large garden was carefully landscaped. A stone cupid energetically spouted a fountain of water from his penis into an ornate pool at the far end of the recently paved patio. Waters was familiar with Reg Stirling's success story from the *Gazette*: he was one of Thatcher's self-made men and one of the many that had brought the Iron Lady back with a landslide for a second term that May. Stirling Equipment Hire had bucked the trend at the start of the decade and now, in the summer of '83, the firm was flourishing as brightly as the owner's garden peonies.

Waters and Clarke walked across the lawn towards the entrepreneur, casting a shadow that caused him to stir, prop himself up and raise his hand to his eyes to see who was disturbing his precious moment of peace.

'You have got to be the police, right? Only coppers would have the nerve to affront me unannounced in me own back garden, lying here without me strides on.'

'Your wife let us in, Mr Stirling.'

He propped himself up. 'Can a man get no rest, eh?'

'We won't be long, sir. Just a couple of questions about your complaint on Saturday night.'

'Harrumph.' The man rose from the lounger and reached for a shirt. 'An Englishman's home is his castle.'

He slipped his feet into flip-flops and moved under the shade of an umbrella. He poured a drink from a jug containing soggy pieces of fruit drowning in an unknown concoction. 'A man should be able to enjoy a bit of 'oliday in his own bloody castle, especially when it is such a beautiful castle as this, know what I mean?' He gestured with the jug towards the large ornate rockery with running water.

'Absolutely,' Waters confirmed.

'I mean that's why I live out here, and not in the middle of town – that's why I've not joined the bloody stampede down to Marbella. All I want is a bit of relaxation, a bit of P and bloody Q.'

'Nobody's disputing your complaint, Mr Stirling,' Clarke interrupted, 'we only wish to clarify a few things.'

'Oh, I see.' The man relaxed, and now assuming they were on his side, offered the jug to them. They declined, anticipating a nasty cocktail mix. 'Glad to help.'

'Do you know Mr Holland, sir?' Clarke asked.

'Nah, not really, exchanged a few words when he moved in, like, but he's not my sort of man, know what I mean?'

'So you weren't invited to the party?'

'He didn't invite us in so many words, but let us know it was 'appening and said to pop in if we fancied it.'

'Weren't you curious?' Clarke asked. 'All that London glamour?'

'Nah, bunch of fannies.'

Waters let out a small laugh.

'Besides, the ol' lady's got a bad back; that was the reason I called your mob. She has an 'ard enough time getting some kip as it is, without all those hoorays partyin' like a bunch of kids . . .'

'Fair enough. Now, I see Mr Holland's place is indeed opposite, but not quite directly. The properties are set well apart – three hundred yards or more, would you say?'

'Exactly so. They'd seriously cranked up the volume, you know what I mean?'

'Was it like that all night? It started at six, I believe.'

'I didn't notice until later, the sound don't carry round here. It weren't a problem till I went to bed. Our room is at the front of the house. I became aware of the din around midnight.'

'So you became aware of the noise at midnight and called the police at twelve fifteen,' Clarke suggested. 'And what time did you go to bed?'

'Eleven. No, wait, I think it was half past. After *Kojak*.'

'But you weren't disturbed until midnight.'

'I saw it on the clock, on the button, twelve o'clock.'

'It was a hot night. Did you have the windows open?'

'It was a hot night, right.'

'Right. So would it be fair to say it was unlikely the party moved outside to the front lawn before midnight, yes?'

'Yeah.'

'And would you also think it fair to assume that something must have triggered this?'

Stirling pulled a garden chair out from under the umbrella and sat down. 'I guess so.'

'Mr Stirling, it's very important, try and think back – was there anything that could have been a catalyst for the disturbance?'

The man ran his fingers through his thin damp hair. 'A motorbike. Yeah, a bike revving, someone was thrashing a bike.'

'Are you sure it was just one?'

'I didn't get up to count, but yeah, I reckon it was just the one.'

'Good. One more thing, Mr Stirling. You were in Bennington's Bank on Monday morning, right?' Waters did not have Stirling as the type for lifting a couple of grand out of a cement mixer, but he might have seen something . . .

'What of it?' He leaned closer, away from the parasol.

'Did you happen to see Dominic Holland in there?'

'Nah.' He shook his head.

'Tell me, did you know Holland is having some building work done?'

'Swimming pool. Terry Todd is putting it in.'

'How do you know that?'

'Fella asked me if I knew anyone that could put in a pool when he moved in, I recommended Todd.'

'That's very decent of you,' Clarke said.

Stirling shrugged. 'Not really. I hire out equipment for a living, don't I. Terry needs a digger for a job like that.'

Superintendent Mullett had got wind of the Benson arrest. 'A chat', as Frost had painted it, was an understatement. Releasing Martin Wakely and pulling in the dead warehouse worker's widow was a careless move, even for Frost. The press were all over it already, tipped off by the woman's solicitor.

Frost assured him he had a witness. Someone had spotted Maria Benson arguing with Curtis on Market Square.

'Who is this witness?' Mullett had cornered Frost on his way to interrogate the widow.

Frost looked at the floor. 'A woman.'

'Yes, but who, and why has she only now come forward? Did she see the television appeal? A poster?'

Frost fidgeted uneasily.

Very unusual, Mullett thought. Why did he look so shifty? 'Frost? *Who* is she?'

'A lady friend of mine.'

'I see.' Now it was Mullett who didn't know where to look.

Personal relationships of this nature were out of his comfort zone; the thought that Frost might have elicited this new information during some idle pillow talk was extremely unpleasant. 'Well. I hope you've got more than that to go on. This could be highly embarrassing.'

'I'm working on it.'

'How old is Mrs Benson?'

'Late forties.'

'And do you suspect her for the murder? It's a bit obvious, isn't it? She was very public in her hatred for Rachel Curtis, but just because Mrs Benson was seen arguing with the woman doesn't mean she'd kill her.'

'But she has denied that the argument took place – which is suspicious.'

'Is she up to jumping out of first-floor windows then?'

'I think it's well within her capabilities – she's quite slender and very lively.'

'Have you found the motorcycle?'

'No. I'm working on the theory she ditched it after I gave chase.'

Mullett was not convinced. 'Well, let's hope something concrete turns up, eh? From where I'm sitting you appear to be randomly pulling in anyone who rides a motorcycle. First Martin Wakely, now Bert Benson's widow. Evidence, Frost, evidence.'

Maria Benson sat stern and hard-faced in the interview room. Her solicitor, a young chap, fidgeted at her side, looking considerably less composed than his client. He was sweating and red in the face. Admittedly it was a hot airless room but the man was more than mildly uncomfortable. Benson's obstinacy clearly baffled him; he obviously didn't think silence was the most effective tactic. If she was innocent, why not speak up? For ten minutes they'd sat there, neither side uttering a word.

'You ought to loosen your tie,' Frost offered in a friendly tone of voice.

The solicitor, Smythe was his name, touched his tie self-consciously. Maria Benson glanced over at him – the first time she had acknowledged him.

'I'm fine, thank you. Though a glass of water would be jolly nice.'

Frost swung round on his chair and directed a WPC to fetch him a glass.

'See, the thing is, when I asked you the first time on Monday whether you'd seen Rachel, you said no. I then discover you did run into her, on your way into Boots to drop off Gary's holiday snaps. And you had a very public barney. Not the sort of thing you'd forget. Now, what am I to think?'

Smythe focused on her. She must have felt the intensity of his stare. She jolted forward and said, 'All right, I did see her, what of it? Charge me then and have done with it—'

Smythe leaned across and whispered in her ear.

'I got an alibi.'

'Thank heavens for that.' Frost made a show of pulling out his notebook. The solicitor gave a faint smile. Frost guessed the solicitor had told her that a lack of cooperation on her part might be disadvantageous to her, even if she was proved to be innocent.

'I was in the pub Saturday night.'

'Which one?'

The WPC handed Smythe a glass of water.

'The Cricketers.'

'Chucking out time is eleven. Did you go straight home?' Drysdale had estimated Rachel's time of death at no later than midnight in his final pathologist's report.

Smythe tapped her hand. This time she bent towards him. Her brows knitted.

Eventually, sitting back and releasing a sigh, she said,

'I don't want anyone else getting in trouble here. All right?'

Frost played dumb, and pushed his bottom lip out.

'It was a lock-in. Don't go hassling Taff.' Taff was the Cricketers' surly Welsh landlord.

'That's fine,' he said jovially, 'I know Taff, I'm sure he'll vouch for you.'

'My son was just back from Spain,' she added – unnecessarily, he thought.

'Yes, had fun out there too, apparently. Which reminds me.' He slid the packet of photographs across the desk. Maria Benson looked bemused for a moment. 'We'll leave it there for now. Gives us something to follow up.' He smiled. 'But before I go, tell me about your motorbike.'

She frowned again. 'What do you want to know?'

'How long have you had it?'

'Is this relevant?' Smythe interjected.

'Yes, very. So, you're the happy owner of a bike with the number plate KAT 93N?'

'Well, I was. But it got nicked, didn't it?'

'*Eh?*'

'June twenty-fourth – check your records, if you don't believe me.'

'So what were you riding on Saturday afternoon then?'

'I had one for the day to try out.' The woman had an answer for everything. 'Ask the garage if you don't believe me. I went back and paid for it on Monday.'

Wednesday (6)

'Coincidence?' PC Simms asked.

'It would look that way, wouldn't it?' Frost said. 'Having the flamin' machine nicked in June, but not buying a new one until late August?'

Maria Benson claimed to have acquired a new motorcycle only on Monday morning, despite the theft of her previous one back in June. Frost wanted proof. Not of the new bike, no, that they had, but evidence that the other one had been stolen in the first place. She could still have done it, used the old bike and ditched it following the pursuit across Denton. There was an insurance claim outstanding, but there appeared to be a problem. In order for her claim to be validated, the theft would need to have been reported, and she would need the relevant incident number. And the insurance company had yet to obtain confirmation from the police records department that the crime had, indeed, been processed.

All of which confusion meant that now, on this stifling hot afternoon, Simms was hunched in front of the computer terminal in Frost's claustrophobic office, searching for this same confirmation. The inspector was hovering uneasily behind him, making it difficult to concentrate. A cloud of cigarette smoke washed across the screen, rendering the flickering green digits even harder to read than usual.

'Flamin' heck, there can't be that many motorcycles get nicked in Denton, can there?' Frost exclaimed.

'It's not as easy as that, I'm afraid,' Simms said.

'Nothing's ever bloody well *easy* since these bleedin' things arrived!' he exclaimed and banged the large grey box to emphasize his point. 'I mean, is it even in here? The theft was apparently in June – are you sure it's there? I thought all records up to June had been transferred.'

'Yes, right, everything from January to June has been input so there's just the one system in operation. So, yes, it should be on here.'

Finding it, however, was proving impossible. Frost groaned loudly. Simms understood the man's frustration; he needed proof her bike had been stolen – the insurance claim wasn't enough on its own. How embarrassing not to be able to find the incident report in their own files.

'Would you mind if we opened a window, sir?' There was a distinct tang in the room, and Simms wondered whether the inspector had access to washing facilities at the Asian restaurant where he was staying.

'The window's buggered. The only reason we're suffocating in here is that DC Clarke's not got one of these wonders of technology on her desk.'

'Where is it . . . damn, come on.' Simms hit the carriage-return button again, then over and over. The keyboard was sticky, resistant. He turned his attention from the flickering screen to his fingertips and suppressed a grimace. 'Do you use the machine often? It seems . . . seems reluctant to cooperate.'

'It's no bleedin' reason to,' Frost puffed, 'this is the first time the bastard has been on.'

Simms raised the keyboard to eye level. Various keys were afflicted with congealing substances – viscous, sticky matter mixed with breadcrumbs, coated with what he assumed to be cigarette ash; substances that were not conducive to the efficient operation of any computer.

'Err . . . would you have spilt coffee on the keyboard, by any chance?' He blew down the keys.

'What?' Frost snapped.

'It's slow going because the keystrokes are not always connecting with the CPU, so I am wondering if you might have knocked liquid over—'

'Oh, so it's my fault? Flamin' typical!'

'It's not waterproof,' Simms offered, pulling out his Swiss Army Knife from his trouser pocket.

'Is that my fault too?'

'Not at all, sir – you weren't to know.' Simms probed underneath the unyielding keys, repressing an exclamation of disgust.

'Quite right,' Frost said, 'forcing this technology on folks is just plain rude, without a by-your-leave.'

In his role as Technology Liaison Officer, Simms knew Inspector Frost had not attended a single computer training session. He tapped the return button repeatedly until it was freed up. 'There, no harm done.' A stream of green asterisks flew across the screen. 'Right, let's begin again.'

Frost pushed a pile of paperwork off the visitor's chair and scraped it across the floor. The pair sat down and laboriously went through the various routines to access the incident database.

After half an hour Frost stood up. 'This is bollocks!' he pronounced.

'The program runs its search on surname, and there is

no Benson. If it ran on incident number it would be—'

'I don't care if it runs on Castrol GTX, it's all bollocks.' He got up. 'What's more, I'm running low on lubrication myself and fancy a trip to see Taffy and quiz him on—'

'Am I interrupting anything important?' DC Clarke entered the room, eyes sparkling.

The cocktail stick from Dominic Holland's kitchen was the same grade of wood as the sliver extracted from Curtis's foot. Clarke was delighted with this evidence; it reassured her she was back in the game – her wits had not been dulled by the endless nights of broken sleep, feeding her infant son.

Now the police desperately needed someone who could confirm Rachel was there, at the party, and who she was with. Martin Wakely had been ruled out, but Maria Benson was under suspicion. Would this play out right? If Rachel Curtis *was* at Holland's party, did it mean Benson was there too? It seemed unlikely . . .

And then there was the mystery of how Rachel's body had ended up in St Mary's churchyard over in Denton – a matter Frost was keenly aware of. The evidence from Forensics and Drysdale supported the theory that the death had taken place elsewhere.

He had a map of the county open on the desk and was working out the possible routes from Holland's place in the village of Two Bridges to the Denton church.

'The only way Rachel Curtis would have got wind of the party would have been through gossip over in town,' Frost said, scratching his forehead.

'Do you really think Benson went too?' Clarke asked.

Waters slid off the desk. 'I can't imagine her tearing up his lawn on her motorbike, can you?' he said.

Frost was using a ruler on the map. 'The woman's practically insane with grief,' he countered.

'She'd have to be,' Clarke said uncertainly, 'to risk such a public display, then carry out a murder. I mean, she's an obvious suspect . . .' She'd not met the woman but it struck her as a bizarre hypothesis.

But Frost wasn't listening. 'What do you make of this neighbour, Stirling?' he said suddenly.

'Sound, and unconnected to this,' Waters answered quickly. 'Stirling knows the builder that's putting in Holland's pool, but I don't make him for stealing the guy's cash. I'd rule him out for now . . . he knew about the party but didn't go. His wife was sick.'

'We need someone who was actually there, and compos mentis enough to make any sense of it,' Frost mused, stepping back from the map. 'What did Holland supply by way of witnesses? Surely some of his London pals weren't completely blotto?'

'He gave us two names.' Clarke consulted her notebook. 'Bruce Reynolds and Matthew Noose.'

'Noose? What sort of name is that?'

'A Somerset one, apparently. They run a flower shop.'

'What, together? Are they, you know . . . ?'

'That's right, Jack, leap to conclusions,' Clarke said.

'It's my detective's brain. Can't help it. Get on down there, only a couple of hours' drive. Take Arthur Hanlon.'

'Me,' said Sue, 'why me?'

'You're forging the trail on this – scoop with the toothpick?' He winked playfully but this only annoyed her.

'Hanlon's in Sheffield,' she snapped.

'Someone's got to go. I agree, it's a bloody nuisance: a big party in the middle of Two Bridges; the host passes out and there's not a single local guest.' He looked to Waters. 'Run back up there first and see if Mr Holland has any recollection of Rachel, I mean if he was conscious until nine—'

'Sorry, Jack. I can't, I've got to split, pay for the cake.'

'Cake? Oh, err, yes, sorry, for the big day. Well, get your cake first?'

'What about Maria Benson?' Clarke asked. 'If we have her in custody, should we not be building the case against her?'

'Once we've looked into her alibi,' Frost mumbled. 'I need to check it.'

'Which is?'

'She claims to have been out Saturday night with her son who'd just got back from Spain.'

'Is it solid?'

'No alibi that can only be corroborated by family and mates is solid. We'll need to check it out. The Cricketers had a lock-in Saturday.'

'Taffy's straight?' Waters queried.

Frost grunted. 'Yes, but he's also a publican, and we all know that he'd rather not be asked – it's bad for community relations to be on the side of the Old Bill, and it's not in his interest to see anyone behind metal bars when they could be propping up a wooden one.'

'But we still need to check it,' Clarke insisted. 'Maybe they went on to Two Bridges after the pub? Holland said there weren't meant to be any locals at the party, but that doesn't mean the word didn't get out.'

'Smart thinking,' Frost said. 'Maybe Maria Benson knew Rachel was intending to crash the party and planned to lie in wait outside the house, but having too much to drink in the pub beforehand, she lost her cool, and tore over there . . .'

'What about the churchyard?' Waters asked. 'How'd she end up there? Why? That doesn't make sense.'

'No murder makes any sense,' Frost said, sparking up. 'We'll map out the possible routes from Two Bridges to Sandpiper Close as well.'

Frost had dispatched Clarke and Waters to Somerset, and

remained alone in CID with the map. How on earth had the victim's body ended up in the churchyard? The body had obviously been moved but there were too many loose threads and nothing pulling them together. But there was one person he'd not questioned yet – Kate Greenlaw's boyfriend, Adam King. With all the fuss surrounding the prostitute in the bath he'd forgotten to follow it up.

As it happened, King was a mechanic in the Eagle Lane garage right next to the station; it was where Frost's Metro currently resided. The DI left the office. A light breeze was blowing and he hoped the weather would hold for Waters' big day on Friday. He must work on his speech tonight. Can't let the man down. He approached the large open doors from the garage forecourt and was greeted by a pair of feet protruding from underneath a jacked-up orange car. He wondered briefly where the Metro might be.

Adam King slid out from underneath a Hillman Imp, got to his feet and wiped his hands on the thighs of his oil-stained boiler suit. Frost was surprised; the man was in his early forties, short, about five foot four or five, and quite slight. He had a beaky nose. Not the sort of chap he'd expect to be courting a feisty woman like Kate Greenlaw.

'You here about Rachel? Kate said you might come by. How can I help?' Polite too, that made a change.

'We're looking for anyone that might have seen Rachel Curtis on Saturday.'

'Other than Kate?'

'Specifically anyone male. Kate mentioned that Rachel had men swarming all over her, and she was available, as it were, once she was released; thing is, we haven't a single name.'

'Not me, if that's what you're implying.'

'No, no, I'm not suggesting that, I only want help putting together a picture of what she was like as a person, so I can know where to look. Kate said you'd known her ages.'

'Yep, I introduced them.'

'How long?'

'Years. From school.'

'Ah, the formative years. She was quite a looker. Did you and her . . . ?'

'Nah.' He shook his head. 'Not my type.'

'Hard work, I'd imagine. Bit of a tearaway?'

'She had her moments. Complicated maybe, but not hard work, just always made dreadful choices in men.'

'You can say that again,' Frost said, thinking of Robbo Nicholson.

'Huh, they were all like that.'

'Like what?'

'Controlling.'

'Why's that, you think?'

'Her dad died when she was eleven,' King said and shrugged. 'She was always in and out of the doctor's after various prescriptions. Maybe talk to them?'

'I will.' Frost remembered his own appointment tomorrow. 'Can you think of anyone that might have leapt in since she got out? An old boyfriend or someone she might have hooked up with?'

'There was the fella at the club.'

'Gazzer Benson?'

'I don't know his name, but he was pretty persistent, though they only went out once or twice.'

'Young, early twenties?'

'Yeah, he was a bit younger than her . . . she wasn't that keen, but he was persistent.'

Maybe the link with Maria Benson was right under his nose! Would explain why the widow would not say anything – mother protecting her son. It was plain as day. The gentle giant on Harry's door. Powerful and protective. Frost didn't know why he hadn't made the connection sooner.

'By the way, Adam, had you heard about a big party at Two Bridges on Saturday night?'

King scratched the back of his head. 'Posh London arty-farty type? Designs clothes?'

'That's the chap.'

'Yeah, I did hear about it.'

'Really? Who from?'

'Me sister. She's a hairdresser. Want the local gossip, she's the one'll have it.'

Wednesday (7)

The police seemed no nearer to catching the thief. Indeed, they didn't seem that concerned at all; after he'd offered them a snack they promptly left, with not so much as a suggestion that the cement mixer would be examined (not that he knew what it could possibly reveal beyond caked mortar, but still . . .).

Holland sighed and poured himself a generous Bacardi and Coke; it was the weather for it, all right . . . It was a very pleasant evening, the temperature had dropped sufficiently and it was blissfully quiet. He'd never imagined he could endure near silence like this – nothing apart from the odd tweet from a bird. He sank into the luxury patio chair. Could he grow to like the place? Probably not – he was tired and stressed and easily bored without distractions. The harmony was broken by the sound of a motorcycle, but it soon passed.

As he contemplated the unfinished pool he grew maudlin. He knew they'd never recover his two thousand. Maybe the police's lack of interest was in fact self-interest. Maybe they were in cahoots with that rogue of a builder? One heard of these things, on the television. They'd probably split the cash? This would never happen in the anonymity of London; but out here everyone was crooked, even the vicar . . . Hello, was that the side gate? He swung round, spilling the Bacardi, to confront a man in a flat cap and sunglasses.

'Oh, it's you.' Holland rose from the chair. 'Wait a minute!' He stepped back. 'You're not . . . who . . .'

But before he could say another word, Dominic Holland toppled backwards into his unfinished swimming pool.

'But that was the name on the computer print-out you gave me,' Sergeant 'Wally' Wallace complained.

'That was the name in the log book,' Bill Wells replied defensively, though it was the night sergeant's handwriting, Johnny Johnson's, so he couldn't vouch for anything more than what was on the page.

The uniform sergeant was in a flap; the traffic in town was severely congested, and as the officer responsible for traffic he was answerable. It had transpired that illegal parking was a major cause. The yellow 'no parking' lines in some areas were no longer visible and when quizzed the council said they had been stymied by the theft of paint from the depot five weeks ago. A theft they had reported. The night security guard at the depot had been napping on the job, and hundreds of tins of what was known as 'hospital green' and 'mellow road yellow' had vanished. Suspicion was at first levied at the guard – but further investigation uncovered an empty Teacher's bottle in the wastebasket in his hut. The old boy had been sozzled.

Wells huffed as he reached under the desk for the records he'd typed up on Sunday.

'Can you believe it,' Wallace, a beefy man in short sleeves, moaned, 'I twig there's a problem with the markings – after the traffic wardens complain about getting more aggro than usual when dishing out tickets. So I get on the blower to the council and get a right earful! There's naff all they can do because the paint has been nicked and we've done shag all to recover it!'

Until last week that is, when an area car reported finding a damaged tin of said paint on Foundling Street.

'Nobody's heard of a Rick Corner on Foundling Street,' Wallace continued. 'Right, what you got there?'

Wells placed an A5 index card on the counter. ''Ere you go.'

Wallace held the card up and adjusted the distance until the words written on it came into focus. *Found on Brick rd. corner.* He looked at Wells in disbelief.

'It's his bloody handwriting and this bloody machine, and it's bloody impossible to concentrate, somebody reporting something every five minutes!' Wells stuck to his guns defiantly. But it would be a different thing altogether if Superintendent Mullett got wind of it. Clearly he'd cocked up – mistaking 'Found on' for 'Foundling Street', and reading 'corner' as the name of whoever had reported it, when in fact there was no mention of any name whatsoever, only a location: Brick Road on the Southern Housing Estate. He picked up the phone. 'I'll ask Control to send an area car or two down the Southern Estate for you . . .'

The shop was long shut by the time they arrived; the traffic was appalling even in Somerset and it had been a good two hours' drive.

Waters rapped on the glass door of Always Flowers. Movement from inside indicated that the proprietors had waited for them.

'Thank god for that,' Clarke said.

'Do come in,' a small, dapper man said politely.

Immediately Clarke's senses were overwhelmed by a dozen different scents. 'Thanks for waiting for us.'

'Our pleasure, how exciting, a visit from the *po*lice!' A taller man appeared from behind a huge display of lilies, sporting what Clarke recognized as a wedge haircut – a male version of a bob with a side parting – and beckoned to them.

'Yes, well . . . Now, Mr Holland, you know him well?'

'I should say, since Design College in seventy-five.'

'How was the party?'

'A riot! Boy, does the man know how to entertain! I'm Matthew, by the way,' Wedge-head said, offering a well-manicured hand.

'And I'm Bruce,' said the little fellow, who had a surprisingly deep voice.

'Yes, even out in the boondocks, Dom really knows how to throw a good one,' Matthew continued, clearly the chatty one of the pair.

'Hmm, I'm sure, he's quite the one,' Clarke said. 'So you've been to Mr Holland's parties before?'

They both nodded emphatically. 'But never to one outside SW3.'

Clarke glanced at Waters, who clarified, 'Chelsea.'

'Absolutely. But all the usual crew were there.'

'So you knew everybody?' Clarke asked.

'Oh *yeah*,' Matthew answered boastfully. She'd never come across two such affected men in her life.

'There were no surprise new faces, then. No local colour?' Waters asked.

Matthew's expression grew perplexed. 'Err . . .'

'How can we help?' Bruce said evenly. 'It's a long way to come just to ask whether Dominic can throw a good party.'

'Do you remember this lady being there?' Clarke held out a photo of Rachel Curtis. The pair shuffled together to take a look.

'It was a bit of a frenzied affair. It's all a bit of a blur . . .' Matthew said.

'We think she may have arrived with a man on a motorbike,' Waters offered.

'I remember something about a bike. A man lost his cool because he couldn't find his lady friend at the party. He was supposed to pick her up, at whatever time it was . . .'

'At midnight,' Bruce said, 'and there was quite a kerfuffle outside over it all. He was charging about looking for her.'

'But you do recognize the lady in the photo?' Clarke insisted.

Matthew frowned. 'Maybe, I'm not sure.'

'I'm afraid they all look the same to us,' Bruce said haughtily.

'Who do?' Waters asked.

'Women,' Clarke answered quickly, though she didn't actually believe them. Then she added, 'Would you recognize the man on the bike if you saw him again?'

'Yes, big fella – tanned. She was supposed to meet him outside, apparently,' Bruce said.

'Ooh *yes*, it's coming back to me: he got in an awful strop, just awful.'

'Big fella with a tan?' Clarke said as they got back in the car.

'Gary Benson.' Waters started the engine. 'But Gazzer doesn't strike me as the fairy godmother type.'

'How do you mean?'

'Cinderella. Insisting on her leaving at midnight.'

'But she'd already left before then, he couldn't find her, that's the whole point.' Clarke flicked down the sun visor. 'You'd think he might have brought this information to us by now, given Jack's got his mum banged up?'

Mullett stood on the golf-club veranda. It was a beautiful evening, the sun dropping down below Denton Woods in the distance, the faint smell of cut grass in the air, and the sky an array of pinks and oranges. Still, the superintendent hadn't come here to admire the view. The board of the club had assembled for the AGM and related dinner. The nominations were in, but the voting couldn't proceed without the presence of the outgoing chairman . . . And Hudson was nowhere to be seen.

'Where the devil is he?' the superintendent muttered.

Laughter erupted in the lounge behind him. Dawson, the treasurer, had no doubt made some lewd joke, causing the secretary, Captain Hughes, to regale them all with his vulgar bellow. Dawson had a mind like a sewer; juvenile, seaside-postcard sense of humour. Since Dawson was an accountant at a respectable firm in Market Square, Mullett was of the opinion that he should have left that sort of puerile nonsense behind him. Mullett's wife, who bore his complaints on a regular basis, would always say a chap needed to unwind from a busy day at the office and that was Dawson's release. Letting off steam the super understood, but reverting to playground humour? Hell's teeth, he got enough of that at the station. Was there no respite?

'Come on, Stanley, have a drink?' Captain Hughes said.

'I'm just worried about Michael.' That was patently untrue; the overweight banker was always late.

Then, as if on cue, in he walked, puce-faced and sweaty. 'Robbed, I've been robbed!'

'A bank robbery?' Mullett said, aghast.

'No, you fool, me personally!'

This was a surprise; the man's house was like Fort Knox.

'When, how and what?' Mullett stepped back from the perspiring portly man.

'My safe – empty!'

'Calm down, Michael, take a seat.'

'Don't you tell me to calm down! This is *your* fault, Mullett. Denton is a thieves' paradise!' He glared at him with little piggy eyes. 'You have no business being here at the club with the town in such a lawless state.'

With that, Hudson turned his back and went off to join the others, drown his sorrows and no doubt drag Mullett's name through the mud. The evening was not going as planned.

The superintendent marched to the bar and ordered another double gin and tonic.

'Gary Benson,' Frost muttered and replaced the telephone receiver.

Waters had stopped at a motorway café to call the station, and Frost now decided to wait for his pal at Eagle Lane. He was beginning to wonder whether he'd been focusing on the wrong Benson; that Gary might have had a relationship with Rachel and had not been forthcoming about it cast a very different light on the matter. He sighed and yanked the ringpull on a can of lager, took a swig and started leafing through the Tête-à-Tête appointment book on his desk. Adam King's sister had indeed been obliging; she had readily met Frost at her salon and lent him the diary.

'Well now, Mr Holland, this is very useful,' Frost mumbled to himself; nothing like a good old gossip at the hairdresser's. Tête-à-Tête was one of these upmarket joints, where punters had to make a booking, not like Ted the Shear's place on Finger Alley, where Frost could stroll in for a trim whenever the mood took him (not that it took him often). In the appointment book, in neat curly writing, there was a record of every client. Holland, it transpired, had been in on the Friday; the hairdresser said he came in fortnightly for a beard trim.

Frost was half expecting Rachel Curtis's name to leap out at him, but was relieved that it didn't. It must have been another customer who got wind of Holland's party, someone who would presumably still be alive and together enough to remember something useful. Tête-à-Tête was pricey. It struck Frost as unlikely that the sort of clientele that could afford the salon would also be the sort to crash a party out of town . . . but there must be a connection. Frost recognized a number of names but one in particular stood out: *Mullett*. Chuckling to himself, he reached for the Rolodex. He checked his watch: eight o'clock.

'Got to start somewhere.' Frost stuck his nicotine-stained finger in the dial.

After three rings a polite female voice answered the phone.

'Ah good evening, Mrs Mullett, it's Jack Frost at Eagle Lane.'

'Inspector Frost, this is becoming a habit,' she tittered. Of course, he'd called on Sunday. 'How can I help?'

'I was wondering about your last trip to the hairdresser's,' he said obscurely.

'Well . . . that is an extraordinary question.'

'Did you happen to hear about a party in Two Bridges on Saturday night?'

'Saturday just gone?'

'Yep.'

'No, I've not been in since July, actually. Why?'

'Oh,' Frost said, thrown, 'you didn't have an appointment at Tête-à-Tête?'

'Goodness, no. Mind you . . .'

'Yes?'

'Stanley had a trim Saturday, but I thought he went to the barber's at the end of the road . . . Tête-à-Tête's a bit extravagant for him.'

Frost couldn't help but snigger at the thought of Mullett getting his whiskers trimmed at such a place.

Suddenly there was a commotion at the other end of the line, and he heard Mullett's wife exclaim, '*Stanley!*' This surprised Frost – Mullett was back? He thought the super was off with his golf chums for the evening.

'Oh, is the superintendent there?'

'Yes, I just heard the door – hello, dear, it's Inspector . . .'

The familiar nasal rasp of his boss echoed down the line. 'That woman,' he barked, 'has gone tonto.'

'Your good lady? She seems all right to me. Probably a bit miffed at you selling the MG.'

'This is not the time for japes, Frost.'

'But it's out of office hours?' Mullett had been drinking, Frost could tell. Perfect: he'd enjoy winding him up.

'Karen Thomas.' The mention of the name swept away any levity. 'Frost? Are you listening? Have you seen her recently, he thinks someone's spoken to her?' Mullett said, and then muffling the receiver, added, 'Grace, fetch me a gin and tonic. *Now!*'

'Sorry, sir? I don't think I . . . "He"? Who is *he*, sir?'

Silence. Then a big sigh. 'Hudson, the bank manager. Has been robbed. At home.'

Frost spat lager all over the paperwork in front of him; so it was Hudson, the filthy manipulative git, who had lost Karen her job. That was what Sandy Lane had been hinting at on Sunday evening; Frost, already having enough on his plate, wasn't interested in gossip and had only half listened to the newspaper hack's intriguing.

'Are you all right?' Mullett asked, taken aback at the choking sounds.

'Why . . . would she need . . .' Frost stuttered, ignoring the super's question. The fact that there was a relationship between Karen and Hudson, however warped, had struck home.

'Eh? I have no idea what you mean, but now you know as much as I do.'

'Far from it – what does Hudson have to say about the theft?' Frost said, regaining his composure.

'He says there is no way Karen would have done it unless someone put her up to it.'

'"Put her up to it"? What are you implying?'

'I'm repeating what he said.' Mullett slurped noisily on his drink. 'The fool believes the woman is in love with him, and wouldn't do anything to harm him unless coerced.'

'Do me a favour!' Frost snorted. 'Cavorting with Hudson? She must be crazy!'

'It takes all sorts,' Mullett replied defensively; his own involvement in the saga must be beginning to grate.

'I have heard that, yes. But there are limits!'

'Have you seen her since the unfortunate incident in front of the cameras?' the super asked.

'Briefly.' Frost thought it best to admit this now while Mullett was weakened by booze, rather than risk it later when he was sober and irritable.

'And?'

'She apologized.'

'That's it?'

'I didn't tell her to turn over Hudson, if that's what you mean.' But I might have done, if I'd known, he thought, and fumbled with a pack of Rothmans. It was beyond belief that a woman like that could consider Hudson in an amorous way. But what was even more deplorable was the way Hudson, a wealthy bank manager, thought he could control the young woman's life, having her fired and thus causing her to lose her independence. As Mullett relayed the conversations he'd had with Hudson, it became obvious that what the banker craved was total owner-ship of the girl; he was driven by lust and jealousy, like that crazed loon who sought to embalm the dead prostitute in his bath. Not that anyone would see it that way, of course; this perverse parallel would slip by unnoticed.

'What's she made away with?' Frost said finally, feeling battered by a wave of exhaustion.

'Contents of his safe. Jewellery, chiefly.'

'Whose?'

'What?'

'Whose jewellery? If she's the love of his life? Whose are the baubles?'

A pause. 'Michael Hudson is leaving his wife of thirty years for this individual.'

'I see, *really*,' Frost said caustically, not believing a word.

'Well, maybe Karen Thomas wants to make sure he does? Pretty stupid though, to give her the combination to his safe, eh?'

'If you hear from the woman again, make sure you recover Hudson's property,' Mullett said stiffly, and hung up.

Frost rocked back on the chair, and sucked long on the cigarette. He didn't know what to think. *Nothing*, that was probably the best course of action. Karen Thomas had been on his mind since he first saw her under the lights of the Coconut Grove – but he had to remain detached . . . Though it was difficult to avoid unpleasant speculation over her entanglement with the Bennington's Bank manager. Forget about it, and do the job.

He tutted, stubbed out the cigarette, and leaned forward to consult the hairdresser's diary. He now realized he'd not quizzed Mullett about his own appointment at the weekend – he toyed with calling the super back, but thought better of it. Instead, he lethargically flipped back a page or two, through to the previous week. And there to his surprise one familiar name sprang out . . .

Frost grinned. 'Needed a haircut before you went on your holidays, did you?'

Wednesday (8) _____

'So, how do you want to play it?' Waters was weary, the drive
back had just about finished him off for the day. It was nearly
nine o'clock. Only he, Frost and the night sergeant remained on
duty at Eagle Lane. He'd dropped Sue back at home to see her
kid.

'So, do we pull Gazzer in? I mean, it's a party – if he was
there, he was there, right? He knows we'll get a witness, set up
an identity parade, if he won't play ball.'

Frost shook his head. 'No, with the mother already in the
clink we need to play it very carefully. We could maybe let
Maria out on bail . . .'

'Are you sure that's wise? If she is the killer, won't she do a
bunk?'

'Not if she's worried about her son.'

'You figure she'd not risk dragging him into it?'

'That's a theory.' Frost sighed. 'Maybe we let her sweat a bit
longer. The fact that Gary has not come forward about his
relationship with Rachel troubles me.'

'Maybe he was hiding it from his old dear? That would only add fuel to the flames?'

'Huh, I can't imagine Maria Benson's flames leaping any higher, can you?'

'Good point, Jack,' Waters conceded.

'It could be an act: maybe they're both guilty. One covering for the other? The fact that Gary's been silent thus far is making me increasingly suspicious . . . Anyway' – he yawned – 'let's leave it for tonight. There's always tomorrow. Here – look at this before you go,' Frost said and passed him an appointment book of some kind. 'Your friend Dominic has been gassing at the hairdresser's. I'll bet you half of Denton knew about his party. Check out these names in the morning, see who else knew about this do.'

'Right you are.'

Waters made to go and Frost himself rose.

'And remember, you've drinks with the lads tomorrow evening, before your special day?' Frost said, picking his cigarettes up off the desk.

'Hey now' – Waters backed away – 'no way – I promised Kim I'd . . .'

'You'll be making young Kimbo enough promises on Friday, and they're the for-evermore kind. Trust me on that.'

'What, and breaking them, just as fast?'

For once Frost had made it home before they closed the kitchen. He thought he might even sit at a table and be served.

'Ah Jack, good to see you,' Kenny Fong said, as Frost shut the door behind him. 'Can I have a quick word?'

'Of course, Kenny. Do you reckon I can grab a bite to eat in the dining room? Been a while since I've sat down for a proper—'

'Sure, sure,' the boy said softly, 'it's just that—'

'*Flamin' knickers!*' Monty the parrot announced proudly to

the diners. Going by their faces, Frost could tell it wasn't the first time he'd been vocal this evening, either.

'Err, that's what I wanted to talk about, Jack. He would never say things like that before you . . . it just wasn't in his vocabulary.'

'I see, oh dear.' Frost rubbed his jaw in surprise. 'I could correct his, err, unfortunate vocabulary, Ken . . . if there were a chance of getting a Kung Po with Extra Ping first?'

He fiddled with the latch and pushed open the flimsy plastic door. Even now at just past ten, it wasn't quite beyond gloaming and probably wouldn't reach pitch black at all this time of year. Still, Weaver felt hidden enough to step outside. The sky was visible here and there, through patches in the oak-tree canopy. From the air the place was not visible. Likewise, the grounds were well hidden from the road. Unless one knew the caravan park was there you'd drive straight past it, maybe noticing only the old red-brick wall.

Occasional lights twinkled through the trees, but all was silent. The caravans were well spaced out, the nearest one to his was quite some way off and appeared unoccupied. He breathed in the woodland air. Nice. He'd not ventured out since arriving that afternoon. The curtains remained pulled to, and with the car behind the toilet block he hoped there was nothing to suggest he was there.

But . . . but how long could he stay? A shiver ran through him as he played back yesterday's close call. If he hadn't recognized the policeman's car he'd be locked up by now, never to breathe air as fresh as this again. Right up to the point when he had shaved her he could have claimed it was all a terrible accident. He could have come up with a story to explain the needle in the neck – but bald, naked and bathing in a bath of meths? There was no explaining that away as accidental . . . However, for now he was safe, and that was all that mattered. He hadn't given

Janey a second thought since discovering the police at his flat.

This place was devoid of technology; he'd not even seen a call box on the way in. The radio reception in the car was poor and the television picture in the caravan was snowy. There was no running water, though, and that was considerably more problematic. He had figured out the foot pump in front of the basin for now, but the tap itself was dry as dust.

'Ah, I thought there was somebody there.' A voice out of the dark startled him.

'H-hello? Who might you be?'

'I'm the caravan park warden – more to the point, who are you?'

'Cassidy.' Weaver had assumed the old stroke victim's name with ease.

'I know Cassidy, and he's a good deal older than you,' came the reply.

'Oh sorry' – he faked a laugh – 'I'm *Mark* Cassidy, the caravan's my uncle's. He said I could borrow it for a week.'

The man stepped closer. 'Ah, that's grand, but you ought to let the warden's office know. He shoulda told you that.'

'Oh, maybe he forgot. He's getting on a bit.'

'Aye, that's so. Well, you'll be needing the key to the lavvies.' He tossed up a key.

'Very kind, thank you.'

The man turned to leave.

'Anything else I need to know?' Weaver ventured.

'Power goes off at midnight till six in the morning, and the water tap is up yonder.'

'Water tap?'

'He ain't told you much, has he?' The man laughed in the darkness. 'We ain't on the mains, you know. You'll have to take your trolley and fill up the tank. It'll be stored under the van.'

'Oh, thanks for telling me.' Well, that was something, but he didn't fancy fiddling with water carriers at this time of night. He had picked up a couple of pints of milk and some tins of lager.

This really was a good hiding place, so primitive, but he couldn't stay for long. He'd need somewhere equally remote but much further away. Strangely enough, he did miss his routine contact with the church and old Father Hill. OK, the establishment itself had not been kind to him, but he did miss the closeness to God, which manifested itself through his relationship with the elderly vicar and the ancient building itself. Maybe there was another way to pursue his calling in the Church itself . . . Jonathan had always said the 'other lot' were more tolerant of their bent, or at least they kept it behind closed doors. Yes, if he could get across the water he might be able to start again . . .

Thursday (1)

'Here?'

'No.'

'Here?'

'No.'

'He—'

'Oww!' Frost howled. The doctor pushed again, and again Frost yelped in pain.

'Hmm.' The doctor moved back to his desk. 'You can put your T-shirt back on, Sergeant Frost.'

'*Inspector*, Dr Mirchandani, I've been promoted since we last met.'

'Hmm.'

Frost jumped off the couch with a wince. It was a while since he had troubled the surgery; he'd not seen his GP, the affable Mirchandani, since recovering from his appendix operation over two years ago. The family practitioner now sported a carefully sculpted beard.

'On the scales, please.'

'I used to have one of those,' Frost said, over his shoulder.

'A stethoscope? Unusual equipment for a policeman.'

'No, a beard. Shaved it off yesterday, in fact. I didn't carry it with the same dignity as you.' Frost couldn't help his ingratiating behaviour; he was always like this the moment he stepped inside a consulting room – be nice to your doctor, flatter him, and he'll tell you you're in good shape.

Dr Mirchandani didn't answer. Frost had always found the fellow genial, if haughty on occasion. Very clever no doubt, judging by the certificates on the wall.

'Like I say, Doc,' Frost continued, 'I've been sleeping on a friend's settee for a good few months. Very soft, can't be good for my back. Then I moved to this Chinese fella's place I know, and the bed is like concrete. Seems to have got worse. I'm sure a couple of painkillers will make me right as rain again.'

The doctor's attention was on the scales. 'I don't think there's anything wrong with your back . . . That will do, Inspector. Please take a seat.'

'Excellent.' Frost beamed.

'How much alcohol do you drink?'

'I don't.'

'Don't drink?' The doctor stepped back, surprised.

'Neat alcohol, no. Always with a mixer, hops and grain, that sort of thing,' he joked unconvincingly.

'Every night?'

'Only from habit – I rarely get drunk.' Frost had thought his back was much better, until the doc started prodding around.

'A high tolerance does not immunize your body from damage by alcohol.'

He shouldn't be wasting the good doctor's time, not when there was Gazzer Benson to deal with. He'd be out of here in five minutes, though.

'Your kidneys are suffering; that's your back pain. Your liver, not that you're aware, is swollen. And you are overweight.'

'Too much of the good life.'

'How much are you smoking?'

He had never counted. 'Thirty a day?' he guessed, knowing the truth to be closer to forty.

'Try to limit what you drink. It is all right to drink in moderation.'

Moderation? If there was one thing Jack Frost was, it was moderate! He was rarely drunk; the doc can't have heard him.

'Do you drink, Doc?' Frost asked.

'Only white wine, and only when I'm eating out. Not at home, I do not keep alcohol at home.'

'I don't have a home,' Frost muttered, aware it sounded pitiful.

'Then I suggest you find one, stability in one's domestic life is good for one's general health and well-being. In the meantime, I want a urine sample and a blood test, just to be sure.' Only a doctor could come out with a sentence so rounded as that. 'And watch what you eat. For a man of your height, you're carrying too much weight. Have a night free from beer, and cut down on the cigarettes.' The doctor moved back behind his desk, the consultation was at an end.

'Yes, but what's the worst that can happen – I burst the odd shirt button?'

The doctor paused in his scribbling. 'A stroke, heart attack, diabetes. I can't comment on the state of your liver until I see the blood test result. But apart from that, you're in remarkably good shape, considering. Go easy on the takeaway curries, and try and ease off the alcohol.'

He should never have asked. 'You don't pull any punches,' Frost said and took the slip. He was hoping for some painkillers for his back, but that clearly was not going to happen. 'I'll cut out the fry-up in the mornings – how does that sound?'

'A good start. You're as strong as an ox, but you're not a young man any more. Time to slow down a bit, that's my advice. Take that to the General as soon as you can, and we'll call you with the results.'

Outside the surgery, Frost sparked up a cigarette. It had clouded over. There seemed to be an inordinate amount of traffic on the road. He held up the cigarette and considered the glowing tip. A raindrop caused it to fizzle. 'As strong as an ox, eh?' he said and ambled off down the street, thinking maybe he ought to get a flat some time soon. He'd noticed one for sale in Sue Clarke's block . . .

Cones. There were orange cones everywhere.

'What in the blazes?' It was nine o'clock and the super-intendent's ten-minute car journey had taken half an hour already. The entire Market Square – the centre of Denton – was at a standstill. The superintendent switched off the ignition and opened the Rover's door. He was in a foul mood. The election of a new golf-club chairman had been postponed. He emerged from the vehicle to hear a sharp blast of hooting from behind him. Placing his cap firmly on his head he turned and glared at a big man in a string vest at the wheel of a grimy Ford Transit. The man adopted a 'Who, me?' face, and the senior policeman turned his attention to the cones that lined the outer perimeter of the square. Parking was usually permitted on either side of the square, but not right now: someone had set out their orange cones, and that was that.

That was inconvenient but didn't explain the gridlock. He strode briskly through the traffic, to be confronted by two delivery vans in the middle of the road outside Aster's depart-ment store. PC Miller was on the scene. Miller nodded at his approaching station chief just as the store manager started to make his protestations to the constable. Two men went about the business of unloading a floral sofa in a lackadaisical manner. The unmistakable figure of Frost in a pink polo top stood on the pavement in the shade of the shop awning, puffing away on a cigarette. Mullett ignored him. The store manager, a neat little man by the name of Perks, was addressing the slouched figure of Miller.

'What the devil is going on here?' Mullett demanded.

'This delivery lorry is holding up the traffic, sir.'

'Because there are cars parked here, on double yellow lines.' The store manager pointed at a white Maxi. 'We have permission to unload.' He raised his arm to a sign.

Mullett stepped up to the kerb. He couldn't see anything. Market Square had always had double-yellows. Why were they not there?

'Last winter did away with most of them,' the store manager lamented, 'should have been repainted ages ago.'

'Does the council know?' Mullett snapped. The police, he knew, should have been taking action rather than letting things get this bad – this was not an overnight erosion. The situation had clearly been made worse by incompetence of the very highest order. The traffic cones should have been placed overnight by uniform in carefully selected trouble spots and not, as it appeared, randomly scattered without any thought at all. He considered the smartly dressed store manager before him, and wondered whether he might have subsequently moved the cones to suit his own delivery purposes.

'I have repeatedly told the council bods,' the manager said, 'but they ignore me, like your very own officers . . .'

'One minute, sir, if I may consult my junior officer.' Mullett called PC Miller to one side and issued a very plain instruction. The store manager was to have his delivery, and he, Miller, was to expedite the process.

'What, like, carry stuff?' he said, dismayed.

Mullett nodded and handed him the keys to the Rover. 'And then as a special treat you can bring my car round to Eagle Lane.' He smiled as sweetly as he could.

Finally he had a new victim! Someone upon whom to unleash

the indiscriminate fury he felt towards everyone and everything. The super was going to walk to Eagle Lane and crucify Wallace.

Waters thanked the smartly dressed woman for interrupting her morning routine to speak to him. Amanda Booth, Rachel Curtis's neighbour from two doors down on Sandpiper Close, was one of the names in the Tête-à-Tête appointment book Frost had given him to check out.

'You didn't fancy the party yourself then?'

'Naah.' Although she was smartly turned out with a perfect bob, the woman was chewing gum and had a coarse twang to her voice. He guessed she'd have got on with Rachel Curtis. 'I 'ad something on meself, but thought Rach might fancy a bit of fun, having just got out. I'd never have mentioned the party if I thought . . .'

'When did you last see her?'

'Friday morning. I popped round to see how she was doing before we went away for the weekend.'

'Right, and how was she?'

'In good spirits.'

'And when you mentioned the Two Bridges party did she seem keen?'

The woman shrugged. 'Yeah, but she reckoned she'd get grief from her probation officer, who was being a bit of a pain in the arse.'

'Fergusson?'

'Didn't say his name.'

'Any men friends around the house?'

'Not that I seen.'

'Thanks for your time, Mrs Booth.'

'No problem, love.' She winked and gave him a crooked friendly smile. Then she jumped in a 500 SL.

'Wonder what *you* do for a living,' he said as he waved her goodbye and watched the Merc two-seater back out of the drive.

After Amanda Booth had roared off, he became aware of his car radio crackling through the Vauxhall's open window. He reached inside and grabbed the handset. There'd been a fatality up at Two Bridges.

'Can't someone else take it?' he said, thinking he wanted another word with Fergusson.

'You already know the address, is the thing,' Wells said distantly. 'I believe the fatality took place over at that London fella's house, Holland? And you're that side of town.' Wells then started to grumble on about the traffic.

Waters wasn't listening any more. *Holland*. He checked the time – ten past nine – he'd call Sue Clarke first from a phone box, she might still be at home.

Thursday (2) _____

DC Sue Clarke had craved a quiet hour with her infant son before heading for the station. She knew that Frost, if he remembered, was at the doctor's and thought she'd not be missed. Guilt had washed over her on the long drive back yesterday evening from Somerset; she'd abandoned her child for the job faster than a Navratilova serve. Three days in and she'd barely seen the little mite, except for the night feeds. And that was starting to take a toll – she'd overslept this morning; her mother had woken her when John Waters called.

Could she check in with Curtis's probation officer? His offices were on the London Road, near her flat. She shucked on her raincoat and said goodbye to her family. She would have to get Philip into a nursery. Her mum looked how she felt. After a vague promise of being home by mid-afternoon, she left, Philip's cries following her out of the door.

The weather had broken, and there had been showers throughout the night. Typical, wonderful all week, then when it really counts, with John and Kim's wedding tomorrow, lets you down. Spots of rain caught her lapels as she hovered outside a grimy sixties office building on the London Road. There was only a satellite probation office here; the main office was in Bath, and Denton shared Fergusson and another officer with three other towns, including Rimmington. She asked at the desk for Fergusson.

'Fridays and Mondays only,' came the short reply. The man lived in Denton, she could call on him this evening, but that would be a nuisance. She flashed her badge.

'I'm investigating the death of Rachel Curtis. I understand her case was being handled by Mr Fergusson, and I would like to see further details of her parole conditions, restrictions on movements and so forth.'

'We can tell you that; the admin clerk will have access to the records, bear with me.' She reached for the phone. 'Take a seat, please.'

She did as requested and sat down next to an old man who was fast asleep. The reception area reminded her of the doctor's surgery, the air heavy with dead waiting time. Her mind turned to Frost. Would the doctor discover something wrong with him? He'd been moaning like billy-o about his back. God knows, he was fantastically unhealthy. She had worried he'd contaminate Philip when he was in the flat; he was forever blowing smoke rings at the baby, who appeared delighted by the game, but surely it was terrible for his health. If Frost had stayed any longer the kid would be smoking before he could walk . . .

'Detective Clarke.' A buck-toothed ginger-haired woman appeared with a buff folder. 'If you'll come with me.' Clarke rose and followed the woman down a corridor. 'I'm sure you'll understand we cannot divulge this sort of information in public. So . . .' She held the door open to a small room not much larger than a toilet cubicle. Clarke had barely sat down before the woman began reciting the contents of the file, the conditions of the release, and the dates and times of the meetings with the probation officer. The restrictions placed on Curtis were ones of distance: she was not allowed beyond a ten-mile radius from Denton, with a dispensation to visit her mother in Sheffield on a prearranged basis. Two Bridges was five miles outside Denton.

'There's nothing there about a curfew?'

'I have just read you the conditions, miss,' she said curtly.

'Mind if I have a read?'

'I can't let you have the file, it is to remain with me.'

'I only want a quick scan, you'll be right there . . . I'm hard of hearing, too much loud music.' She had heard Frost pull this one in the past.

The woman slowly turned the report round on the desk. 'Very well, but be careful not to mark it.'

Admin assistants. She had always thought them a self-important mob.

On the first sheet, the dates and times of meetings were recorded. There had been three of them. She flipped over to the next page where the rules governing Curtis's release were typed up. Aware she was being watched like a hawk, she read slowly and carefully. But nope, there were no time constraints, only the distance of ten miles, and that she was not to drive, which they knew already. She turned to the next page, headed 'Observations'.

'If you want any more information, you'll need to make an appointment with Mr Fergusson himself,' said the woman and whisked the file away.

That was the last straw. 'Anyone would think we're not on the same side,' moaned Clarke.

The builder stood outside the front of the house, wearing a flat cap in the drizzle. Though his face was weathered by years of toil outside, shock and fear were still discernible on the worn features.

'I just come round to see the guy, you know, after the money went missing . . . to see what could be done.'

The panel van's side door was open and Waters suspected the man had come to collect gear he'd left behind, rather than to enquire after Holland's well-being or to negotiate a reasonable settlement.

'I found him, just lying there.'

'Where?'

'Round the back. In the pool.'

At the excavation site, Waters peered over the edge and winced. Dominic Holland lay skewered through the stomach on a steel rib jutting skyward from the earth eight feet below.

'He might have fallen?' Todd offered. 'You know, after having a few.' He gestured to the glass tumbler lying on the grass. The two men stared at one another.

Forty-five minutes later the entire pool area was cordoned off and crawling with Forensics. The property backed on to fields, and was easily accessible from there – Saturday night's party had reached the perimeter hedgerow, as was evidenced by the discovery of discarded drinks bottles and condoms.

Waters was in conversation with Harding, the forensics officer. 'If an attacker approached from out there, there's the risk Holland would have seen them coming.'

'Well, there are no footprints through the house – looks like the place has just been scrubbed from top to bottom,' said Harding. 'I imagine the garden gate was used – and of course this all presumes there was another person involved. There is only one glass. He could have fallen backwards. There's a half-empty bottle of Bacardi over there. Or he could have been pushed. I would suggest he was taken by surprise either way. I will let you have a summary tomorrow.'

The old houses were secluded enough, set back on a leafy road, for the neighbours not to be aware of all the comings and goings. This much they'd established from the Curtis investigation. Waters watched Todd finish giving his statement to a

PC. Todd readily acknowledged he'd been put in touch with Holland by the neighbour, Reg Stirling, gruffly admitted he now wished he'd never taken the job, then immediately apologized for his insensitivity.

The builder caught Waters' eye and strolled over. Harding made to go inside.

'I'll be off then,' Todd said, playing with his cap. 'But know where to find me. I'm sorry about earlier.' He fumbled and dropped his cap to the ground. 'Oops.'

Waters bent to pick it up. 'Here.'

The man gave a slight laugh, and fixing on the hat said, 'I wonder if he ever got one.'

'What?'

'Mr Holland. Was thinking of getting 'imself one of these.'

'Oh yeah, why would that be?'

'He told me he'd seen someone else wearing one. He said it was a taxi driver who came to the house Saturday night to collect someone. Same cap as me. Thought it might help him blend in, you know, with Denton life.'

'A taxi driver?' Holland claimed to have passed out at nine, Waters recalled. 'What time? To collect who?' Could this have been Rachel Curtis's departure?

'Didn't say.'

Should be easy enough to trace. Then Waters asked, 'And where did you advise him to get one? A cap like yours?'

'Castleton's, in the town.'

'You know, I've a good mind to make an official complaint,' Detective Clarke said, arriving at her desk with a bucket of warm soapy water she'd brought across from the canteen.

Waters didn't respond. He wore a frown as he sat at the desk opposite, clearly in the middle of something: he'd already been phoning round taxi firms when she'd first arrived in the CID office ten minutes earlier.

'What's up?' she prompted.

He looked up. 'Dominic Holland is dead.'

On reflex she raised her hand to her mouth in surprise. 'You're kidding. How?'

She listened to his account of Todd's discovery at Two Bridges.

'Of course, it could have been an accident, he could have slipped, but with everything else leading to his doorstep, you can't help but think . . .'

'He was pushed,' she finished his sentence.

Waters nodded in agreement. 'Where's Jack?'

'He was at the doctor's first thing.'

'Doctor's? He's not had a day off sick since I've known him. What's wrong with him?'

'Oh, forget him,' Clarke said dismissively. 'What about Holland?'

Waters sighed. 'Can't do anything on that yet, but if it turns out it's suspicious you can bet it's tied up with Rachel Curtis's murder.'

'Or the thief that took the money from the cement mixer.'

'Huh, yeah,' he said, shifting in his chair. 'You're right, maybe they came back for more dosh, we've sweet FA to go on there . . . but we are learning more about who knew about that party of his. Turns out Rachel found out from a neighbour of hers.' He hefted the phone book to one side and got up.

'Where you off to?'

'Castleton's.'

'In the High Street?'

'So it would seem. Why?'

'It's an outdoor-clothing place, for farmers and—'

'Excuse me, chaps.' The round face of Sergeant Wallace appeared.

'Yes, Wally, what's up?'

'Superintendent Mullett, he's suspended me.'

*

'You're late.' They had seen each other recently in Market Square, and Mullett himself had arrived only minutes earlier, just time enough to summarily suspend Wallace. He felt better for it; not being disposed to hear the buffoon out, he issued his marching orders pending an immediate inquiry. And now from one incompetent to another.

'Sorry, sir, doctor's appointment.'

'Oh.' This was unexpected; he'd never known Frost to have a day off sick during his whole tenure as superintendent at Denton – he wondered what it would take to prompt a man like him to visit a GP. 'Are you OK?' he asked, his mind suggesting all sorts of terminal possibilities.

'Just age, I'm afraid,' Frost said, 'sore back, mainly.'

'Well, there's no escaping age; what age are you exactly?' Mullett said, sagging with disappointment.

'Forty.'

'Is that all? Never mind.' He himself was fifty-three and wearing it considerably better. The super touched his moustache lightly in smug satisfaction and tapped out a Senior Service. 'If there's nothing to worry about,' he puffed, 'then we'll continue with the business at hand.'

'No, I've a few more years left.' Frost beamed. 'Strong as an ox, in fact.'

'Fabulous. Have you seen the newspaper this morning?'

'No, why?'

Mullett slid the morning paper across the table. 'Read there.' He pointed to the second paragraph, alongside a picture of Maria Benson.

'"Maria Benson, forty-seven, who has been recuperating at her home off the Wells Road from an operation on her ankle following a motorcycle accident was arrested by—"' Frost stopped. 'Oh,' he said.

'Oh indeed. Ankle operation. Unlikely to leap off a porch roof now, is she?'

'No.'

'I thought that reporter Sandy Lane was a chum of yours?'

'So did I.'

'Well, what do you have to say for yourself?'

'The arrest wasn't made public. Sandy'd see that as fair game, I suppose. Had I told him we'd got her, then maybe . . .'

Frost scratched the back of his neck. Mullett noticed Frost was in the same polo top he'd been wearing at the start of the week, and he doubted the pink Fred Perry had seen the inside of a washing machine yet.

'I'm not interested in why Lane didn't talk to you. Be thankful he didn't report on Wakely too. What is your next move going to be? Are you going to arrest another motorcyclist at complete random?'

'I think we slow things down.' Frost laced his fingers together and twiddled his thumbs. 'All this charging around isn't getting us anywhere. Look at the situation from a different angle. Forget motorbikes. The person I saw bolting from the house might just have been a common-or-garden house-breaker. There's other avenues to explore.'

Mullett sat back in disbelief, trying to remain as calm as possible. 'So you suggest taking your foot off the pedal' – he leaned further back in his executive chair – 'and taking time to think the situation through?'

'You could put it like that, sir. And let's be honest, it's a bit hot to be charging around here there and everywhere.' Frost ran a finger round the inside of his collar.

'I see. And Weaver, Jane Hammond's murderer, who has disappeared; we just leave that, too, and hope he pops up somewhere?'

Frost suppressed a yawn. 'Yep, we've done as much as we can.'

'That's not good enough. All leave is cancelled until you get a result.'

'But Waters is off on honeymoon—'

'No, I mean it. Dominic Holland's demise precipitates a crisis. As I said, all leave is cancelled,' Mullett reiterated. It felt good saying it. 'I'm sure you'll explain the situation. Or maybe you can tell Waters that his best man's usual slipshod approach has landed the whole team in hot water; do you even begin to comprehend the mess we're in? The mess *you've* put us in? That woman found in the churchyard made the national press! The *nation* is watching us, and all they can see is your bumbling incompetence.'

Mullett felt light-headed as Frost left the room. Maybe it was the heat. Where were his pills? He seemed to be losing his cool every instant . . . He clutched at his chest. Booting Wallace out was a short-lived relief. His doctor had warned him about displacement behaviour. He tried a light laugh. It didn't work. Damn Hudson. Damn the golf-club chairmanship. *Damn bloody Jack Frost.*

Frost was incensed at Mullett's pigheadedness over his decision to cancel all leave. It was directed at him and he knew it. He had to try to let it go. He made his way back to his own office, rather than the general CID office, and sat down to study the forensics report on Sandpiper Close from Tuesday. He couldn't engage with Holland's death or anything else, not until he'd got as near to the bottom of the Curtis case as he possibly could. Though he'd told Hornrim Harry he was exploring new avenues on the Curtis case, he was still sure the motorcyclist held the key, and that the rider was Gary Benson. Maria Benson might not be strong enough to leap out of windows, but she was steady enough on her feet to ride a motorcycle, though he hadn't picked Mullett up on that – it didn't matter anyway as he was now thinking it should be Gary, not the mother, they should be after. But if it *was* Gazzer tangled up in this, Frost had to be one hundred per cent sure – he couldn't face Mullett again unless he was certain.

Fingerprint analysis was what he was after. He flicked open the manila folder from Forensics and lit a cigarette. There were a number of miscellaneous prints taken from around the front door (possibly his own, or the cleaner's), but the person he'd seen leg it might have been wearing gloves – he wasn't sure . . . In any event there was not much to glean from the report in front of him now; it was disappointingly short. The cleaner had earned her two quid, it seemed; the house was practically free of prints. There was nothing that could link Benson or his mother to the place, and the report concluded there had been no forced entry.

The intruder must have had a key? Gary might have had one, if they were dating— An exaggerated knock broke his concentration. It was Waters. He couldn't tell him yet about Mullett's ban on all leave. Damn Maria Benson and her son. The evidence might be thin, but instinct was telling him it was Gary. Maybe the mother knew, or was on some level complicit, and hence the over-the-top behaviour, allowing herself to be arrested . . .

'All right, pal?' Sergeant Wallace's grim news had delayed Waters heading into town. 'What a morning!'

'Hornrim Harry is overdoing it, that temper of his is getting worse,' Frost said, 'it'll do his blood pressure no good. I've been on the receiving end in the past, now poor Wally got it today.'

'And how about you, are you OK?'

'Of course I'm OK, why wouldn't I be?' Frost said, surprised.

'The doctor's . . .'

'Pah, fit as a fiddle.' Frost reached for his cigarettes, and then jabbed at the open file before him. 'The house at Sandpiper Close is clean of prints, but then our boy may have worn gloves and could have let himself in with a key. The mother's out of the frame on account of a gammy leg, but I'm now thinking

young Gazzer . . . I'm working on the idea that if he was courting our Rachel, that would fuel the mother's hatred, and perhaps
explain her peculiar behaviour.'

'But at the same time explain why she was protecting him, by
keeping shtum?'

'Exactly.'

'That makes sense. I checked in the Cricketers. Taffy confirmed a lock-in Saturday night but was hazy on specifics: who
was there until when.'

'Did he vouch for the Bensons?'

'Yep, they were there to start with . . .'

'It takes about fifteen minutes to get to Two Bridges from
there,' Frost said.

Waters smiled. 'As any taxi driver would corroborate.'

'You've got something.' Frost put the file to one side. 'What
are you not telling me?'

'Todd, the builder, remembers Holland talking about a taxi
driver who came to the house on Saturday night. It's all to do
with caps, but you don't need to know that bit.'

'Caps?'

'Forget caps for a moment. I just checked with every taxi
firm in Denton, and guess what? There were no calls out to
Two Bridges that night. Whoever it was that arrived at Holland's
was pretending to be a taxi, which has to be significant?'

'I hear you. Crack on with that line of enquiry then.
Meanwhile, I'm going to nail our Gazzer once and for all.'

Waters was concerned that Frost was growing obsessed with
the Bensons, to the point where he was not giving alternative
possibilities sufficient consideration. 'Glad you're OK,' he said,
leaving the office.

The inspector, muttering curses under his breath, didn't
answer.

Thursday (3)

David Simms entered High Fields care home rather sheepishly. Why he felt now he should hide his profession he did not know. He was proud to be a policeman. Nevertheless, it was now nearly eleven, an hour later than he usually visited. He made his way through the day room, smiling at the pale-faced residents as he went. Frost was right, the patients here might benefit from some fresh air; he was sure they had the heating on even though it was still August. He requested a wheelchair for his mother and helped her climb in. The beautifully landscaped grounds to the rear of the home were empty, unbelievably, apart from a couple of nurses smoking underneath a willow tree.

He found a small rose-clad arbour and pulled up a chair. As was his practice, Simms told his mother about his week. However, he lacked his usual enthusiasm and his voice was tinged with sadness; her disorientation at seeing him in uniform yesterday had given him grave doubts as to whether she actually understood a thing he said – did she even realize he was a policeman?

'You know it's me, Mum, right?' he said directly to the shrunken woman. A frail hand reached out to touch his cheek. He thought he saw a sparkle pass across the surface of the heavily medicated pupils.

The moment was then interrupted by a male nurse approaching at some speed. 'Mr Simms?'

'Yes?'

'The gentleman your colleague was interrogating yesterday, Mr Cassidy?'

Simms had to pause. Yesterday. Frost. Yes, Weaver's patient. Though 'interrogating' was a bit strong. 'Yes?'

'His speech, you see . . . He's talking,' said the nurse. 'Coherently,' he added, with emphasis to denote the significance.

'Right. Mum . . .' He looked uncertainly at the nurse. 'She always did like the sun, loved her garden.'

'Of course. You can leave her here, she'll be fine. I'll make sure.'

The nurse gave Simms a brief outline of Neil Cassidy's history as he followed him back inside the building. Cassidy was in rehabilitation after suffering two massive strokes. His recovery had been plagued by seizures, which could leave him speechless for weeks.

'Often what he's thinking is not what comes out; the right words elude him. So yesterday he was repeating the same word over and over again, because it wouldn't come out right.'

The man in his sixties turned and greeted them with a broad smile. 'Caravan!' he said brightly, then after a pause, added, 'Water . . . Caravan.'

The nurse nudged Simms. 'Pleased as punch he is.'

'Thank you.' The PC wondered what bearing this might have, if any, on the Ben Weaver case. Frost hadn't got a word out of Cassidy. The man then pointed to a pot plant.

'He wants his plants watered?' Simms said. 'Have you a phone I might use?'

Cassidy remained at the window repeating the word 'caravan' elatedly to the wider world beyond as Simms hurried to the reception desk.

'Won't be a tick,' Wells said, heading for the Gents at a brisk trot. Clarke was processing the release of Maria Benson at the front desk with PC Miller and Smythe the solicitor.

'That's it, you're free to go.' Clarke signed the final papers. 'Inspector Frost will speak with Gary. Please remember it's for the best.'

The woman remained silent but Smythe nodded; he had impressed on his client the necessity of questioning her son. Frost had gone on ahead, in the hope of having a word before the mother returned home and possibly escalated the situation.

Clarke watched pensively as Maria Benson left Eagle Lane.

The detective might not be well disposed towards Frost at present, but she did not enjoy seeing him make a hash of things. And, unfortunately, this was how people were seeing the Curtis case unfold. She wondered whether had he not stumbled upon an intruder at Curtis's place the investigation might have developed in other directions. Because when it boiled down to it, that's all it was: there was an intruder, probably thieving, and it had nothing whatsoever to do with the woman's murder.

Maria Benson was followed out of the building by Sergeant Wallace, head bowed, into the rain. Wally raised his hand solemnly as he left. Events and moods had altered in line with a change in the weather.

The telephone rang urgently behind Clarke.

'Bloody unfair, poor Wally,' Miller said, ignoring Wells' phone right beside him. The departing sergeant was the constable's boss. All to do with a council depot being raided, and road markings being left unpainted. 'If CID were up to snuff and caught the buggers that nicked the paint in the first place it'd never have happened. Should be them being marched out the door.'

'And what's your contribution been so far this week, eh?' said Clarke. The sharpness in her tone took the PC aback. 'Answer the bloody phone, why don't you, it's the least you can do.'

'Right there! Slow down!' Clarke ordered, but they'd already overshot the entrance. Simms braked hard, then shifted the car into reverse. The entrance to the caravan park was set back from the road, and obscured by dense overgrown foliage. As they passed under the dark green oak canopy, Clarke saw two forgotten stone lions sitting upon ancient red brickwork to either side of the entrance. Once upon a time they must have heralded a gateway to a much grander setting than an unsightly twentieth-century caravan park.

'Caravan parks,' Simms remarked. 'Never been to one before.'

'Why would you?' Miller said from the back seat of the Golf. They drove along an unmade gravel road, passing by the white rectangular vans. Although they were relatively well spaced out, they were altogether at odds with the serene woodland setting. 'Jeez, this place is the back of beyond. Why would anyone come here to spend their summer in a sardine tin?'

Half an hour ago Simms had called from the High Fields care home: Neil Cassidy, one of Weaver's patients, had recovered his speech and was able to communicate some information. The sharp-thinking off-duty PC had made a vital connection, and a quick call to Cassidy's daughter had led them to Cravensea Caravan Park, nine miles south of Denton.

A white-haired couple made their way slowly along the roadside, regarding the people inside the passing car with curiosity.

'You might not like it now,' Clarke remarked, answering Miller, 'but in thirty years' time when all you've energy for is mowing your patch of grass and watering the geraniums, before a quick sherry, a bowl of peanuts and nodding off to James Galway at noon, things might look different.' Clarke was exaggerating, but she remembered a similar place in Suffolk she'd visited as a child with her grandparents, and more recently, her parents.

'Sounds like you've got it all mapped out.'

'Huh, let's just say I can appreciate the attraction,' she said, thinking of her unhappy mother changing her grandson's nappies back in her Denton flat.

When Clarke had picked up Simms's call at Eagle Lane she'd not even heard of the place. Nobody had. So the collective intelligence of CID had resorted to consulting the Yellow Pages to find the location. Cravensea Park, they had learned, was in the grounds of a Tudor manor house, thought once to have been owned by Anne Boleyn. But for all its historical resplendence it had been a devil to find.

'Which one could it be?' Clarke asked, peering through the trees.

'Hmm. A white one?' said Simms, helpfully.

'Well thank you, Sherlock.' Clarke glanced at the boy. For an instant she saw his brother, Derek, with whom she'd been in similar situations many a time. 'It's no time to be funny, David. Pull over here, next to this one . . .'

It was the young policeman's day off, but such was his enthusiasm to be involved, he'd insisted on driving. Her gaze lingered on the young man; she didn't know how she felt towards him. He was sweet and boyish, lacking the brash arrogance of his older brother. She wondered what he had heard about Derek's relationship with her . . . and Philip. There was a conversation to be had, this she knew. But now was not the time for such thoughts.

Simms parked the car under an enormous oak that bordered the gravel road and afforded the caravans privacy from passing cars. Cars were parked in between the mobile homes, indicating which might be occupied.

An elderly gent gingerly descended the two steps down from the next caravan, pausing to consider the new arrivals. 'Be on the lookout for a maroon Volvo,' Clarke said, 'Weaver more than likely drove it out here, but he may have hidden it from view . . .'

Simms switched off the ignition. 'Look, there.' He pointed towards a signpost marked *Office and Toilets* near a single-lane track breaking off the main drive.

'Miller, you keep your eye on the road,' Clarke said, taking control of the situation.

''Ello, 'ello . . . what have we got here, male, under sixty-five,' Miller said from the back seat, 'shortish ginger hair, bit of a beard?'

Clarke and Simms swung round together, almost knocking heads.

'Bloke coming this way tugging a trolley with a large plastic container on it.'

'Stay put,' Clarke whispered, unnecessarily, 'he's coming straight towards us.'

Weaver, and it was definitely him, had been to fill up with water; here he came ambling back into their line of vision.

Just then, a squirrel hopped on to the track to inspect an acorn and sat there, right between Weaver and their car.

'Ah, look at that,' Miller said in mock tenderness.

'Damn it – he's seen us.' There could be no mistaking three adults sitting in a strange car in the middle of the day. The man darted between two caravans. Clarke burst out of the Golf. She signalled to the others to circle behind as she gave chase. She rounded the caravan as Weaver slipped between the trees beyond. He didn't have too much ground on them. She must be able to catch him – if she didn't lose sight of him. She entered the woods and ran through the trees, following what she thought was a path until her foot caught in brambles. Stopping dead, she panted heavily, hands on knees. Christ, she'd not run like that, since . . . God knows, well before Philip was born.

Weaver was gone. Or was he? She couldn't see him, but then perhaps he wasn't visible through the dense foliage. Clarke stood still, blood pulsing in her ears. A bird called in alarm to her left. Beyond a thicket of hazels was a large fallen tree. Crouching low, she edged her way towards the horizontal trunk. It was moist underfoot and she moved soundlessly until she was able to reach out and touch the crumbling bark. The bird – a blackbird – was still audible on the other side. She glanced left then right along the fallen tree: one way a tangle of branches, the other a mass of roots and earth. Her choices were limited. She let the trunk take her weight and breathed deeply.

After a minute, or it could have been two, when the roaring in her ears had subsided, she took stock of her position. Should she wait for the others? No, there was nothing for it but to get over to the other side. She felt her way along the bark until she found a foothold, then with her hand she grasped the stump of a branch. In two swift moves she was over, landing not more than three feet away from a startled Ben Weaver. The two faced each other, both crouched catlike in equal amazement. Weaver made to lunge but thought better of it, which prompted Clarke to cry out, 'Here!' and again, 'Over here!' Weaver turned and fled further into the woods. Clarke gave chase again. She could hear her colleagues' calls in the distance but she hadn't the breath to respond. Branches and brambles whipped her face but she was gaining on her target when, abruptly, he vanished. She stopped dead for a second in disbelief, and called faintly, 'Over here,' but with little conviction, before moving on cautiously. In less than twenty paces the grass underfoot gave way to fast-flowing water – a riverbank, hidden from view by low-hanging branches. Below her a lily-white hand was clutching desperately at a tuft of grass.

'Help!' Weaver spluttered. 'I can't swim. I can't . . .'

Clarke edged forward, raising her foot . . .

'Got the bastard!' Miller said. 'You've got a pair of legs on you, Detective, we had trouble keeping up.'

She glared at the pathetic figure in the water, then turned away, leaving the men to pull the murderer out of the river. She wasn't sure they shouldn't have just left him to drown.

Thursday (4)

The celebration at Ben Weaver's arrest was short-lived, much to PC Simms's dismay. His quick thinking had got CID a result, but that success was overshadowed by some major bust-up between Frost and Mullett. Nobody knew what had gone on in the superintendent's office, only that there had been an almighty row.

Simms entered the canteen dejectedly. It was his day off but he might as well grab a bite to eat here before disappearing off home. In the queue he spied Mullett's secretary, Miss Smith, talking with two WPCs. Simms strolled over with a confident demeanour, hoping she might offer a congratulatory word. But the woman was visibly shaken, and paid him no heed. Simms stood there like a spare part and found himself enquiring what was up.

'Jack Frost. Blowing his top at the superintendent,' Liz Smith said tersely, unappreciative of the interruption. 'I was,' she continued, 'sure he was going to punch him, and if Sergeant Waters hadn't intervened, who knows how it would have ended. I was sure I'd have to call for help . . .'

How big a deal could this be, he wondered.

'You all right?' Clarke now stood behind him.

'Sure.'

'Let's grab a coffee.'

The pair took a table in the far corner. Having asked Simms to join her, Clarke then sat and said nothing, opting to stir her coffee in silence. This was the first time they'd been alone since her return to Eagle Lane. The pursuit of Weaver had been adrenalin-fuelled, and he'd felt only the excitement and a desire to impress. Now, presented with the woman herself, the one person at Eagle Lane he'd wanted to get to know and perhaps connect with in some way, he couldn't think of anything to say.

'That was something, eh, back there?' he said eventually, thinking of Weaver. He couldn't very well ask about her child in the staff canteen.

She placed her spoon on the saucer. 'Sure was,' she said as if she'd just remembered he was there. 'Well done for acting so promptly when visiting your mother, not everyone would have the wherewithal to put two and two together like that.'

He couldn't help but smile. It was all he wanted to hear, really. The whole thing was over so quickly – Weaver was carted off to County almost immediately to be questioned over another similar case – 'Oh, it was nothing really. Anyone would have done the same – besides, you're the one that actually caught him.'

'Teamwork,' she said with a faint smile.

He'd never considered Sue Clarke at close quarters before, but for the first time now saw how pretty she was, and why his brother had been so smitten. Tired though, eyes marked by dark shadows. He changed tack. 'What's all the fuss with Inspector Frost?'

'Good question. After we brought Weaver in, Jack caught Mullett in the lobby, and demanded he change his mind.'

'Over what?'

She shrugged. 'Well, that's the mystery, nobody knows. They disappeared into Mullett's office and had an almighty barney.'

Simms felt a hand on his shoulder. 'Sorry to interrupt,' Sergeant Waters said, 'but might I borrow Detective Clarke?'

'What's up?'

'Jack's going into interview room one with Gary Benson; I thought a calming influence might be needed . . .'

'Not sure I've got it in me,' she said wearily.

But off she went and David Simms was left with two cold coffees. One crime quickly replaced another, and one small victory was soon forgotten. All the same, the young policeman was moved in ways he found difficult to explain, and fought hard to resist the temptation to run after Clarke.

'Do you know how much patience I have with you and your dear old mum, Gary?'

The man shook his head.

'This much.' Frost pursed his thumb and forefinger tightly together, and held his hand high so all in the room could see.

Clarke had never seen Jack this angry before; whatever the bust-up with Mullett was about, it must have been monumental. To his credit, Gary Benson had come in of his own accord, not that it appeared to win him any favour with Frost. And this was only preliminary questioning – Benson had not been interviewed prior to today.

'Now, I'm going to ask you a series of questions that require a yes or no answer, so it's very straightforward. Got that?'

'Yes, Mr Frost.'

'If you give me a wrong answer, you will at the very least lose your job. I assure you Harry will see to that, understood?'

Clarke watched Frost in amazement; she had never witnessed him threaten a suspect in such a way. She tried to catch Waters' eye, but he stood observing calmly at the back of the room.

'Right, off we go. Did you know Rachel Curtis?'

'Yes, Mr Frost.'

'Did you go to Dominic Holland's party?'

'Yes, Mr Frost.'

'With Rachel?'

'No.'

Frost gave it a moment's pause, then said again, 'Did you go to the party with Miss Curtis?'

'Err . . . yes and no,' Benson said, looking confused.

'Jack—' Clarke wanted to interrupt. The bouncer was clearly terrified.

Frost ignored her and prompted, 'Gary?'

'I went to get her but she'd already left.'

'What?'

'On me bike. I knew she was going, I said I'd pick her up at midnight. But she'd gone.'

'Gone where, with who?'

'I dunno, I went in the 'ouse but they were all bladdered.'

'Did you speak to anyone, is there anyone who could confirm your story?'

'Yeah, a couple of woofters were hoovering coke in the front porch. A little fella and a big gobby one with a spastic haircut.' The florists.

'Gary, we've spoken to them already,' Clarke said calmly, aware that Frost was pacing furiously, 'and they might not be entirely credible as witnesses.'

Benson turned to Frost anxiously. 'It's true, Mr Frost, they were munted, but that's hardly my fault. She never left with me! She weren't there no more. I was well narked, tore up the geezer's lawn on me bike.'

'Why oh flamin' why did you not say this earlier!'

'I thought you'd think I'd done it, because of me mum. Her making threats, an' all.'

'What time was this?'

'About midnight. Rachel had already gone by then, I'm tellin' ya—'

'Could have been in that taxi,' interrupted Waters.

Frost looked at the sergeant. His theory about the man pretending to be a taxi driver. A man they'd not been able to identify but who allegedly was wearing a flat cap of the sort sold at Castleton's.

'How much earlier?' Frost turned back to Benson.

'Well, early, one of them fellas said she'd left about nine. I dunno.'

'All right, you two can go,' Frost said, addressing Waters and Clarke. He leaned in to Waters. 'But not too far . . .'

Frost calmed down after his colleagues departed and he was left alone with Gary Benson. He understood the man's predicament; mother and son were each protecting the other. At the same time, though, he was disappointed that neither felt they could trust the police, or him personally, with the information. Gary said he'd picked Rachel up at the Codpiece around sevenish and then dropped her off in Two Bridges and agreed a time to collect her. So Taffy was telling the truth – Gary and his mother were there at the lock-in.

'Why did she want to go to the party?'

'Could smell money, couldn't she. Always smart, that one. Not my sort, rather be in the pub with me mum and me mates. I'm sorry about the geezer's lawn – I was just pissed off that she'd dragged me out there again for nowt.'

'But why would she ask you to come get her, then leave sooner without letting you know?'

'Maybe she didn't feel well.'

'Maybe.' Frost lit a cigarette and passed the packet over.

'The morning after, I did wonder whether it was part of 'er parole or something. You know, home before midnight an' all that.'

Frost let out a jet of smoke. 'Good point. But nine o'clock? She's not a flamin' schoolgirl.'

Gary just shrugged. 'I dunno,' he said eventually, 'that probation geezer was always on her case. Right menace.'

'So he should be. It's his job.'

'He really didn't like her seeing me,' he said mournfully.

'Why was that?' It struck Frost as unusual that someone from the probation office would express such a forceful opinion on who one of his charges was seeing, unless they were a known villain.

'I dunno,' he said again and scratched at a shaving rash under his chin. 'She was *always* having to see him, though.'

'Hmm.' Although Frost took what Gary was saying with a pinch of salt, what he was hearing was not in accordance with what he had been told. Fergusson was to see her once a week, was his understanding. He'd check that with Waters, who was waiting outside for him.

Frost tossed over his pack of Rothmans. 'Here.' He rubbed the back of his neck, he wasn't really angry with the confused bouncer, no, his real anger now was directed at Mullett. Despite the spectacularly swift arrest of Ben Weaver, the superintendent was refusing to lift the blanket ban on leave. Apparently, the super did not consider the arrest of a murderer a significant enough result; no, in his eyes the real problem was the Rachel Curtis case. Apparently, this case would have all sorts of 'ramifications' were it not brought to a quick resolution. The bungled television appeal had only added fuel to the flames and delivered Mullett his favourite target on a plate: Frost.

Frost saw Waters wave at him through the small window in the interview-room door. 'Now. I'm guessing, although you might not have killed Rachel, you do have a front-door key to her house?'

He nodded guiltily.

'And I'm guessing that it was you leaping out of the first-floor window when I arrived the other day? Stop me if I'm very much mistaken, but you weren't there to water the plants, were you. You went to pick something up, something that might incriminate you.' Frost couldn't think what. Something small and personal, that would fit in a jacket pocket. 'What was it?'

The bouncer remained silent.

'Come on!' Frost glanced at the window again. 'I haven't all day.' He had his money on a lighter, stuffed away somewhere they'd overlooked.

Benson mumbled a word Frost didn't catch.

'Cat got your tongue?'

'Pants. I was looking for my Y-fronts,' he said meekly.

'You what? What on earth? How could you leave without your grundies? I know it's been a bit on the hot side, but all the same . . .' Having said that, Frost had mislaid his spare pair himself. He'd left Sue's wearing the only pair he now had to his name.

'She . . . errr, wanted to keep them, as a souvenir, like.'

'Jimmy Hill!' Frost rubbed his chin in distaste – 'What the flamin' heck would a girl – even a nutter like this – want with your pants?' Gary was embarrassed. 'Well, it takes all sorts, I suppose. You gave me the right runaround.'

'Yeah, but you can see why I didn't want to stop.'

'Why'd you even risk it? It's not that we could identify a man from his underwear . . . not unless he had his name written in them.'

Gary blushed to his roots. 'It's Mum,' he said. 'She always gives me personalized pants for Christmas, since I was a nipper.'

Frost looked at the hulk of a man sitting next to him. There was no explaining the relationship between a mother and son, but this took the biscuit.

'Go on, get out of here.'

*

'What about this phantom taxi driver then?' Frost said, watching Benson shamble off down the corridor.

'Well, the old boy at Castleton's said he'd not sold a flat cap like that one since Terry Todd bought his at the beginning of August. Not much call for them in the summer.'

'Is he sure?'

'He'd done a stock-take the other day.'

'So where does that leave us?'

'There was one missing though.'

'Oh . . .'

'His daughter sometimes minds the shop for him during the holidays. It's possible she sold it – his records aren't great; the till was prehistoric. Trouble is, she's now on a French exchange with the school. He'll try and call her tonight though.'

'Hmm, schoolgirls on a trip to France doesn't sound promising.'

'Sorry,' Waters added.

'It's not your fault. I'm going back to the churchyard later. Whoever killed Rachel must have had a reason for leaving her there.'

'How do you arrive at that?'

'I don't know for sure, but since we have established she was at Holland's party – regardless of the time she left – the simple fact she ended up in the churchyard must have some explanation. Originally I had thought she might have been the victim of some horseplay that had gone drastically wrong, you know, a bit of hanky-panky in the graveyard.' He caught Waters' eye. 'Now I'm thinking maybe she pulled a posh London type at the party and left early to take him home – nice big house and comfy bed, who wouldn't rather that than get a sore arse banging up and down in a cemetery.' Frost paused, giving the possibility some further consideration. 'No,' he pronounced, 'there has to be a reason for it: it's not on her way home.'

'But we don't know that she left the party with anyone. We *think* she left with some geezer purporting to be a taxi driver, who came to collect her early.'

'Granted. The question still stands though – there has to be a logic to the churchyard. Look at the map. St Mary's is so far out of the way, between her place and Two Bridges, it has to be significant.'

The pair stood in the corridor, considering the next move. Footsteps approached, and along came the large silhouette of Arthur Hanlon. 'Where the bleedin' hell have you been?' said Frost.

'Sheffield!' the man shouted back.

'Right, the mother, at last.' Frost puffed out his cheeks. 'OK, I better attend to this. But you go get ready for your big day . . . wait, there was one thing. Fergusson, the probation officer.'

'What about him?'

'Gazzer said that old Fergie was a bit of a pain in the arse, demanding on Rachel's time?'

'Funny, that's exactly what the woman I saw this morning on Sandpiper Close said – "a pain in the arse".'

'Which woman?'

'A neighbour of Rachel's that used Tête-à-Tête – reckoned Rachel got an earful about staying out late . . . so Clarke checked it out. Went to the probation office. Fergusson wasn't there but she saw the file, there were no curfew restrictions.'

'"Curfew"?'

'Yeah.' Waters paused. 'You sure I can go off now?'

'I insist. But remember: back at the Eagle for six thirty sharp.'

'Ah, wait – is this your way of making sure I come, by letting me get the preparations out of the way?'

'You've caught me out!' Frost clapped his friend on the back. Frost had chosen not to tell Waters of Mullett's moratorium. His pal would get a station send-off tonight, marry at noon and then jet off on his honeymoon to Barcelona if he had to fly him there himself. In any event, if he did not communicate the super's edict to CID officers under his command, then the only person who'd be for it would be him and him alone.

'I'll be at Kim's. You'll call if you need me?' Waters hesitated.

'You can count on it,' Frost called over his shoulder.

Thursday (5)

Generally, when he remembered, Frost would always have a woman officer in the room whilst interviewing a female suspect. He had long since realized that he was ill-equipped for deciphering the mysteries of the female mind. Still, there were some occasions, like with Maria Benson, when he forgot. He had to concede that the outcome might not have been so long drawn out if he'd had some help at hand. So, given Mrs Curtis's very vocal reluctance to travel down to Denton, he was not taking any chances this afternoon and had two female officers present; DC Clarke and a WPC. Thus far, Mrs Curtis had answered every question in a straightforward fashion, which was a blessed relief after the aggro of Maria Benson. He could only assume her initial resistance was down to Hanlon's incompetence. Though Frost loved the ageing detective dearly, he was proving himself less than useful as time moved on. Or, to coin the super's phrase, the older he got, the more he turned into 'an absolute cretin'.

'And Rachel's father?' he said, hearing his voice growing hoarse. Too much talking and shouting.

'Pah, he was never there,' the woman answered as the WPC placed a cup of tea before her. Frost was struck by the parallel with the murdered prostitute and her orphaned son, and wondered if the outcome might have been different in either case if there had been a man on the scene. He was firmly of the view that one had to lie in the bed one made for oneself.

'I'm sorry,' Frost said, 'it can't have been easy, raising a kid on your own. I'm all for castrating the wandering male of the species.'

Clarke shifted in her seat. Frost felt himself prickle with embarrassment; he was a thoughtless oaf, at times. He coughed a smoker's hack to cover his shame.

'Huh, no, it wasn't that,' Mrs Curtis said after taking a sip of her tea, 'though, sure, legging it would have crossed his mind given 'alf the chance. No, he was in Strangeways for thieving. When is anything ever easy? Better off without him anyway, he was completely useless. Always disappointing the girl.'

'Thank you for coming down, Mrs Curtis,' Frost said, not wishing to dwell on absent fathers any longer, 'what we need help on is fleshing out Rachel's character, to help us work out her tragic final hours.'

'What she hankered after was discipline. Unlike most little girls, Rachel wanted guidance, to be told what to do, but her father was useless, vain and arrogant, only interested in himself . . . still is.'

'Yes, I have heard that an authority figure was lacking in her life.'

'But she always picked rotters, see; that Robert, and before him, Darren. Making her do things that were . . . unseemly.'

'We know about Robert Nicholson, Mrs Curtis,' Clarke said, moving closer, 'but tell me about this Darren . . . What sort of things?'

'When she was still at school.' She took a deep breath. 'I know she was only a youngster, and he was a lot older, but she should have known better.'

'What happened, Mrs Curtis?' Clarke asked solicitously.

'Always taking risks, doing silly dares. It's ironic she ended up in a churchyard: that was just like the first time she was in trouble with the law. Broad daylight too, indecent it was.' Frost had known it had to be significant.

'I'm sorry' – Clarke leaned forward – 'I'm not with you.'

'Well, put it this way. Her reputation in ruins at fifteen. Vicar caught her and Darren at it. In the churchyard. Called the coppers.'

'Did she . . .' Frost didn't know how to phrase it carefully, so didn't bother trying. 'Like a bit of kinky stuff, you know.'

The woman was aghast. Luckily Clarke intervened. 'She was easily led into doing silly things, is that right, Mrs Curtis?'

'Yes, always looking to be led and wanting to impress at the same time, a fatal combination for a pretty girl,' she said defiantly.

'This lad that led your Rachel astray, what did you say his name was? Darren?'

'That was all of seventeen years ago,' Mrs Curtis said, surprised, 'besides, as you said at the start, she'd not, you know . . .'

'Quite, Mrs Curtis,' Clarke said calmly. 'Don't you worry, we just need to rule out all possibilities. We will get whoever did this.'

'Leave no stone unturned,' Frost said, and then added quietly to himself, 'Grave or otherwise.'

'Call West Yorkshire Police, get on to them to find this Darren Tandy.'

'Really? I see from the path report she'd been sexually active recently but there was no sign of her putting up a struggle,' Clarke said as they entered the CID general office. 'Besides, Rachel has not seen the man in over fifteen years?'

'Think about it. Tandy sees Rachel's name splashed all over

the press and thinks to himself, maybe it's time to get reacquainted?'

'What, after she's released on mental health grounds? It's not exactly winning a gold medal at the Olympics, is it,' Clarke said doubtfully.

'Benson died from a heart attack in hospital.' Sue Clarke watched him scratch around for his cigarettes. 'Maybe Tandy was curious, likewise our Rachel about him, but when they met up things got a bit out of control.'

'That's not your desk any more, Jack.' She had binned a pack of stale Rothmans earlier. 'Do you think you're going to change that polo shirt any time soon? You've been in it all week,' she said, noticing an unsightly stain.

'Will do. Tomorrow, for sure. Anyway, we won't know what happened until we speak to him, will we?' he said, giving up the search. 'It's a lead and we're not getting anywhere with the mystery taxi driver. By the way, where was the probation officer this morning?'

'Fergusson wasn't there,' Clarke said. 'I saw the conditions of release and there were no curfew restrictions, only distance.'

'I heard. Where was he?'

'He works out of Rimmington and County most of the time, apparently.'

'Of course, I forget we see him around as he lives locally . . . Right, there's two other murdered-prostitute cases we're reopening in the light of Ben Weaver's capture – well done on that, by the way. Still got it, ain'tcha. I need an hour or two to run through the files down in Records and then I'll meet you at St Mary's churchyard. Have a meander round the graveyard while you're waiting, see if we've missed anything.'

'Why don't we go together from here?'

Frost shook his head vehemently. 'No, no . . . I've to make a stop on the way. Personal matter.'

'Personal' was not a word Jack Frost had used before, at least not with her. Maybe something was wrong. Maybe she'd been too dismissive. Maybe the doctor had bad news. He didn't look too clever, but then again he never did . . . 'Are you all right, Jack?' Her phone started to ring. Frost reached out on reflex, but caught himself in time and stepped back, gesturing for her to answer it. 'Detective Clarke speaking.' It was a woman asking for Frost. She held the receiver out. He took it without comment.

'Ah . . . hello . . . how are you? Good, good.' He turned his back on Clarke, but she could hear him mutter that now was not a good time to talk. After a brief apology he hung up and left the office without another word. Clarke instantly grew concerned and a wave of guilt washed over her for turfing him out of her flat.

The superintendent paced his office.

He'd been marching up and down for the best part of an hour. Frost had really wormed his way under his skin this time. Mullett was overcome with a feeling of faintness. He stopped to loosen his tie, something he would never normally do – usually the Windsor knot remained secure beneath his Adam's apple until he crossed the threshold in the evening – but needs must. His breathing had become laboured, the room felt airless and yet the temperature had cooled significantly.

He was absolutely right to hold steadfast on the leave issue; Frost had no right, no right whatsoever, to dictate how he ran his station! The capture of Ben Weaver had absolutely nothing to do with it. And as far as that was concerned Frost wasn't even involved in the arrest. Mullett eyed his pills in the small container on the desk. He'd had today's dose already, another might do more harm than good. He needed a holiday, desperately, that was all. The golf-club chairmanship was a setback, but not the end of the world. He looked to Margaret Thatcher on the wall, noble and resilient. She'd not be thwarted by the kind of morons he had to put up with . . . Not for turning and all that. All the same, he might go home early for a lie-down.

Frost thanked the WPC for the lift to the motorbike garage. He gave a crafty wink to a pretty blonde and alluded to her riding pillion. She tittered and said her dad used to run her to school on a bike. He wondered if that was a brush-off – was he old enough to be her father? He watched her pull away. Not that he'd know where to start with a girl that young any more. Shame. A wisp of a thing like that on the back of a bike tearing through the countryside was an appealing thought . . . She was similar in build to Karen Thomas, in fact. He still couldn't get her out of his head. Karen had called him at Eagle Lane unexpectedly just now, wanting to meet up on Friday. But Frost's enthusiasm had dwindled after learning of her entanglement with Hudson. She was obviously a gold-digger, how else to explain the banker. No, Julie was more his speed, a bit broader across the beam; he'd need to have a bike with some oomph there, he chuckled, thinking of her cherries as he ambled across the forecourt.

Yes, his mood had altered significantly. The rage he felt for Mullett only lasted while he was cooped up at the station. Anyway, since he'd resolved to disobey the super, there really wasn't anything to get worked up about. Indeed, now he was out of there, he felt rather perky. En route Frost had even nipped into Topman and bought a clean shirt, discarding the filthy Fred Perry one in the store bin. He'd dabbed on a bit of Blue Stratos at the till on the way out. He had to host John's booze-up tonight and after Clarke's comment on his attire he thought he should make an effort to be presentable. He did listen to her but didn't like to let on – any more than he'd tell her what he was really up to now before meeting her at St Mary's churchyard . . .

For the last six months all Frost's personal mail had been directed to Eagle Lane, and this morning Bill Wells had handed him a solicitor's letter, which for once he'd opened straight away. To date all envelopes marked with a Thwaites and Co. frank he'd parked under the computer keyboard, the contents un- doubtedly pertaining to all manner of sad and grim reports in relation to Mary's estate. But this one he knew to be different; this envelope contained a cheque. For all her bitterness, Mary's mother had conceded that Frost's income had paid for the upkeep of the house, and though not a handyman himself, he had at every turn paid what was required when necessary, from a new boiler, to roof insulation, to recarpeting. The house had been well maintained, and as such it had fetched a good price. After his trip to Topman he'd banked a cheque for £2,000, with- drawn £250 in cash, and now he was going to buy himself a motorbike.

The imminent purchase was not necessarily something that required secrecy, but he'd not told a single soul; not that he usually cared what anyone thought, but the fact that he was still technically homeless might draw scorn, a bike seeming frivolous in comparison. The truth was, he felt he deserved a treat, and given he was without a car it struck him that a motorbike had its merits. Especially with the traffic in town this summer – he'd certainly get about quicker. Besides, he thought as he perused the rows of brightly coloured fierce-looking machines, he was hardly going to blow the whole whack.

'All right there, buddy' – a slender long-haired salesman approached him – 'what can I interest you in?'

'I'm after a bike,' he said openly.

'You've come to the right place.' The salesman waved across the array. 'What you after?'

'I'm not sure. I can ride but not been on one in ages.'

'That's all right, lot of blokes your age decide they fancy a bike.'

Bleedin' cheek, Frost thought but secretly he was pleased the boy recognized his seniority. 'Talk me through what you got.'

The guy happily delivered chapter and verse on an array of foreign bikes with names he'd never heard of – Suzuki, Yamaha, Kawasaki. 'Gordon Bennett, these sound like Chinese to me.'

'Japanese, all of 'em.'

'Haven't you got anything made in Great Britain? My old man rode a BSA during the war, he'd turn in his grave if he thought I was on a machine from the land of the rising sun.'

'They are the best. British bikes, like British motors, are basically a pile of crap.'

'Wait a mo, what's that over there?' Frost pointed to a black bike to one side.

'That? That's a trade-in. Nah, not what you're after. Now take this Z250, a good entry-level bike for such—' But Frost had wandered off.

'Tell me about this one.'

'Well, it's made in India for a start.'

'Hmm, that's good enough for me.' He ran his fingers along the worn seat. 'I like it.'

Frost had not returned to Eagle Lane. In truth, he thought it extremely unlikely Darren Tandy had anything to do with the death of Rachel Curtis; but it was an avenue that needed to be investigated, and would occupy Clarke while he checked out a hunch of his own.

He stopped the newly acquired motorcycle in the communal parking area outside Baron's Court, the block of flats behind Market Square. His legs were a shade wobbly; the old bike vibrated like hell, but the sensation itself while riding was not an unpleasant one.

The elegant Victorian building before him was a stark contrast to the ugly concrete blocks on the Southern Housing Estate where Jane Hammond and Weaver had lived. No, a different class of people resided here, mainly retired folk with a few bob tucked away, or younger professionals with respectable jobs in the community. However, here as with the housing estate over the canal, Frost sensed darkness.

The flat he wanted was on the second floor. And the resident, a single man, was working out of town today. Donal Fergusson, a fifty-six-year-old probation officer, had been in the district for over ten years, and today was at Rimmington. On the occasions Frost had come into contact with the Scotsman, he had found him charmless and brusque. How the fellow had ended up here in Denton was a mystery. A solitary individual who kept himself to himself; the consensus was he had fled his native Glasgow following an acrimonious marital break-up. Frost was no judge of others' domestic circumstances, but a man's history was a consideration when fathoming an inexplicable situation. Gary Benson's throwaway remark had led Frost to think Fergusson's relationship with Rachel Curtis unusual enough to warrant scrutinizing the public servant a little more closely. But it was tricky to get a handle on, the very nature of their relationship being confidential, with no witnesses to their meetings. No, Frost had to chance it, and delve into the man's life if he was to glean anything at all. The final nudge had been Rachel's mother's description of her daughter: that she had always been susceptible to a man with power . . . one that might make her leave a party early at nine and not midnight?

Frost checked the walkway was clear, before hurrying to Fergusson's door. Not a soul. This was CID's second illegal entry this week, and as such he'd undertaken this operation solo; it was extremely dicey, because if Fergusson caught him here, there would be all hell to pay. Frost needed to be nimble. Fortunately the locks to these doors were ancient, and he'd been in other flats in the block before. He deftly picked a master key from one of many hanging from an enormous bunch that he yanked out of his jacket pocket (a new leather number he'd bought at a discount with the Royal Enfield). The door gave easily and he was inside the cool apartment in seconds.

Fergusson's place was clean and neat, with not much in the way of ornaments on the G-plan furniture. There was a bookcase and record player. The books were fiction; nobody he recognized, the swirling type and period costumes on the cover led him to believe they might be romances. He flipped up the smoked-plastic hood of the turntable – Robert Schumann: *Fantasie in C.* Classical, Frost sniffed, his knowledge of such music did not stretch much beyond what he'd read of the tastes of Napoleon (which was Italian opera. Not that Frost had listened to that either), with whom he'd been fascinated for years. He replaced the lid, and not wishing to hang around any longer than was strictly necessary, moved into the bedroom at the back of the flat. The room was in semi-darkness with thin curtains half drawn, possibly to keep the room cool. Beyond the window would be the well-maintained courtyard down below. The bed, of wrought-iron construction, was immaculately made.

Opposite it was a heavy free-standing wardrobe; so large that the inspector wondered how Fergusson had managed to get it up the stairs and through the flat entrance. Frost pulled a handkerchief from his back pocket and gently pulled open the wardrobe door. Drab-coloured suits hung lifeless, with winter coats at one end. Beneath the clothes lay a mixed array of shoes; large feet, size eleven or twelve, quite a few pairs, too. At the back, partially hidden, was something with a patent-leather finish. A dress shoe? Unlikely. He bent down and parted the long winter coats to reveal a woman's stiletto. There was nothing else in the wardrobe, or indeed the whole flat, to indicate a woman's presence. Frost slowly leaned inside and delicately, as if retrieving something incredibly fragile, lifted the shoe. Size four. Rachel Curtis's size. He gently put the shoe back, and exited the flat as quickly as he could, heart pumping as if about to break out of his chest.

Thursday (6)

He wasn't at the churchyard entrance where they'd agreed to meet. Clarke paced the cobbled street and breathed in the scent of recent rain on the trees. Maybe he'd gone ahead alone. The DS walked round the side of the church, weaving through the wet grass and in between wonky headstones. But neither was Frost waiting for her at the grave where she understood the body had been discovered. She glanced at the headstone: *Norah Elizabeth Wilkins, 1860–1892*. There was more, but she couldn't make it out, the lettering eroded and faint. Why this became Rachel Curtis's final resting place was a mystery. It did seem peculiar, she had to admit. She stepped closer to get a better look at the stonework; she was curious about Norah. A movement to the right caught her eye. Under a yew tree towards the back of the church, she saw a silhouette.

The portly figure was one she was familiar with. Frost turned to face her in the greying light. He raised a hand and fluttered his fingers. He'd not mentioned Mary once to Clarke in the whole time he'd stayed with her. Clarke knew Frost's wife was buried here and now she felt she was intruding. He made his way over.

'Sorry, Jack. If you wanted some time to—'

He dismissed her apology. 'Just checking she's still there, don't want her creeping up on me unannounced,' he joked chirpily. 'I wanted to forget she was here, to be honest. How did you get on?'

'Darren Tandy is dead,' Clarke said flatly. 'Died years ago.'

Frost nodded. 'Hmm.'

'Just "hmm"?'

'What do you want me to say? Excellent, another dead end?'

'No . . .' She was at a loss for words.

'But I wonder all the same if Rachel being left lying here might be significant – that incident with Tandy from her past . . .'

'But who would know about that, other than her mother – it's not public knowledge . . .'

'We found out soon enough. Since we discovered she was at Holland's party, I haven't stopped thinking that her body being here is meaningful.'

'How, though?'

Frost turned full circle, slowly surveying the grounds. 'Look around you, what do you see?'

Clarke scanned the churchyard, not sure what she was looking for. 'A load of old headstones.'

'Correct. But how many are this ornate, with both the headstone and slab intact?'

'None that I can see . . . maybe at the front?'

'Nope, there is only the one. Belongs to a rich widow.'

'I saw, aged thirty-two; is that the age Rachel was?'

'Yep.' He slapped the moss-covered stonework and started off down the path. He was grinning.

'Wait!' She hurried after him. 'What's going on?' She'd seen that cheeky smirk before. He was on to something.

'This was premeditated. The murderer saw this slab, and earmarked it for Rachel.'

'Why?'

'Why?' They'd reached the entrance. 'I haven't a clue *why*. But this is the place to start looking for an answer.' He handed her a piece of paper listing three sets of names and dates. Two dates were from earlier that month, and one was from July.

He surprised her by mounting an old motorcycle parked by the church's stone wall.

'What's this?'

'The list of recent burials. Poor sods.' He gave the bike a kick-start, to which it responded by roaring into life and emitting a cloud of black smoke. 'Speak to the next of kin.' He pulled on a pair of old-fashioned goggles.

'I thought you were staying, to visit Mary's . . .'

'Nah, told you, I forgot the old lady was even here . . . Pretty bad form, eh, given her mother has finally coughed up.'

Clarke didn't get the reference and Frost chose not to elucidate.

'What about a helmet—'

But it was pointless, her words were drowned out as he revved the engine, pulled out and rode away.

'And then he just roared off on an old motorcycle.'

'I didn't know Jack Frost had a motorbike,' Kim Myles said, topping up Sue's wine glass. They were having a cheese and wine night at Kim's sister's house on Bath Hill before Kim's big day. The six women sat in a circle in the spacious front room.

'Nor did I,' Clarke replied.

'Does it come with a sidecar?' A woman with sandy-blonde hair that Clarke didn't know asked. 'Frost likes to be chauffeured around, so I heard.'

'Me too,' confirmed another. 'Heard he likes a drink or two.'

Apart from Kim's sister Lorraine they were all on the police force and based at Rimmington. The conversation inevitably turned to work – with most questions being directed towards Clarke and the goings-on at Eagle Lane, a perennial source of interest at Rimmington.

'He likes a drink as much as the next man. He likes to think, too,' Clarke said casually, not wanting to be seen to be leaping to his defence. 'Can't drink and drive, can't think and drive either. Typical man, I guess, terrible multi-tasker.'

'Poor lamb,' said a woman Clarke didn't know, 'but a woman would never get away with it.'

'A woman would never make inspector, full stop,' another said.

'Sue had Jack Frost sleeping on her settee for a couple of weeks,' Kim said, sensing an awkwardness, smiling at Sue. Clarke didn't correct her on the timescale – she thought the other woman was being tactful by making their connection clear without raising any eyebrows.

'Really? What was that like?' asked Jenny, the quieter brides-maid. 'He's a bit of a ladies' man.'

'Wouldn't know . . . I've got a baby, and they didn't quite hit it off.'

'Didn't he have two girlfriends when his wife was ill?'

'Not that I know of.' She prayed she wasn't blushing. 'He's always on the job.'

'Exactly!' They laughed. The double entendre lightened the mood.

Sue watched them all giggling but didn't have the heart to join in. The conversation quickly returned to the other infamous Eagle Lane character.

'Is Mullett really that much of a stiff?'

'He runs a tight ship, no question,' she said, thinking of her own recent predicament and that of poor Wallace, the super's latest victim.

'But a good policeman?' Kim said, pulling a dubious face.

'Just dry . . .'

'. . . as sandpaper.'

'He's not his usual chirpy self at the moment, it has to be said,' Clarke conceded, 'he suspended Wallace and then went home sick.'

'What's the wife like? Word at our nick is she's a bit of a looker, but well-to-do, like Jean Simmons.'

'The actress?' Clarke said, aghast. 'Really? I have no idea! Nobody's ever seen her.'

'Like Arthur Daley's "'er indoors".'

'Men: always a woman behind the scenes clearing up. Like children, they need looking after.'

'And all hell to pay when they're kept tied down.'

'I wonder how the boys are getting on?'

PC David Simms was not used to drinking.

Detective Sergeant Waters' send-off at the Eagle was well under way, with policemen from all over the district, many still in uniform, filling the spacious pub to capacity. Cigarette smoke hung thickly in the air, obscuring the ceiling, absorbing the laughter and banter of the assembled crowd. Simms's head was starting to spin. Nevertheless he took another swig of his beer and turned his attention back to the conversation between two men from Bethnal Green. Both were detectives Waters had worked with before moving to Denton eighteen months ago. The taller of the two, in his fifties and now retired, was talking at length about 'Nipper' Read, the Met's Murder Squad super-intendent who had arrested the Kray twins. Simms had never met anyone who had actually worked with Nipper or had come into contact with the twins themselves. Simms had hoped the two coppers might share some little-known fact, some intimacy kept from the public, but after twenty minutes of listening he was starting to think they were both full of hot air.

He was growing restless and eager for conversation with

someone his own age. Though it was his day off, he'd been determined to come to the drinks. He'd never been to a proper policemen's bash before. The first disappointment was that it was to be held at the Eagle, the pub across the road from the station where every copper spent their spare time and money as it was. The second and greater disappointment was that it was to be a 'men only' affair. Simms was single, and he had hoped this would be an opportunity to chat up girls, especially after the week he'd had. A roar of laughter reached him from the bar, catching his attention. He made his apologies and moved on.

'Down it! Down it! Down it!' Waters slammed the glass on the bar, and let rip an enormous belch to huge applause. He was, there was no denying it, completely smashed.

'I think that's my lot,' he gasped and wiped his mouth with the back of his hand.

'Nonsense!' cried a rosy-cheeked Frost, cigarette dangling from his lower lip. 'We're only just getting warmed up.' Frost was very jolly indeed.

Waters had completely lost track of time; they might have been in here forty-five minutes or four hours. 'I can't get too bladdered, Jack, I'm getting married in the—' Before he could finish his sentence he was greeted with a raucous rendition of 'He's Getting Married in the Morning'. At which point Waters realized several things at once. Firstly, that they'd serenaded him with that song twice already this evening because, secondly, he'd made the mistake of uttering the trigger phrase twice, ergo, thirdly, he must be well and truly smashed to have been dumb enough to set them off on a third round.

God help him.

Frost was kicking with all his might just to keep his head above water. Why in hell's name did he agree to go for a midnight dip?

314

He couldn't even swim. What a ludicrous idea! A figure appeared at the water's edge.

'There you are,' a woman's voice called softly. He looked up. The clouds parted in the sky above, allowing moonlight to reveal the ex-dancer Karen Thomas.

'I'm so sorry you lost your job,' Frost spluttered.

'Don't worry about that. Shall I join you?'

'I was rather hoping you'd help me out of here . . .'

'Nonsense. I'm coming in.' She started unbuttoning her blouse, moving seductively. Frost kicked harder, but his feet were caught, tangled in something. Perhaps he was in a lake, not a swimming pool, as he'd first thought. He struggled to see beyond the lapping water. He could just make out stone slabs to his right. No! Beyond the girl's silhouette loomed the unmistakable bell tower of St Mary's Church. A pond in the graveyard?

'Wait! Wait!' Frost shouted, panic causing his voice to tremble.

Out of nowhere, a loud noise sounded and drowned out his cries for help. Mullett appeared next to the girl, holding a long fireman's hose.

'He's mine,' he said and grinned maliciously, shoving the woman aside.

The awful noise grew louder and louder – what was it? – but Frost had no time to consider it further as the superintendent unleashed a high-powered jet of water down on his head. The force thrust Frost deep underwater. He was helpless to resist. He couldn't breathe . . .

The gagging sensation woke him from his nightmare. His face was pressed hard against a cushion and his feet were tangled in the blanket at the end of the sofa.

A sofa?

It all came flooding back. He was in Sue's flat. He'd shown up late last night, three sheets to the wind and clearly under the impression he still lived here. He had woken up all three of them. Rudely.

Mrs Clarke fidgeted in her camp bed underneath the window, the springs gave as she settled, and after an enormous sigh she commenced to snore profoundly: the noise, from his dream!

'Flamin' heck,' he said, pulling the cushion over his head to muffle the sound. He lay back on the couch. Rather a nightmare than listen to that all night! Then he had an idea. 'Where's that little crumpet gone? I reckon I could forgive her for fancying fatty Hudson, just this once . . .' And with that, he was asleep in a flash.

Friday (1)

'You cannot go into work this morning, Jack!'

'I'll just nip in and out, won't be five minutes,' Frost said, still groggy on the sofa. 'Some loose ends to tie up.'

'What do you mean? There's only a skeleton staff on today and whatever it is, it will all still be there for you tomorrow. And tomorrow's Saturday, you can have the whole place all to yourself. Jack, you can't give us all time off for the wedding, then go in yourself, for heaven's sake. You're his best man!'

'No, you're all right. There's something I have to . . . oooh, flamin' Nora, I forgot how uncomfortable this bloody sofa is.'

'Nobody forced you round here at one o'clock in the morning, and certainly nobody asked. You can leave the bloody key on the side when you leave.'

'Ahem, yes, sorry about that, force of habit.'

'You gave Mum a terrible fright.'

Mrs Clarke had screamed her lungs out when Jack Frost had loomed over her in the middle of the night. It was her screams that had woken up mother, child, and probably the entire block.

things had only got worse when Frost started singing 'We Have all the Time in the World' and tried to get Granny Clarke into a slow-dance. The poor woman still had not recovered. Though she had tried her best to make light of it this morning, as she stood in the kitchen doorway nursing a coffee, her pale face spoke volumes. She was heading back to Colchester this evening and Sue Clarke feared she might never return. She tried a smile, but her mother did not respond in kind. Instead her gaze, a blend of distaste, curiosity and fear, remained unwaveringly on Frost, bare-chested and busy scratching himself in a most unseemly fashion.

'The service is at midday. I pick John up at eleven. It's eight thirty now – I've got bags of time.'

'Uniform should have details of the next of kin of the recently buried in St Mary's you asked for,' she said resignedly, 'if you insist on going in.'

'Excellent,' he said through pulling on his new Topman shirt, which was not a pleasant sight. Her mother was wisely busying herself with Philip in the bathroom.

Then it struck Clarke. 'But remember, you've to get ready in time for the ceremony. Look at you! It's going to take the best part of a morning to get you straight. You need a shave again too . . . And, seriously, where is your morning suit?'

'Good question.' He stood up. 'Very good question.'

Frost was alert – more with it than he had any right to be, considering how much he'd put away last night. He took a deep breath of fresh morning air as Sue slammed the door behind him. He was pleased to note the weather was fine again. Not something he usually paid much attention to, but today was his pal's special day. He chuckled as he remembered the previous evening and what the lads had done to Waters. No time to dawdle. He had to put things right with Hornrim Harry; he had a vague sense of a bad dream involving the super. He couldn't put his finger on the specifics, but he had awoken with some presentiment that left him uncomfortable.

Nevertheless, he bounded down the steps two at a time to reach the ground floor. The exertion shook the dormant alcohol within him. He reached for the stair rail to steady himself. Too late – prickly cold surged through his body and he gagged momentarily. Fortunately he had sufficient presence of mind to lift a nearby dustbin lid before vomiting generously into the metal container. The ripe smell of uncollected rubbish prompted a swift second wave, more violent and eye-watering than the first.

When it was over he felt much better, although parched. He hurried down towards the main road, lifting a milk bottle from a doorstep on the way. He needed a toothbrush. His mind was not necessarily on the impending wedding, but rather on his appointment with Karen Thomas that afternoon at five. He'd thought he'd let the matter go, but he couldn't. He had to warn her that Hudson had her marked for emptying his safe.

On arrival at Eagle Lane Frost discovered Superintendent Mullett was not there. Nevertheless he had to get into his best man's attire. His morning suit was hanging up on the back of his office door. Living a transitory existence as he had these last few months, he had prudently chosen to keep anything of importance in the place he spent the most time – at work. He quickly changed, leaving off the tie, which could wait until later. Then he looked down at his shoes. To say that his scuffed brogues could do with a polish was an understatement. He'd tap Bill for a tin of polish and a brush from behind the desk on his way out. Anything else? He patted down his hair. Cigarettes. He reached inside the desk drawer and grabbed a fresh pack. All set. Wait. The ring! The ring was on the fob with his car keys. He reached down, picked up the trousers he'd just removed and emptied out the pockets to reveal . . . a solitary motorcycle key. Flamin' hell. The ring would be in the garage with the clapped-out Metro. He had remembered this on Tuesday after the rehearsal, but had been so distracted with the Ben Weaver arrest that he'd clean forgotten to collect it. Never mind, he still had time; he'd make his peace with Hornrim Harry then zip over to the Bull.

But there was still no sign of the superintendent. He walked to the front desk.

'Traffic problems in town, Bill?' Frost guessed, as he took the tin of Kiwi shoe polish.

Desk Sergeant Bill Wells shrugged uneasily. Wells was implicated in the traffic foul-up by association with Wally Wallace.

'Haven't heard, Jack.' He checked his wristwatch. 'Not yet nine, but he's usually in by eight thirty.'

'My, my, Bill, you do look smart,' Frost said, smearing a worn shoe brush with paste, 'the super will be impressed.'

'Hmm, it ain't for him. Want to look proper for John and Kim, don't I?' He moved back from the desk and gave his tunic a tug. 'Does it really show? I even polished the buttons with Brasso last night.' The desk sergeant was obviously pleased that his effort had not gone unnoticed.

'You look good enough to eat, lad. Which reminds me, I need some nosh . . .' He was starving. They'd not eaten last night and he was still missing the fry-ups at Sue's. He'd skipped two meals, no amount of nicotine would stave off this hunger. He buffed each shoe in turn, not even bothering to take them off his feet, and replaced the polish and brush on the desk. He slapped his paunch. 'I need refuelling. Not so much as a cocktail sausage on offer last night.'

'And we know why that is, Jack,' Wells bristled. 'The collection money was used for a present. It was put to the vote.'

'Hmm,' Frost sneered. '*An iron*. As if he'll iron those tatty denims he lives in . . . Anyway, the canteen beckons.'

''Ere, Jack, what's this I hear about a motorbike?' Wells leaned across the desk. 'Your motor will have had the clutch done by this afternoon, and you'll be getting another pool Sierra any day now.'

'Fancied one, didn't I?'

'What you get?'

'A Royal Enfield Bullet,' Frost said proudly.

'Never 'eard of it, sounds flash, though.'

'A classic, mate. A steal, too – fella only wanted . . .' Frost trailed off, noticing a figure hovering at the desk. The WPC who had ferried him around yesterday. 'Hello, young lady,' he said.

'I've got some names for you, Inspector.'

'Names?'

'Next of kin? Detective Clarke said . . .'

'Ah, just what I was after, let me have a butcher's . . .' Frost snatched the paper from her hand. One name was familiar, and took him by surprise. 'Well, well, well. I wonder what *that* could mean?' Wells's blank face met his stare. 'Constable,' Frost addressed the WPC. 'Dig a bit deeper on this fellow.' He handed the slip of paper back. 'In particular, I'm keen to know whether he has a daughter. Of school age.' With that he made for the exit.

'Jack, you've duties to attend to. Best man and all that!' Wells called after him, before adding, 'What about the super, Jack?'

'Tell him to get a motorbike to dodge the traffic,' he said. All interest in the station commander had evaporated and he left the building.

Detective Sergeant Waters stood before his soon-to-be-wife's full-length mirror. There was something different about his reflection; was it the whistle that was so transformative? He cut a fine figure in a morning suit, even if he did say so himself. The jacket was a shade too tight, but not so you'd notice. He took a swig of water – his head pulsed with dehydration – and regarded the L-plate on the bed. He had little memory of last night, couldn't recall getting home, but was thankful he had made it back in one piece. He remembered the last Eagle Lane stag do all too clearly – a young copper had woken to find himself padlocked to a lamp-post. Poor blighter had missed his train to Dundee – and thus missed his wedding. A similar fate could have been on the cards for Waters, but he trusted his best man wouldn't leave him high and dry. He knew there had to be *some* benefit to having Jack Frost in the key role, though Kim had argued against it. No, Jack had kept him out of harm's way . . . wait, what's this? He placed the water glass down and stepped closer to the mirror.

'Fuck a duck.'

Simms was on duty with Miller in an area car, cruising through the Southern Housing Estate. The pair had both been at the knees-up the night before. They were not invited to the wedding itself, but were welcome at the reception when they'd finished their shift, which at this point in time seemed an infinity away.

'It's going to be a long day,' Simms observed, elbow jutting out of the car window. Waifs and strays drifted along the pavement regarding them as though carriers of the plague. 'Not that I wish them crap weather,' he said as he flipped down the sun visor, 'but I could do without another scorcher. The heat with this hangover is going to make this a grim shift – the seat's already stuck to me back.'

'Cheer up,' said Miller and pressed Play on the cassette deck. Fleetwood Mac's 'Oh Well' piped up.

A bare-chested man wearing a scarf knotted round his head was loading a flatbed truck outside a row of council-house garages. There was nothing suspicious in the action other than the man's haste, which appeared out of kilter with the slow, sultry morning.

'Hello. Why's he in such a hurry?' Simms edged the car slowly towards the truck, but as they had the windows wound down the burst of music alerted the man to their presence. He stopped in his tracks, hesitated, then carefully placed the tins he was holding down on the ground and slowly walked around the front of the vehicle and out of view.

'Speed up,' Miller said, his perspiring face growing animated. Simms swung the car in front of the truck. They both leapt out but he'd gone. There was an open garage door.

They looked wildly around.

'There!' Simms shouted, pointing down an alleyway. He had caught a glimpse of the man's white trainers disappearing round the corner at the other end. They exchanged glances then gave chase. Anyone that keen to get away was up to no good.

Simms felt the concrete jar against his feet as he pounded down the alley. Pain shot up through to his knees. Either side were gardens that backed on to the alley; washing lines and potting sheds flashed past. Miller was hard on his heels, breathing fast. The man disappeared into a garden to their right. A child on rollerskates (the man's son, perhaps?) watched in amazement as the two policemen careened through the back gate.

A woman's voice cried out, 'Spike, Spike! *No!*'

It took Simms several seconds to realize he'd been attacked by a dog. A big one. The animal had knocked him sideways into a plastic slide. Miller kept up the chase. Simms could feel saliva on his face, and was vaguely aware of fangs, but the dog did not bite. He found its collar and threw the beast to one side. He sprang to his feet and, without thinking, kicked it sharply in the ribs with his heavy police shoe to deter a second assault. The dog yelped, and the boy called out, *'Mummy!'*

Simms, getting his bearings, jogged up the garden path to the house after his colleague.

'Don't you boys ever knock?' said a woman at the kitchen sink scornfully as he passed through into the hall to discover

Miller in action. He had cornered Martin Wakely, whose escape had been scuppered by a mountain of paint tins blocking the front door.

Simms felt distinctly woozy. Behind him, the woman said, 'You'll get a bill for that dog, if you've hurt 'im.'

It was the end of her first week back at Eagle Lane. Sue Clarke was thoroughly exhausted, but pleased with herself for pulling it off. She watched her mother patiently change her infant son's nappy, as he thrashed about irritably.

'I'll do this for you today, Susan, but honestly, I'm not sure for how much longer I've got the energy. I really need a weekend back at home.'

'I know, Mum.' Clarke was repositioning her hat in the mirror. It was Frost's fault the older woman was so irritable, after disturbing her sleep. He was so irresponsible, everything he did lacked thought and consideration – like declaring CID shut for the day. When questioned whether this was a wise decision his response had been, 'What is the point of bleepers if not for use in an emergency?' Not that he ever reacted to his . . . Still, Clarke was regretting not exiting the flat with him earlier. Her mother had slowly been grinding her down. It was selfish, she knew, but she felt bad enough leaving the baby without her mother complaining too. She commanded herself to stop thinking about it, then said out loud to the mirror, 'That'll have to do.'

Clarke turned to face her mother and forced a smile. The other brightened, picking the baby up, who also smiled, content with a fresh nappy.

'You do look *so* lovely. Try and catch the bouquet?'

'I'm not a bridesmaid, Mum.'

'Well, try and find yourself a man, in any event.'

She kissed her on the cheek. 'You'd hardly approve if I did – they're all policemen today.'

They walked to the front door, her mother holding the baby. 'Enjoy yourself then, the weather has sorted itself out for you.'

Yes, Clarke thought, everything was set for a perfect day.

Mullett hung on to the phone as his wife fussed around him with a thermometer. Having left the office early yesterday, he'd slept like a baby until midnight, but then woken up and had not caught a further wink let alone forty. Anxiety coursed through his every vein, making his extremities tingle unpleasantly. He had decided to check in with the doctor this morning; his fears over his blood pressure had escalated. He'd not felt right since the argument with Frost. How was that barbarian apparently so bullet-proof? 'Strong as an ox,' his doctor had pronounced him. Mullett would be happy with the creaking of old age . . . The phone continued to ring unanswered. Where the devil was everyone?

'Ahh Wells, Superintendent Mullett here. I shall be in this afternoon. Anything I should know?' He saw no reason to explain he was under the weather. The desk sergeant proceeded to give an account of Martin Wakely and the council-depot paint.

Wakely. That explained his behaviour earlier in the week.

'Make sure that paint is restored forthwith to its rightful owners. And I want Frost in my office at four o'clock. Yes, yes, I know about the wedding. The reception will be through by then.'

'I think it's mean of them not inviting you,' his wife said when he replaced the receiver.

'Nonsense.' He sniffed, though he knew for a fact that Kelsey, Rimmington's super, was on the guest list. Did it bother him? Would he have been more lenient on the leave situation had he been invited to the reception? 'Criminals will not pause in their activity, nor should we,' he said, thinking of the recovered paint. He was especially pleased with young Simms this week . . . No, what troubled him through the night was the girl that had cleaned out Michael Hudson's safe. The woman stood between him and the golf-club chairmanship. He needed her captured. Try as he might, he could not let that rest for another year. Mullett was intuitive enough to know Frost's prickliness was down to his own feelings about the woman in question.

His wife disturbed his thoughts with a damp flannel.

'I'm fine, darling, honestly.'

'I think you ought to go back to bed,' she said, concerned, 'and change out of those pyjamas – I'll fetch a clean pair from the airing cupboard.'

He wasn't listening. Must he be the one to apologize and back down? Maybe if he was less aggressive, he might get what he wanted more often? But he wasn't in tip-top condition and it was difficult to be agreeable under such circumstances . . . If he apologized to Frost (or at least pretended to) they could start afresh with the whole of CID back in the office on Monday. Then again . . . His mind flipped back to the wedding: *why* hadn't he even been invited to the confounded reception, was he really that disagreeable?

Detective Sergeant John Waters stood alone in the saloon bar of the Bull pub in town, across the road from St Mary's where, in less than an hour, he was to be wed. That the pub was empty was not a surprise, it was just after eleven and the place had only just opened up. What did surprise him was that he was still on his jack jones; he glanced at his watch again – eleven fourteen. The minutes were whizzing past.

'Come on, Jack,' he said quietly to the large Scotch sitting on the beer mat before him. *Don't let me down, pal.* He lifted the glass to his lips. The barman gave him a curious look. He'd taken the perhaps rash move of shaving off his other eyebrow. Better to have none than one. Or so he'd decided, in a moment of panic. On reflex he rubbed the patch where the brow should be. Only after he'd done it did it occur to him that his appearance could be considered effeminate . . . Then, even worse, as he'd been tying his salmon-pink tie in front of the mirror, he'd remembered Jane Hammond's shaved body lying in the bath. A drag queen or a corpse; either way Kim was in for a big shock. Shock was the wrong word to describe his betrothed's likely reaction – fury was nearer the mark. Indeed, it would be a toss-up as to what she was likely to be more furious about, his lack of eyebrows or lack of best man.

Friday (2)

Frost waited patiently in the probation service offices' reception, sipping a cup of tea. He could count the number of times he had visited this sort of place on one hand. It was not his sort of scene: he loathed all manner of officialdom. Just being here made him feel guilty, for some reason.

At least the motorbike had cheered him up, although the sight of all the clogged-up traffic this morning made him think of Wally Wallace. He must have a word with Mullett about that too, when he'd cleared things up. His eyes darted around the waiting area, seeking distraction everywhere, but avoiding the wall clock. He knew he was running late. He hadn't banked on the man having official appointments (but of course he would!), and he knew he couldn't simply barge in. The man would get spooked. But come on, he really didn't have that much time . . .

'Mr Fergusson will see you now,' said the receptionist, and indicated the route he should take within the building. Frost thanked her politely before making his way down the corridor.

The receptionist eyed him warily – she must have thought him a jilted ex-con, sitting there in a morning suit.

Fergusson sat in an anonymous office lined on each wall with battleship-grey filing cabinets, all unmarked and revealing nothing about their contents. The Scotsman could just as easily be about to issue a parking permit in a council office as tick off one of his charges.

'Inspector Frost, it's been a while.' The man in his late fifties glanced fleetingly up from his paperwork. If he'd noticed Frost's attire, he didn't show it.

'Do you mind?' Frost placed his hand on the plastic chair.

'Be my guest,' he said, head back in his business.

Frost sat down and watched the man as he furiously scribbled a report of some kind.

'Hope you don't mind me finishing off here, it's just I'm only in Denton Mondays and Fridays and the paperwork piles up.' The man's Glaswegian burr was warm in tone.

'Not at all, you scribble away.' Frost pulled out a Rothmans.

'I'd prefer it if you didn't do that.' The probation officer raised his head for the first time. Frost, holding the cigarette between his lips, met a hard stare, which lingered for a second before being replaced by a smile.

'Of course,' he said in friendly fashion, and sat for a minute longer, while the man continued to write. The casualness and lack of urgency was part of the inspector's ploy, but he was conscious of the time.

After a further minute he cleared his throat. 'Sorry, but I thought the receptionist sending me through was an indication you were ready? And I'm expected elsewhere, very soon.'

'Quite right,' Fergusson said, pointedly placing the pen to one side, and lacing his fingers in front of him. 'I'm sure you too are a busy fellow. My apologies. How can I help?'

'Rachel Curtis.'

'Yes, poor wee lass. I spoke to your colleague at the weekend. Black fella.'

'Indeed you did, but further information has come to light.'

'She certainly had no shortage of enemies, it would seem. I'm sure you have your work cut out,' the probation officer continued. 'I'm not sure I can be of much help; as I said before, I only saw her once or twice before she died.'

Frost made no comment on that. 'I'm interested in her psychological state. How would you describe her state of mind – those times you met her, that is?'

'You're talking to the wrong person. I'm a probation officer, not a psychologist.'

'But she was released on mental health grounds. You must have been briefed?'

'Yes, of course . . .' he stuttered. 'But I hadn't seen her for long enough that I'd feel able to – to establish her state of mind.'

'Once or twice, yes, you said.' Frost twiddled the unlit cigarette between his fingers. The other man watched. Frost pointed towards the filing cabinets with the Rothmans. 'Dig the file out, then. Let's see what it says?'

'Look, Inspector, I know very well what it says.'

'Enlighten me then: what sort of person was Rachel Curtis?'

Fergusson pushed himself back in his chair, and took a moment to consider. 'She was vulnerable. Easily led.'

'Go on.'

'A lack of parental guidance as a teenager allowed her to slip under the influence of ne'er-do-wells. But a willingness, or desire to be led, meant that she repeated her mistakes time and time again, into adulthood and, alas, we know how it ended.'

'Very good,' Frost complimented. 'Can you expand on *lack of parental guidance*? Her mum's alive and kicking – we just dragged her all the way down here from Sheffield, somewhat reluctantly, but people express their grief in different ways . . .'

'Her *father*,' Fergusson said, lowering his voice. 'The father was, I believe, in and out of prison.'

'Ah, so it was a *man* about the house she was missing.'

'Yes, if you must put it in those simple terms.'

'Thank you.' Frost smiled, then said, 'But . . . taking this a step further: do you think she craved a strong disciplinarian, a man who would tell her what to do, to compensate for the lack of structure in her home life? Good or bad, right or wrong, that was irrelevant so long as someone else took control. That made her feel safe, so that was all that mattered.' He let his words sink in and lit his cigarette. 'That's why she stayed with Nicholson, regardless of the pain and trouble he caused her. Now, though, with him off the scene, banged up, she found herself feeling unstable again. Without her anchor, as it were, she was all over the place. Getting a tattoo one minute, roaring off to crash a party on a motorbike the next.'

'Yes. I guess so.'

'But' – Frost held up his cigarette in full view, then delivered his punchline – 'in the final two weeks of her life there *was* a man. A man with authority. A man she would kick out against, a man she would try and resist, but ultimately a man who would make her do as she was told. Even leave the first party she'd gone to as a young, free, unattached, attractive woman.'

A bead of perspiration appeared on Fergusson's forehead. 'That's a remarkably well-thought-out assessment. Have you considered branching out into psychiatry?' he said coolly.

'I suppose her death might have been an accident.' Frost looked for an ashtray.

Fergusson offered a teacup. The man had forgotten his own objection to the inspector smoking, an omission that in itself betrayed his inner tension.

'It comes to us all, we cannot say when.'

'Indeed, that reminds me – my condolences on your mother,' Frost said.

'I'm sorry?'

'Your mother passed away recently, I gather . . . ?'

For a moment Fergusson struggled for words, then said, 'All terribly sudden. How did you know?'

'My wife is buried in St Mary's.'

The answer appeared to settle Fergusson down, but it did not explain, as they were both well aware, how Frost could know. His mother was, after all, buried under her maiden name of Mackenzie.

'Perhaps I might dig out the file after all,' said the probation officer and rose to his feet. 'Might I offer you a cup of tea?'

Frost nodded. 'Lovely, two sugars.'

After Fergusson slipped out of the room, Frost sprang over towards the filing cabinets. He squinted at the tiny labels. *A–D* was the one he wanted. There it was, as Clarke had said it would be. He pulled the file out, and then followed Fergusson into the corridor where the probation officer's departure had been curtailed by DC Hanlon and a uniformed officer.

'On second thoughts,' Frost called out, 'only the one sugar. The doctor says I've gotta lose a few pounds.'

The church was packed. Clarke stood in the second pew from the front. Across the aisle there was a startling array of afro hair. She considered herself modern, but never in her life had she seen so many black people in this neck of the woods, least of all in a church. Not that she set foot inside a church more than once a year.

A sense of unease was palpable on both sides of the aisle, bride's and groom's, black and white. Not for the first time, Waters paced the stone floor. Handsome bugger, she thought to herself. He cut a slick figure, no doubt about that, but there was something else, she couldn't put her finger on it. Abruptly, without warning, the church organ piped into life. The bride was almost here, but the best man wasn't. Waters looked at her, his eyes pleading for reassurance she couldn't in all honesty give. She shrugged and smiled. It could be worse . . . better Frost be missing than the bride. Still, she couldn't help but worry. He wasn't used to that new motorcycle, and he'd refused to hear of wearing a helmet, anything could have happened. That man was a poster boy for irresponsible behaviour of all kinds.

Waters took his place at the front of the church; all eyes were now on the groom. Clarke cast a quick glance behind her – Kim was there in the doorway. This wedding was happening with or without a best man. It was a perfunctory role after all, only of any value for toe-curling speeches and, on occasion, supplying the ring. And John wouldn't be daft enough to have entrusted Frost with the ring . . .

Frost wasn't aware of the church bells until he'd switched off the Bullet's engine. Its finer qualities were, Frost now realized, more aesthetic than practical: he'd be more comfortable mounting a lawnmower, and the noise was deafening, but hell, it looked the part. He pulled his hip flask from his pocket. It was sterling silver, somewhat tarnished, engraved with the words *Drink me* in Victorian calligraphy. He took a swig to calm him down. Motorcycling would take some getting used to. Frost's legs were still jelly as he ran into the church. The bells had stopped. Come to think of it, so had the organ. He was either just in time or too late. A speech was echoing throughout the stone nave.

'He's more popular than I thought,' said Frost, and grinned at frowning guests. At the far end of the aisle, the happy couple stood before the good Father. Frost adjusted his jacket, and walked as calmly and nobly as he could towards the altar, each footstep echoing around the space. The congregation couldn't decide whether to be furious or relieved. Consistent as ever, Frost certainly knew how to make an entrance.

He slipped into place. The vicar raised an eyebrow as he started on the vows. Frost gently elbowed John, who greeted him with a sly smile of relief. Frost could barely suppress a childish snigger, but was brought swiftly down to earth when Father Hill requested the ring. With all the excitement of nailing Fergusson and in his haste to get to the church on time, he had forgotten to collect his car keys. Balls. All eyes were on him. The silence grew stronger with each passing second.

Frost, always resourceful in a crisis, linked his hands behind his back and deftly began to twist his own wedding ring free from his finger. Initially it proved unwilling but eventually it gave in. See, sometimes a little sweat on a bloke was a good thing! He plopped the hot metal band into the vicar's palm. Had he had any eyebrows, Waters would here have been seen to raise them. This was not the elegant band he'd spent a small fortune on. This . . . 'ring' wouldn't have looked out of place in a mechanic's workshop!

The service proceeded to its natural conclusion, the grubby ring having slipped on to Kim's elegant finger effortlessly, as opposed to Frost's short stubby ones, and the happy couple exited the church.

'Cut that fine, Jack,' Hanlon said as they both launched confetti aimlessly into the air.

'Perfect timing, by my reckoning.'

'Bothered to turn up then?' Clarke joined them.

'Nice hat,' Frost said.

'Well, what have you got to say?'

'Eh?'

'Come on, you've got that look about you.' Clarke appraised him. 'Some say it's a twinkle, I say it's smug . . .'

They moved with the crowd, the sun beating down on them. The reception was at Chadwick Hall, a couple of miles south of Denton. Frost considered the Bullet; he didn't trust himself on it after a few drinks. He'd doubtless end up in a ditch.

'I'll drive you,' Clarke said, reading his mind.

'Donal Fergusson killed Rachel Curtis.'

'The probation officer?' Clarke opened the Escort door for him. Hanlon jumped in the back.

'Exactly.'

'How did you reach that conclusion, Jack?' Hanlon asked.

'Rachel desperately needed a controlling influence in her life – when Nicholson got banged up, she was left adrift.'

'But he was a homicidal maniac.' Clarke pulled out, joining the throng of vehicles.

'Yes, but she still needed a guiding influence, remember what her mother said, lacking a father she fell victim to wrong 'uns? Fergusson knew this from her psychological assessment. And he was well placed, an official guardian, if you like, to keep an eye on her.'

'Disgusting abuse of power,' Clarke said.

'How'd you twig, Jack?' Hanlon asked from the back seat.

'Curtis had been caught having it off in a graveyard as a teenager,' Frost said, turning round in the car. 'That's not a fact anyone would know unless they had access to her personal history. By dumping her body there, the killer no doubt assumed we'd be asking questions, and her mother might implicate the old boyfriend in Sheffield.'

'But he's dead . . .'

'And it wouldn't make sense anyway,' Frost continued. 'She's not a kid any more.'

'Might be kinky, that's what you assumed, isn't it,' Hanlon said.

'True, but I think it was just opportune. Fergusson buried his mother there only two weeks ago. St Mary's churchyard is secluded, screened from the road. Curtis was placed dramatically, on the only flat tombstone in the whole place. It was a stage. He'd have to have planned it.'

'I'm with you, but I still don't get why he killed her?'

'They had a row. He came to collect her under the guise of being her taxi driver – Castleton's daughter did sell that flat cap, by the way, but not to him – to Rachel, who wanted it for a 'grumpy old man'. She thought the pattern some sort of tartan that would remind him of home. Go figure that. Rachel would have chosen not to cause a scene at the party; remember, this woman is vulnerable, used to being ordered about. And she'd be unlikely to argue with her probation officer in public, wouldn't she? These are all London types that know nothing of her history. The only one who knows about her is Gazzer Benson, who'd agreed to pick her up at midnight.'

'But she'd already left. Hence him ripping up Holland's lawn.'

'Right.' They pulled into the grounds of a grand country house. 'I reckon they had a row in the motor. He either pushed her out . . .'

'. . . or she jumped?' Clarke suggested.

'Maybe. And ran along the road. Until he caught up with her. But either way, he left her body at the church to fool us – it's nowhere near Two Bridges, his place or hers. But actually, it's the key that gave him away . . . Forensics are all over his Vauxhall Viva as we speak.'

'Could it have been an accident?' Hanlon interjected.

'I really think she might have tried to do a runner; remember Dr Death said she had marks of new tarmac on her feet? Well it's not just outside the Codpiece there's roadworks – no, there's been a ton of resurfacing on the back roads between Two Bridges and town, in particular the fork that runs towards St Mary's. But you'd not be able to make that out in the dark as there's no streetlights. Maybe he stops by the river and tries it on with her, she resists, they argue and she makes a bolt for it. She gets a short distance, falls on the unmade road surface, breaks her ankle . . . He then picks her up, and well, you can fill in the rest. Poor woman.'

Clarke parked the car. No one said a word. Rachel Curtis had been a victim all her life. She never had a chance. Outside it was a beautiful day. The setting was sumptuous and all around them wedding guests wearing colourful clothes were emerging from their vehicles.

Frost was the first to break the silence. 'Flamin' heck, this is a bit posh. Very classy.'

All eyes were focused on the impressive mansion before them. 'Yes, like your speech will be, I imagine,' said Sue. 'Are you thinking of putting your tie on before then or what?'

'Collar's already on the tight side.'

Frost could reduce the finest tailoring in all the land to something befitting a Dickensian pauper, but she had to hand it to him – he was a bloody amazing detective. As they got out of the car she admired him as he swigged thirstily from a hip flask.

'Ahh . . . I love a good wedding.' He beamed. 'Come on!'

Friday (3) _____

Mullett sat staring at the front page of the newspaper. He'd completely forgotten about Holland, or more to the point, he'd forgotten about Holland's high profile. The fellow was a Somebody in the fashion business and his death was sure to make the national news. And so it had. The front page of the *Daily Mail* in fact. *DESIGNER'S DEATH SHROUDED IN MYSTERY* read the headline, with an accompanying photo of Holland hobnobbing with a popstar Mullett had never heard of. There was no mention in the report of the missing money but no doubt that would follow. He expected Eagle Lane would be teeming with reporters any second. It was four o'clock in the afternoon. He stretched then rose, folded the paper and left the office – it was high time CID returned from the festivities.

Mullett had been in a little over an hour. The doctor had prescribed him more medication – something he was loath to take. Maybe he didn't need it; his doctor suggested he take up another form of exercise, something more energetic than golf (and it was true, golf had not helped his stress levels – not that he had explained precisely how unhelpful it was proving on that front). He was determined to dust off his tennis racket. The very thought of it made him feel calmer. He nodded to a pair of uniformed officers who stepped aside as he rounded the front desk.

'Wait a second,' he stopped in his tracks, 'Where's Wells?'

'Sergeant Wells has the afternoon off, sir. I'm Constable Dawson.'

'Yes, of course.' Mullett knew the lad, a recent addition to Eagle Lane. What he didn't realize was that Wells had abandoned his post to a constable fresh out of Hendon. He continued on to CID but it was fast becoming obvious that he would be greeted by an empty office. He was not wrong. Nevertheless he moved along the desks searching for signs of recent activity. One desk in particular was unusually tidy. Waters, he thought. On close inspection he saw a note stuck on to the computer screen that read, *Gone for tapas – back on 4th. JW.*

Mullett balled his fists. Right. The absolute last straw. Frost clearly hadn't told Waters that his leave was cancelled. Not that the super had anything against Waters, lack of wedding invite aside, he was a nice chap and good at his job, but a direct order was not to be disobeyed. He considered the note left by the detective sergeant. If Waters had only approached him directly, if he'd made the case for his honeymoon . . . he might have been persuaded. But Frost had never given Waters a chance, just as he'd never given Mullett the respect he deserved.

Frost was for the high jump.

A presence was hovering. He spun round to discover the young lad from the front desk.

'Yes,' he snapped.

'Sorry to trouble you, sir, there's a lady in reception and—'

But before the boy could get the words out an elegant tanned woman with a blonde perm barged past him.

'Oh, *oh*, Superintendent, I simply must talk to you!' Her vibrant pink lipstick was horrible and mesmerizing.

Mullett set his anger at Frost aside. Here was a lady of some refinement, requiring his assistance. He adjusted his tie and said, 'Please, this way, to my office. Mrs . . . ?'

'Beswetherick. And it's Miss.' She beamed.

'And how may I help?'

'Simply dreadful news. Dominic. Dominic Holland is dead!' She grabbed Mullett's arm, took hold firmly and began to sob. The superintendent was quite taken aback, and offered to make her some tea.

It transpired the lady from South Kensington was Holland's business partner. She and someone called Niles had played a practical joke on the late Mr Holland, which may or may not have precipitated the poor man's demise.

'So, when he arrived at the office late on Monday, bragging about his swimming pool *again*, I thought, Right, I'm going to teach you a lesson, young Dombo, your Tightspots were so last year and those bloody Dagenham Drainpipes *simply* have not worked. If you spent more time at work, focusing on the marketing, rather than out in the boondocks fannying around over the colour of your pool tiles, our figures might be a tad more rosy.'

Mullett sat speechless. He was enchanted with the creature before him, but had absolutely no idea what she was talking about.

'And . . . ?' he offered tentatively.

'I dispatched Niles in the Porker, didn't I? On Monday night, while Dom was prancing about at that party with those celebs – I asked Niles to find that cash, and bring it straight back, see how funny *that* is!' She then proceeded to forage in an enormous handbag. 'And here it is.' She flopped a Bejam bag on his desk, then burst into sobs once more. 'Oh I can't believe that he's *dead*! I only meant to teach him not to be such a . . . such a bloody *knob* about things!'

Mullett tried to calm Miss Beswetherick down, but to no

avail. She was inconsolable and it was not surprising. He really couldn't quite grasp the situation. He needed Frost, and rose to ask Miss Smith to page the absent detective. He paused with one hand on the door and glanced back at the Londoner's shaking frame. With his other hand he reached into his trouser pocket, and with a sigh of defeat pulled out the Valium he'd collected from the chemist that morning.

Waters sat down next to Frost and draped his arm across the other's shoulder as they watched his wife Kim get on down to 'Jungle Rock' with Arthur Hanlon in the Tudor hall.

'So you think Fergusson went on to kill Holland for fear he might be recognized?'

'Reckon so,' Frost said. 'The investigation into Holland's missing cash would be on the police bulletin, which all probation officers receive; he knew we'd be questioning Holland and he'd not want to risk it. It was all too close for comfort.' He paused. 'It's like Baloo tossing Mowgli around,' he added, nodding towards the dance floor.

'But without the rhythm and style.'

'I dunno, she's a bit of a mover, your missus.'

Waters smiled. 'Tell me, the eyebrow. It wasn't your idea, was it?'

'Never.' Frost shook his head vigorously. 'A terrible thing to do to a fellow the night before his wedding. Just the one, I told 'em, she'll never notice standing next to him.' The pair fell about laughing. It had been a fabulous day, ring and eyebrows notwithstanding. Frost checked his watch, four o'clock. The party was in full swing; the reception-only guests had started to arrive, their sober demeanour and air of slight surprise making them stand out from the other rosy-cheeked well-wishers in the sumptuous banqueting hall.

'Well, old buddy, I got to make a move.' He nodded across to

Bill Wells; they'd arranged a changeover so the rest of Eagle Lane might get a chance to celebrate.

'Hornrim Harry?'

'Yes, there's him.' Frost had completely forgotten about Mullett. He was thinking about meeting Karen Thomas in an hour. 'Your Errol's making quite an impression on our Sue.' Sure enough, in a corner DC Clarke was talking animatedly to John's brother. 'He's even taller than you. He's not a copper too, is he?'

'Nah, he's an airline pilot, got back from Sydney yesterday. Lives the life, I can tell you.'

'Good for him,' Frost remarked, 'and good luck to you too, Sue.'

Frost rose and hugged his pal. The music changed tempo, couples drew closer together; a good time to be off. It had been a wonderful day and he was relieved they'd all made it through the week. He swelled with emotion seeing his friends and colleagues shine with alcohol-tinted happiness as he crossed the dance floor; they all deserved to let their hair down, and what better way to do it than celebrating a wedding. He passed behind Sue Clarke who was now swaying gently to 'Ticket to the Moon' with Errol. It pleased him to see her enjoying herself, given the way the week had started for her with Hornrim Harry. ELO reminded him of his Metro still in the garage. He thought he might leave the car there, but collect the cassette. This track was on *Time*; he'd keep it as a memento of the day.

Frost had not really drunk that much alcohol at the reception, by his own standards, and so had asked Wells to drop him back at the church to collect his motorbike. It was five twenty as Jack Frost turned into Eagle Lane, goggles on, heading to his rendezvous with Karen Thomas. And though it was Karen he was meeting now, it had been Julie who had crossed his mind as he left Chadwick Hall – if he was to have a boogie, god forbid, he could imagine swinging *her* about but, strangely, not the pole-dancing beauty. He'd call Julie soon. There was no rush, he was a free man and this was the first time he'd felt it.

As he passed the station, he was surprised to see Superintendent Mullett on the front steps – a remarkable sight this late on a Friday. Even more unusually, he was deep in conversation with a blonde lady standing next to a black Porsche convertible. He tooted on the bike horn and gave a friendly wave. Mullett looked over – and his jaw dropped in disbelief. Frost was tempted to stop, but . . . well, why spoil a very enjoyable day. Nothing was so urgent it couldn't keep till tomorrow, eh?

He cruised along the road and found himself wondering if he shouldn't take the weekend off. It was a strange feeling. He couldn't think of the last time . . . Perhaps the motorbike was more than a symbol; perhaps he would just bugger off somewhere, anywhere. Go visit his old aunt Crystal in Devon maybe . . .

Karen Thomas was waiting for him outside the Jade Rabbit as arranged, wearing a floppy hat and big sunglasses.

'Hello,' he called.

She was clearly surprised to see him astride a motorcycle, but didn't mention it. 'Unusual place to meet. It's closed.'

'I've heard quite a bit about you in the last twenty-four hours, eh?' Frost said.

'I thought you might, that's why I wanted to see you.' She smiled. There was a gap between her two front teeth, and they were a little too large for her mouth. He hadn't noticed this before, perhaps because he hadn't seen her smile, but he found it endearing.

'To tell me what?'

'I'm off to Amsterdam.' It was then that he noticed the duffel bag sandwiched between her sandalled feet.

Frost paused and considered this information for a moment.

'I see. Want a lift?'

'A what?'

'I'll give you a ride if you return what you stole from old Hudson.'

'What, on that?'

They both considered the Bullet.

'Yeah, why not?' he said. 'It's a very healthy way to travel, plenty of fresh air.'

'What, all the way to Holland?' she asked, her expression a mix of surprise and concern.

'I never said that; chuck Fatty's jewels in his front garden and I'll take you as far as Harwich first. And take things from there.' He placed his hands on the gleaming fuel tank, still warm in the late afternoon sun. 'It's a lovely evening for a ride.'

'All right!' She picked up her bag, but Frost got off the bike, and approached the front door of the Jade Rabbit. 'Where you going, then?' Karen frowned.

'Just got to feed the animals, so they don't starve, and leave a note to say I'm off.'

'You're living *here*?'

'Sort of.'

'You *are* a strange man, Jack Frost.'

He unlocked the door. 'Not really, I'm very ordinary. Hop on and make yourself comfortable, won't be a tick.'

Acknowledgements

Thanks to Sarah Castleton, Frankie Gray, Phil Patterson, Felicity Blunt, Elisabeth Merriman, Kate Samano, Bill Scott-Kerr, Tash Barsby, Dominic Wakeford, Emma Beswetherick, Andreas Campomar, Ravi Mirchandani, Bob Fritz, Martin Wakley, Sarah Neal, Katie Gurbutt, Martin Hughes-Games.

James Henry is the pen name for James Gurbutt, who has long been a fan of the original R. D. Wingfield Frost books and the subsequent TV series. He works in publishing, and enjoys windsurfing and long lunches.

After a successful career writing for radio, R. D. Wingfield turned his attention to fiction, creating the character of Jack Frost. The series has been adapted for television as the perennially popular *A Touch of Frost*, starring David Jason. R. D. Wingfield died in 2007.